The Blackdog King

The Blackdog King, Volume 1

Livia E. De Souza

Published by Livia E. De Souza, 2024.

This is a work of fiction. Similarities to real people, places, or events are entirely coincidental.

THE BLACKDOG KING

First edition. May 31, 2024.

ISBN: 979-8224091430

Written by Livia E. De Souza.

Table of Contents

For my family

Prologue

The only sound in the room was that of leather boots pacing across a rough, stone floor. Alderic was not accustomed to failure, yet his every attempt to gain the map had been thwarted. The sun was setting, casting the stark room in the blushing glow of evening hours, and the perfume of the flowering vines that crept along the castle walls hung heavy in the air. On another day the fragrance might have pleased Alderic, but now he only found it suffocating.

His fingers absently traced the rough gouge mark at the center of his sword's hilt. The defect that rested against his palm in battle was a reminder of the indignation he had suffered, and of the price he was willing to pay to right the wrongs done to his father.

Still, the map lay so far out of his reach, that it might as well have rested at the bottom of the ocean. The earl had always been an effective adversary to Alderic, making skillful use of his limited resources to spite the king at every turn. Yet, Alderic would not relent.

The raw, crushing smell of water saturated the air of the castle, but it had been a long time since Alderic had noticed the scent. He had grown accustomed to the cold and damp, the sickening feel invading even the marrow of his bones. Yet, he could not bring himself to stop the water from seeping into the foundation of Ashen Castle.

Throughout the castle were reminders of his destroyed family, and the loss of Severin had been undeniably difficult. His brother's death had left him a stray in his own kingdom. Alderic was aware that most in Vesia believed he had killed Severin. He was not surprised that his own people had reached his conclusion, as they often failed to see him as human. However, he was interested to find that carrying this blame did nothing to worsen the pain.

In mourning, he had closed off the wing of the castle that led to Severin's quarters and moved the widowed Moirin to a new suite. The empty rooms gathered dust, and Alderic himself had not entered these quarters since the day of his brother's death. He would not allow grief to end his search before it had even begun.

As if summoned by a thought, he could hear long skirts brush the floor of the hallway passing the door to his chamber. Alderic did not need to look to know that Moirin was near. He could feel her enticing presence as surely as he might the weight of a boulder resting on his chest.

His hand tightened on the sword hilt, his thumb pressing hard against the jagged metal edge of the wretched hollow. It cut into his finger, and he could feel the wet blood trickle across his hand, running down the groove of his unsheathed blade. He let the crimson liquid pool on the stone floor and watched silently as it disappeared into a crevice, his dread of the woman's nearness gradually dissipating.

He pressed the injured thumb to his mouth, wetting his teeth with the fresh blood. The metallic taste brought him back from his self-indulgent reverie.

His time was at hand.

1

The sun beat down in the dusty alley, its white rays nearly blinding. Blake wiped the sweat from his brow, wincing as grit entered his eyes. His heartbeat felt sluggish in the afternoon sun, his blood thickened from the heat. His mouth was dry, and his throat clutched insistently for a sip of water.

A gathering of nearly twenty red-flushed faces looked back, keenly watching his every move. Some had carried with them wares from the marketplace as they followed the murmurs leading them to this opportunity to try their luck at a game of chance.

Blake did not recognize any of the faces, which he always took to be a good sign. He had begun the game nearly ten minutes ago, and was losing more than half the time. His modest wins did not yet cover the coin he had seemingly squandered on his own diversion, and he knew the others were keeping a mental tally. His voice faltered, and his hands shook so even the farthest member of the crowd could see.

"Excuse me, I must take a drink before continuing," he said, offering them his most charming smile. "You all understand, of course."

Blake's dry voice cracked, as he turned his back to those gathered. He riffled through the bag on the ground, searching for the leather canteen he had placed there earlier. Every half-second he could not find it increased his sense of desperation.

A man in a canary yellow shirt stepped forward, after checking that Blake truly was distracted. He took the moment to surreptitiously mark two of the three shells on the table by scraping them with his fingernail. He made a small dent in one, and a broad, horizontal line on the other.

"What is he doing?" a child whispered, before being quickly hushed by her mother.

Blake heard a silence fall over the crowd and, in spite of himself, he felt a smile steal across his lips. He resumed his position behind the makeshift table and self-consciously straightened his sweat-soaked clothing, tugging slightly at the neck of his shirt.

"I'm afraid this will have to be the last game of the day. Who would like to play?" he asked, his eyes scanning the crowd eagerly.

Those assembled rushed forward, their spirits bolstered by the sureness of their bet, money gripped tight in outstretched hands. Though he should have known better, Blake still felt surprised by the response.

"Please, ladies and gentlemen, only one may play," he laughed lightly. "But don't worry, other days will bring other diversions."

His eyes landed on a particularly well-dressed man. This gentleman's conspicuously wealthy air was incongruous with the grime of the alley. Blake quickly assessed his appearance, noting that a single button on this man's jacket was worth more than the handfuls of coins pressed in his direction combined. When Blake sensed an opportunity, he did not hesitate to seize it.

"You, sir!" he called out, pointing at the man. "I'll let you play the final game of the day, if you can match the highest bid."

An expression of surprise crossed the man's face, but he masked it instantly, replacing it with a smirk. He sauntered forward, lazily looking through a coin purse he held in his hand. The small crowd parted quickly to make way for the evident nobleman.

"If I heard right, that would be fifteen. I'll double it." He dropped the small purse onto the table. "Thirty pieces."

The weight of the bag tilted the warped board, and Blake smiled. Thirty pieces would more than cover the losses of the day. He poked through the contents of the bag, though he had no doubt it truly contained thirty pieces. This nobleman didn't look daring enough to attempt deception.

"I will match that, though you know it could be my ruin," Blake responded with only a moment's hesitation, laying his own money down beside the purse.

His fingers lightly grasped the playing pieces, and he lifted the center shell to reveal a withered pea lying on the rough board. The nobleman nodded in confirmation, and Blake shuffled the shells against the tabletop. His hands continued to shake, as shell scraped quickly against wood.

Confident the pieces were well transposed, Blake stood back and crossed his arms.

"Alright my good sir, an intelligent man such as yourself should have no trouble telling me which shell the pea is under."

The man made a great show of thinking, the self-contented smile stretching across his lips. He played to the crowd, tapping his fingers on his chin, and they laughed in response.

"I suppose I will guess: that one." He pointed to the unmarked shell. His voice raised on the last words, displaying a comically overdrawn insecurity. Again, the crowd laughed.

"Are you sure?" Blake asked, eyebrows raised.

"I am."

"I will give you one more chance to reconsider."

"That will not be necessary. I am certain of my choice," the man responded with an eyeroll.

Blake picked up the shell, revealing the empty board beneath, and the smile fell from the man's face. Blake lifted the remaining shells, revealing the pea by his right hand. He was careful to look as surprised as the spectators at the discovery.

"Better luck next time." Blake said, pulling the coin purse towards him on the table.

Blake took in the growing sound of whispering amongst the crowd, along with the look of confusion turning to anger on the face of the well-dressed gentleman. Blake was filled with a familiar sense of unease.

"The city guard is coming," the man in the yellow shirt cried out, as he quickly made his way from the alley into the city streets.

In a single movement, Blake swept the money and shells off the table into his open bag. He threw the bag over his shoulder and made his way from the alley, not even bothering to collect the table. He was able to disappear amongst the rabble as the spectators quickly dispersed, each knowing well the penalty associated with gambling.

Blake cast a glance back at the angered man as he made his retreat. The wronged nobleman was within moments obscured from Blake's view by the harried movement of the crowd.

When he was sure he was out of sight, Blake ran through the backroads until he spotted the tavern. He rounded the corner, pulling himself behind the modest building. Dust filled his lungs, and he coughed drily before taking a long drink from his nearly empty canteen.

"That took you long enough, I've been waiting here for ages."

The man in the yellow shirt stood in the shade of the building, leaning against the wall. He twirled a few small coin purses on a string around his index finger. Blake hunched over, trying to catch his breath. He was struck by the vividness of the dust clinging to the brown leather of his boots.

"And I'll bet you my take was greater than yours," the yellow-clad man continued.

Blake could hear the laughter in Hugh's voice. Gathering himself, he straightened up and outstretched his hand, accepting the knotted purses. He weighed them against his own bag and shrugged.

"Perhaps," he admitted, tossing the bags back, "but, it's close."

Hugh caught them, grinning widely. "I never thought I'd live to see the day."

"You keep wearing that shirt, and your life will be considerably shortened," Blake said, striking a more serious note.

Their trade relied on being practically unrecognizable, and Hugh's love of color placed them at considerable risk. Were canary yellow shirts typical in Vesia, it would not have raised many eyebrows. However, in all his twenty-four years, Blake had yet to encounter so bright a shirt on any other person.

Hugh's smile was not faded by this criticism. He'd heard it many times before, but he was unmoving on the topic. "It hasn't hurt me yet," he responded with a shrug.

"Yet," Blake repeated, grimacing.

Hugh, like Blake, had been raised far from the capital of Vesia. The son of a farmer, Hugh was strong and fast. Though he and Blake were near same age, Hugh possessed a naiveté that could prove fatal to a criminal. They had met only the year before, but their quickly formed partnership had nearly tripled Blake's earnings.

"I think I need more practice with the shells," Hugh said, changing the subject. "Watching you today, I think I know what my problem is. I have to stop my thumb from getting in the way, it just seems to stick out most of the time."

"The whole thing is simple enough," Blake answered, "but, you think too much. When we have time, I'll show you how to fix it."

Blake was continually impressed by Hugh's dog-like loyalty, and willingness to take on the most menial of tasks while he waited patiently to learn the finer art of deception. Yet, Blake found that he resented his role as mentor. He purposefully stalled in the instruction of his companion, even though he knew in his heart that it was wrong to use Hugh as a simple cutpurse.

While much of their money was found in these games, they often participated in more conventional methods of thievery. Blake picked locks while Hugh acted as a lookout and distraction, the latter proving himself invaluable to the enterprise. Blake grew accustomed to this way of operating and, as the months dragged on, he found himself endlessly rewarding Hugh's loyalty with unfulfilled promises.

"We have only a little time before sundown. Get food and fill the canteens. I'll find us a new pair of horses, and we'll meet here at sunset. I don't want to stay in the city too long," Blake said.

Blake was reluctant to spend any more time than necessary in Conrisia, the capital of the Vesian Kingdom. Only a few miles to the west, lay the castle of King Alderic, a man with a reputation for barbaric cruelty. It was a large city, but Blake found himself unable to quell his irrational fear that he might somehow find himself before the chilling Blackdog King.

Hugh nodded and turned to leave, stopped suddenly by the appearance of a well-dressed man who stepped forward proudly from the corner of the tavern walls.

"Blake!" Hugh called out.

Blake turned to Hugh, freezing when he perceived the newcomer. The feeble wind carried the smell of amber perfume, and Blake cursed himself for not noticing the intruder's presence sooner.

"What have we here?" the man asked gleefully. His cheeks were ruddy, and he appeared to be near bursting with delight.

"Excuse me sir, you must have me mistaken for another," Hugh said.

"I think not," the man responded.

Blake recognized him as the final player of the shell game. He kept his eyes locked on the embittered face, while his fingers sought blindly for the dagger he kept well hidden in the folds of his shirt. It was not the first time one of his marks had tried to repay his kindness in like, though it was the first time he had been caught so unaware.

The nobleman drew his sword and pointed it with disdain at the pair of criminals. He kept the blade fully extended, as though half-afraid he might cut himself with the sharp edge. Blake was not particularly skilled in combat and avoided fighting when he could. However, through enough street brawls he had learned to quickly assess an assailant and their vulnerabilities. Though the sword made the nobleman ostensibly dangerous, his bearing showed that he would fight from a place of weakness.

"When the peasants dispersed, and the aforementioned guards were nowhere in sight, it occurred to me that I might find the two of you together." He sneered down at the pair. "You can steal from them all you like, but you were foolish to try the same on me. By the end of the day, I'll see you hang."

The man continued to put forward threats, but Blake found his attention slipping away from the swindled man's words, his interest growing instead in the sword pointed at him. It glinted in the little sunlight present behind the tavern building, and Blake squinted to make out a diamond encrusted hilt, the stones laid in what he assumed to be silver.

The soft fingers of the nobleman already seemed to weary of holding the weapon out, and the blade had begun to dip.

"Though you are mistaken, I would be glad to assist you in any way I can," Blake said, edging toward the nobleman with each word. "We will help you find the thieves who cheated you, and be sure the rogues pay for their crimes."

The man laughed. "A liar too, by the gods you shall hang."

Seeing an opening present itself, Blake lunged forward. He used the flat of his palm to strike the nobleman's wrist, and the weapon slipped through the other man's weak grip. It landed on the ground with a dusty thud.

A scramble for the blade quickly ensued. Blake dove for the sword, just as the nobleman stooped to reach. The thief used his knee to shove him out of the way, knocking him to the ground. Blake's boots skidded in the dirt, as he seized the hilt and drew back his arm, pointing the tip of the blade at the fallen man's throat.

Hugh kept the man on the ground, pressing the sole of his boot against the nobleman's shoulder, while Blake stood up, keeping the weapon trained on their victim. Blake's chest rose and fell with heavy breaths, as he looked down the length of the blade at the disheveled noble.

"I'm sure he has more than he wagered in the game, as he seems like an otherwise cautious man. Perhaps you should search him," he said to Hugh with a laugh, "though this might put your earnings for today ahead of my own."

"As if they weren't already." Hugh shot him a mocking grin. "Besides, the day's not done; you might catch up yet."

Hugh searched the man, collecting a few valuable pieces of jewelry as well as a coin purse containing seventeen pieces. These he crammed hastily into his pockets. He pulled the rings off the nobleman's fingers, and loosed the fine gold-link chain around his neck.

The nobleman glared up at Blake from the dirt, his teeth grinding in self-righteous anger, while he submitted to Hugh's fleecing.

It was now Blake's turn to smile.

"A bit too decorative for my tastes," Blake said, turning the blade over in his hands, making a show of admiring the craftsmanship. "But, it is a beautiful sword. What a shame it is that no one taught you how to use it."

The man sputtered in rage, as Hugh finished procuring the last valuables from his person. Hugh pulled off the nobleman's belt and tossed it to Blake.

Blake fastened the belt around his waist, sheathing the brightly glittering sword by his hip. He turned jestingly from side to side, displaying a sword by any estimates far too fine for his person.

Through with his joke, Blake turned to Hugh, and an unspoken signal passed between them. The pair of thieves ran through the streets, away from the nobleman who was only just beginning to climb, shaking, to his feet.

They ran in the direction of the stable Blake had located earlier in the day. In a pinch, Blake knew the owner would trade him two horses for the sword. He could tell that it was likely worth ten horses but, should the city guard catch them, bartering for an additional eight horses could not buy them back their lives.

The stable was a little farther away than Blake had remembered, and he felt himself beginning to panic as the city streets seemed to stretch out endlessly before them. They ducked into backroads for as long as they could, before the alleys ended, leaving them in full view of the thriving metropolis.

The only building in sight was a temple of Rubelytte, goddess of fire and ruler of the gods. However, Blake was hesitant to use the place of worship as a refuge for thieves.

Cries sounded out behind, and Blake became aware of the thunder of approaching hooves. It was too late to think of hiding in the temple; in a matter of seconds, they were encircled by the royal guards who patrolled Conrisia.

Blake stood with his back to Hugh's, wielding the ornate sword. It suddenly occurred to him how odd a figure he must cut, dressed in the clothes of a peasant and brandishing a weapon easily worth one hundred times his own life.

Despite the increasing seriousness of the situation, he smiled when he realized that, by his own calculation, he was worth less than one tenth of a horse.

A woman, the Captain of the Guard, stepped down from her saddle, and approached the pair. Her grey hair was bound in a long braid that disappeared into the folds of her cloak, and her face fell into pleasant creases at the corners of her mouth as she smiled at them. She held her hand out to Blake, who wordlessly passed her the decorative weapon. She had an easy command about her that he could not imagine disobeying, even were they not surrounded by armed guards.

The wronged nobleman was riding on horseback, behind one of the guards. He dropped down from the back of the saddle and broke through the small audience that had gathered. He was reddened by the exertion, and he heaved for air, spitting at the ground as the city guards' attention became fixed upon his comically disheveled figure.

Blake tried hard to maintain his composure as he laid eyes on the nobleman. He knew he was not one for staying level-headed in these situations, but if he had any chance of leaving the city alive, he would need to remain as calm as possible.

"Sir, are these the men who robbed you?" the captain asked, her tone measured. She seemed to be a reasonable person, and Blake hoped that an even temper would impress upon her both his and Hugh's innocence.

"Robbed me?" the man shuddered as he looked at the pair. "These thieves tried to kill me."

"What?" Blake shouted, his air of calm disappearing as quickly as he had adopted it.

He surged forward to strike the nobleman with his bare fists, but a guard grabbed him around the waist. Blake was airborne for a moment as he struggled. Once he had stopped resisting, the guard set him back down, though the guard's hand stayed wrapped painfully tight around Blake's upper arm.

"Yes," the man said as he turned to Blake, a terrible leer stretching across his face. "First, I saw them running an illegal game in an alley. Not only were they gambling, but they were manipulating it so they were sure to win."

"So, not exactly gambling," Blake could not help but interject.

"Quiet," the Captain of the Guard warned, before turning back to the nobleman.

"When I confronted them, they dragged me behind a tavern and tried to murder me. Luckily, I was able to fight them off."

Blake began protesting, as did Hugh, and their combined objections increased in volume until they were shouting over each other. The captain, with a wave of her hand, ordered them to be silent.

Blake obeyed, but pulled stubbornly against the guard holding his arm. The guard's grip tightened, and he silently shot a threatening glance at the new prisoner. The look of warning was enough to subdue Blake.

The captain looked at the nobleman with scrutiny, her eyes narrowing slightly as she assessed the accuser's appearance. She took a deep breath, as she turned her attention back to Blake and Hugh.

"Very well, we shall take them to the castle prison to await sentencing." She turned to the nobleman, her tone somewhat caustic, "I must admit, I am impressed by how well you managed to fight off these two young men," she said, the corners of her lips twitching upward, "especially given they had taken possession of your weapon."

The nobleman squirmed beneath the speculative gaze of the captain. He opened his mouth, as if to speak, before closing it again. He shifted back and forth, before his eyes again made contact with hers. Though his discomfort was evident, he stuck out his jaw in defiance.

"I suppose I managed to scare them off." The now familiar smirk returned and he surveyed the two thieves, before continuing, "they seem rather easily frightened to me."

The captain nodded, though with a look of knowing. "That must have been the case."

Hugh and Blake's wrists were bound with rope, the other end of which was tied to the saddle of the captain's second in command, a young woman with straw-yellow hair. A handful of mounted guards began the journey back to the castle, and Blake and Hugh were pulled roughly along at the horses' gait.

2

From the shelf, Alderic took a book: the worn pages showing its age. He held the leather-bound volume carefully, as he turned to a story he knew by heart: The Tale of the Beast of Erkynon.

It was his favorite legend, and one his father had told to him often in his childhood. His eyes passed over the familiar page, as he read again the disquieting tale.

The Beast of Erkynon, Death Sin, is a wretched thing, born of profane union between the death goddess, Erkynon, and a mortal man. Love drove Erkynon to leave her underworld kingdom, walk amongst the living, and bear a child.

Erkynon broke with divine law in bringing forth this abomination. Rubelytte banished her from both the heavens and the land, imprisoning Erkynon in her own kingdom below, never again to speak to any living.

Had Rubelytte killed the baby, she would only have reunited mother and child; the Beast of Erkynon would reign as prince of the underworld, rewarding Erkynon for her misdeeds.

Instead, Rubelytte cursed the child with immortality and named it Death Sin. It was confined to the earth: to suffer the pain of living. The Beast of Erkynon will bleed when cut, but will never die. Any weapon raised to kill Death Sin will annihilate only the instrument.

Erkynon could not undo the curse placed on the child, but she gave Death Sin a gift of her own. Though the child could never enter the afterlife, she imbued it with the ability to bring forth the dead into the land of the living. She spat upon the other gods, and prayed that the child would raise an army from the hordes of the departed to wage war upon mankind: those most beloved of Rubelytte.

As the death goddess cannot speak to any alive, the Beast of Erkynon will live unaware of its power until, one fateful day, a king of kings meets Death Sin. This great king will bring his sword to cut off Death Sin's head, but the blade will shatter upon striking the skin.

Then will the gift of raising the dead awaken within the Beast of Erkynon.

Alderic's eyes passed over the ink illustrations that covered the pages, showing the signs and symbols associated with Erkynon and her child. They were strange, bearing no resemblance to anything on earth: dark lines pulled together in a disconcerting manner.

Some markings were used to buy time from the goddess, stalling the inevitable passage to the underworld, others to ensure the prosperity of a loved one in her kingdom. The most complicated of these markings was used to gain her favor by binding a human sacrifice to her, placing them in her eternal service: a hideous fate for an unlucky soul.

Though Alderic hesitated to rest his faith in folklore, there was an undeniable potency to these images; a mere glance could bring a wavering heartbeat or a frigid breath.

His obsession with the Beast of Erkynon had begun early in his reign. He was fascinated by the Beast, this inhuman capable of bringing about great suffering. Upon assuming the throne, Alderic had faced challengers on all sides, each vying to kill him and seize his title. He had met these threats with force, perhaps more than was necessary.

As many souls as the Beast of Erkynon was prophesied to bring forth to the land of the living, Alderic had sent far more to the land of the dead. Though perhaps regrettable, this show of strength accomplished his goal: no one questioned his efficacy, and he quickly became unstoppable. He surpassed his father's ambition to expand Vesia and he had brought about peace, as so few would dare to defy him.

He cast a final glance across the markings of Erkynon, before closing the book. There were more important matters to attend to, and he could not allow himself to become caught up in tales surrounding the demigod, however enthralling.

Alderic walked out onto the turrets and looked out at the water crashing on the cliffs far below the castle walls. The sound soothed his restless mind, as the cold wind tugged at his cloak and swept his hair. For the first time in months, he had hope.

His soldiers had kidnapped a wayward, lovesick guard: the second in command of the earl's protection. This second guard made the mistake of leaving the fortress to meet with a lover, but was abducted long before reaching his destination.

After only a little pain, the second guard had revealed everything he knew about the hiding place of the map and the magical, liogan force that kept the earl's fortress safe from the king's spies. Alderic was almost disappointed by the poor caliber of the earl's trusted man. Though he did not take pleasure from the manner in which he had returned the second guard's body, Alderic knew there was no room for laxity where the earl was concerned.

In the past week, he had thought long on the unique obstacle presented by the fortifications. He knew he chanced losing any spy he sent, just as he was sure that he could not send any in his employ. Even a bare knowledge of the legend, or memory of meeting the king, posed a significant risk to their concealment.

After consideration, he had come to the conclusion that he needed someone skilled, but oblivious to his intentions. Alderic had crafted a means by which a spy could extract the map without compromising themselves, though the king had yet to test the efficacy of this plan. A single failure would destroy any potential the method might hold, and risked setting his purpose back significantly.

The long search for an abettor was possibly nearing an end, as the Captain of the Guard had sent word by rider of two thieves, accused of attempting a nobleman's murder, who were to be brought to the castle within the hour. The king would watch them from the turrets, and reach a judgement. Little known to one of the newest prisoners, he could be crucial to the king's plans.

Alderic circled the castle, reaching the highest point overlooking the drawbridge. He had spent too much time away from the crumbling black walls of Ashen Castle and, though he commanded from the seat of the kingdom, he would not yet sit in his father's throne.

He had returned to Conrisia over one year before, his efforts dedicated to finally learning the truth of Ethin's liogan weapon. He was pressed, not only by the possible existence of the weapon, but by mounting legends and prophesies foretelling the end of his reign: the death of the king.

Though his grip on Vesia was unrelenting, the people told tales amongst themselves. It was said that a high ruler would arise from the eastern kingdom of Elsin, to slay the Vesian king and free every neighboring land from the looming threat of Alderic's rule. Such stories had plagued his reign from the moment he had taken the crown, yet this prophesy held the people's minds in a way none had before.

He stared into the dark depths of the still water winding around the castle walls. He knew the moat's waters seeped into the foundation of the castle, gradually eroding the stronghold, but he could not bring himself to touch it. Even the most minimal suggestions for improvement brought before him were met with an unceremonious rejection. Since his ascension to the throne, not a stone nor blade of grass had been changed on his orders and he had no intention of relenting.

The derelict stronghold stood as a testament to his annihilated family. Alderic had no heir, and his devastating aversion left him with no hope of ever conceiving a child. The king knew that the royal bloodline become extinct upon his death.

The walls could fall to ruins around him.

3

Blake's wrists and shoulders ached as he watched the dirt beneath their hurried feet slowly change from the dust of the city, to the damp grass of the hills. The temperature dropped as they began their ascent to Ashen Castle, a dark stone edifice that cut a bleak outline against the grey sky and the windswept grass of the country.

He could hear the crashing of waves against the cliff which lay to the other side of the castle, and taste the approaching rain in the air as the sky filled with dark clouds. The wind sent a chill through him. Ashen Castle seemed to exist in a climate of its own, the cold sea air and green grass untouched by the scorching sun of the city below.

Blake could not help but admire the heights reached by the expansive black walls, and protruding turrets. He looked upwards to study the surroundings, though each glance ended with a rough pull at his bound wrists. Even from a distance he could see archers pacing, and the bows ready by their sides.

He could also see another figure. This man stood above the archers, dark and brooding against the pale sky. Blake could not explain why, but he was overwhelmed by the feeling that this man was watching him. Though the person was far too high to discern clearly, Blake felt his breath catch in his throat and he turned his eyes away. Somehow, it felt safer not to look.

"You can get us out of this, can't you?" Hugh whispered from beside Blake.

"I will know better once we are inside the castle, for now it is best you stay silent," Blake cautioned.

They finally reached the moat. Looking up again, he found he was no longer able to see the archers atop the walls, his view of the sky blocked by the dark stone.

A large drawbridge lowered, the chains creaking as they bore the considerable weight of the worn wooden boards. They stepped across the bridge, over the cool, shadowed water that encircled the castle. The moat was wide, and he could see the water resting against the walls of the castle. Blake looked over the edge of the bridge, and could see a large, black shape move quickly beneath the surface. He shuddered, as the rope yanked him forward.

He had heard stories of the monster which lay in King Alderic's moat, but he was surprised to find they held truth. He was increasingly coming to believe the Vesian tales of magic surrounding the dilapidated castle. Small, blue flowers sprang from the moat and wound around the castle walls, their vines creeping into cracked stone. The blooms wilted on the vine, yet lost nothing of their midnight vibrancy. There was something distinctly unstable and frightening about the place.

They were led through the gates, and into an abandoned courtyard. The captain dismounted, and handed the prisoners over to a guard, who led them into an inner passage of the castle walls, and down a dark flight of steps.

Blake's eyes had not yet adjusted to the dim light of the prison's interior as they were led down. He slipped on the steps when the guard pulled the ropes, and struggled to stand, bracing his elbow against an unseen edge. As he righted himself, he noticed the stone steps were slick with condensation, and he could hear the faint trickle of water coming from the heart of the prison.

They were thrown into separate cells, across a narrow passageway. Blake could hear the metal grate doors slam shut, and the key turn in each of the locks. A faint sound of whistling followed the guard up the stairs and out of the prison, until Blake could hear the noise no more.

He rifled through his pockets, thankful they had not been searched before their incarceration. He found flint and steel, string, and a few coins, but nothing helpful. As his search moved lower, he came upon his lock picks, tucked safely in his left boot, and began working to open the door to his cell.

"How soon until we are free?" Hugh whispered loudly across the hallway.

"Not long, but longer if I have to talk to you."

"Hurry. The walls seem close, and I don't think I can stand it."

He cast a glance through the dispiriting darkness of the prison, and could tell Hugh was watching him expectantly from across the hallway. Blake knew the subject of lock picking had always been of interest to Hugh, but it was also one of the many lessons Blake had neglected to teach him during their time travelling together.

As he thought on his failure as an instructor, he felt the satisfying give of the crafted metal parts beneath his fingers. He pushed the door open slowly, keeping a downward pressure with his right hand. This pull kept the control of the creaking sound within his grasp.

He padded lightly across the narrow hallway, and crouched down to bring the lock on Hugh's cell to his eye line.

"I can't see what you're doing," Hugh whispered. Even in the face of sizeable danger, his desire to apprentice himself was evident.

"This is hardly the time," Blake responded, curtly.

Given that he was now facing the lock, rather than blindly working through a door, it seemed as though this task should be easier. Yet, Blake found the lock was entirely unresponsive to his efforts. He squinted, trying to gain a better view, but he knew this was not the reason. He had encountered this type of lock many times before, and could pick one blindfolded and backwards if needed.

Hugh shifted back and forth, and Blake could sense his companion's agitation growing. He had tried to mask his frustration, but he let it out, striking the lock. The metal clanged, resounding throughout the prison, causing both men to freeze.

After seconds that felt like a lifetime, no guard came bursting through the door, so Blake resumed his efforts. It felt as though something had been lodged in the lock, making it impossible to open with simple lock picks. He could think of no other explanation.

"How much longer?" Hugh asked again.

He could feel Hugh's eyes watching even his smallest movement. Hugh's aspirations had been anchored to Blake for the past year, and Blake could not help but feel he had failed miserably, though he supposed his shortcomings as a mentor no longer mattered.

"Give me a minute," Blake whispered, his annoyance with the situation directing itself at Hugh.

Blake knew he would not be able to open the lock. He continued to move the metal pieces, now more for Hugh's benefit than in a true effort, as he tried to formulate a new plan for escape. He focused his ears on the sound of trickling water surrounding him, but he could not avoid the inevitable conclusion. With a creeping sense of dread came the realization that there was nothing else he could do. If he stayed even a moment longer, he risked discovery by the guard, leading both of them closer to the gallows.

Blake stood, tucking his lock picks back into his boot. He could feel Hugh's anticipation mount, and he kept his eyes downcast to avoid meeting those of his companion. He put his hand between the metal bars, and took Hugh's forearm in a reassuring grasp.

"I have to leave," he spoke slowly, his eyes still averted. "I will return for you if I can."

There was a part of Blake that hoped that this was not a false oath, even as he knew better. Were he able to escape from Ashen Castle, nothing could lure him back to its treacherous confines.

He let go and took a step back, summoning the courage to look Hugh in the face. Despite the low light, Blake could see Hugh's eyes were wide with disbelief.

"You cannot abandon me." Hugh's voice shook. "I am begging you for mercy, for my life, don't do this."

Blake nodded, even as he backed away. "If I stay, we will both die."

Hugh's eyes filled with tears. They fell, staining his cheeks, as his chest was torn with rough, ragged breathing.

Blake felt a pain growing in his chest as he looked on his imprisoned partner. Hugh had followed him unquestioningly from city to city, trusting Blake to train and defend him. Neither could have predicted such a parting.

"Please," Hugh whispered. His fingers wrapped around the metal bars of the door, and his shoulders hunched over, wracked with quiet sobbing.

Blake turned, and made his way to the bottom of the steps leading to the inner passageway of the castle.

"If you do this, I will never forgive you," Hugh whispered after him. "I will carry your betrayal deep within my heart; I will bear it even into the underworld."

Blake took a deep breath and climbed the steps, feeling carefully to find his footing. He could hear gentle sobbing echo through the cavernous prison, and he forced himself to ignore the sound. Soon, Hugh's weeping faded into the background.

Blake was able to pull a strip of metal from the railing, and readied himself to attack the guard who was doubtless stationed in the hallway. He turned the handle of the door, keeping the metal piece held high beside his ear.

He pushed the door open, so only a sliver of light fell inside the prison. He could see the guard's back facing him, but found he had enough room to slip past. While he was able to leave the prison undetected, he was forced to move in the direction opposite the courtyard. He knew this was for the best; had he entered the courtyard, he would likely have been immediately recaptured.

The hall ran through the length of the castle walls and, as he passed through, it adopted the appearance of a coarse tunnel. The rough-cut walls were lit by flickering torches and Blake's shadow followed, jagged, behind.

He clung to the wall, his heart racing. He knew his recapture could be the result of a single glance by even a servant of the king. He passed doorways, and a window that looked to the outside of the castle. Each of these was an opportunity for escape, but the risk was too great. He had seen the archers posted along the walls when he entered the castle. Any escape pathway that released him within clear view left him vulnerable to their attack.

There was no place in the known world where Blake would less like to be than in Ashen Castle. While he had never seen the king himself, the legends surrounding the warlord were gargantuan in scope.

The people called him the Blackdog King, though never in his presence. The face of a wild blackdog with bright red eyes was the symbol of King Alderic's family. Those of his bloodline had risen from leaders of a brutal tribe to rulers of the largest extant kingdom. It was King Alderic himself who had accomplished this prodigious task, by building endlessly on the territory his father had secured.

As a child, Blake was often told of blackdog ghosts. These phantoms were seen in the countryside and said to be harbingers of ill-fate, though Blake had never glimpsed one himself. He wondered whether the evil associated with such apparitions was due to the influence of the Vesian king, or whether the king's epithet was simply a reflection of his nature.

In the early years of King Alderic's reign, any who opposed him were massacred, and he conquered the surrounding kingdoms with impunity. Though there had not been a Vesian war in years, the fear and hatred of those early days burned in the minds of the people.

Vesia could do nothing: their warlord king might as well be a god.

The sounds of footsteps approaching from behind drew his attention, and Blake quickened his pace. He caught sight of a small niche cut into the wall and, looking around, knew there was nowhere else to hide. He tucked himself into the alcove, and sank to the ground. Sitting on his heels, he tried to remain motionless in the shadows. His mouth was dry, and he could feel his heart pounding in his chest.

Two guards passed by the niche. They were absorbed in conversation, and did not notice Blake hiding in the shadow as they crossed the entrance. He waited until the sound of their voices had faded before he dared to breathe again.

He stayed on his heels, trying to formulate a plan. His palms reached out to the wall, and rested a moment. The marks in the stone were sharp, and his fingers came away coated with rock dust. He squinted against the flickering light, and could clearly see the cuts in the niche were made more recently, and crudely, than those of the walls. He shifted weight between his two feet. He could feel a wavering in the floor, and heard the faint grating sound accompanying the movement.

Making sure the hallway was empty, he stepped out, and dropped to his hands and knees. He felt a small dip in the center of the niche's floor, and found a hold within the recess. He placed his fingertips in the hold and braced his legs against the walls of the alcove. He pulled with all his strength, and he could feel the stone disc move an inch, before he lost his grip and stumbled backwards. The stone dropped back into place.

He waited and, when it was clear the noise had not drawn any guards, he tried again. This time, he was able to lift the stone. He could only hold it a moment, but when it fell, it landed askew. From there, he was able to grab the edge and drag it along to uncover an opening in the floor.

The scraping sound of the dragged stone was considerable, and Blake knew he had little time. He stepped over the cover, and dropped down through the hole without a moment's hesitation.

The fall was surprisingly long, and his knees buckled at the landing. He found himself in pitch black surroundings, with only a little light coming from the alcove above. He moved blindly through the space, his arms outstretched. He was seeking only to place distance between himself and the prison. Besides, he knew he could not return to the niche, both due to the height of the ceiling and the attention the misplaced stone would doubtless attract.

He felt along the stone wall as he moved forward, until his hand struck a wooden beam. He was able to discern he had come to a door and, finding the handle, turned it. He breathed a sigh of relief as he felt the tap of the latch opening.

He spilled into a small room. His dust-covered shoes landed on a red woven carpet, and a time-worn tapestry adorned the wall opposite. The room was lit both by candles and the dying light of the rain-clouded sun. He headed for the door, but a movement from the corner of the room caught his eye. He froze in place as he realized he was not alone.

"I see you made it."

A man stood in the corner of the room, his eyes fixed on the tapestry. Blake opened his mouth to speak, but found he was without words. He turned to run, but the man touched the hilt of his sword. The implied threat was enough to stop him from leaving.

"Have a seat." While spoken as an invitation, the words were unmistakably a command.

Blake sank down into a nearby chair. From this position, he was better able to take in the appearance of the man who stood before him. He was tall, at least a foot taller than Blake. He wore an indigo shirt, and a dark grey cloak. His nostrils flared slightly, and his skin was pale as that of a corpse. His straight black hair fell to his lower back, and Blake self-consciously ran his fingers through his own untidy brown hair.

"Do you consider yourself a skilled thief?" he asked.

The man's deep, unwavering voice broke Blake from his examination of the other. Blake leaned back in his chair, as he knew the importance of appearing self-assured.

"The best." He smiled. "I've made it past nearly every type of lock Vesian blacksmiths have crafted, and stolen more valuables than even I can recall."

The man was visibly unimpressed by this display, frowning. This swept the smile from Blake's face, replacing it with an expression that was practically earnest.

"You run rigged street games, and failed to evade discovery by a nobleman who is a nothing but a fool on his best day. That does not speak well to your supposed skill."

"Unless it was my aim to get inside these castle walls," Blake joked, immediately regretting his flippant tone as the words left his lips.

"It wasn't," the man sighed, looking the thief over once again. "I have a proposition for you. If you can complete a simple task for me, I will give you your freedom in exchange." His baritone voice was exceedingly measured, a mannerism that in other circumstances Blake might have mistaken for boredom.

Blake's heart skipped, and he could taste metal against his tongue. Nevertheless, he knew better than to discard with caution.

"Only King Alderic can pardon me," he responded, making a deliberate effort to imitate the steady speech of the other man. "Am I to be given this task on his orders?"

The man nodded, though seemed mildly surprised. "I can ensure that he gives you a full pardon."

"What is the task?" Blake asked.

"It is a simple retrieval. You will break into an earl's fortress, and retrieve an iron chest that I am told is hidden within Lord Wesley's private cellar."

"Will I be able to carry it?" Blake asked. "If not, I may need more time."

"That is irrelevant," the man responded shortly.

"Why did you choose me?" Blake asked. Given the man's description of his criminal activities, it was clear that he did not hold the thief in high regard.

"Because you made it to this room." He responded, seating himself behind the desk. "This is one of the few places in the castle you could have reached that would not have ended in your death." He spoke these words with a casual nature that unnerved Blake. "You were merely lucky to find the entrance to the passageway, I have no doubt of that, but there is something more important that kept you from using the window."

"The archers," Blake said quietly.

The man nodded. "The fact that you deliberately turned away from more obvious means of escape shows you kept in your mind a vision of the threats to your person both within the castle walls and without. A handful of others have attempted to escape, but each was lured into such a trap." He paused. "Though I suppose you may feel you have fallen into a trap of your own."

The man's thin lips twisted into a smile, and Blake felt his stomach turn. There was something about this man that made the air in his lungs turn cold, and all Blake could think about was getting away.

"It is not a particularly challenging trial, yet it would prove me to be the kind of master thief needed for such a mission?"

The man shook his head. "Not a master, it shows you are merely adequate. For this task, a master thief would only prove more trouble than they are worth."

"What if I refuse your offer?" Blake asked.

"You will die," the man shrugged as he answered.

In truth, Blake had no intention of turning him down. In addition to a natural aversion to his own death, he found the idea of breaking into a stronghold and stealing a guarded valuable undeniably exciting. It was only his unfounded dread of the man before him that gave Blake a moment's pause.

"I will do it, but I ask one more thing in return." Blake resumed his cocky pose, eyeing the much taller man down the length of his nose as best he could.

The man stayed silent.

"The other prisoner who was brought to the castle with me, Hugh, will be released."

After a moment's thought, the man nodded. "He will be released when you bring me the chest."

Blake stood and held out his hand, forcing himself to smile. The man took his hand in a strong grasp, and Blake was taken aback by the coldness of the man's skin.

Blake was led by servants to the courtyard and a carriage harnessed to four horses. The sky was dark, and rain was falling across the cracked cobblestones. He took a final look at the derelict, though royal, surroundings before being guided roughly into the carriage. He sat down inside, flanked on either side by guards, and braced himself for the journey ahead.

"Where are we going?" he asked the one to his left, but received no response.

The carriage pitched as the horses were driven forward, and Blake was jostled between the guards. He smiled apologetically, but both of his escorts merely stared ahead.

His thoughts turned to Hugh, and to the state of despair in which he had left the other. He had no doubt Hugh cursed his name, but he smiled when he thought on the deliverance his success would bring.

4

It was early morning when they arrived at the fortress. The walls rose high, though to only half the height of Ashen Castle's walls. There were no archers patrolling the turrets, and the gate was open. This made the courtyard accessible to the people of the land, who moved freely in and out of the fortress.

Still, Blake could see a porter by the gate, who watched those entering the walls closely as they moved to the courtyard. Guards stood on either side of the porter, though no one seemed to take notice of the carriage nearing the walls.

The castle guard handed him a doublet made of green velvet.

"This is the uniform of the earl's staff. Wearing this should allow you free movement within the walls," the guard to his right explained.

Blake stepped outside the carriage, pulling the uniform on over his clothes, and took a closer look at the scene before him. The porter seemed better defended than the fortress itself, which at a glance had nowhere near the fortifications Blake had seen at Ashen Castle. A chill ran down his spine as he wondered what method of defense could stay the hand of the seemingly invincible Blackdog King.

"We will be waiting outside," the guard spoke to him from the carriage. "We have soldiers posted outside the walls, so do not think of trying to escape."

Blake took these words as his dismissal, offering a mockingly cheery wave as he walked away. He could hear the horses pulling the carriage, though he knew that they would not go far. It must have rained that night, because the muddy grass squelched beneath his boots.

The fortress was located in a rural area removed from the capital, surrounded only by small villages and farms. The fortress was built from sandy colored bricks, and was welcomingly golden in the light of the new sun. The air was clear, with the fresh scent of recent rainfall in the pleasantly warm air.

He approached the gate, careful to appear at ease. As he passed through the entrance, he gave a nod to the porter, who gave no sign of suspicion.

Inside the courtyard walls was a bustling crowd of people. A night's ride from Conrisia, the courtyard seemed to have adopted the function of a small marketplace. The people came with carts, and bartered for food and goods. The sound of laughter and idle chatter filled the space, and Blake found he could move freely beneath the cover of the merry crowd.

Glancing upward, Blake took in the extent of the enclosure. Doors indicated rooms and hallways contained within the walls, and each wooden door was carved with delicate etchings. He touched the surface of one of the closed doors, his fingertips running over an embellishment depicting a sleeping lion.

Simple drawings adorned every other stone in the wall, and Blake could not help but contrast the warmth and adoration evident in these surroundings with the broken, yet undeniably intimidating, Ashen Castle.

It was odd that a presumed stronghold would allow such free passage to the civilians and, while entry to the courtyard had been simple, Blake soon realized that access beyond this point would prove to be more difficult. Every door he located was straddled by two watchmen, their eyes fixed vigilantly on the crowd ahead.

He watched a servant dressed in a worn velvet uniform similar to his. She stood in the middle of the courtyard, making what appeared to be painfully polite conversation with a woman selling orchard fruit from a cart. When the exchange ended, Blake followed behind her as she approached one of the doors. The servant passed through the entrance, and Blake kept close on her heels.

Blake let out a sigh of relief as he entered the cool, candlelit hallways. The noise of the crowd outside faded, and was replaced by the muted sounds of the earl's servants going dutifully about their daily tasks.

He felt a movement by his elbow and he jumped. A woman had come to stand by his side, and indicated with a crooked finger that he should follow her. He could not risk raising suspicion, so he allowed himself to be led into the kitchens.

"You're new here, aren't you?" she asked. Her face was turned away from him, as she critically took in the activities of the kitchen, one hand resting on her hip.

Blake nodded silently.

The woman pushed a tray of food into his hands, and straightened his collar. "The earl likes to meet the latest additions to his staff. You will bring him his breakfast this morning."

Blake nodded again.

"You don't know where to go," she said with a reflexive eyeroll. She grasped his upper arm, careful not to upset the tray, and led him into the hall and to the bottom of a staircase. "Up three flights, second door on the right. Knock twice and wait for Lord Wesley to tell you to come in."

Blake thanked the woman, and focused his efforts on keeping the tray upright as he brushed past servants and guards in the bustling hallway. The smell and sight of the food on the tray brought Blake's attention to his own empty stomach, and he tried to ignore the butter dripping across the piece of fresh bread that sat at the side of the plate.

When he came to the earl's door, he balanced one end of the tray on his knee and knocked twice.

"Enter," said a voice behind the door.

Blake let himself into the room, finding himself in the presence of Lord Wesley. He set the tray down on the breakfast table by the window and offered a small, courteous bow to his feigned master.

"I don't recognize you," the earl observed plainly.

Lord Wesley sat in an armchair beside the bed. His cheeks were freckled, framed by curls. His face was careworn and enervated, and he watched Blake through drowsing eyelids.

"My mother was proudly in your employ, but has been taken ill. She sent me here to earn money for the family in her stead. It is a testament to your lordship that I was so graciously welcomed by all in your estate," Blake said.

He sensed that Lord Wesley would have a softness concerning his staff. However, given the number of servants he had seen in the hallways, Blake knew that the earl would not know the name of each.

"You are most welcome, boy," the earl responded, his eyes crinkling. "I am sorry to hear of your mother's illness." He reached into a drawer by his bedside and retrieved a small pouch. He motioned for Blake to come nearer. "Please accept this money. I hope it will serve your family as well as your family has served me." He pressed a few coins into Blake's hand.

"Thank you, my lord," Blake said, pleased to have been right in his assessment. "This is truly a great kindness."

"Think nothing of it," responded Lord Wesley, waving his hand airily.

Blake took this as his dismissal and made to leave the room. His hand was on the doorknob when he paused, a question wavering on his lips. He was reluctant to call further attention to himself, but his curiosity had gotten the better of his sense.

"Forgive me, my lord, but may I ask you a question?"

"Certainly," the earl responded.

"My mother told me that King Alderic has tried to enter the fortress. Why would the king concern himself with this place?" he asked, turning back to the seated Lord Wesley.

The earl's expression darkened for a moment, before he offered a small, sad smile. "You have nothing to fear from the king. For reasons I cannot explain to you, neither he nor any of his soldiers can enter these walls. Truthfully, you are safer here than anywhere else in Vesia."

"My mother told me that the king has committed horrific acts in his attempts," Blake pressed; it seemed a reasonable presumption.

"She is doubtless talking about the second guard," the earl said, as he brushed his brow with the back of his hand. "Yet, that is no reason for unease."

"Is the king really so terrible?" Blake continued, trying to provoke Lord Wesley. He had already risked himself, and was unwilling to leave the room with unanswered questions. "Perhaps he is merely trying to protect his kingdom."

The earl's eyes narrowed. "You are still a young man, yet even for your limited years you are foolish. I can tell you of the second guard, and perhaps you will amend your unnaturally generous opinion of the king."

Lord Wesley settled into the chair and interwove his fingers. "The highest-ranking guards are not allowed to leave the walls of the fortress," he said. "One man, my guards' second in command, disobeyed this order. He wished to visit his sweetheart in the village and thought he could slip away for a few hours, unnoticed. He was incorrect. The second guard was missing for several days, and we believed that he had been kidnapped by the king's soldiers, likely tortured for information. These fears were only confirmed when we saw him next."

"So, he returned?"

"In pieces," Lord Wesley responded bitterly. "Every day for one week, the king's soldiers sent a wild horse running loose into the courtyard, dragging behind it a piece of the second guard. The Blackdog King aimed to unsettle us through this repulsive act."

Blake felt a knot twist within him at this description of the king's brutality. He knew he should leave, but he pressed on.

"And you think he got whatever it was he sought from the second guard?"

"I do not know," the earl said, looking sadly at Blake. "Still, I promise that the fortifications we have in place can withstand any soldiers or spies the king sends our way. He will not find what he seeks and, without this, we are of no consequence to King Alderic one way or another."

Blake half-heartedly wished he could share the earl's optimism. He did not understand the nature of the fortress' defenses, yet the thief's mere presence was proof that King Alderic's man had found a way past such resistance.

Blake excused himself from Lord Wesley's room, thanking him for his words. He was sorry to deceive the earl, but his thoughts turned back to Hugh and he knew he had no choice.

The earl was simply far too trusting.

Blake entered the main hallway. He heard a movement and the sound of voices approaching. He went through one of the wooden doors that lined the hall, deciding to pass a few minutes in the small room until he could be sure the hallway was again unoccupied. He could not afford to waste time on another assigned task.

The only source of light was a small crack in the wall, through which filtered the pale rays of the sun. In time his eyes adjusted, and he was better able to look around the room. The walls were lined with shelves, each holding stacks of books. On the floor were wicker baskets containing carefully rolled scrolls, covered by folded, yellowed linen.

Blake was unusual; though of low birth, his education was as good as that of any Vesian noble. His mother had insisted that he learn to read, write, and speak as well as any in Conrisia. A learned woman, she had taken it upon herself to provide such instruction, and these abilities had served him well in his career as a swindler. Despite his humble upbringing in a fishing village on the Isle of Ang, a small island within Vesia, he could blend easily with all ranks. He doubted this was the use she had predicted when she spent long hours teaching him to read and speak as she did.

He removed an old book from the wall, and thumbed through the crumbling pages. He leaned back and held the book beneath a shaft of light. The writing was archaic, but he was able to piece together the meaning well enough. He kept hold of the book, as he idly scanned the rest of the room.

His eyes landed on a green glass bottle, tucked behind a basket in the corner of the room as if hastily hidden by an errant servant. He picked up the bottle, brushing away the accumulated dust with his shirtsleeve, and removed the cork. His nose was struck by a sharp, alcoholic scent. It smelled of the rye drink he had enjoyed in the past: a crude but potent swill.

Nevertheless, the container looked respectable, so he kept hold of the bottle and the book as he peered around the door into the hallway. There was no one in sight, nor could he detect the sound of approaching voices, so he slipped from the small room.

As he moved through the fortress, it became clear he would not find the private cellar by chance. He had no recourse but to ask for assistance. Blake ran a hand through his hair, and straightened his clothing, as he spotted a guard at the end of the hallway.

The guard was leaning against a doorframe. His spear rested in the crook of his arm, and an ornamental dagger that distinguished him as one of the earl's higher-ranking guards was stuffed awkwardly into his belt. He looked Blake over as the other man approached.

"I have been ordered to bring this to Lord Wesley's private cellar, but I must confess I have become rather lost." Blake kept his eyes down, a practiced look of worry gracing his brow. "Today is my first day in the earl's employ and, when I was given this task, I was embarrassed to admit I am too unfamiliar to find my way."

The guard stretched out his hand. "Give me the book, and I will deliver it for you."

Blake was taken aback. He held the bottle in plain sight, yet the guard assumed the book was the object of discussion. He knew he had taken too long to respond, so he flashed his most humiliated smile.

"Sir, I appreciate your kindness, but I could not ask you to leave your post. I am sure I can find the way if I am given direction."

The guard sighed. "You can go down two flights to find the cellar. No one is permitted to enter, but you can leave the book with the posted guard," he said as he stepped aside, seemingly tired by their conversation.

Blake thanked him, and walked past the guard to the stairs. When he was out of sight, he balanced the green bottle on a windowsill in the stairwell. He descended two sets of steps, and came to a guard standing outside of a door which was secured by a large padlock.

Blake glanced behind him, noticing that the stairs continued their descent, leading to some place far beneath the cellars.

"Sir, I have been asked to bring this book to the earl's private cellar," he ventured, holding the book reverently with both hands.

The guard wordlessly outstretched his hand.

"I would like to carry it in myself, if it is all the same to you," Blake began, bringing the book back to his chest.

The guard shook his head. "No one gains access to the cellar. Give me the book, and I will ensure that it is properly stowed."

Blake could see that arguing would be useless. He was significantly smaller and more poorly armed than the guard, so fighting him would likely be a fatal attempt. Besides, the smallest shout would leave Blake mobbed by armed members of the earl's protection.

He looked the guard over, and noticed a large key that hooked onto an old, rusted chain around the guard's waist. The key seemed to be the right size for the lock, and Blake devised a second plan. He only hoped the guard would not try to put the book in the cellar immediately.

"Thank you for your help," he conceded.

Blake loosely held the book out to the guard, but dropped it to the floor just as the other man reached his hand out, with the appearance of an accident. The book landed at the guard's feet.

"I must apologize," Blake stammered.

As the guard bent down to pick it up, Blake touched the stooped man's shoulder with a shaking hand in apology, while simultaneously lifting the key from the chain, catching it with his smallest finger as it dropped toward the floor. He hid the key within his sleeve, and shook the guard's hand before taking his leave.

Blake knew he had little time before the cellar guard discovered the key's absence. He walked slowly until he was out of sight, at which point he raced up the steps two at a time. He came to the windowsill where he had stored the bottle, a plan half-formed in his head.

He pulled up the velvet servant's garb, tucking the hem beneath his chin to keep it out of the way. He took his own cotton shirt, and used his fingers to tear away a thick strip of fabric. He quietly removed the bottle's cork and tucked the fabric in, turning it over briefly to ensure it was soaked through with alcohol. He reached into his pocket, and removed flint and a small piece of steel, items which had not been confiscated from him before his imprisonment. He struck the two together, trying to make a spark, and wincing at the abrasive noise that echoed through the stone-lined stairwell.

He quickened his striking until, finally, he got a small spark. The fabric lit quickly, and he sprinted down the stairs, dropping the bottle onto the landing beneath that of the cellar door. He watched as the fire flashed, and the guard left his post to investigate the source of the flames. The fire would not spread, given the stone surroundings, and Blake knew he had to act during this short window of time.

He could feel the heat of the blaze as he made his way quickly to the door. The air was filled with the sweet, sharp smell of rye, and he could hear a commotion growing on the landing below.

He inserted the key, checking again to ensure the guard had not returned. He opened the lock with ease, and stepped through the door, closing it fully behind himself. He looked around to find he had entered an extensive underground library. The walls were covered in shelves, each of which buckled under the weight of the tomes stacked to the ceiling. The air was thick with dust, and a small oil lamp lit the center of the room.

Blake searched the room for the iron chest, but was unable to find it. He knew it might be concealed behind the rows of books, and worried he would not have time to conduct a thorough exploration before the guard noticed the missing key.

As he scanned a bookshelf at the far end of the room, he noticed that it sat at an odd angle with the wall. He examined the shelf from top to bottom and, as he crouched down, he noticed that it did not meet the floor.

He tugged at the edge of the shelf and leapt out of the way when the section of wall swung forward, revealing a small doorway. The hidden room was dark, so he retrieved the oil lamp before proceeding.

The floor was filled with baskets of ancient scrolls, and at the center lay a small iron chest. He walked cautiously toward it, the lamp casting a yellow glow on the rusted metal box, which was secured with a padlock.

He tried to lift it, but could not. He pushed against the side, ramming it with his shoulder, but it was as though it were welded to the floor. He took a step back, before falling on the chest with renewed efforts. He shoved, kicked, and pulled until it became clear that it was unmoving.

Sweat beaded across his face, and he could feel a bruise forming on his abused shoulder. He may not be able to bring the chest from the room, but perhaps he could bring its contents to the king's man.

He turned his attention to the padlock, an unwieldy thing that had succumbed to the same rust covering its bearer. He found a long piece of metal decoratively attached to the chest, which he was able to pry loose. Finding the weak point of the lock, he drove down with this piece of iron and felt the safeguard give way beneath his tightly gripped fingers. He slid the remaining lock piece from the loop, and lifted the lid of the chest. The hinges creaked, and Blake could feel his heart racing.

He held the lamp next to his cheek, resting the base against his shoulder, and tilted it to cast light into the chest. He was surprised to see it contained nothing more than a red roll of leather wrapped around a piece of parchment. He extended his fingers to pull free the contents.

"I wouldn't."

Blake froze at the sound of the voice, his fingers only inches from the parchment. He withdrew his hand slowly, the thud of his heart echoing in his ears.

An old man stepped out from one of the shadowed corners, his walking stick tapping the stone floor with each step. He wore a long, tattered robe, that pooled at his feet as he came to stand before Blake. His hand shook, even as it rested on the top of the cane.

Perceiving the man's frailty, Blake felt his usual brashness reemerge.

"Why not?" he asked, puffing his chest out.

Silently, the old man rested against his walking stick. Blake lifted the lamp, using the light to perform a thorough examination of the man's face. The eyes were white as shells, their color not broken by the darkness of a pupil. Blake waved his hand inches from the cellarman's face to test his sight.

"You may lower your hand," the old man's dry voice cracked on the words. "You are here on the king's orders, is that not so?"

Blake declined to speak, and the cellarman seemed to take Blake's silence as assent, because he continued, "if you bring this to Ashen Castle, you will irreparably alter the course of history, and cripple our pursuit of freedom for the Vesian kingdom."

"I suppose we shall see," Blake said with a smirk that would probably go unnoticed. "Or rather, I shall. After all, I doubt you will see the end of the year." With this, he snatched the leather roll from the chest, and tucked it into his shirt.

Blake would not be distracted by the old man's idealistic rambling: too much relied on his success. The smell of dust and old paper filled his nostrils, and the cellarman swayed unsteadily before him. The foreign nature of these surroundings served to better focus Blake on his goal, as it was more difficult to fall beneath the spell of false comfort.

If the cellarman was bothered by Blake's obvious contempt he did not make it known. Instead, his face fell into a pitying, though blank, stare. "You will not be able to leave this room. The door is closely watched."

"There was only one guard," Blake spoke, though mostly to himself. "If this is so important, why is it not better secured?" He turned to the old man. "Has anyone tried to steal the parchment before?"

"Of course," the old man barked out a laugh, "you think you are the first sent here on the king's orders? There have been many before you, and after you are caught there will doubtless be many more to come."

"Then why are more guards not posted?" Blake questioned, his curiosity growing.

"You are the first to make it past the porter," the cellarman admitted. "He holds the intent of this parchment in his mind, and any who aim to steal it, or can so much as recall meeting the king, are immediately known to him: they do not last long. If the king were to try storming the fortress, I would destroy the parchment myself."

"A liogan?" Blake mused. "I thought they were all killed during childhood."

Liogans were individuals with greater than human capabilities. Though they were typically born to ordinary families, after only the first few years of their lives, they would begin to display magical talents. In ancient times, liogans were powerful and feared by all. However, the fear they inspired soon became their curse and the practice of killing liogans the moment their gifts betrayed them became widespread.

"It is true that were his abilities known, he would not last long outside Lord Wesley's protection." The cellarman responded, his unsettling white eyes rolling in their sockets, seeming look Blake over. "I wonder how you made it past."

Blake pondered this, and his mind seized on a piece of information unknown to the cellarman: he had not been sent in search of the parchment.

"Would he search minds for the iron chest?" Blake asked.

The cellarman's mouth opened a fraction of an inch, betraying his revelation. "The second guard must have told the king where the parchment was kept," he murmured.

"The man who sent me expected that, were I unable to lift the chest, I would settle for stealing the contents. He did not care about the iron chest, he only needed my ignorance of the parchment." Blake felt pride at having pieced together the reasoning behind his assignment.

"And I suppose you have not met the king," the cellarman continued, his voice conveying his defeat.

"Never," Blake responded.

Blake had made it past the cellar guard once, but knew he could not do so alone again. "You will help me escape," he said, turning to the cellarman.

"I will not," he responded, his jaw visibly tightening, "and you will never make it past the guard without me."

There was a firmness to the cellarman's response that made Blake realize it would be impossible to coerce him. Only one recourse remained. The old man must have been of great importance to the earl. He was charged with a presumably precious object, something the entire stronghold had been designed to protect.

Blake grabbed the old man by the front of the shirt, pulling him roughly toward the door, but the bony shoulder slipped from his grasp, and the cellarman stumbled backwards. The walking stick had fallen from his aged hand and the cellarman fell against the wall, his head striking a shelf.

The old man sank to the ground, and lay there unmoving. Blake rushed forward, and crouched over him. He took the aged face between his hands, relieved to find that the cellarman was still breathing.

Blake was sorry to have done him such harm, even without intention, but he knew he was running out of time. Devising a new plan, he slung the unconscious cellarman over his shoulders, and adjusted his cap to partially obscure his face.

He entered the larger room, undid the lock, and pushed the heavy door forward, knocking deliberately into the guard. He shoved through the doorframe, as the guard recovered from the unexpected jostling.

"How did you get in there?" the guard demanded, an angry red hue growing on his cheeks.

"There is no time. I found him on the floor, and fear he may be injured. Where is the doctor?"

"But how did you—" the guard stubbornly challenged.

Blake lowered the tone of his voice, inching toward the guard. "We cannot delay. You know as well as I what will happen to you if any ill befalls this man. I will ask once more: where is the earl's doctor?"

The guard ceased his stammering; it was obvious Blake had struck upon at least a facet of the truth. The guard gave directions as quickly as he could talk, while Blake dropped the key to the top of his own foot and rolled it carefully to the ground, ensuring it would not clank tellingly against the floor.

"Thank you for your aid, Lord Wesley shall hear of your vigilance."

The guard practically bowed to him, as Blake carried the cellarman up the stairs and into the courtyard. He knew the guard would immediately alert the rest of the staff, and that he could not afford to hide anywhere on the grounds. He caught sight of a horse-drawn wagon laden with goods that was preparing to leave the courtyard.

Blake waited until the owner had taken her place behind the horses, before opening the back of the wagon. He lay the unconscious cellarman upon one of the softer looking bags, before climbing into the wagon himself. Blake pulled a cloth over the pair of them, and ducked down as the wagon lurched forward at the pull of the horses.

From beneath the cloth he could hear the hooves click against the courtyard cobblestone. He waited until he was sure they were out of the porter's sight before lifting the covering. It seemed the liogan did not search the minds of those departing the fortress.

He briefly considered just leaving the cellarman on the wagon. However, it occurred to him that when the old man regained his senses, he would likely remember everything. Blake assumed the king's man would not look kindly on loose ends, and Blake would not jeopardize the promised pardons when he was so close to achieving his end.

The wagon was travelling forward slowly, so he was able to roll the cellarman to the edge. He hopped from the wagon to the ground, and brought the unconscious man again across his shoulders. He kept to the brush as he searched for the king's carriage stationed outside the fortress walls.

Finding it, he opened the door. The guards he had travelled with seemed surprised to see him, and Blake wondered whether the watch on him was as vigilant as described. Perhaps they had assumed he would fail as had those who tried before him.

He set the still unresponsive cellarman on the floor of the carriage and climbed in, resuming his place between his quiet attendants.

The guard signaled to the driver, and the horses were stirred to action. The unconscious man's body rolled against Blake's feet. Blake pushed back with his toes, and the body slumped forward.

Blake closed his eyes. He tucked his hand inside his shirt, and pretended to fall asleep. After a few minutes had passed, he cracked his eyelids open and confirmed that the guards were no longer watching him. Careful to keep his arm and wrist still, he used his fingertips to gradually and noiselessly tear off a large corner of the parchment that stuck out from the leather roll. He pulled the torn piece into his palm, and stole it into his sleeve before actually falling asleep, the thrum of the horses' hooves lulling him into repose.

5

That night, Alderic returned in dream to a memory that often crept its way to the forefront of his mind. The king was not by nature reticent, but something forced him to revisit Owen's final day in his service. The day he had learned of Owen's betrayal.

The dream was always the same. Alderic received word that a condemned prisoner was left alive by the king's knight. Never before had Alderic questioned the loyalty of Owen, but even a brief moment of softhearted defiance was a liability to the king's rule.

He summoned Owen to his quarters. The time he spent in wait seemed to stretch days, rather than the mere minutes he paced restlessly through the room. His body flushed, and he loosed the cloak around his shoulders, discarding it violently in frustration.

He had never before trained a knight with Owen's skill, and he felt the impact of this loss as a throbbing in his skull. Owen's failure to fulfill the ambitions of the kingdom was borne absolutely by his king.

A knock came at the door, and Alderic gave the unseen visitor permission to enter.

Owen stepped through the door, closing it promptly behind him. His blond hair was tied back in a loose braid, and his shirt bore the sweated markings of the chain mail armor he had only minutes before removed. He cast a harmless smile at the king, clearly unaware that his traitorous act had been detected.

Alderic stood before the knight, one of the few who neared his stature, and cast a regretful glance over his failed protégé.

"Where were you yesterday?" he asked, praying his words would not be met with a lie.

Alderic could see a nearly imperceptible change cross Owen's face. The warrior's smile wavered slightly, but his eyes did not leave those of the king.

"You would not ask me such a question if you were unsure of the answer," Owen responded, his tone cautiously light.

"This is true," Alderic said. "Yet, I would hear it from your mouth."

Owen's lips drew together, his face drained, revealing his unease. He paused a moment before answering.

"My king, I fear I have done you wrong. I was weak, and I failed in my duty towards you. I can only beg your forgiveness."

"Why should I not have you executed this minute?" Alderic breathed the words, as he stepped closer to the devoted soldier.

"You will not execute me. You would find no satisfaction in committing me to so common a death." The possible impudence of such a statement was undercut by both men knowing that this was merely the truth.

"Perhaps you are right," Alderic murmured. He stepped closer, until there were only inches between them. "However, I cannot rely upon you, and without trust you are worthless to me." It pained him to say this, but he would not lie to the knight.

Alderic, in one swift movement, pushed Owen to the ground. Owen tried to stand, but the king was upon him in seconds. Alderic bestrode the knight's chest, his knees digging into the soft of Owen's elbows, pinioning him against the stone floor.

Owen instinctively tried to pitch the king off of him, but it was of no use. Alderic was heavier and stronger than he, and his efforts only ground the joints of his arms harder against the floor.

"Do not struggle," the king commanded.

Owen submitted immediately to the king's directive. Alderic had long before fashioned the knight to follow his orders without hesitation. This was all the more reason Owen's disobedience was unforgiveable.

Alderic removed a knife from his belt. With one hand he held Owen's throat, while the other brought the blade to Owen's face. He set the knife point on Owen's forehead, above his temple. Applying a firm pressure, he dragged the blade against the skin, slicing deftly in a diagonal downwards.

Blood spilled from the incision, cascading across his forehead and cheeks, and Alderic watched the knight for a reaction. Owen's breathing became quick and shallow, but he stayed still. He made no movement to challenge Alderic's control.

Alderic paused as the knife neared the warrior's eye. He lightened the pressure slightly, bringing the blade to skim across Owen's open eye, slipping across the surface of the vividly blue iris and through the pupil. The force behind the knife was not great enough to puncture the eye, but it left a mark deep enough that Alderic knew Owen would never see through it again.

He brought the knife across the bridge of the nose, and down to the jaw, slicing the corner of Owen's mouth. He could feel Owen completely motionless beneath him, and he released his hold on the knight.

Alderic rose, and walked back to the chair in the corner of the room. Sitting down, he rested his chin against his hand, as he looked down at the warrior who lay unmoving at the center of the room. Blood streamed from the fresh cut, matting in the long blond hair that had come undone during the exchange.

Hours passed by, and neither man stirred. Alderic watched Owen, transfixed, while the knight made no attempt to stand. The sun set, and the scent of flowers faded into the cool night air.

Every time he dreamt like this, he awoke with the clear image of Owen's bloodied face.

6

When the carriage stopped inside the courtyard of Ashen Castle, a guard seized Blake by the arm, waking him roughly. Blake could hear the old man awakening in the carriage, and the grunt another guard made as he hoisted the elderly cellarman to his feet.

He stepped down from the carriage and the guard kept alongside him, escorting Blake across cracked courtyard cobblestones. Blake lost sight of the cellarman as he neared the side of the castle.

Blake forced a stumble as they approached a door. He landed on his left knee, yanking himself from the guard's grasp. As he was helped to his feet, he surreptitiously slipped the paper fragment into a crack between the stones of the castle walls. He glanced at it briefly to make sure it was well hidden, just as he was thrust forcibly through the doorway.

The guard showed him into a small room, the same room where Blake had been tasked with the strange retrieval. The guard closed the door and Blake could hear a few footsteps before the guard settled in a waiting place outside.

Blake rubbed his neck, the bumpy carriage ride had caused a crick to form, and he turned his head back and forth trying to relieve the annoyance. The small motion helped to calm his nerves, and prepare him for this meeting.

The door finally opened, and the man entered unaccompanied. His long, black hair was smoothed back, and his grey cloak wavered behind him.

Blake straightened his head, and pleasantly greeted the arrival.

"Do you have it?" the king's man asked, his direct tone dismissing any thought Blake might have held of small talk.

Blake reached into his shirt, and retrieved the parchment. The voice of the cellarman rang out in his head, and he felt a moment of hesitation as he looked at the pallid, outstretched fingers of the man.

He handed it over, though something of regret accompanied the action.

The torn section was not immediately obvious. Blake held his breath, as he watched the man turn the red leather roll upside down, and tip the parchment into his palm.

"Our deal was for the entire document," he said quietly, looking over the incomplete sheet.

"Of course," Blake smiled, "but, as I am sure you understand, I will not hand over the only thing keeping me alive in its entirety. I need assurances that you intend to uphold your end of the deal."

"Such as..."

"I need a signed order from the king, and I will need a witness."

"Do you have a witness in mind, or will any party do?" the man asked, a bitterness to his voice.

"The Captain of the Guard," Blake responded, knowing he had not been expected to answer the question in earnest.

The man said nothing, but after a moment he nodded and stepped from the room.

Blake could hear low voices through the closed door. He was suddenly aware of an alkaline scent permeating the air. It was the fragrance of water encircling the castle, something he had noticed first in the leaking prison.

The man did not look at Blake as he reentered the room, seating himself at the desk. His broad frame relaxed in the chair, as he scanned the unrolled parchment. Blake could tell his focus was more on the absent corner than on the markings before him.

Blake was left to stand ineptly in the center of the room, unsure of where to turn his gaze. The man at the desk seemed to have forgotten about his presence entirely, and was examining the parchment with an intensity that fascinated Blake.

A knock at the door preceded the captain of the guard's entrance to the room. She glanced at Blake, before turning to the man at the desk. She carried with her a piece of paper, which she laid out on the edge of the desk. The man looked it over, before the captain invited Blake to examine it.

Blake scanned each inked line. It was a pardon for the attempted murder, and any crimes he had committed prior to his arrest by the royal guard. Blake finished reading, and set the pardon back on the table.

He had never been more grateful for his mother's insistence that he learn to read and write as well as any noble Vesian.

The man pulled the paper toward himself, and dipped his quill into a nearby inkpot, signing his name with a tense scratch at the bottom of the page. He stood, and took a lit candle from the desk. He dripped wax next to the signature, before pressing the ring on his finger into the cooling red substance. He pulled his hand back, and the imprint of a blackdog's face stared back from the page.

A chill swept over Blake as he turned his eyes to the man seated before him.

"You're King Alderic?" The reckless words fell from Blake's lips before he had mind to stop them.

The captain turned to him, her mouth open in astonishment. "Do you not recognize your own king?" she asked.

Blake's sought desperately for something that could make up for his indiscretion. "I was only surprised a man of his youth could have reached such infamy," he said.

Blake had found flattery to be a useful tool in escaping all manner of binds, but this was hardly a lie. He had heard such tales of King Alderic's barbaric rule and colossal kingdom, that he never considered King Alderic could be a man not much older than thirty years.

King Alderic did not react, to either the reference to his age or Blake's questionable choice of the word infamy.

"Why would you meet with me?" Blake asked. "The liogan porter was searching minds for a remembered meeting with the king. Was that not dangerous?"

King Alderic looked up, "You know about the liogan porter," he said, though seemingly to himself. He sighed, indulging Blake's curiosity. "While it may seem counterintuitive, I needed you to see my face to ensure we had not met before. When you had no reaction to me presenting myself as another, I knew you would evade detection."

Blake nodded, understanding this reasoning. He could imagine how quickly he would have faced the hangman had he recognized this man as the king.

"You have your pardon," King Alderic spoke steadily, drawing their conversation back to the point. "Where is the remaining piece?"

Blake led them to where he had secreted the fragment. King Alderic followed directly behind, and Blake's shoulders tensed. Now that he knew the man's identity, he could not shake off an oppressive awareness of the Blackdog King's presence.

He led the king and captain through the halls to the outside of the castle. He moved as quickly as he could, having no desire to prolong his time in Ashen Castle.

When they came to the place in the wall, he pulled the piece of parchment loose, careful not to scrape it on the rough stone. The Blackdog King himself assisted Blake to his feet, before accepting the parchment fragment. He examined the corner closely, while the captain stood behind Blake.

King Alderic nodded, satisfied that it was the genuine article. "You may go, your friend will meet you outside the castle walls." His eyes remained on the paper as he dismissed Blake.

Blake turned to go, a giddy relief flooding his body. His hands shook slightly, something he had previously managed to control. As soon as he found Hugh, they would acquire a pair of horses and ride to the next city without delay. He hoped he would never find himself in the Blackdog King's presence again.

"Wait."

Blake froze and his heart sank, as he turned back to the king.

King Alderic motioned for the captain to search Blake. "I must take precautions around a thief," he said, raising his chin as though challenging Blake to contradict him.

Blake nodded in response. His body had grown strangely numb, and he stood still as he helplessly submitted.

The captain searched him in a perfunctory manner, seemingly satisfied that Blake had not taken anything from the castle. Blake knew that she had doubted the nobleman's accusation of attempted murder; he felt he might almost be able to trust the woman.

The captain reached into one of Blake's jacket pockets, and he felt her freeze. The captain drew her hand out, her fingers grasping a small, silver clasp. Her expression, turning the clasp over, was one of recognition.

"Captain?" the king spoke, his eyes locked on Blake and a telling note of knowing in his voice.

"This is mine," the captain responded, clearly astounded by the discovery.

The king spoke to Blake, gazing over the pardon he had written up only moments before. "While you have been pardoned for your past crimes, stealing from one of the king's officers is a hanging offense."

Before he knew what was happening, Blake's arms were seized by two guards, who pulled him in the direction of the prison. His feet dragged against the cobblestones, the leather of his boots scraped by the rough surface.

He was hauled down the steps and thrust back into a cell, blinded by the sudden darkness. He called out for Hugh, but received no response.

The prison guard turned the key in the lock, and made to leave. Blake's hand darted through the metal bars and seized him by the shirtsleeve.

"Where is Hugh?" Blake asked, his voice hoarse. The sleeve slipped through his cold fingers.

"Who?" the guard responded.

"The man who was brought here with me yesterday."

"About this tall," the guard held his hand out somewhere below his own hairline, "dark hair, bright yellow shirt?"

Blake nodded fervently.

"He was hanged yesterday."

The words did not make sense at first, but, when the realization of what the guard said struck him, Blake fell to his heels, bracing himself against the wet stone. He could not summon the strength to look up at his imprisoner, and he could hear his own voice shaking as he spoke.

"When?"

"A few minutes after you made your little escape." Blake could not see the guard's face, but he could tell the man was laughing. "I've never seen a prisoner break down like that. Most here accept their fates, they get real quiet, full of regret. Everyone knows the king's prison is just the last place you see before the gallows. This man, it's like he shattered. He was still sobbing when they tied the noose.

"The drop kills most of them, breaks their necks. Not this fellow. He was left kicking for a few minutes, before he finally just stopped fighting."

The guard walked away, his chuckles echoing through the prison as his feet tapped up the steps. The wet prison walls glistened with light as the door was opened, darkening just as quickly when it closed.

Blake felt as though the floor had fallen out from under him, the damp of the leaking prison soaking into his clothing.

Hugh was gone, and it was Blake's fault. He had chosen the city, the alley, and the marks. He had baited the nobleman, found the rendezvous location, and had not thought to bring the horses earlier.

Yet these past failures paled in comparison to the betrayal he had committed in the prison. Hugh's last moments were spent believing himself abandoned, left to die by the only friend he knew.

Even after his travels with Blake, swindling and thieving, Hugh had never lost his devotion and optimism. The kindness and practicality he possessed as a farmer's son was not diminished by the dishonest way they made their living. While Blake had been a reluctant master, he knew he would never meet another like Hugh.

Blake pulled himself to his feet, and paced the length of the dark cell. He was walking from one corner to the other, when he felt his foot connect with something solid and soft. Blake knelt down, and put his hand out. He could feel nothing but air, so he held his breath and inched forward. His fingers landed on a coarse tangle, and he realized he was holding human hair.

The mass shifted beneath his hand, and he sprang back. In the darkness, he could barely make out the form of a man. This prisoner was bound by the wrists and ankles to the wall, with so short a length of chain that he could not move more than a few inches.

"I...I'm sorry," Blake stammered, backing away.

The other prisoner was silent and his head rolled forward to lie on his chest, before he became very still. His limbs sagged, useless, in the chains.

"You!" a venom-filled voice called from across the hallway.

Blake moved toward the cell door, squinting to make out the shape of the one who cried out to him.

"You did this." The voice trembled with both indignation and age. "Our single opportunity to place the crown of Vesia upon the brow of one better suited to rule, squandered by a mere thief."

Blake wrapped his hands around the metal bars and leaned his weight against the door. From what little he could see, the old man from the earl's cellar sat cross-legged on the floor of the opposite cell, his garments wrapped tightly around him.

"What does the king want with the parchment?" Blake asked. He kept his voice low and level. Even in the darkness, he could sense the old man's livid glare.

"What good will understanding do you now? Do you plan to tell the hangman as he slips the noose around your throat?" the cellarman spoke at a whisper.

The hallway separating them was only a few feet wide, allowing Blake to hear the cellarman with ease.

"Can you think of a better way to pass the last moments of your life than telling me exactly how I have failed Vesia?" he said, goading the cellarman into a response.

A sigh came from the darkness, and he heard the cellarman pull himself to his feet. The metal groaned, as the old man pressed against the cell door to further reduce the space between them.

"King Alderic comes from a long line of kings and queens. Beginning as tribal warlords, they have ruled Vesia for generations, though I doubt I am telling you anything you do not already know." His voice was hoarse, as he struggled speak. "King Alderic has amassed the greatest kingdom known to mankind, and thus far has been unstoppable in his conquests. Rulers hand him their crowns to avoid enduring the brutal warfare in which King Alderic excels.

"The tale of the parchment you stole begins when King Alderic was only a boy. His father, King Conri, returned from one of his many military campaigns one night. Busy drinking and carousing, the late king did not notice his closest confidant, Ethin, disappear from the castle. Ethin took with him silver and gold, but, perhaps more importantly, it is said that he tore the blackdog head emblem from the hilt of the drunken king's sword. To this day, King Alderic carries the same roughly gouged bronze sword at his side."

"I have heard of Ethin before," Blake began.

"I am sure you have. He is a hero to those of us who would see the kings of Vesia dead. Ethin was the son of a conquered ruler; King Conri took the young man in, taught him the ways of Vesia, and made him an advisor to the throne. While King Conri may have believed Ethin's loyalties would lie with his newfound home, the young man's blood drew him toward rebellion."

"So, he gouged the blackdog's head from the sword. I understand the insult, yet I fail to see what this has to do with the parchment," Blake interrupted.

Blake could see the outline of the cellarman's head shaking.

"Those of today have no patience." Nevertheless, he continued, "some years following his disappearance, a rumor spread that Ethin, knowing he would not live long enough to see King Conri overthrown, had hidden these treasures alongside an object of far greater value than all the wealth of the Vesian kingdom."

"What could that be?" Blake asked.

"A weapon unlike any known of today, something ancient and powerful, beyond mere human comprehension."

"Liogans," Blake whispered to himself.

"Yes," the cellarman said, responding carefully to the breathed word. "There was a time many centuries ago when magic held a place in warfare. A clever and resourceful liogan could aid the weakest child in becoming ruler of a nation. As those born with this ability are killed, the worth of magic has become forgotten altogether."

"So, Ethin created a weapon using liogan power," Blake began, "but what makes you think this is strong enough to stand against the might of Vesia?"

"King Alderic has no experience fighting against liogan craftsmanship, his outwitting of the earl's porter aside. It seems there is no greater weapon against an undefeatable king than one that history itself has left him so ill-equipped to face."

"The king knew that the porter at the earl's fortress is a liogan, why did King Alderic not have him killed?" Blake asked.

The cellarman shrugged. "The king, like his ancestors, do not seem to care one way or the other regarding liogan. Most people, like yourself, seem to be under the impression that liogan simply no longer exist. Besides, the moment King Alderic understood the liogan's role in protecting the parchment, he would know killing him to be foolish."

"But the king let Lord Wesley know he had kidnapped and killed the second guard," Blake countered. "He sent the guard's body back in pieces."

"Yes, but we believed that was an attempt to force Lord Wesley to move the parchment from the fortress to somewhere less protected. When this failed, he may have realized that the earl's reliance on a liogan porter presented a unique weakness he could exploit." The cellarman paused. "But, you well know of this vulnerability. After all, you were the one used to circumvent it."

"You have still not told me why the parchment is important," Blake reminded the cellarman, quick to divert the conversation from his own blame.

"Haven't I?" The cellarman seemed genuinely bemused. "Perhaps I supposed you would have figured it out by now. It is a map, leading to the mythic liogan weapon and stolen treasures. Desire to possess this map has haunted the royal family since its creation.

"Rumor has it King Alderic's younger brother, Prince Severin, shared the king's obsession with finding the map, and locating the weapon. King Alderic would lay waste to it, where Prince Severin would have used it to usurp his own flesh and blood, placing himself on the throne. Prince Severin died before he could have taken any action. Poisoning, it was thought, and the cook hanged for it. Despite this, many believe Severin's life was taken by the Blackdog King himself."

"How did you get the map?"

"Ethin went into hiding after the theft, though as you can imagine King Conri spared no expense in locating the treasonous confidant. He finally found him five years later, and tortured him until his spirit gave out. But, before his capture, Ethin passed the map to a servant, who brought it to us years later for safekeeping. By this time King Conri had passed away, and his eldest son had ascended the throne. We planned to locate the liogan weapon, and overthrow the king while his reign was still young, but we were betrayed by one of our own and could no longer risk retrieval. Besides, the map is far from a simple depiction of landmarks."

"What is it?" Blake asked, his interest piqued.

"We believe the first marking is a place, and the second a person. We hoped that if we could locate the first point, we could make sense of the rest." He shifted closer to the bars, his voice dropping again to a whisper. "I believe the map represents a chain of trust. That each point can only be accessed by someone true to Ethin's cause, and that sense can only be made of the map in order."

"I understand despising his mercilessness, but what about his rule warrants a blood-soaked uprising? It seems that, despite the king's once violence-bound ways, there is peace in Vesia," Blake asked.

"King Alderic is dreaded by his people. To be ruled by the Blackdog King is to be ruled by a ghost. His absence from building order is somewhat mediated by the shadow he casts across the kingdom, but the people must govern themselves, mob rule replacing the law of the land. It should not be this way."

A slight rustling sound came from the corner of the room, and the old man's tongue was stilled as both listened with rapt attention. Something moved forward slowly, close to the ground.

The shape stood, revealing a human figure. Wrapped in a cloak which dragged on the wet prison floor, the figure approached Blake's cell. Staring eyes looked past him to the figure chained in the corner.

"He has the map," a woman's voice spoke out from beneath the hooded fabric. "I will return for you soon."

Blake could sense a shift in the chained prisoner. Whatever the movement had been, it satisfied the woman, who nodded and began to retreat.

All Blake knew was that this woman could represent a means of escape, from Ashen Castle and the noose. It appeared that she planned to rescue his fellow prisoner, leaving Blake only little time to act and possibly save himself.

"Wait," Blake whispered.

The woman stopped and turned back to face Blake.

"What are you going to do?" the old man asked her, his voice shaking.

The woman ignored the cellarman's question, and strode quickly to where Blake stood. His heart leapt into his mouth, as he reflexively took a step back.

"You are the one who brought him the map, is that not so?" she asked, her words dripping with vitriol.

"I am, but I can assure you that had I known the consequences, I would never have done so." He was unsure himself whether this was true, but he knew that honesty would not help his cause. He moved back to the door, a further plea entering his voice. "Let me go with you."

"You can stay here and rot." She turned again to leave as she spoke, "we have no use for one loyal to Alderic."

"I beg you to hear me."

Blake's hand reached out, and gripped the cloaked woman by the wrist. He was sorry to find himself in the same position Hugh had suffered moments before his hanging, and Blake could only hope this woman would be more yielding than he had been.

"I am highly skilled in my trade. Were it not so, the king would not have wasted his time on me. I could be useful to you," he petitioned.

She pulled back forcefully, causing Blake's shoulder to collide with the metal grid. He removed his arm from the door, rubbing the stinging flesh.

"I don't know who this man is, but it seems he has been chained here for a long time. He likely cannot walk, let alone fight." Blake lowered his voice, "I know that, if you want to stop King Alderic from retrieving the weapon, you will need a thief; you will need someone of great skill." For a moment, he allowed a small smile to appear on his face. "You will need me."

She looked past Blake, to the chained man. "Owen," an unspoken question lay in her voice.

Blake was blind to the prisoner's response, keeping his eyes fixed on her face, but a moment later the woman's eyes returned to his.

She motioned toward the chained man. "Set Owen free from his restraints. I will retrieve you both as soon as I can." She stalked toward Blake, halted only by the metal gate. "One word to the king or his guards, and I will see that you join your friend in the afterlife before the hangman has even woken."

At the callous mention of Hugh, Blake felt as though his body had numbed. The familiar taste of metal sat against his tongue, and a creeping sickness grew in his chest. He watched in silence, unable or unwilling to speak, as the woman retreated into the darkness.

He felt the damp beneath his boots, and wondered at the fact that the entire castle had not sunken into the drenched foundation.

7

Alderic had spent the afternoon in the throne room making arrangements for his absence from Conrisia. He would leave his decisions in the hands of the Captain of the Guard, his proxy. It was an odd arrangement, but he was more trusting of another practiced in maintaining order than in the exercise of politics. His true right hand had always been his one knight, but this knight accompanied him, and therefore could not be left in charge of the kingdom.

Evening was falling by the time he returned to his private quarters. He had not yet crossed the threshold of his rooms when he knew he was not alone. His breath hitched in his throat when his sight landed on Moirin sitting in his chair. Her fingers idly ran the length of her skirt hem, and she looked up at him slowly, her dark eyes hypnotizing as they watched him.

Her mere presence was enough to incite a desire which turned to terrible dread within him. Taking a deep breath to brace his senses against her onslaught, he strode forward. Her proximity to the newfound map was disconcerting. He had already created one copy, but he knew she could not be trusted.

"What are you doing here?" he growled.

She smiled sweetly, cocking her head to the side as she looked at him. She radiated devotion when addressing him. Her dark hair was twisted over her shoulder, and her copper skin glowed golden in the candlelight. Her smiling lips were half-parted in greeting, and to any observer she would seem nothing but affectionate toward her ruler.

He often wondered why she carried on with this pretense.

"Would you believe it if I told you I wanted to see you?" she asked, her words cloying. She twisted the end of her loosely braided hair between her fingertips. "I heard a rumor that you are leaving tomorrow."

He took her by the shoulder, and gently moved her to the side of the bureau. He opened the drawer to check that the original copy of the map was still accounted for, using his body to impede her view of the contents.

It was still there.

"Yes, I will be leaving," he responded curtly, reluctant to engage her further. "Is that all?"

He leaned back against the wall and looked her over. Alderic knew that Moirin would never pay him a social call without an underlying reason. Once, she had wanted something from him, something he could not grant her. Though she masked her ever-growing resentment of him, it had nevertheless become clear through the years following Severin's death.

Alderic found her detestation of him to be a relief.

It disturbed him that she had gained entry to his quarters, and he would speak to the captain about this indiscretion.

Moirin made to leave, but Alderic was still unsure of what she had gained through this conversation. He knew there was a reason she was in his quarters.

As she passed by, he caught her by the wrist and pulled her to him.

"Have you taken anything from me?" he asked quietly.

"Of course not," she answered, pulling back, but he did not release her.

Her wrist felt small within his hand, and he kept it locked in a crushing grip. His long black hair fell forward to obscure half of his face, but he could not bring himself to brush it aside. He could feel the jutting bone at the side of her wrist beneath his broad thumb, and he mechanically pressed the pad of his finger against the fleshed point.

When he failed to let go of her, despite her resistance, her smiling mask slipped for a moment. She took his free hand and drew it to her waist. She stepped closer and stood on her toes, so her lips were only inches away from his neck.

"You can search further, if you wish," she spoke the words softly against his skin.

His hand tightened where she had placed it on her waist, his nails dragging against the fabric of her dress. A terror rose in his throat, and his vision darkened. He released her wrist, pulling his hand back as if burned.

His heart thudded painfully in his chest, and his skin soaked with sweat.

He grabbed her by the arms and pushed her roughly from the room, into the hands of a passing castle guard. The sound of his slamming door echoed through the hallway, and Alderic strode back to the center of the chamber.

He sat down in the chair, seeking to regain command over himself. His heartbeat was still rapid beyond his control, and he ran a hand through his drenched hair.

The panic had quickly overwhelmed him, as it always did at the slightest suggestion of sensual pleasure. He became acutely aware of a physical weakness within himself that he fought to control. His mind and body conspired against him; they would kill him given the chance. He had long since abandoned hope of overcoming this failing, accepting the asceticism forced by his nature.

Alderic was not prone to anger, nor was he predisposed to happiness. In moments like these, he was driven by fear, as surely as he was by his need to breathe, and little brought him alarm as Moirin did. Yet, despite the horror her presence induced, he could not stop thinking about her.

His jaw tensed and his tongue began to bleed, caught between sharp, unyielding teeth.

Wanting to shake this sense of infirmity, Alderic stalked down to the prison, his heart still racing and blood welling in his mouth. As he descended into the leaking depths of the castle, his eyes adjusted quickly to the lack of light. He instructed the prison guard to open the old man's cell.

The cellarman cowered in the corner, as he saw Alderic near. He whispered beneath his breath, a series of repetitive phrases. The rate of his mutterings increased the closer Alderic grew, and the old man seemed to press into the wall, as though he could melt his body into the cold, wet stone.

Alderic knew he had drawn the attention of the map's thief, who leaned forward against the opposite gate, watching every move the king made. Alderic turned his back to the younger man, his attention fully on the elderly prisoner before him.

"You've lost the map." The king crouched down to better look into the face of the defeated cellarman. "In a few weeks' time, I will tear to pieces your mythical weapon, and you will have wasted your years in protection of nothing. However, I think I might keep you alive." He brought his fingertips to gently squeeze the prisoner's throat. "You'll see your world fall apart, as every hope your sentimental friends hold dear is ripped from them."

Alderic was not one to waste words on the condemned. Satisfied he had instilled terror in the elderly cellarman, he left the small cell.

Mockingly, he tipped his head towards Blake in thanks, before his face twisted into a cruel, thin-lipped smile. He watched the thief's face blanch as it stared back in the darkness.

In truth, he regretted his dishonorable tactics in handling Blake, but he could leave no room for failure in his destruction of the liogan-made weapon: he would not tolerate a threat to his rule. The fewer people alive who knew of his goal in leaving the castle, the better.

He returned to his quarters knowing a sleepless night lay ahead of him. The smell of Moirin's perfume hung thick in the air. He kicked the bureau. The wood panel broke at the force, and he ran his fingers through his hair. He was still unable to rid himself of the angst her visit had incited.

8

After King Alderic left, Blake took off his belt. During this, his second imprisonment, his lock picks and other tools had been confiscated, though the prison guard had left him with the belt. He supposed there was no objection to him doing a job the hangman would accomplish anyway. While it was not the ideal tool, he bent the belt buckle beneath his shoe, until the corner broke apart and the metal contorted. He drove the thin strip until it became malleable, and turned his attention to the bound man in the corner.

Blake began work on loosening the chains binding the man's feet. The chain was threaded through an iron hoop set in the wall and the only way to remove it was to open the locks.

Blake slipped the bent metal into the keyhole. He pushed the leather belt out of the way, but it still managed to obstruct his already poor view, given the darkness of the prison. He pressed down, trying to make the metal conform to the depth of the keyhole, and breathed a sigh of relief when he finally felt it give way.

He was able to slip the chains away from Owen's feet, but Owen remained motionless against the wall. Blake wanted to check whether he was still alive, but began to fear the answer.

Instead of confirming the other man's breathing, he turned his attention to Owen's wrists. Given the belt buckle had already been molded into a usable pick, this task was accomplished in half the time. Owen was still and Blake decided to leave him in the corner. It was for the best that they did not make a demonstration of the man's freedom in case a guard did return.

He left Owen, where he lay collapsed against the corner, and began to work on the cell door. He could no longer see the cellarman across the narrow passageway between the cells, but, from what he could tell, the cellarman had not returned to his feet following the king's visit.

A chain of trust.

This was perhaps the only thing that could put one like King Alderic at a disadvantage. Ethin was clever, Blake had to grant him that. However, Blake suspected any effort would be in vain. Even a successful escape did not mean they would recover the weapon before King Alderic did, in fact it was unlikely that any would be able to outmaneuver the Blackdog King.

In the minds of the people, King Alderic occupied the space between a force of nature and a god.

The cloaked woman was again outside the cell. This time, Blake had not heard her approach. She emerged from the shadows, and Blake unlocked the cell door with the warped belt buckle.

"Move quickly, we don't have much time," she whispered.

Blake hauled Owen to his feet, surprised by how light he was. When Blake reached the outside of the cell, the woman slipped Owen's arm around her neck, and pulled him toward the concealed egress. Blake opened the old man's cell door; he would not have another lost life on his conscience.

The cellarman was sprawled on the floor. His body was cast in shadows, and Blake shook him lightly. "We need to leave," he spoke under his breath.

The cellarman did not respond, so Blake grasped his arm and pulled the man to his feet. The old man's body was limp, and Blake noticed that his own hand, where he grasped the cellarman's wrist, was wet.

He lowered the elderly man back to the floor, and looked at his hand. It was covered in a dark, slick liquid that was unmistakably blood. He moved his hands to the old man's wrist, and found a rough-edged bolt in the restraints which bound him.

The old man had killed himself, working his wrist against the jutting bolt until it had cut through the flesh. He had bled out onto the prison floor.

"He's dead," Blake said, stunned.

The woman grabbed Blake by his collar, and hauled him from the cell. She had already gotten Owen through the aperture, and Blake was similarly propelled through the opening.

Blake crawled through a narrow passage concealed within the wall. He followed Owen, who only moved forward with great effort. The cloaked woman shoved him roughly when they took any longer than necessary.

They seemed to be going deeper into the earth; everything grew cold around them, and the stone passage was slick with condensation. Blake's hand slipped, his elbow slamming against the carved rock.

"Be careful of the water; we're passing beneath the moat," the woman said. "This escape tunnel was built many years ago and I do not know what condition it will be in the further we travel from the prison."

Sure enough, the further they travelled, the rougher and weaker the cut stone grew. At one point, Blake was up to his elbows in the cold, stagnant water that had pooled in the passage.

Finally, they emerged in a forest, under the blanket of night. The castle was visible just beyond the cover of the tree line. Blake could see the burning fires in the walls, and glow of candlelit rooms, finding them unavoidably welcoming. He was nevertheless glad to put distance between himself and the castle's formidable inhabitant.

Owen had collapsed as soon as they left the passage, and the woman dragged him across the grass until she was sure they were out of sight. She propped the weakened man up against the trunk of a tree, and called Blake to her side.

"Wait here until I return," she ordered, turning to leave.

"Where are you going?" Blake asked.

"I am going to Conrisia to get weapons, supplies, and horses." She nodded towards Owen's slumped figure. "Watch him."

The woman disappeared through the trees, and Blake turned his eyes to the man half-lying on the ground. Owen was unmoving, and Blake sat down beside him. He kept his eyes fixed on the lights of the Ashen Castle's walls, as he listened for the woman's return.

A stream ran nearby, its water diverted from the moat, and joined with a larger river that wound its way through the woods. Owen pulled himself to his feet, and made his way on shaking legs to the water's edge. His breath came in ragged gasps, as if his lungs were stinging from the fresh air. Blake wondered how long Owen had been locked in the cold damp of the king's prison.

Blake did not want to follow Owen, nor appear to be watching him closely, so he merely glanced from the corner of his eye as the man stooped to drink from the running stream. The thin, long-limbed shadow gradually discarded the dirty rags wound around his body, before bathing himself in the icy waters.

Owen's body was pale and gaunt. He was nearly as tall as King Alderic, though he was lanky where the king was strapping. Blake's eye was drawn to the jagged, crude scars that covered the prisoner's torso. As the dirt washed off, Owen's hair was revealed to be a light blond, the matted strands extending past his waist.

Owen emerged from the frigid water, and wrapped his body in the cloak their rescuer had left behind. He sat beside Blake, and the silent pair kept their eyes fixed on the castle. Fires burned, and the lights continued to flicker through the leaves of the trees.

For the first time, Blake noticed the scar on Owen's face. The darkness of the prison, combined with the layers of grime that had covered Owen's skin, prevented him from recognizing the disfigurement earlier. A rough, purple mutilation extended the length of his face in a crude diagonal, running directly through his left eye. Lighter in color than the other, it had an oddly twisted appearance, as though the tissue was knotted in the center.

He considered asking Owen about the marks. His imagination ran wild with scenarios in which a prisoner of the king might have acquired such brutal injuries. However, it was not the time for inquiry, so they remained in silence as they waited for the woman's return.

9

Alderic knew something was amiss; he detected an absence within the castle walls. One of the strengths he owed most to his tribal ancestors was the trust he placed in instinct.

It was absolute.

He proceeded to the prison with haste, though he already knew what he would find there. The guard at the entrance nervously accompanied him down the stairs and into the darkened hallway.

The cells were empty, save that of the old cellarman. He was exactly where Alderic had left him, but there was something different about the way his body rested against the wall. Alderic entered the cell, and grabbed the grey hair, turning the cellarman's face upward. When he let go, the head dropped loosely to rest on the reclining chest; the man was dead.

He left the cell, his boots squelching in the spilled blood that pooled on the stone floor.

"Dispose of the body," he ordered.

Alderic knew that, given this massive failure, the guard himself would be disposed of soon enough.

This escape did not alter his plans. He did not need to visit Moirin's quarters to know she was not there. Her presence had something of the oppressive about it, and he could sense her absence from the castle with the certainty that he would know the loss of a limb.

He did not feel betrayed by her actions in absconding with the two prisoners. While her efficacy was unexpected, he could not say he was surprised. Nor, in truth, was he disappointed to see her leave. Since her arrival at the castle many years ago, her presence had filled his senses, lingering in his mind through restless nights, as a creeping nausea that kept him endlessly awake. If she could be forgotten, he might finally be free.

He found the Captain of the Guard to inform her of the escaped prisoners.

"What does Moirin intend to do?" the captain asked.

"Her intention has always been to rule Vesia, and possessing this liogan-made weapon could bring her closer to achieving her end. I can only assume she made a copy of the map; she is far from careless, and would never have left Ashen Castle without this."

The captain's brow creased with worry. "Given her possible alliances, will she have an easier time understanding the map?"

The captain was one of the few people Alderic had entrusted with the information regarding his attempt to retrieve the liogan weapon, and he could count on her bluntness in addressing him. Unbridled candor toward the king was uncommon, and Alderic placed great value in the captain's straightforwardness.

He had considered this possibility. The various insurgents scattered throughout Vesia had enjoyed ample time and opportunity to try locating the liogan weapon. However, they feared leading the king to the very weapon they sought to use against him. While the castle's escapees had the map, nothing in this arrangement had by nature changed.

But then there was Moirin, and she held within her an unparalleled resolve. Alderic had once made the mistake of underestimating her ambitions, and he was not the only one who had paid the price. She had proven that if any presented a dangerous opposition, it was her. Should she command the liogan weapon, there was no doubt that Alderic would suffer.

He pulled the map onto the table, and pointed at the first marking. "Fellridge-Helna." He paused. "I assume Fellridge refers to the town that lies to the north-east, two days' travel from the castle."

"And Helna?"

"I do not know." Alderic frowned. "Waiting until daybreak has now become imprudent. Assemble the soldiers, and ensure they are prepared to depart within the hour."

10

Owen sat by the tree trunk, while Blake knelt by the side of the stream, washing the cellarman's blood from his hands and boots. Satisfied that the last of the blood was gone, he returned to sit by Owen.

"What have you and the woman planned?" Blake asked.

"To find the liogan weapon before Alderic does," Owen answered slowly, his voice soft.

"What will you do with it?"

"I will do nothing, but she will use it to overthrow Alderic and make herself Queen of Vesia." Owen nodded to himself. "She will not be without allies in this effort."

It was true that many would celebrate the end of the Blackdog King's reign. As far as Blake knew, no king or queen had been as reviled as their present ruler, his adept ruthlessness unmatched within Vesia and beyond. While Moirin's desire was understandable, Blake had little faith in anyone's ability to usurp the king.

"How does she plan to go about this?" Blake asked.

Owen shrugged. "I do not know," he said. "I will simply follow where she leads."

"Why are you helping her?" Blake asked. Though he knew little of their plan, its inherent danger was obvious.

"Beyond her saving me from a life wasted in a water-drenched, underground prison?" Owen paused. "She provides me with something I cannot live without."

"The cellarman said King Alderic will destroy the weapon if he finds it," Blake continued, pressing no further on Owen's cryptic answer. "Do you not worry that he will, instead, use it to further his own aims?"

"He will not use it," Owen said, after a weighted pause.

"Why not?" Blake asked.

Owen kept his eyes on the castle. He spoke absently, as though to himself.

"Alderic uses the same weapons as his ancestors, and his only improvements on these basic materials are strategic. He has never shown any interest in advancing the arms his soldiers bear."

Blake had half hoped Owen's answers would provide some clue as to why the other man was imprisoned by King Alderic. From the tales he had been told, he assumed no one was kept more than a few days in Ashen Castle's prison before meeting their end through a drop from the scaffold.

"The woman who freed us. Who is she?" Blake asked.

"Moirin?" Owen responded. "She was married to Alderic's brother, Severin."

"Which would make her a princess," Blake said, surprised.

Owen let out a harsh laugh. "Even when Severin lived, she would not accept that title."

"And he was poisoned?"

Owen nodded.

"The cellarman told me the cook killed him," Blake said as he studied Owen's face, searching for a reaction that never showed itself.

He wanted to ask more questions, but was silenced by the muffled sound of approaching hooves. Moirin rode a horse and led two others behind, all three steeds heavily saddled. She tied the reins to a branch, and tossed a fabric bundle to Owen, who stepped away to clothe himself.

She removed a bag from one of the saddles and dropped it to the ground, unrolling the bound leather. Inside were a variety of weapons, glinting in the light of the rising moon. She removed a sword, and slid it into the sheath at her belt. She put a knife in her boot, before her fingers moved to the handle of a double headed axe. She lifted it, her arms tensing beneath the heavy weight. She handed the weapon to the returned Owen, who accepted it with shaking hands.

"I thought you might enjoy the feel of an axe once again," she said with a slight smile.

Blake sensed that something sinister lurked beneath her smile. He could see the blood drain from Owen's face, as the man held the weapon, shuddering, before him. He had the distinct impression that Owen's trembling had less to do with his weakened state, than with whatever the axe symbolized to both of his escaped companions.

"You are cruel," Owen whispered, his voice barely audible over the sound of the running stream.

Moirin's smile grew. "Perhaps, but I need you at your best. No one in this land or another wields an axe with your expertise." She turned her attention to Blake. "I don't suppose you have much weapons training."

Blake shook his head. "But, I can use a dagger if the need arises."

"The weapon of a common street thief." She scowled, handing him a small knife from the pack.

Blake bristled at the contempt in her characterization of him, but he let the insult go, given the considerable debt he already owed to her. Besides, he knew she had every right to be angry with him. He was the reason King Alderic possessed the map.

"I'll need you to handle a sword as well." She weighed a few swords in her hands, passing him the lightest. "I cannot have you armed with only a small knife, so this will do for now."

He took the sword, which felt heavy in his hand, and looked around for somewhere to stow it. Moirin, anticipating this, handed him a brown leather baldric. He slung it over his right shoulder, so the sheath rested at his hip. He slid the sword into the leather and felt the hilt at his fingertips, the blade eager to be drawn.

She lifted the outer layer of her skirt, revealing the white fabric that lay beneath. The cloth was covered in ink markings, resembling those on the parchment Blake had stolen. Moirin cut the section of fabric free with a knife and folded it carefully, tucking it into her pocket.

She tossed each of them a canteen, which they filled from the stream. Bubbles spilled from the opening of Blake's flask, as it grew heavy with water. When they had finished, they mounted the horses, and set out through the woods.

"The first location on the map is Fellridge, a small town to the north-east," Moirin spoke, as the horses plodded along. "We can reach it one day before Alderic. This path is unreliable and unstable. He will likely choose the wider path, more easily travelled by even his smallest party. These horses have been rested, and will be able to ride through the night. Still, we must be careful as Alderic will know of Fellridge as well as I."

Blake felt exhaustion fill him, as he had slept no more than a few hours since the day of his first arrest, but he forced himself to remain focused on the journey. The path had already narrowed, and branches threatened to strike him down at every turn. His horse faltered on the uneven ground, and he held his breath as he followed the line they had formed. He could understand why King Alderic would be barred from travelling this route. For the three of them, travelling the path was arduous. It would be impossible for a small army.

11

Rain fell across the valley, making the ground dangerously soft beneath the hooves of Nahia's horse. Her steed had already slipped twice in the mud, and she was immensely grateful to see the castle in the side of the mountain rising up before her.

As the path turned from earth to stone, her horse found surer footing. Nahia's cloak was soaked through, and her hair was clinging uncomfortably to her face.

Alderic hated Lord Richard, and Nahia had to smile as she thought on the king's detestation of the baron: something she had never understood herself. Lord Richard made for pleasant enough company and, while his appetites did tend towards the perverse, she had never found him to be particularly objectionable. In fact, she made it a point to visit whenever she returned from the eastern kingdoms.

She wondered where Alderic was. The last time they met, he had indicated a new lead on the map. However, he had been sold false promises before, and she hoped that he would not again be searching in vain.

Once in the baron's courtyard, she was greeted by servants who took the reins of her horse, and brought her into the solid warmth of the castle. She was given dry clothes and a meal, while Lord Richard was made aware of her presence.

Nahia was sat at the table. She had travelled through the past night and day, and the feeling of her weary muscles relaxing was almost painful. Though there was little she enjoyed more than adventuring through the kingdoms, there were times when she appreciated the luxury of familiar surroundings.

Lord Richard was aware of Nahia's love of tea, and servants brought forward a pot of the steeped amber liquid, which they poured into a porcelain cup on the table.

The heat of the cup between her palms helped to ease the bone chill she had experienced only moments before, as she made the journey from Elsin. The way to Rieville would only present a greater challenge and, while she was well-acquainted with the path, she appreciated the chance to rest herself before resuming the journey to her own estate.

The baron entered the room and, rather than stand, Nahia simply nodded from her seat at the table and Lord Richard sat down opposite.

"You visit is abrupt, though welcome as always," Lord Richard said through smiling white teeth.

Nahia grinned back. "It has been over two months since I last visited." She reached into the satchel at her side. "I brought you this, a small token from the eastern kingdoms."

Nahia passed Lord Richard a knife. The handle was studded with sapphires, the blue gems shining out from bright silver. Lord Richard turned the blade over in his hand, admiring the metalwork.

"Elsin craftsmanship, no doubt. It is beautiful," he mused, setting it down on the table, a smirk rising to his lips. "I'm sure I can find a use for it."

"I'm sure you can," Nahia responded.

"Perhaps sheathing itself in the neck of our dear king." Lord Richard said, his tone provocative. Nahia shifted forward in warning, and Lord Richard narrowed his eyes at her. "I will never understand the affinity you feel toward King Alderic," he said, staying her with his words.

Nahia did not respond, instead watching Lord Richard warily.

"You bear him nothing but friendship, yet you know that he sent assassins to destroy my mother and father for the resistance they raised against him." Lord Richard's fingers toyed with the dagger. "It would be understandable for me, in my grief, to arrange the death of the king."

Nahia's darted forward across the table, her knuckles striking Lord Richard's hand. The blade of the dagger cut into his palm, and the table was stained red with quick flowing blood.

Lord Richard withdrew his hand. He closed his fist around the wound, concentrating the blood into a stream of thick drops, which he allowed to pool on the bench. He stared, transfixed, at the steadily growing crimson puddle.

"Tell the lies to your people," Nahia's tone darkened in warning, "but do not mistake me for a fool. I know as well as you that the blame for their deaths does not lay with the king."

"You hold him in too high esteem."

"And you do not offer him the respect a king demands of his subjects," Nahia responded.

"Though, if the rumors from the east are true, his days as king may be numbered."

"You speak of the Rock of Briggid," Nahia said. "Passing through Elsin, I found this to be on the lips of every hopeful inhabitant. What do you hear of it?"

"That it will identify the Blackdog King's orphan usurper. Whether true or not, it gives hope to Elsin, and every kingdom besides," he said, smiling. "Given your loyalty to the tyrant, I should keep such knowledge to myself."

"Do you put stock in such tales?" she asked.

"No, but so long as the rock stands, it gives courage to all who would set themselves against our conquering king. It is this hope I place my faith in. The overthrowing of King Alderic cannot come quickly enough."

Nahia regarded Lord Richard coolly.

"Don't worry, I will not say another word against 'father', though I know he disapproves of me," Lord Richard responded sarcastically.

"Father!" Nahia laughed. "An odd way to speak of a man easily thirty years your junior," she said, before looking Lord Richard over carefully. "Though, you seem not to have aged in years."

"Do you want my secret?" Lord Richard responded lightly.

"Not particularly. When it comes to you, I've found the less I know, the better."

Lord Richard looked for a moment as though he might protest the implied accusation, but he merely shrugged.

"Where do you journey next?" he asked, abruptly changing the subject.

"Rieville."

"Perhaps you shall pass by Linwood. When were you there last?" Lord Richard asked.

"Not for many years. Why?"

Lord Richard leaned back, steepling his fingers against his lip. "Then you have not heard of the 'Horror.'"

Nahia shook her head.

"The Horror of Linwood. It kills their people in the night, leaving the bodies in the lake covered in bizarre markings. The people cannot leave the town, even travelers passing through are killed when they try to depart Linwood."

"If none can leave, how is it you know of this so-called 'Horror'?" Nahia asked skeptically.

"Only one, as far as I know, has made it from the town alive. He reached my castle some days later."

"And yet word of this did not spread even as far as Rieville," Nahia pressed.

"No," Lord Richard said, smiling roguishly. "I'm afraid the secret died with him."

Nahia nodded, understanding his meaning perfectly. "I am now tempted to pass through Linwood, if only to see if your words hold truth, yet I cannot waste my time on such distractions, as my presence is required in Rieville."

He laughed. "I've never known you to willingly return to your own estate."

"I am only rarely called back to my duties, and these days they seem few." She shook her head. "But, I am there on a different business this time. Do you know the Earl of Eskemn?"

Lord Richard nodded. "I have heard of him."

"He and his advisor are dueling, and I have been asked to act as the Earl's champion."

"But you are not a good fencer," Lord Richard said, smiling as the words left his lips. "Why would he ask you? Perhaps it has to do with your reputation as a dauntless adventurer."

Nahia shrugged. "He made a mistake in selecting me, though I believe his choice may have little to do with my abilities. If he is seeking my aid or influence, he will find I am not so easily swayed by flattery. I'm afraid it is a lesson he will learn at personal expense."

"You intend to lose," Lord Richard mused. "It seems a strange thing to put yourself out for."

"I am headed in that direction anyway, and will pay a visit to my manor. I need to at least give the appearance of interest in my assets. Besides, I am planning to visit Alderic in Conrisia." She sighed. "It has been a long time since I've found myself in the heart of Vesia. Between Alderic's military campaigns and my journeys, our paths only rarely cross."

"For how long do I have the pleasure of your company?" Lord Richard asked.

"A day or so," she responded, "if I am not intruding."

"Quite the contrary; my castle is rarely frequented by outsiders, and it gives me pleasure to hear of your adventures in the eastern kingdoms. Besides, I have some innovations I think you might find entertaining," he said, "assuming you still do not share your regal friend's distaste for my diversions."

"You know that I do not. His disgust with these pursuits does border on the extreme," Nahia conceded, though on edge at the mild derision of Alderic. She paused. "In fact, I've brought you a second gift."

She picked up a large object from where it had been resting beneath the bench and set it on the table. It was wrapped in black silk, and tied with a red lace ribbon.

Lord Richard carefully pulled away the silk wrapping, and looked eagerly upon the contents.

"What is it?" Lord Richard asked.

"It was made after a design originating in the west, a rather ingenious device. I thought you might have some use for it." Nahia said. "Though I must admit, I do not understand your enthusiasm for such interests."

"Perhaps after tomorrow you shall. I promise this will be more interesting than last time."

12

They journeyed through night and day, stopping only briefly to rest the horses. It was near evening by the time they reached Fellridge, a small town run through by a single, overgrown dirt road.

It was clear to Blake that Fellridge experienced little passage by travelers. Looking around, he could not see any established tradesmen or shops. The town was seemingly comprised of farmers and cattle-herders. While he could hear the sounds of the nearby animals, there was little noise besides. After his harrowing experience in Conrisia, Blake found the secluded, rural town to be a comfort.

They reached a trough of fresh water at the center of the town. Moirin signaled a halt, and swung down from the saddle. Blake's knees buckled as he dismounted. He was unused to spending such time on horseback; his legs felt weak, and his entire body ached for rest.

Moirin left them immediately to begin her search for Helna. Earlier, Blake had told her about the cellarman's suspicion that Helna referred to an inhabitant of Fellridge, and Moirin would waste little time in seeking this presumed ally.

Owen stayed on horseback, impassively watching Moirin depart, and Blake sat down on a felled tree by the side of the dirt road. The sword at his hip knocked against the wood, jolting him. He was still unused to having so cumbersome an instrument at his side.

A shawled woman with loose, light colored hair, and wind-ruddied cheeks, walked up to them. A small boy clutched at her skirts, hauled along as she approached them with curiosity shining in her eyes.

"Where are you from?" she asked, looking them over. "You're not from around here."

Blake stood. "We come from the Conrisia." He offered his hand. "My name is Blake, and this is Owen."

She looked at his hand for a moment, before taking it in her own. Her grip was firm and her hands bore the calluses of hard labor.

"My name is Bethen. If you've not eaten, you and your friend are welcome to come to my house for supper, as is the woman you were with." She gestured in the direction, the shawl slipping from her shoulder. "I'm afraid you won't find much else in these parts, and we could always use another pair of hands at the farm."

Blake was famished. He had not eaten since daybreak, and they were carefully rationing their food. He could not see the harm in enjoying a brief meal, and doing a little work in return. Besides, the woman seemed agreeable enough.

He looked to Owen for permission to leave, and was offered an inattentive shrug in response. Owen said he would wait by the horses. He seemed reluctant to leave without Moirin.

"And how is our capital city?" Bethan asked as they walked through the road.

"Conrisia is thriving," Blake answered, though wondering if Bethen had ever seen the city for herself.

From what Blake understood, the ancient capital city had been renamed in honor of each Vesian ruler, the day they took the throne. Only King Alderic had broken with this tradition, leaving his father's name upon the city.

Blake followed Bethen back to her home. They stepped through a fence, and passed between several brown cows, to reach the front door. The air was cold, and the smells of cattle and grass flooded Blake's nostrils. The peaceful sound of the countryside lulled him, and he was again struck by the exhaustion he had been fighting off for the past few days.

He was ushered into a small home. The floors and walls were crafted from a bare, rough-cut wood, and a table sat at the center of the room. Half of the table was littered with freshly harvested vegetables, and bread dough rose in a cloth-covered bowl.

Blake sat down at the table, and took off his jacket. The place reminded him of his parents' home, which he had left behind many years ago. He felt homesickness rise in his chest, and he wondered if his family still resided on the Isle of Ang.

The boy set a small fire in the hearth, while Bethen busied herself in the kitchen. When the flames were lit, the boy sat next to Blake, watching him curiously.

"What's your name?" Blake asked.

"Jacob," the boy informed him matter-of-factly.

"Well, Jacob, would you like to see a trick?"

The boy nodded, and drew closer.

Blake propped his foot up on the bench beside him, and unlaced one of his boots, taking the cord between his fingers. He gave the boy his knife, and held a section of the lace taut between his hands.

"I want you to cut the string here." He indicated the section with his forehead.

The boy sawed clumsily through the string, smiling when it finally broke. Blake brought his hands together, and drew them apart, revealing a whole cord.

Jacob's eyes widened, and he ran to his mother. She was busy preparing supper, but he pulled at her shirtsleeve until she could no longer ignore him. Bethen bent down, while Jacob whispered excitedly in her ear.

Blake grinned, and re-laced his boot. It was a relief to be able to use his skill of trickery without worrying that it would be mistaken for real magic, a misunderstanding with likely fatal consequences. He knew the boy was too young to have developed a fear of liogan.

Jacob returned from the kitchen with a piece of bread, torn from a freshly-baked loaf. Salted butter melted inside, and the boy pressed the bread into Blake's hands.

"Thank you," Blake said, before the boy ran back to the safety of his mother's skirts.

Blake busied himself over the next few hours washing and cutting vegetables. Bethen whistled over a pot of water hung over the crackling fire, adding vegetables as quickly as Blake could prepare them. The sweet smell of yeast-risen bread and boiling vegetables quickly filled the small Fellridge home.

Looking at Bethen, Blake was again reminded of his own mother, whom he had not seen in several years. He sometimes wondered how different his life would have been if he had stayed in his village. While he probably would not have faced the hangman's noose, he could never have been satisfied with the simple tranquility of rural life. Still, he was able to enjoy the moment of peace in Bethen's home for as long as it lasted.

There was a knock at the door, and Bethen called for the visitor to let themselves in. Owen stepped through the door, looking around the room until his eyes landed on Blake.

"I've tied the horses up outside. Is there any word from Moirin?" he asked.

Blake shook his head.

Bethen came over, handing Owen a piece of bread. "You don't look much good for work; why don't you sit down," she said brusquely.

Blake was suddenly struck by how sunken Owen's eyes were in his skull, bordered by a muted darkness revealing how little he had rested. There was still a frailty to Owen's body that undermined his stature, a failing that even the axe he carried could not mask.

He moved over on the bench so Owen could sit beside him.

"Thank you for your hospitality," Owen said to Bethen.

Blake continued completing whatever odd tasks Bethen gave him, while Owen fell asleep seated on the bench, his head resting awkwardly against the wall.

Jacob looked at Blake, and pointed at the scar across Owen's face. He mouthed a question, to which Blake shrugged. Blake was just as curious, but afraid to ask. Perhaps he would be able to question Moirin about it later.

Moirin arrived at the house after suppertime, having noticed the horses resting in the paddock. Bethen welcomed her, and set a bowl of soup for her on the table.

"Thank you for offering us the shelter of your home," Moirin said. She pulled a golden necklace from her pocket, and handed it to Bethen. "Consider this a small token of our appreciation."

"Thank you, though a gift was hardly necessary," Bethen said, before stepping away to put Jacob to bed.

Moirin sat down opposite Blake.

Owen was still asleep, and Blake turned to Moirin. He raised his eyebrows in question, but Moirin shook her head fleetingly in response.

"Helna is a nickname. The woman lived here many years ago, and was known to be a friend of Ethin. She died over a decade ago," she said. Her voice was low, though neither Bethen nor Jacob was at the table. "I had to convince many distrustful people of my intentions to find this information, so it will likely be difficult for Alderic to find the same."

"Did she have any children?" Owen was awake.

"None living. She has one grandchild, Geils, but he no longer resides in Fellridge."

"Does he know anything?" Blake asked, hoping the question was not too foolish.

"Perhaps," Moirin responded, shrugging. "Helna burned her own house down before she died, and there are few in the town who even remember her. Her grandson is the only prospect we have."

"How long will it take us to reach him?" Owen asked.

"He is believed to live in the city of Brecktvin," Moirin responded. "Three days' travel from here."

Bethen was in the kitchen, and approached the table to bid the guests goodnight.

"The nights are cold, and you'd do best to stay under a roof," Bethen said. "I have no extra beds, but you're welcome to sleep on the floor by the fire."

They thanked her again and Blake brought the bedrolls into the house, where they lay them side by side in the small room. The embers in the hearth kept the room warm, and soon Blake had fallen asleep, grateful for the simple pleasure of a roof over his head.

In the morning, they took their leave. Bethen put two loaves of bread and a wheel of black-waxed cheese into a jute bag, and handed it to Blake. He thanked her for her generosity and the comfort of her home. He waved to Jacob, who peered out from behind his mother as he watched the company depart the farm, and leave the town of Fellridge.

The road was a little wider, and Blake brought his horse to ride beside Moirin's.

"What will you do if you find the liogan weapon?" Blake asked.

"I will use it to overthrow Alderic," she replied. "His bloodline has been far too long on the Vesian throne."

"This much I know," Blake responded. "Yet, where will you go? Will you bring the weapon to another kingdom?"

Moirin shook her head. "I do not want another king or queen to seize Vesia. My brother, Roland, is a duke. He and his husband, Thomas, wield great influence in Vesia. With their aid, and the weapon, I can raise the support and arms to overthrow the tyrant king."

Though he doubted it still, Blake supposed it was as good a plan as any.

13

After spending days and nights, on horseback, resting only as required by their mounts, Blake was grateful to see signs for the port city of Brecktvin, anxious to walk on his own two feet again. He had fallen asleep during one ride and found himself carried along by the horse, as she followed dutifully behind her fellows. He awoke when he leaned too far to one side, and nearly tumbled from the saddle into the road.

Morning was breaking when they reached Brecktvin. Light brick buildings rose high overhead, with green metal roofs that shone bright in the new sun. People of the city, on foot and horseback, travelled through the roads, paying little attention to the newcomers in their midst.

They walked through the bustling streets, until they came to a tavern near the city's center. The small building was dwarfed by those on either side, and inhabitants lazed in the sunlight sipping cups of tea in the store front, only a foot away from the current of traffic.

Their stomachs empty, and bodies tired, the travelers stopped in the tavern for breakfast. They tucked themselves into a darkened corner of the room. A barmaid approached, bringing three steaming bowls of porridge, each with a dollop of dark honey at the center, and a fresh pot of black tea.

Moirin thanked her, before signaling for her to come closer. "I was wondering if you knew of a man named Geils, originally from Fellridge. He would have arrived in Brecktvin around three years ago."

The barmaid appraised the group. "Why are you looking for him?" She rubbed a hand across the back of her neck, her discomfort apparent.

"We are friends of his from many years ago, and bear an important message," Moirin responded, unfazed by the unusual reaction of the server.

The barmaid let out a quiet, bitter laugh. "You will have little trouble finding Geils, but you must pray he does not find you first," she leaned close, "friend or not."

"What do you mean?" Blake asked, drawing the barmaid's attention.

She looked around the room, before seating herself in an empty chair by the table, her voice dropping to a barely audible whisper. "Geils of Fellridge is both known to and feared by all in Brecktvin. Years ago, a plague swept the city. All suffered, and those of us who survived bear the marks to this day."

She lifted her shirtsleeve to reveal a series of small blue streaks that marred the skin of her arms. Blake had never seen such an affliction before, and looked curiously on the strange disfigurement.

"Geils arrived, demanding to meet with the city elders," she continued, bringing the fabric back down over her arm. "He said he was a liogan, and swore he knew of a cure for the ill that plagued the city.

"He said that the liogans in Brecktvin had placed a curse on us that could only be lifted by appeasing the gods, appealing to a power greater than the sorcery of their cursed kind. Every week, he would bring some poor soul to the town center and make their sins known. Every week they would beg for mercy, and every week their cries would be extinguished only by the quick work flames made of their living flesh."

"This was three years ago. Do the human sacrifices continue to this day?" Blake asked.

"We have walked through your city, and see no signs of sickness," Moirin noted.

The barmaid shook her head. "It ended long ago," she sighed. "But, we are afraid of returning to a plague state. The sacrifices are less frequent, only every month or so. In return for finding the cursed among us, Geils has been given the largest home in Brecktvin. If you still wish to find him, it's difficult to miss. He lives in an old house of worship bordering the main square."

"If he is a liogan, why has he not been killed himself? It is uncommon for one to be allowed to live past childhood," Blake said, sorry to be speaking so bluntly. However, he had seen this to be true. Liogans had trouble controlling their abilities when they first presented, and were typically put to death immediately. Geils had lived in a town of the ordinary, so protecting himself would have been impossible.

"They are afraid that if anything happens to him, they will all be cursed," Moirin answered, watching the barmaid for confirmation. "I doubt they have allowed word of his powers to spread beyond Brecktvin, in an effort to protect him."

"Is such secrecy possible in a port city?" Blake asked.

"It would seem so," Moirin responded. "I had heard no tell of Geils before now."

"We are all warned to keep outsiders away from the marketplace during the sacrifices. It is rumored that some of Brecktvin would have spread word beyond the city, but they were killed by their fellows before they could," the barmaid interjected. "These tales alone are enough to continue the city's protection of Geils."

"It is the rule of the Blackdog King," Moirin said. "In the absence of order, the people are slaves to superstition, and take it upon themselves to carry out justice as they see fit."

"Geils of Fellridge will be in the marketplace this afternoon. If you would like to see him pass judgement on the latest sacrifice, you will not have to wait long," the barmaid remarked, before standing. "If I were you, I'd stay as far away from him as I could. I've seen his kind of magic with my own eyes, and have no doubt that he is a powerful liogan."

Moirin offered thanks and passed her a few gold coins, in exchange for the barmaid disremembering the nature of their conversation. The barmaid accepted the payment, tucking the coins into a small pocket in her shirt.

When the barmaid had left, Blake spoke up. "It is unlikely that a liogan would make his nature so public, and it seems even more doubtful that he would be willing to burn others of his kind."

Moirin shrugged. "We will see him this afternoon. We can only hope that he knows something of his grandmother's dealings with Ethin, and that he is willing to speak with us."

14

Alderic led his troop of twenty to Fellridge. He knew that Moirin would have taken the shorter route through the woods, aided by the small size of her company. He would not make her time but, as king, he could expect other advantages.

The journey ahead would be a suitable testing ground for the new knight, his novice second-in-command. The young man was still inexpert with a sword, but his loyalty and resolve were the reasons Alderic had chosen him for the role. Skill with weaponry would come in time, and the king trusted his intuition. This new knight could, with training, become an unsurpassable warrior.

One they had arrived in Fellridge, it took little time to find someone who had seen the band of scrappy challengers, and the townsfolk were anxious to assist the king in any way they could. However, a few refused to speak with his soldiers, and Alderic feared that these were the ones who knew the most about Helna.

He was told repeatedly of Bethen, a dairy farmer, who had been seen speaking to a stranger. This outsider was described as a swarthy man of average stature, wiry, with unevenly cropped brown hair.

Needing no further confirmation that Blake, at least, had been in Fellridge, Alderic rode past the waiting townsfolk to Bethen's farm. His soldiers and knight waited in the dirt road, collecting whatever information was offered by the villagers.

Alderic rode to the gate, where he saw a young boy playing beside the cows. He called the boy over.

"Did you see three travelers pass through here yesterday?" he asked.

The boy nodded, half-hiding his face behind dirt-covered hands.

"Did you hear where they were going?"

The boy shook his head and nervously looked up at Alderic.

"Is your mother home?"

This time the boy hesitated, looking timidly at the house. To Alderic, this was as good an answer as any. He had little time to waste in Fellridge, and his patience was beginning to wear thin. Still in the saddle, he reached down and grabbed the boy by the scruff of the neck.

"Bethen," he called, holding the boy in the crook of his arm.

A woman stepped through the door, still clutching vegetables in the scoop of her apron. She dropped the vegetables into the mud at her doorstep when she caught sight of her son. She cried out, and ran towards the king's horse, halting when Alderic held up his hand.

"The travelers who were here yesterday. Where did they go?" He kept his voice steady, as he watched her face contort in fear.

Bethen pursed her lips, and shook her head. Her eyes filled with tears that ran down her cheeks. Her lower jaw shook and her hands balled into fists at her sides, the knuckles turning white.

Alderic was never one to circle a purpose needlessly. His horse shifted beneath him, echoing his own impatience. When it became clear a vague threat would not suffice, he made it more specific. He pulled a knife from his belt, and raised it to the boy's throat.

"I will only ask once more," he spoke deliberately, his eyes locked with hers as the blunt of the knife pressed against the boy's throat. "Where did they go?"

Bethen's son struggled, and Alderic brought the knife back a quarter of an inch so the boy would not cut himself.

The woman broke down, dropping to her knees before him.

"A woman and two men lodged with me a few days ago. I heard them speak of finding a man named Geils in Brecktvin." The words came strained, choked within her throat. "I swear to you: that is all I know."

Given the profuse tears and cries springing from her shattered form, Alderic was inclined to believe her.

She held her arms out, and Alderic tossed the boy from the saddle. Bethen pulled her son close and wept. The boy did not cry, but he clutched his mother tight all the same. He looked up at Alderic from beneath his mother's arm. The king knew there was nothing more they could offer him.

He returned to his soldiers, who were watering the horses at the trough, and led the troop back to the road.

Moirin had identified Geils of Fellridge, and unintentionally passed this information to the king. Alderic smiled to himself, as he wondered whether the escaped prisoners staying ahead might prove beneficial.

15

They arrived at the Brecktvinian center, just as a large crowd was beginning to gather. The square was paved with smooth stone and bordered on each side by buildings towering above. The sun glinted off the greened-copper rooftops, which seemed to nearly brush the blue sky, and a salty sea breeze spread warmly through the city.

A wooden platform had been erected at the edge of the square, appearing to have been there for years given its wear. At the center of the square was a conspicuous pit filled with old charred wood and bone. The stone beneath the debris was scorched from years of use, and an iron stake stood eight feet high in the midst of the fired detritus.

The crowd quieted, and murmurs gave way to a deadly hush, as everyone became steadily aware of the man climbing the steps to the platform. Reaching the top, he stood before the crowd. He was cloaked in rich blue-violet fabric that was laced with gold, the lowered cowl obscuring his face, and he held in his right hand a tall, iron staff.

"People of Brecktvin, for years now, we have been blessed with good health, and bountiful food. Yet, when I arrived in this city, it was struck with sickness and famine. Women left their newborns to die, a fate more merciful than life, and men perished in search of remedy for their stricken bodies." He smiled and raised his arms. "Looking at you now, I am reminded of all the good we have accomplished. Yet, good comes at a grave price. We cannot forget the sacrifice we must make, nor neglect our duty towards each other. The few will suffer, so that the many may live." He stepped forward, striking his staff against the boards.

Blake watched with rapt attention, and he could sense Owen tense beside him. Moirin stood to his other side. Her arms were crossed in front of her chest, and her eyes narrowed as she assessed the man on the platform.

Geils, as Blake assumed the man to be, passed a hand over the top of the staff and fire sprang forth. He ducked beneath the cowl of his robes, before flinging the cloth behind him. He opened his lips, and let escape a current of breath which turned to flame upon contact with the staff.

The people watched in silent amazement and Geils smiled back at them, his slick teeth showing for only a moment.

"Hold in your hearts no doubt; the gods speak through me. It is by their will that I fulfill this terrible destiny. Through their intervention, and my love of Brecktvin, I find the courage to do what is just."

The crowd parted, and two heavily armed men stepped through. They were dressed in the same brilliant cloth that Geils wore draped across his shoulders. Between them, they held a scrawny youth by the elbows; he could not have been older than seventeen. He struggled with all his might to free himself from their grasp, and his bare feet dragged against the ground.

Wrenching his arm, he broke free for a moment. He sprinted a few paces, before the crowd seized him, hurling him back into the clutches of Geils' men. He was again dragged to the pit. Once there, his hands were bound with rope, and another man tied the youth to the stake and piled wood at the base.

The youth was frantic. He tugged at the bindings, his strength failing against the strong cord. Blood was beginning to run down his hands, the skin breaking beneath his struggle for freedom. He beat the back of his head against the stake in frustration, and his hair became wet with the same red that pooled between his wrists. Despite his thin, weak stature, he did not give up his efforts to free himself.

"Are we going to let him burn?" Blake whispered. He was unsure to which of his companions he directed this question, but the sick feeling growing within him could not be ignored.

"Saving him does not bring us closer to Geils," Moirin answered, her eyes fixed on the youth at the stake. "Some sacrifices must be made."

"Those are nearly the same words Geils spoke moments ago," Blake responded bitterly.

Moirin seemed taken aback by this comment and turned to Blake, her eyebrows raised. "I am surprised to find you the voice of justice and compassion."

"Am I incorrect?" he responded, choosing to ignore the implication.

Her mouth opened a fraction, before closing again. She seemed to be considering the choices laid out before her, and Blake held his breath as he observed her deliberation.

"I suppose it does not make us any worse off." She shrugged a shoulder. "If needed, he could be used as a bargaining tool."

"How can we free him? We are surrounded by Geils' men and the Brecktvinians, who would gladly see the youth dead," Blake asked.

Geils was descending from the platform, a flame still flickering at the top of his iron staff. With bodyguards on either side, he ceremoniously made his way to the freshly prepared pit.

"Draw your sword," Moirin whispered to Blake.

Blake looked away from the fire pit, and saw Moirin had already drawn her weapon, and Owen held out the axe. Blake pulled the sword from the sheath, and realized his hands were trembling. He was accustomed to the occasional brawl, but he tended to engage in fighting only when it heavily favored his victory.

Owen walked to the pit, and held out his axe, the sharp blade pointed at Geils. His eye stared down the handle at the violet-cloaked man.

"We're taking him with us," Owen said, his voice still hoarse from disuse.

Geils laughed, and signaled to the bodyguards. Both drew their weapons and charged at Owen, who cut them down in a single, fluid motion.

Blood splattered the ash surrounding the pit. Geils drew back, the death of the two men leaving him momentarily unprotected.

Blake kept his sword drawn, his eyes on the crowd. A bodyguard tried to intervene, and Blake took a step toward him. He withdrew instantly, out of the reach of Blake's weapon. This retreat sent a surge of power through Blake's body, and he found his hands had stopped shaking.

This feeling of strength was somewhat lessened when he realized that the man was looking past him. His eyes were fixed on Owen, who held the gore-spattered axe. Blake's blood ran cold when he saw the expression ravaging his companion's face. The near comatose countenance he had grown accustomed to was distorted by a monstrous, primitive force. Owen's face was blanched, and he shook with a barely-controlled struggle. His excruciating stare turned briefly to Blake, who wondered if this visceral creature could even recognize him as an ally.

Owen turned away, and Blake was struck by something he saw in his eyes: agonizing pain, an all-consuming torment that wracked the man's body. Blake could scarce move as his mind raced, trying to make sense of the sudden change that had overcome his companion.

Owen strode through the crowd, which scattered before him. Moirin followed, pulling the sacrifice along by the remaining bindings at his wrists. Blake held the back of the attacking party, his sword drawn.

No one approached, and they were able to retreat to the horses. The youth's hands were still bound, so Moirin helped him onto the front of her saddle.

They rode to the outer limits of the city, taking cover in the woods, and continuing to where the Brecktvinians would not easily find them. They took out their packs, and prepared to camp for the night. All were silent, and the youth looked nervously from one face to another, hardly believing his rescue.

"This is, perhaps, an advantage," Moirin said, breaking the stretch of silence. "It is unlikely Geils will send the people after us, as he will fear again appearing impotent against three strangers. We have his attention, and are practically guaranteed an audience with him." She sighed. "I will go tomorrow to meet with him, and see if we can strike a deal."

"Will I be returned to the stake?" the youth asked, speaking for the first time since the square.

"We will do what is necessary to further our mission," she responded, summarily dismissing his concerns.

Moirin retrieved the map and studied it by the light of the fire, without a second thought spared for the fate of the sacrifice. Blake turned to Owen, who was wiping blood from the blade of his axe. He did not look up or show any interest in the proceedings.

The youth seemed to notice the indifference that had become evident to Blake, because he leapt to his feet and began to run away. He was surprisingly fast given the injurious ordeal he had undergone only moments before.

Blake sprang up and sprinted after the youth, bodily knocking him over after only a few paces. Blake grabbed him by the elbows, and dragged him back to the others.

"We cannot send him back," Blake said, as he pushed his prisoner to sit on the ground.

Moirin looked at him. "You continue to surprise me, yet a mere thief cannot hope to understand the necessity of protecting the common good. I will meet with Geils tomorrow to make the exchange, assuming the man is even in possession of his grandmother's charge. By tomorrow evening, I will have the information, though the youth may have to pay for our knowledge." She smiled coldly. "I'm sure Geils can arrange a burning for the afternoon."

Blake's ire was piqued, but he stifled his resentment and pressed on.

"You name me a mere thief, yet I have never been a murderer." It was Moirin's turn to flinch in insult. "I can secure the information we need without sacrificing a life."

It was a bold promise on Blake's part, and one he was not entirely sure he could fulfill were he given the opportunity. His ability to mimic a certain level of confidence was key to success in his trade, and it appeared its efficacy prevailed even against Moirin.

She sighed, casting a glance at the disinterested Owen before turning back to Blake. "If by tomorrow evening you are not successful, we will move ahead with my plan."

Blake nodded, letting out a breath he had not known he was holding.

The captive visibly relaxed by his side, though that may have been premature. Despite his words, Blake was without a strategy. Yet, he had never been one for thinking ahead.

Owen was still cleaning the blade, though the blood was long since gone. There was something meditative in his repetitive motion and Blake watched, transfixed. The monster he had glimpsed in the fight was vanished, leaving behind this vacant soul.

Blake brought his attention back to the captive. "What's your name?" Blake asked.

The young man seemed to have edged closer since the thief's defense of his life, sheltering himself beneath the protection Blake represented.

"Ian," he responded.

"How did you come to be in the square?"

"I was in the jailhouse of Kritnin." He looked down. "Late last night, those two men in the square grabbed me from my cell, and brought me on horseback to Brecktvin. We arrived in the afternoon and, within minutes of being taken from the saddle, I was dragged to the stake."

"No one said anything to you?"

"No."

"And you've never been to Brecktvin before?"

Ian shook his head.

The pieces were beginning to come together for Blake, offering a possible answer to a question lurking within his mind since they had first learned of Geils' cruel practice.

"Is it, therefore, safe to assume that no one in Brecktvin knew you, or would intervene on your behalf?"

Ian nodded.

"This explains why the people of Brecktvin do not protest the sacrificial murders. No one they care for is ever harmed by Geils. You are not a liogan?"

Ian smiled for the first time since their meeting. "If I had any power, wouldn't I have used it to save myself?"

"Why were you in jail?" he asked Ian.

Ian hesitated before he responded. "I was part of a bandit raid on Kritnin. I was the only one captured," he stated this simply, avoiding the eyes of the small company.

"Did they not try to get you back?"

"I was moved before they had a chance. When they find I am here, they will come for me."

Blake was surprised by the certainty in Ian's voice.

"How did you come to be in the company of bandits? You don't exactly seem an outlaw," Blake said, surveying the weakly frame before him.

"And you don't seem a noble," Ian shot back, though appearing to regret his impertinence immediately. "I apologize, I only mean that—"

Blake interrupted with a slight laugh. "No offense has been taken. I do not run in my companions' circles, and have no delusions that I am of similar stock. I was merely wondering how you came to the fugitive life."

Ian relaxed, leaning back against his elbows. "They took me in when I was an orphaned child. I never grew as big or as strong as they would have liked, but I suppose they developed a liking for me. They've always treated me differently, protecting me more than the others, and I've been their cook for as long as I can recall."

"What would they do if they were to find you had been burned?"

Ian winced at the mention of his closely avoided fate. "They'll do what they see fit. It's best for the city if I remain unharmed."

Blake nodded. The fire was beginning to die. Owen had pulled a cloak around himself, and appeared to be sleeping, albeit lightly. Moirin stirred the embers with a stick, before retiring.

Blake knew Ian would not sleep, and used the remnants of Geils' bindings to tie him to a saddle on the ground. He did not make the knot too tight, trusting Owen to hear Ian if he attempted another escape.

Satisfied that he had done what he could, Blake allowed himself to slumber. He would need to be well rested for his meeting with Geils.

The next morning, Moirin accompanied Blake to the city, and Owen stayed behind at the campsite to ensure Ian neither escaped nor was harmed. They had decided to proceed to Brecktvin on foot, not wishing to draw unnecessary attention to their presence.

"How long have you known Owen?" Blake asked. Given the fact that he would be putting his life on the line for them, he felt he deserved an answer.

"Many years."

"How did you meet?" he asked. Moirin looked at him, her eyebrow raised. "I only ask, because you seem such strange company. You are a lady of the highest nobility, while Owen seems more suited to something else entirely," he continued, though himself unsure of what that would be.

She sighed, finally indulging his curiosity. "I was married to Alderic's brother, Severin. I was there when Owen was first presented to the king."

"By whom?"

"Owen's father, an earl. Owen had been given high levels of training in council, and was sent to Alderic's court as a demonstration of loyalty to the king." She smiled, though there was something sad to it. "I still remember seeing Owen the first time he was in the court. He and Alderic may have been near the same age, but already the king's heart had been hardened through as yet unfelt years. Owen was a mild-mannered man, in truth more suited to idle pleasantries than to the battlefield.

"The king saw something in Owen: a facet to his disposition that, if properly exploited, would make him a great warrior. In previous years, the king had taken a single knight to act as his right hand on the battlefield, though all were killed within only months of service. Owen was different. He responded to Alderic's harsh training with a fervor, adapting rapidly to each challenge the king threw his way. He was poised to become a powerful ally in Alderic's fight to expand his kingdom. Through each battle, his incredible skill allowed him to thrive, yet he avoided killing, doing so only when he could find no other recourse."

She paused. "I believe it was Owen's adoration of life itself that Alderic distorted, twisting it to serve his ends."

"I can imagine Owen's remaining reluctance to kill did not sit well with the king."

"It did not. Owen could survive, engaging in little bloodshed. Battles would go by, and no lives were ended by Owen's hand. A taciturn knight is of little use to one like Alderic; he needs someone to whom loyalty means complete obedience.

"However, Alderic found a solution to this perceived weakness. One day, their army captured a rebel city. Alderic had the soldiers of the opposition who refused to submit to his authority brought to the center of the city. He handed Owen an axe, and forced him to behead each of the conquered soldiers in succession. Alderic made Owen a gift of the axe to use as his primary weapon in battle from that day forward." She smiled. "Owen may despise it, but he is never more powerful than with an axe in his hand."

"When I saw him the other day—"

Moirin nodded, cutting Blake off, "he changed."

"You saw it too?"

"The scars he carries on his body are exceeded only by those within his mind. That kind of damage is unpredictable; what protects him one moment may endanger him the next." She paused, considering, "perhaps that shift in demeanor exists to shield him from the acts he knows he must commit."

Blake was suddenly reminded of something Owen had said when they first escaped from Ashen Castle's prison.

"Owen told me that he follows you because you provide him with something he cannot live without," Blake said.

Moirin nodded. "Owen needs a leader. His torments and capabilities make him dangerous, and no one is more aware of this than he. It is why Owen does not trust himself to make decisions. He would as soon place himself back under Alderic's leadership as my own, provided he has someone who will direct his every action."

Moirin paused. "Indeed, I believe Owen's brief moment of weakness, his single betrayal of Alderic, is the greatest regret of his life. He will never again find such a master."

Their conversation had brought them to the edge of the square. Vendors had set up their stalls, carefully avoiding the area surrounding the stake. People walked by the pit, keeping their eyes averted. It had become part of the city landscape, yet no one would acknowledge its existence.

"I will be here at midday to meet you." She offered a reassuring nod. "I wish you luck, and I truly hope you find success."

Blake thanked her, and headed into the colorful, bustling marketplace. Asking the first merchant he saw, he was pointed in the direction of Geils' residence, an imposing structure which, in hindsight, he could hardly have missed.

It was a broad building, arched as though modeled on a halved barrel. Two spires climbed to great heights from the body of the building, made from the same light brick that covered the rest of the home. Ancient statues of the gods sat on the walls, high above Blake's head. He wondered to himself what the architects of the structure might think were they to meet its newest inhabitant.

A brass loop was nailed to the imposing door, and Blake knocked it hard against the wood. He could hear the faint echo resound within and the tapping of footsteps across the floor, nearing the entrance.

A servant opened the door and looked Blake up and down. Blake knew he was not the image of respectability, so he spoke before the servant could make any inquiry.

"I am here to see Geils," he said.

"He does not wish to be disturbed," the man responded without hesitation, stony faced.

"I have the sacrifice who was kidnapped from the flames. Geils will want to speak with me," Blake said forcefully. He kept his eyes locked on those of the servant, unwilling to yield.

Blake thought his words had given the other man pause, but within seconds the door was being closed in his face. His heart sank, and he wondered whether the man would return. Still, he refused to leave so easily. He would wait on the steps all day if he had to, whatever was necessary to gain access.

The door opened again, minutes later, and two servants ushered Blake into a wide atrium. The walls were painted with a black pigment depicting religious scenes across wide wooden panels. A glance at the room overwhelmed the onlooker with the occurrences of flames shown throughout.

One wall bore a black painting of the fire goddess, Rubelytte. It made sense that Geils would turn his devotion to Rubelytte, but the familiar depiction was unsettling given the charred pit that lay within the square, just beyond the door.

Blake was led up stone stairs before he had time to study the room in greater depth. The two servants walked on either side of him, as if afraid he would dart away. They exchanged a look over his shoulders, and seemed to be on edge in a way that Blake did not fully understand.

At the top of the steps, a long blue carpet ran the length of a dimly lit hallway. They walked to the very end of the hall, Blake's apprehension steadily growing, reaching a room with an open door. The servants stood back, and Blake stepped through the threshold. The window was curtained, and the walls glowed hazily with the light of candles.

Geils stood at the far side of the room, before a mirror. He was no longer wearing the blue-violet cloak from the previous day's ceremony. Instead, he was dressed in a simple shirt, tucked neatly into trousers. His chestnut brown hair was slicked back into a tie at the base of his skull, and grey showed prematurely at his temples.

He leaned forward against a small, round table, staring into his own reflection. The metal mirror carried spots of tarnish, and Geils looked past these to study his own face. He could see Blake's reflection in the mirror, but made no move to formally address the visitor. His eyes moved upward, perhaps assessing what risk the smaller man posed. Still, he did not directly acknowledge Blake's presence.

A third servant brushed past Blake in the doorframe, and walked to where Geils stood. He carried with him a bowl filled with water, and he stepped carefully to avoid spilling even a drop on the blue carpet. He set the bowl down on the table, moving aside shaving instruments to make room on the wooden surface. He was dismissed with a careless gesture from Geils and stepped past Blake again as he retreated from the room.

Blake watched, as Geils wetted a shaving brush and used the bristles against the bar of soap in a silver tray. He applied the thick lather to the lower half of his face, pausing only to inspect himself in the mirror. He took the blade from the table into his hand and ran the edge across his chin. The straight blade left smooth skin in its wake, and he tipped the collected lather into the side of the bowl before bringing his attention back to his face. The man was fastidious, leaving no part of his barely emerging beard untouched by the cool metal.

"I prefer to keep no remnant of this hair," he indicated his chin. Geils spoke to Blake, though his eyes remained locked on his own reflection. "It is a worldly impurity that impedes the divine force channeling itself through my words."

"Odd, since I have met bearded firebreathers in the past," Blake countered with a grin. "It never seemed to harm their performance."

Geils gave no indication he had heard Blake's taunting words, his complete attention focused on his task. Once he had finished shaving, he stooped forward, immersing his face in the basin of water. He patted his face dry, before splashing a little fresh water on his newly shaven skin.

Watching the precision with which Geils approached grooming, Blake touched the slight beard on his own face. He typically kept himself clean-shaven, but since his imprisonment his hair had been allowed to grow. He kept it short using the blade of his dagger, as it irritated him if it grew more than half an inch, but he knew his appearance was even more unkempt than usual.

Looking up, Geils finally turned to face Blake. "I sense that you are skeptical of my liogan power."

"It is only that I have observed that type of performance before. Though, I will admit that I have never seen an act quite so convincing." Blake looked hard at Geils. "My name is Blake, and I believe that you and I can communicate more effectively if we begin with a clear understanding of one another."

"Why have you come here? You have the sacrifice and, clearly, I have made no attempts to pursue him. I thought you would be pleased with the outcome."

"If saving him were my goal, I would agree. It is not."

Blake was not fooled by Geils' show of nonchalance. If Ian were allowed to live, it would be unavoidably embarrassing for a man who claimed a direct connection to the gods.

"What is it you're after?" The unease Blake knew existed beneath Geils' calm demeanor was beginning to show itself.

"I believe Helna, your grandmother, was in possession of something before she died, something given to her by Ethin, a man of King Conri's court. I will trade you the youth for this, assuming it is within your possession."

"You are in search of Ethin's hidden treasure," Geils said with a self-satisfied smile. "My grandmother would tell me the stories when I was a child. I am surprised there are any foolish enough to believe them."

"My beliefs are not your concern. However, the success of your liogan sacrifices are. Do we have an agreement?"

"How do I know you still have the sacrifice? Besides, if I do have the item, though I make no such claims, how do I know you will not leave me empty-handed?"

Blake dug through his pocket, retrieving a lock of hair he had cut from Ian's head that morning, and tied with a small piece of cord. He handed it to Geils.

Geils turned it over in his hand. "This could be from anyone."

"True, but take it for what it is: a gesture of good faith. As a man of belief, you should realize the extent of the trust I am placing in you."

The token's significance must have reached Geils, because he relented. "Very well, but how shall this exchange be carried out? I will not go forward if I fear betrayal."

"Tomorrow, have the people of Brecktvin gather for a burning. We will bring the youth to the square, accompanied by your bodyguards. I will stand by your side on the platform, and you will give me the item at the same moment the sacrifice is marched forward to the stake. If there is any sign that my people will recapture the sacrifice; not only can you withhold the item, but you can take my life."

"My men could just seize the youth," Geils smirked.

"After yesterday's display, I don't think so."

"Very well." Geils did not seem perturbed by Blake's calling of his pretense. "Tomorrow at noon, we will make the exchange."

Blake nodded, and turned to leave. He paused, his palm resting on the painted doorframe, and looked at Geils. "Just to satisfy my own curiosity, what is the item your grandmother gave you?"

Geils smirked. "So you can kill me and search my belongings? You will find out what it is soon enough."

Blake politely returned the smile. As relieved as he was by Geils' acceptance of the proposal, he was still apprehensive of finding a way to both acquire Helna's charge and keep Ian alive.

Once out of Geils' home, he looked up at the sun. It was shining bright, with the newness of the still early morning. There were several hours to pass before he was to meet Moirin. While he could easily find his way back to the campsite alone, he knew that she would be displeased if he broke from the plan.

With time to waste, he began to wander through the city. Initially, he was afraid he would be recognized, given the exploits from the day before, but he was relieved to find the people of Brecktvin paid him little attention.

As the hour dragged on, he made his way to the port. He sat down on the edge of the dock, the water shimmering only inches beneath his feet. He watched ships unloading their goods, and listened to the sound of seabirds as they soared overhead. The air was salty, and his skin felt grimy from the breeze. He tossed a stone off the dock, and watched as the rippling water licked the edge of the wooden boards, leaving them darker beneath the sunlight.

16

Alderic was growing impatient. He had stopped to rest the horses, and take refreshment. It was necessary, but nonetheless another inconvenience in his pursuit of the weapon. With no hope of moving forward immediately, he took the opportunity to continue the sword training of his freshly recruited knight.

The man was dressed in new armor: a helmet, breastplate, chain mail shirt, and leather gauntlets. He was strong, but his body uneasily bore the weight of the shaped metal, his movements encumbered by a lack of familiarity.

They stood by the side of the dirt path, surrounded on each side by trees. The king faced him, sword drawn. Every movement of the knight was hesitant, stirring only when Alderic began an attack, and even then, he only acted in defense of himself.

Alderic sent the edge of the sword towards him, deliberately slow, and the knight swatted it away in a sweeping motion that might, under ordinary circumstances, leave him vulnerable to a second attack.

Alderic stepped back, before immediately relaunching his strike on the novice. This time he quickly closed the distance between them, forcing the knight to stumble backwards. Their blades locked, and the knight found himself unable to free his weapon from Alderic's control. The king came within a few inches of him, before striking the knight's visor with the hilt of his sword. The metal rang out and the knight dropped to the ground, dazed.

Alderic looked down at his fallen knight, untroubled by the seeming lack of skill the man possessed. He placed his boot on the knight's breastplate, pinioning the novice warrior against the grass. The king kept pressure squared on his chest.

"Stand," Alderic commanded, "you must finish the fight."

The knight struggled against the king's weight, but found he was unable to right himself. He pushed against the ground, grass and dirt slipping away beneath the heels of his boots. As the king remained unmoving, the breastplate shifted against the knight's shirt, the top of the armor piece coming to press against his throat.

The metal edge wedged against his windpipe, but he continued his efforts to stand as his king had commanded him. His helmet had fallen off, and his cheeks were reddened with the exertion as the compression at his throat began to hinder his breathing.

When it became clear that he would not give up, no matter the pain he experienced, Alderic stepped back and offered the knight his hand. He grasped the gauntlet in his palm, and pulled the knight to his feet.

"Callum." He spoke, as the knight retrieved his fallen helmet and sword from the ground.

"Callum?" the knight repeated, confused.

"You have begun a life in my service, and I need a name to which you shall respond. To me, Callum will work as well as any other. Do you have an objection?" The knight shook his head, and the king sighed. "I hope the name will bring something to your actions, as to send you into battle now would be to send you to your death."

Whether the knight was glad to be given a name by the king was unclear, but he approached his military study with a new vigor. Alderic was pleased to see Callum begin to initiate attacks against him, the intimidation of attacking the king appearing to wear off. While his skill was still greatly lacking, there was a fire lit within him.

He lunged at the king, trying to make contact. Alderic deflected the blow, as he was not wearing any armor, his own sword striking the knight's breastplate with a clang. Confidence without skill was dangerous, but Alderic believed this knight, with even brief training, would live longer than the others.

"Attack me again," the king commanded. He was determined to practice until Callum could complete the assault without any hesitation.

It was rare for Alderic to train a knight during a journey, but opportunity necessitated immediate instruction. Callum had appeared, from their first meeting, loyal and enthusiastic. Alderic knew that these traits would more than make up for any deficit in combat skill. Under his guidance, Callum would learn quickly. Soon he would be prepared for the battlefield.

This confidence in the abilities of another Alderic had only felt once before, and a bitterness rose in his throat as he was reminded of a past failure: Owen. A man with the skill and courage to aid the king in every conquest, though he lacked the nature to do so. With two such opponents as Alderic and Owen, the only outcome was the complete annihilation of one. Alderic would never break, his heart battle-hardened in his unrelenting quest for ascendance, so Owen had left with a fractured spirit and a shattered mind.

Alderic regretted nothing but the weakness Owen had shown in his final moments as the king's knight.

Callum was lunging towards him again, and Alderic averted the hit. The king had been lost in thought, and momentarily forgotten his surroundings. Nonetheless, his defensive movements were almost entirely reflexive.

He kicked Callum back easily and the knight landed against a tree.

Alderic reached his hand out, grasping the knight's wrist, and pulling him forward. He nodded and clapped him on the shoulder. The knight had made significant progress during only a few hours instruction.

He helped Callum out of the helmet, and the knight brushed the sweat-soaked hair from his eyes. There was an intensity in the knight's gaze, a devotion to the king's cause that took even Alderic aback. There was little need for a test of loyalty with Callum; his fidelity was clear. Alderic knew Callum would not repeat Owen's mistake.

Yet, the totality of Callum's quickly formed devotion made Alderic uneasy.

17

As Blake waited by the water, he noticed that his head was beginning to ache. He had not eaten or drunk anything since leaving the woods that morning. While his mind was still preoccupied with the seeming conundrum of Geils and Ian, he knew he would think better with food and drink.

There was a small merchant's stand at the end of the dock, and Blake walked towards it, shielding his eyes from rays of the late morning sun. A man, his face tanned and heavily lined by hours spent beside the sea, was tending to customers as Blake approached. Money and food changed hands as fishermen and sailors collected their meals.

Blake came to the stand and requested the same meal that he had seen each of the previous patrons leave holding. His fingers brushed the coins Moirin had given him earlier; he had more than enough.

The man took a piece of white flatbread, and made a cut in the side. He took a shredded vegetable Blake did not recognize, placing it inside the pocket of the bread, and slid a wooden instrument beneath a piece of fish that cooked beside others over a small but steady fire. The fish meat was yellow, heavily coated in a mixture of spices that scented the air around the stand. The man placed the fish within the bread, and handed it to Blake.

Blake was passing the man his payment for the fish, when a small bottle behind the stand caught his eye. He could not be sure, but the shape was reminiscent of the ones he had often seen during his youth on the Isle of Ang.

"Is that Fisherman's Ruin?" he asked, stepping forward and keeping his voice at a near whisper.

The merchant's eyes travelled from Blake to the bottle, his wariness evident. "Perhaps."

The merchant's reservation was understandable. In the Isle of Ang, possession of Fisherman's Ruin carried a hefty fine. Too many had been lost to accidents involving the substance, and a ban had been instituted. Blake imagined the case was the same in Brecktvin.

"I would like to buy it."

"The entire bottle?" the man responded in disbelief. "I usually sell it by the capful."

"I would like the bottle, and I trust your discretion regarding our transaction."

"Twenty pieces." The merchant extended his hand.

Blake handed over the money, and carefully stowed the bottle within his shirt so it rested against his stomach. He felt an intense discomfort surge within him, as he knew the dangers of having the potent liquid so near. He returned to the edge of the dock to eat, all the while acutely aware of the cold container sitting against his skin.

At midday, Moirin met him at the designated spot, and walked with him back to the others while he told her of his meeting with Geils.

When they had returned to the campsite, Blake retrieved the bottle from his shirt, carefully opened the top, and breathed in the odorless fumes. Fisherman's Ruin was no different than water in its taste, smell, and color. Any difference in this liquid through appearance was undetectable, but he felt slightly lightheaded after only a few breaths. It was an experience he had not had since his childhood.

It was for this reason Fisherman's Ruin had earned its name. There was once a time when the substance was to be found in every home and on every boat, it's uniquely volatile properties making it invaluable. However, fishermen took to bringing the bottles with them to enjoy the more recreational aspects of the liquid. Boats had capsized and the fishermen were too often lost to the watery depths.

Despite the illegality, Fisherman's Ruin remained popular across Vesia. In the Isle of Ang, Blake had known nearly everyone to keep a bottle hidden. He had plenty of experience working with the notorious substance, and it was Fisherman's Ruin's less illicit purpose that Blake required.

Moirin came to Blake's side, and he handed her the bottle.

"What is it?" she asked.

"Fisherman's Ruin," he responded. "I wanted to be sure of its authenticity before I told you. I did not wish to raise false hope."

Moirin took a short breath of the vapors.

"It is genuine," Blake said.

Moirin nodded. "Tell me what do you require of us."

In order for Blake's plan to work, they would need to hand Ian over to Geils' bodyguards. Ian was naturally averse to this strategy, so Blake handed him a small knife.

"Hold it like this," Blake said. He held a similarly sized stick flush with his wrist. He set it down, and adjusted the knife's handle in Ian's finger tips, before returning to his demonstration. He shook the fabric of his sleeve down to cover the stick. "All you have to do is loosen your grip, and the handle will fall fully into your hand. If we fail, and they bind you, you can cut yourself free from the ropes."

Ian practiced the grip, and letting the handle fall from his wrist until he could nearly replicate Blake's action.

"How will I escape?" he asked, still dropping the knife from his fingertips to his palm.

"We will aid you in any way we can." Blake put his hand on Ian's shoulder in reassurance. "You have the knife if something goes wrong, though my hope is that you will never have to use it."

Despite Ian's time with the bandits, it was clear he was entirely unprepared to defend himself. Blake wondered how he had survived an outlaw's life for all those years.

In truth, the knife would do little to protect him. Facing his own mortality, Ian would probably drop the knife onto the ground, though it was still more likely that Geils' bodyguards would discover the hidden weapon when they bound Ian's wrists at the stake.

This did not appear to have occurred to Ian, and Blake was not about to enlighten him. If the plan failed, Ian would suffer an excruciating death, whether he was armed or not, and the idea of protecting himself seemed to ease Ian's mind.

"I won't let anything bad happen to you, I promise," Blake said.

He was reminded of the promises he had made Hugh.

Owen returned from the forest, his arms filled with kindling. He set them by the small, stone circle they had built at the center of the site, and stoked the fire. When it was ready, he began roasting the meat Moirin had brought over the open flame. The smell was sorely welcome, and Blake instinctively moved closer to the fire.

They ate the roasted meat, and Blake spoke a little of the Brecktvin port. Ian fell asleep shortly after supper, while Moirin, Owen, and Blake sat around the fire.

Blake looked at Owen's eyes, and his gaze was drawn to the scar traversing the milky lens. Perhaps it was an injury suffered in battle but, based on what Moirin had told him, and what he had seen for himself in Brecktvin, it seemed unlikely.

Owen was still weak, but he was gaining strength. His limbs were thin and his face gaunt, but his movements had become more fluid. He was able to wield the heavy axe with a grace and force that Blake, in his healthiest state, could never hope to replicate.

Moirin sat beside Owen, her shoulder only inches away from his. They were accustomed to each other's company, and seemed as though they should be at ease with one another. Yet, there was something that Blake could not quite manage to put in words, an underlying disquiet that tainted their alliance: a mutual apprehension.

Moirin saw him staring, and offered a small, reassuring smile. "Are you prepared for tomorrow?" she asked.

"I am," Blake responded.

Moirin retrieved a wineskin from her pack, and they passed it around the fire. It had been days since Blake had had a drink, and it was sorely welcome.

Blake looked hard at Moirin, wondering how she could be so committed to finding this liogan weapon that she could throw aside her lifestyle and nobility in pursuit of it.

"I am sorry, again, for my part in acquiring the map for King Alderic," Blake said.

Moirin looked up, appearing surprised by this sudden apology.

"It is done, and there is little else to say on the matter." She shrugged. "Besides, perhaps it is good that my hand has been forced. Based on the words of the Elsin, time is no longer my friend."

"What do you mean?" Blake asked.

"Have you heard the prophesy from the Elsin kingdom of the high ruler who will overthrow Alderic and peacefully unify the kingdoms?"

Blake shook his head.

"For many years, there has been a legend that one will arise in the east and bring about Alderic's death. Now, the Elsin claim that this usurper will come from their land, and will be identified by the Rock of Briggid."

"The Rock of Briggid?" Blake asked, the name unfamiliar to him.

"I know little of its purpose, only that it will make the high ruler known." Moirin sighed. "Currently, only Alderic stands between me and acquiring the throne of Vesia. If I wait too long, this high ruler may rise, and I do not wish to contend with any prophesy."

Blake nodded and took another drink from the wineskin. He glanced at Owen, but found the warrior appeared uninterested in talk of the Elsin prophesy.

The next morning, they rode into town. Ian sat in the saddle behind Moirin, his wrists loosely bound in from of him, and they made no attempt at discretion. The city's inhabitants stared and scuttled away as the riders paraded through the street, their captive in full view of the people.

They rode to the doorstep of Geils, where Ian was taken into the custody of two bodyguards. As per their arrangement, Moirin and Owen stayed by Ian's side, keeping close watch over Geils' men, while Blake went into the former house of worship and was led immediately toward Geils' chambers. The servants kept a few paces ahead of their visitor.

As he proceeded up the steps, he passed the servant preparing the shaving basin. Blake offered to carry the bowl, but the servant declined the offer. Blake slowed his pace to keep by the water-bearer as they walked up the steps.

Blake feigned a misstep, and bumped into the servant's side. The water bowl collided with the railing, and the servant was momentarily knocked from his feet. Blake caught the bowl against the wooden rail, quickly adding to the water the contents of the bottle hidden in his sleeve.

He held the bowl in one hand, offering the other to the servant who pulled himself hastily back to his feet. Blake handed the basin back to him, and the servant thanked him profusely. If anything untoward was suspected, the servant gave no indication, and Blake breathed a silent sigh of relief as continued up the steps.

He watched tentatively from the doorway as the servant set the water bowl down on the table by the mirror. Geils stood, waiting, and no words were exchanged between the two. Blake was now certain that his actions had gone unnoticed, and that the plan could move ahead.

His hands shook a little, something that, even despite years of experience, he had never been able to outgrow. Geils looked at Blake, as if noticing him there for the first time, before turning his attention to his ritual shaving.

Blake watched the movement of the blade somewhat mournfully. If all went well, this would be the last time his hands drew the fine blade across his skin. Blake was not prone to melancholy, yet he had never faced taking a life before.

"I am told the youth has been turned over to my custody." Geils stopped the blade mid-stroke and looked at Blake through the mirror, one eyebrow raised. "Could I not simply kill him now?"

Blake laughed, masking the doubt he had in his own scheme. "If you wish for your men to be made mincemeat. I can assure you, my companions are more than capable of destroying any opposition your handful of servants pose."

Geils smiled. "So you say."

"So I say," Blake repeated quietly, before raising his eyes to meet Geils' again. "Do you have the item?"

"Right here," he tapped his breast pocket, with a sly grin that Blake did not care for in the least. "Patience, it will be yours soon enough."

Blake paused before speaking again. "May I ask you a question?"

Geils looked at him, clearly surprised. "You may ask," he responded simply.

"Why pretend to be a liogan? It seems to present a great risk to your life."

"Perhaps," Geils laughed aloud, after confirming that no one apart from Blake was within earshot. He lowered the blade from his face, his task completed. "Yet, what is life without risk. When I came to this city, they would not have trusted me had I not claimed an otherworldly power. I chose to pursue a life of command, of influence. The kind of life I never could have lived within the rural confines of Fellridge. I live each day with the knowledge that I balance on the edge of a knife, yet I am unable to regret my choices. To have lived only one day on the path I have crafted for myself is to have lived an entire life."

Blake watched as Geils stopped speaking, and plunged his face into the basin. The thief held his breath, waiting for a sign of recognition that something was amiss. None came.

Blake could understand the desires that prompted Geils to leave Fellridge and pursue a life of deceiving others. After all, it was not entirely unlike that which Blake had chosen for himself.

"I can hardly question your efficacy," Blake begrudgingly admitted. "I am only sorry it came at so great a price."

Geils pulled on the ceremonial robe and straightened out the fabric, ignoring the criticism lodged within Blake's words. He checked his reflection once more in the mirror, smoothing down a few stray hairs, before crossing the threshold to join Blake in the hall.

While Blake had hoped there might be an easier acquisition of Helna's charge, it would be impossible to retrieve anything from the shirt pocket without Geils knowing, now that his violet garment covered his clothing. There was nothing left to do, but see his shaky plan through to the end.

He followed Geils out the door, and into the square. They were flanked on either side by armed men whose sole purpose was to protect Geils from harm, the kind of harm that Blake himself aimed to inflict.

The crowd had already gathered, eagerly awaiting the appearance of their leader. Blake followed Geils up the steps, and onto the platform. The pace was slow, as Geils continued to exude the somewhat timeworn mystical aura attributed to liogans. Blake could not help but be agitated by the meandering pace, the slowness of each step increasing his own trepidation.

Once on the platform, Blake searched the faces until he located Moirin, Owen and Ian. They were surrounded by four of Geils' bodyguards, all with their swords in hand. Moirin and Owen's weapons were not drawn, in keeping with the image of docility they wished to present.

Blake shook his head when he made eye contact with Moirin to indicate he was not in possession of their end. She nodded, and he could see her quietly speak a few words to Owen. Owen looked up at him, his eyes tracking

Blake with apprehension. Timing was everything, and their success or failure rested entirely on Blake's shoulders.

Blake turned his attention to Geils. "You have your sacrifice, now give me what is mine," he said.

Geils shrugged, "I suppose you've earned it."

He reached into the neck of his robes, feeling for his shirt pocket. Blake could see the fingers clasp around something, and Geils tossed a small wrapped package to Blake.

Blake tore open the edge, and glanced inside to see a small gold key. "What is this for?"

"I have no idea." Geils responded. "I was merely told to safeguard it. My grandmother told me to never open the package."

"She told you nothing else?"

"Nothing," Geils responded.

Blake crushed the wrapping back around the small metal piece and tucked it into his pocket.

"Very well, I will leave you now."

Geils placed his hand on Blake's chest. "You are not to leave until the sacrifice is complete. Those were our agreed upon terms."

Blake allowed himself to be stopped. He was prepared to stay on the stage, and had even counted on Geils taking this action. Blake knew the importance of a mark maintaining a sense of control and believing himself to have thwarted deceit. Blake gave the appearance of disappointment.

Geils motioned for his men to bring Ian forward. They seized the boy, and dragged him toward the stake. He kicked and screamed, struggling against the hands that gripped him. Blake stayed on the platform, not wanting to disrupt Geils' practiced routine. With a flourish, Geils lit the end of his staff, and raised it up. He disappeared beneath his cowl, and when he reemerged, he breathed across the flames.

His breath caught light, and a spray of fire appeared before his face. Blake could see a shift in Geils' expression as he realized the fire was changed in character. This registration of surprise lasted only seconds before the fire seized hold of the Fisherman's Ruin residue left across his face, catching the pampered skin in its scorching grasp. Geils let out a horrific scream, as his visage was engulfed in flame.

Geils dropped to his knees, clutching at the blazing skin. He beat his head against the wood of the platform, trying in vain to extinguish the flames. He writhed on the boards, inching toward Blake. It seemed he was no longer trying to end the fire, instead creeping his accusatory fingers toward the man responsible for his agony.

The guards holding Ian rushed forward to protect their master, neglecting the bound sacrifice. Owen grabbed Ian, pulling him away from the pit. Their actions were unnoticed in the commotion that had broken out in the square. There was no time to undo his restraints, so Owen threw the boy over his shoulder.

When Geils' blistered fingers were near the toe of his boot Blake stepped to the side, out of his reach. The smell of burning hair and skin filled the thief's nostrils, as the sound of screaming and hissing flesh inundated his ears. A fire of Fisherman's Ruin could not be extinguished by water, the liquid only prolonging the flame.

Geils was pulled to his feet by a servant who had run onto the platform, his fingers clutching the flaming staff as he was lifted. The servant had taken the cloak, and wrapped it around Geils' face, hoping to deprive the fire of air.

Blake searched for a way off the platform, but the crowd had surged forward, making a discreet exit nearly impossible. Geils swung the staff wildly, still blinded by the cloth wrapped around his head, and the end connected with Blake's chest. The pain burst through his torso, practically knocking him from his feet.

Abandoning his search for an inconspicuous escape, Blake dropped from the stage into the fray. He used his fists and elbows to forcefully clear a path through the distraught crowd. He had long since lost sight of his companions, and pushed blindly in the direction he had last seen them. He shoved his way to the edge of the frenzy, and ran as quickly as his legs would carry him from the marketplace.

At the fringe of the city, he found his horse waiting alone. The others had already departed, he assumed in the direction of the campsite. He followed, urging his horse forward with light taps of his heels against her sides.

When he arrived, he found they had begun packing their belongings. Ian was unbound, but clearly shaken by his second brush with immolation. Owen was tying their bedrolls to the saddles, while Moirin inspected the map. She looked up when Blake approached, her eyebrows raised and lips drawn.

"What is it?"

Blake pulled out the package, and tossed it to her. "It's a key."

She unwound the weathered packaging, searching for some clue. Finding none, she let the key drop into her palm.

"Did he say what it pairs with?"

"No. He said he knows nothing about it," Blake responded, his eyes watching the path for any sign that he had been followed.

"Do you believe him?" she asked.

Blake shrugged. "It is impossible for me to say. He has nothing to gain by withholding information, but he may have kept something back just to spite us."

"Nevertheless, we are in possession of a map piece we previously lacked," she said, clapping him on the back. "You have done well today."

Moirin stepped away from the campsite, to examine the map without distraction, and Ian stared into the burnt-out pit from the previous night's fire. He had not spoken since Blake had arrived, and Blake guessed he had not spoken to the others.

Blake sat down against a tree trunk, pressing a hand against his chest. The spot where Geils had struck him was tender, but his breath was again coming easily. When he pressed against the spot, he could feel a dull throbbing across the ribcage.

Owen saw him checking the injury and approached.

"Let me take a look," Owen said, his voice flat and unaffected. His countenance was far removed from that of the axe-wielding warrior Blake had glimpsed in the square.

Blake pulled up the bottom of his shirt, tucking the rolled fabric beneath his neck, and exposing the growing bruise on his sternum.

Owen touched the skin lightly, his brows drawn together in deliberation. Owen pressed the connected ribs, and Blake winced as pain radiated through his torso. Owen drew back.

"I do not think anything is broken, but it will be tender for a few days. You have doubtless had your share of scrapes and bruises."

With that, Owen smiled. It was a fleeting smile, and Blake was caught off guard by the sorrow that saturated even this small display. It was as though a torment had seeped through Owen's soul, in moments of rest becoming indistinguishable from the man himself.

In a swell of empathy, Blake reached out and touched Owen's shoulder. The warrior's eyes were turned away, and the movement caught him by surprise. He started at the contact, every muscle in his body tensing, and Blake jumped back.

Owen seemed to realize he had frightened Blake, and he bowed his head in apology. The sad smile was back, this time with a hint of regret.

Blake sat beside the warrior, afraid to move, but his eyes travelled to Owen's wrists. The warrior's sleeves were rolled up, exposing the bruises and scars left by the shackles of his long imprisonment.

Those marks would last a lifetime, and Blake found himself wondering exactly how long Owen's life might be.

18

Blake did not sleep that night. Screams and the smell of burning human flesh flooded his mind, and he was unable to shut out the intrusive thoughts. Fisherman's Ruin was inextinguishable, and the flames feasted on Geils' skin for as long as the fuel lasted. It was a terrible way to die, but he was unable to feel sorry for his actions. The world was better off without Geils, and Brecktvin could now heal the wounds that had festered far too long.

They were one step closer to finding the liogan weapon and freeing Vesia from King Alderic's brutal rule.

A twig dug into his lower back and he sat up, adjusting the bedroll beneath him. He was suddenly aware of the approaching sound of horses' hooves, and muffled voices. He looked to stir Owen, but found the man awake, his fingers inches from the axe handle.

Blake roused Moirin and Ian. The sound was drawing nearer.

King Alderic, by Moirin's calculations, should still have been two days behind them. Yet, it was not unthinkable that he could have caught up.

As quietly as possible, they gathered together their possessions. They moved into the brush, and Moirin led the horses to a separate hiding place. They would not be able to outride the king, so they were safest trying to conceal themselves.

The riders approached. In the dim light, Blake could see a dark fabric tied around their heads and faces, leaving their eyes uncovered. Only one rider was bare-faced, a hulking figure who led the group. They displayed neither the customary dress nor discipline of King Alderic's soldiers.

There was a rustling noise as Ian burst into the clearing, leaving Blake's side. Blake tried to pull him back, but Ian was quickly out of reach.

The riders heard the sound, and drew their weapons, forming a circle around the youth in the clearing.

"Hail!" Ian cried out, raising his hand in greeting.

The riders lowered their weapons and the unmasked leader of the group dismounted, walked to Ian, and embraced him forcefully. Ian spoke a few words into the leader's ear, before turning back to his hidden companions and motioning for them to join him.

Blake waited with his sword drawn, rising only when Owen ventured forward. Moirin met them in the clearing, her hand resting on the hilt of her sword. She looked at Owen, something unspoken passing between them.

"I would like to introduce you to Aeron, the bandit queen," Ian announced.

The woman who stood before them had a somewhat unorthodox appearance. Long brown hair was kept in a tangled braid at the base of her neck, and her clothing was an odd mix of fabric and armor. It seemed as though nothing she wore was made for her, rather each piece was salvaged from entirely different men and women.

She was middle-aged and a little taller than Blake, with a strong, bear-like body. She shook Blake's hand, nearly wrenching his arm from its socket in her enthusiasm.

Though her strange appearance made it unlikely that one could forget making her acquaintance, Blake could not shake the feeling he had seen her somewhere before. He looked into her face for some sign that she might recognize him, but she gave no indication of familiarity.

Aeron turned to Moirin, smiling widely. "Ian tells me you saved him from the stake. As it happens, we were on our way to do the same."

"It seems you would have arrived a day too late," Moirin countered, her eyes narrowed.

The grin fell briefly from Aeron's face and she crossed her large arms in front of her chest. "It was difficult tracking him down, took some convincing for the prison guards to tell us where he was." Her smile returned, wider than before. "Had we been too late, we'd have just raided the city."

"Well, there is no need now. I am glad we can leave Ian in your care," Morin said.

"Where are you traveling?" Aeron asked.

"That is none of your concern," Moirin responded, before turning to Blake and Owen. "We had best be going."

Aeron raised her hands in submission. "Of course not. However, I'd like to offer you protection. You have done me a service, and I would be glad to repay that debt." There was a cautious note of suggestion in her manner. "One of our scouts came across King Alderic and his soldiers only a half day's ride from here."

"What makes you think we are concerned with the king's comings and goings?" Moirin responded too hastily, unable to conceal the tension in her voice.

"If you were, you could ride with us for a ways. That's all," Aeron responded.

Blake surveyed the group of what looked to be fifteen bandits. When it was clear no headway would be made, he pulled Moirin aside, out of the bandit's earshot. Owen glanced in their direction, but stayed where he stood, keeping a wary eye on the riders before him.

"It is not a bad notion, concealing ourselves within the bandit ranks. Alderic is looking for three people, not eighteen. Besides, I have heard stories of a network of allies the bandit gangs maintain. I would be interested to see if these bear any truth. We could benefit from their broad alliances."

"I would imagine the street thugs have their own networks to which you are privy," she returned, her restless eyes still fixed on the bandits.

"Were I in possession of a vast array of contacts who would willingly shelter us from King Alderic, you would be in no position to turn them down," Blake responded. He clipped his tongue between his teeth as he struggled to maintain a civil tone. "Ian does not know the nature of our journey, though it seems that their leader is aware that we are trying to evade King Alderic. There is no need to share any further information with the them. They can be used solely for our protection and concealment."

"I suppose we are no less safe with them than with anyone else," Moirin sighed, clearly unhappy to be conceding to Blake's reasoning. "We will stay with them only until we are out of the reach of Brecktvin."

Blake smiled, concealing the surety with which he had known she would relent. "I am glad to hear it."

They returned to Aeron, and informed her of their decision. She seemed pleased with their acceptance of her offer. She told them that she had planned to camp the night outside Brecktvin, but Moirin pressed them to continue their journey away from the city.

If the bandit scout was right, King Alderic was moving more quickly than they had anticipated, and would be in Brecktvin by morning.

Aeron said nothing, but Blake could tell she knew their haste was due to King Alderic's imminent approach, and he wondered whether she had suggested spending the night outside Brecktvin to test Moirin on this point. Regardless, Aeron agreed to move the band onward, under cover of darkness.

A few riders had dismounted and embraced Ian, whose teary eyes expressed the relief he felt to be rejoined with the bandits. They jostled him and ruffled his hair, treating him as one would a younger brother.

After they retrieved the horses and packed their belongings onto the saddles, they set out away from Brecktvin, Moirin riding at the front of the company beside Aeron.

Owen and Blake rode at the back of the party. Owen because he wished to keep an eye on the bandits, and Blake because he felt safest by the warrior's side. The thought nearly made Blake laugh aloud. After all, Owen could be dangerous and unpredictable in his apparent madness.

Blake knew he should keep his mouth closed and be content to journey in silence, but they had fallen well behind the riders and were out of earshot.

"Why do you think King Alderic chose you?" he asked. The words cut abruptly through the quiet, and his shoulders tensed as he anticipated Owen's reaction.

Owen was quiet. Blake could not see his face in the darkness, but he regretted asking the question almost immediately.

After a moment's pause, Owen's rough voice answered through the darkness. "I have asked myself that question nearly every day. The king cannot be understood. He may be ruthless on the battlefield, but he is ruled by the most curious attachments. There was once a time when we were close."

"Then why did he leave you chained in the prison?"

"I betrayed him," Owen stated simply.

"But he allowed you to live," Blake pressed. "Why would he not repay betrayal with death?"

"He will undoubtedly see me dead. However, I was carefully crafted by his hand, and he will not grant me an easy exit from this world." Owen sighed again. "When I die, it will be by his sword in battle. He will not allow me to perish any other way."

"How did you get your scar?" Blake asked, knowing his luck was thinning.

"I have many scars."

"The one across your eye."

His inquiry was met with a deadly silence. Blake could tell he had asked one question too many, and accepted the lack of response from the warrior. The only sounds he could hear were the wind in the trees and the snapping of twigs beneath the horses' hooves. From the front of the company came Aeron's carefree laughter.

19

The pale walls of Brecktvin were bathed in the morning light, the copper rooftops as green as Alderic had remembered them. The buildings towered above, higher than those in Conrisia. Where the Vesian capital reflected its ancient heritage, Brecktvin was imbued with the energy of a fresh, thriving city.

He led his soldiers into the town square, where he was surprised to see only a sparse scattering of people. Upon seeing the soldier who carried the Blackdog banner, the few merchants began collapsing their stands, and parents dragged their curious children into the small streets leading away from the city center.

It was not uncommon for the people to disperse when their king made his presence known. His reputation for severity was something of which Alderic was acutely aware. Rationally, there was little to fear. Vesians lay beneath his rule and he would offer them all of the protections a king traditionally bestows on his people, provided they did not stand in his way.

During the journey from Fellridge to Brecktvin, his company had crossed paths with a group of fishermen who knew of Geils of Fellridge. They had explained the nature of his position, the power he held in Brecktvin, and the deeds he committed in exercise of this influence. Alderic then knew that his meeting with Geils had taken on an imperative extending beyond the map.

The king dismounted from his tall black steed, and idly scanned the emptying square. Those who remained were too afraid to depart, perhaps fearing that to flee would imply disrespect. Catching sight of one merchant who was still trying to gather his wares into a large straw basket, he strode forward and seized the man by his shoulder. The merchant let out a yelp, but did not pull away.

"Where can I find Geils of Fellridge?"

The man pointed to a large building against the opposite side of the square.

"There you will find whatever remains, anyway," the merchant said cryptically, his voice trembling in fear.

Alderic considered questioning the man further, but knew he would understand the merchant's meaning in short time. His sight landed on the pit at the center of the square and the charred wooden platform, half-collapsed before it.

He called to Callum, who dismounted and obediently followed him across the square to the wide bellied edifice. The twin spires cast an oblong shadow across the corner of the marketplace.

The soldiers stayed in the square, as Alderic and Callum approached the structure. Before Alderic had even raised his hand to knock, a servant opened the door and stepped aside, his eyes downcast, to allow the king free entry.

Callum followed at Alderic's heels through the hallway and up the stairs. His short hair and bright face gave him a childish look, which contrasted sharply with the grave countenance of the king. Callum had the aspect of a hunting dog, happily kept by his master's side.

The servant led them to a large bedroom, without a word spoken to the king. The curtains were drawn, and a sickly yellow light filtered through the rich fabric. The room appeared to be empty, but a light wheezing coming from an armchair in the corner told the king otherwise. Alderic stepped closer, his eyes still adjusting to the dull light of the room. His fingers touched his sword, ready for any bid the room's occupant might make for escape.

No such attempt was made. He drew closer, until he could better see the one seated in the chair. The figure was human, but no eyes stared back. Upon closer examination, he could see the head was tightly wrapped with thick layers of bandages. The fabric resting above the mouth was drawn in and pushed away with each pitiful, rasping breath the man took. It was unclear whether this man would be able to give them any information in his condition.

"Are you Geils of Fellridge?" Alderic asked.

There was no response. Callum threw open the curtains, flooding the room with sunlight, while Alderic took the bandaged chin in his fingertips, and turned the head from side to side. This action was met with a muffled scream.

So, he was conscious.

"Are you Geils of Fellridge?" Alderic repeated, squeezing the bandaged skin tighter with each second the man did not answer.

The bandaged man nodded fervently. His body pressed against the cushioned back of the armchair, as if trying to retreat from the king's constricting grasp.

"You met a woman a few days ago. She wanted information, did she not?"

The man shook his head, with a great deal of effort and pain. His body tensed, as if expecting a physical reprimand from the hand of his interrogator.

Alderic paused, surprised that Moirin would not have handled the acquisition personally. "A man then, what was his name?"

Gasping for air, his breath impeded by the bandages, the man muttered a word. Alderic did not hear it, and turned to the knight.

"I think he said Blake," Callum responded with a shrug.

Alderic's attention returned to Geils. "What did you give them?"

Geils shook his head, his shoulders still burrowed against the cushions.

"They would not have left without it. What did you give them?"

Geils shook his head again. The king could not tell whether this lack of response was a form of rebellion, or whether the effort to speak was too difficult for a man in his state.

Alderic could only make speech the least painful of his options.

He found the end of the bandage which wound itself around the victim's face, and began to pull. The fabric clung to the blistered, oozing skin, and Alderic had to pull hard to remove the nearly glued bandage.

Geils cried out as a layer of skin adhered to the gauze, and was pulled cleanly away. The flayed surface began to drip a mixture of blood and a thin, clear fluid.

A servant came to the door, alarmed by the shouts of his master. Callum pulled his sword from the sheath, brandishing it with steady hands. The servant retreated silently, and Callum closed the door to prevent further interruption.

Alderic continued pulling at the bandages, until the lower half of Geils' face was exposed. The pink, raw skin was wet, and glistened in the light from the windows.

"I will ask you again: what did you give them?"

"A key. A golden key," Geils whispered, his voice cracking. "I only looked in the package once."

"Did you tell them anything else?"

Geils shook his head.

"But there is something else to tell," Alderic persisted.

Geils began to shake his head once again, but Alderic grabbed hold of his face. His palm spanned across the other man's eyes, and he pressed his thumb and fingers into Geils' temples. Geils began to scream again in anguish, and Alderic covered the shrieking mouth with his other hand until the cries died down.

"Do not lie to me. What did you neglect to tell Blake?"

He pressed harder; Geils' body writhed in the chair. His legs kicked out, striking Alderic's shins repeatedly. Alderic held firm, increasing the pressure he exerted on Geils' damaged face. Callum watched from the corner, keeping alert for any intrusion.

Finally, Geils stopped kicking and his body became limp, as if every ounce of resistance had left him in an instant. He mumbled against Alderic's hand, and the king let go of his mouth. Geils panted for air, his breath coming quick and ragged. His eyes remained covered in bandaging.

Alderic's hands were sticky from touching the blistered skin, and he wiped the fluids from his palm onto Geils' shirt front.

"It fits a wooden chest," Geils wept, his voice struggling to form the words.

"What else were you told of the chest?"

"It carries the king's insignia over the lock, and wrapped around the center is a band of diamonds," he sputtered through his flowing tears. "You must believe me. That is all I know."

"If you have lied to me, you will not be going far," Alderic answered, standing over Geils. "I understand you were exploiting the superstitions of the people, and burning innocents alive. I will not allow these acts to go unpunished in my kingdom."

Geils repeated the phrase "my kingdom" beneath his breath and his entire body tensed, only then realizing the identity of his tormentor. His whimpering stopped abruptly.

"Were you an able man, I would strike you down. However, I feel that dying now would be a mercy. I will allow you to live, but you are to leave Brecktvin. If I ever receive word you have resumed your malicious ways I will have you torn apart limb from limb, and leave your body impaled on the stake in the town square. Do we have an understanding?"

Geils nodded, and his broken weeping resumed as suddenly as it had stopped. Alderic and Callum left the room, and a terrible cry followed their departure. They proceeded down the steps, curious servants slipping out of sight as they passed.

"We will stay here tonight, it will give the soldiers and horses a night to rest. We will ride out tomorrow," Alderic said.

That night, a feast was prepared by Brecktvinian cooks. Alderic ate a simple meal before retiring to Geils' study, while his soldiers ate and drank in the hall beneath. Alderic allowed this behavior in moderation, though the king himself was never one to partake in such indulgences.

He spread the map out on the desk before him, musing over markings whose counterparts he had yet to encounter. He could hear the scrape of a chair, and knew that Callum had taken a post outside the room. Alderic had not asked him to do so, but he was glad that Callum was refusing the drink offered to the soldiers.

He returned his eyes to the map, and to the sewn corner. He planned to ride out the next morning, yet he was unsure of the next location and of which direction he should take. Thus far, the markings had been placed topologically. As such, the physical arrangement of the markings could be deceptive.

He stared at the map until his weary eyes could make no more sense of it. He ran a rough hand across his face, rubbing the temptation of sleep from his eyes. A candle was set at the edge of the wooden desk, and Alderic stared into the flame. No matter what he tried, he found it impossible to make sense of this next marking, which read only: "Split Oak".

He stood, and paced around the small room. The shelves were covered in heirlooms and trappings, the displays of wealth typically found in such homes. However, one object caught his eye, standing out from the other trinkets.

He pulled it from the shelf, a hot anger suddenly coursing through his veins. He threw open the door, startling Callum, who got up quickly from the chair, sword drawn.

Alderic strode down the hall, kicking the door to Geils' bedroom. The door slammed against the wall, the crashing sound echoing through the hallway.

The injured man still sat in the chair, and started when he heard the rapidly approaching king. Blinded by the bandages, his hands grasped the arms of the chair, helpless to come to his own defense.

Alderic hurled the object at Geils, striking him hard in the ribs. As the bandaged man doubled over in pain, Alderic pulled Geils from the chair and threw him to the ground.

Callum picked up the object Alderic had thrown, and turned it over in his hands. It was a small chest, made of wood, with a blackdog's head over the lock. Around the middle ran a line of small diamonds.

Alderic placed his knee by the fallen man's shoulder and stooped forward to speak to him. "You lied to me about the box, or is it merely a coincidence that an object on your shelf exactly matches your description of the chest," Alderic hissed, his hand tightening around Geils' throat. "You are a vindictive, insignificant fool, and you will tell me the truth." He released Geils' neck, gripping him by the front of his shirt. "What was the message that accompanied the key?"

Alderic half-kneeled, his long, black hair brushing the ground. His hands tightened, lifting the scorched man and suspending him inches above the floor.

Geils shook his head, constricting his burned lips. His fingers fumbled blindly against the king, as he sought in vain to free himself from his tormentor's grasp.

Dropping him back to the floor, Alderic ripped the bandages from Geils' eyes. The stripped skin displayed the full damage inflicted by the fire. The king pressed his thumbs against the singed eyelids, and Geils shrieked.

"Tell me," the king commanded, "what do you know?"

"Linwood," Geils gasped. His mouth was beginning to bleed as the skin split. "I was given the name Linwood." He sobbed, as blood pooled at the side of his mouth. "I swear, that is all I know."

"If I find you have lied to me again, I will return. When I return, I will kill each of your servants, burn down this house, and make good on my promise to have you torn to pieces even as you still breathe."

Alderic kicked Geils squarely in the stomach, and left the room followed by Callum. Geils attempted to raise himself to his elbows, but was still too weak. He was left to lie on the ground, the misery of his newly inflicted injuries matched only by the excruciating pain which had become his existence.

"Why do you not kill him?" Callum asked.

Alderic sighed. "He lied about the wooden chest, giving us details of an object he doubtless saw nearly every day in his own home. Geils had nothing to gain by deceiving me, but it seems as though he cannot help but tell falsehoods. If he has lied again, I cannot risk the information dying with him." Alderic turned to Callum. "Nothing would give me more pleasure right now than to watch the light fade from his detestable eyes as the spirit leaves him, but it is not a chance I am willing to take"

Callum nodded in understanding, casting a final glance back to the dark room. Geils still writhed on the floor, clawing uselessly toward the chair, and Callum wondered aloud whether the man would even survive the night.

Alderic walked out onto the balcony overlooking the square, while Callum resumed his post in the hallway. Candlelight flickered in windows, and lamps colored the street while a few inhabitants wandered past. Some seemed to be simply enjoying the cold night air, while others walked with hurried steps from one place to another, wasting little time in their journeys. The smell of the port was carried on the wind through the city, salt in every breath.

Despite the iniquity that tainted the very lifeblood of Brecktvin, it was undeniably beautiful.

Alderic's hands tightened on the railing. From an early age, he had been told that understanding the lives of his subjects would allow him to rule more effectively, though he had never grasped the benefit of catering to the people.

He knew that a tenuous lawmaking had arisen across Vesia as a result of his neglect. However, until that day he had been unaware that ritual human sacrifice persisted in his kingdom, and he disliked such ignorance in himself.

That Geils could exert control over so great a city as Brecktvin served to remind Alderic of the importance his mission carried. Should the weapon exist, he could not risk it falling into the hands of one like Geils: a man driven by the malevolent hunger for power.

Were that to happen, it would plunge Vesia into the mayhem of civil war.

While he did not ignore the rapidly spreading legend of the high ruler from the east, Alderic would handle challengers for his crown as they arose. However, the danger posed by the liogan weapon was perhaps greater than Vesia could survive.

His ancestors may have been content to rule a small kingdom, but this satisfaction had ended with his father's reign. Conri had begun the work of expanding the kingdom, and had made his two sons vow to do the same.

By Alderic's twenty-third year, four years after assuming the throne, he had expanded his late father's kingdom into the greatest known, raining terror and bloodshed down upon any who opposed him. Eight years later, his hold had not slipped, though this came at the expense of true governance for his people.

Where Conri understood his subjects, Alderic ruled through fear. He had sacrificed admiration in pursuit of this, and found that even his dead brother was better liked than he. Severin had offered assurances of pleasure and prosperity, enticing admiration through vows of fortune.

Alderic had never tried to court the Vesian people, nor disguise the severity with which he would defend his rule. His rigor and ruthlessness, in the absence of placating promises, had built him into an icon of brutality, feared and hated by nearly all. Alderic knew he was resented by his subjects, yet he would not loosen his grip. It was his way.

20

The bandits stopped to rest in a small clearing in the woods, not visible from the main path. They had travelled through night and day, heading east from Brecktvin, and darkness was beginning to fall. Aeron insisted that she would feed and rest her party before continuing. Her riders were unused to travelling such long stretches at a time.

A few bandits went in search of food and, upon their return, Ian immediately resumed his cooking duties. Soon he had a fire burning with fresh, seasoned meat roasting on a makeshift spit. The fat dripped down onto the fire, smoking and sizzling in the cool air.

The others of Aeron's followers kept by the fire, dividing up the spoils of past robberies, drinking liquor, and telling tales of past conquests.

Moirin stood off to the side, studying the map in the dying light, while Owen sharpened weapons a few feet away.

Blake approached Aeron where she was sat, watching the others prepare for the night. She looked up with surprise as he sank to the ground next to her.

"I cannot shake the feeling I've seen you somewhere before," Blake spoke. "Have you been to the Isle of Ang?"

Aeron shook her head. "Not that I remember, but I have travelled."

"Have you always been a bandit?" he asked.

While Blake's curiosity often landed him in trouble, he hoped this would not again be the case. Aeron seemed to be more forthcoming than either Moirin or Owen had been. Despite their only recent meeting, Blake felt more comfortable speaking to her than to either of his travelling companions.

"No, I had an ordinary life once, but, as you can see, I am built for strength." She moved her hand from the top of her head downward to draw attention to her imposing figure, though no such signal was necessary. "I was always brawny, and I turned it into a comfortable living. Men and women from across Vesia would travel to my doorstep and pay to see if they could push me out of a five-foot circle, before I could them.

"I started to travel, making money from spectators and challengers. No one could defeat me and my life became boring, even as I drew larger crowds and wealthier challengers. By the end, they would pay almost one hundred pieces to see if they could beat me."

"I saw your performance when I was a child, travelling with my family to visit Conrisia," Blake said, finally making sense of her familiarity. "With such success, why would you join with bandits?"

"One day, a friend of mine was put in servitude to settle a debt. The tradesmen had nearly made it out of town, when I found them and beat them near to death." She sighed. "We couldn't return home. We wandered for days, afraid we'd be recognized. Finally, we came across the bandits, who gave us the chance to join." She surveyed the men and women before her. "Even now, our company is mostly those who have nowhere else to go."

"Which is how you found Ian?" Blake asked, still puzzled by Ian's presence given his obvious incompatibility with the pugnacious life of an outlaw.

"Years ago, we attacked a caravan on its way to Conrisia. The travelers were more armed than we thought, and our leader was badly wounded: a deep knife slash through his belly. He knew he was dying and named me his successor, so long as I found and protected his son."

"Ian."

She nodded. "Ian's mother died years before, and he couldn't find the child. I swore to him that I would protect Ian. I would raise him in our ways, and be sure he wanted for nothing." The normally jovial expression on Aeron's face lessened. "Had anything happened to Ian, I'd have failed in my promise to his father. I'd have left Brecktvin in ashes."

Her head sank, and her back hunched. The armor clanked lightly against the guards on her shoulders.

Blake did not know Aeron well, but already he hated to see her so sorrowful. He was reminded of his own desertion of Hugh, and the feeling of having failed his former partner. He could only imagine the misery that would follow letting down one you had practically raised.

"I don't suppose you would want to wrestle me?" Blake asked, trying to lighten her spirits.

Aeron raised her arm, placing her hand on his forehead. She pushed, swiftly knocking Blake onto his back. He looked up to see that the same bright smile had reappeared on her face.

"Let's try to keep you out of trouble for now," she said, pulling him to his feet and clapping him warmly on the shoulder. "Looking at your companions, I'd think you've already got more than you can handle without adding a sound beating."

The smell of roasted meat filled the air and, as the blanket of darkness fell, the bandits gradually drew toward the small fire. Ian cut the meat into pieces, making sure each person was fed. While he was far from skilled in a fight, Blake could see the value Ian held within the bandit ranks.

That night, Blake was awakened by the sound of footsteps. His heart began to race, and he sat up slowly, afraid to draw attention to himself. The bandit's night guard was leaning against a tree, awake but unaware of the movement within the campsite.

The figure crossed in front of him, and Blake caught the glint of moonlight reflected on a knife.

Owen lay only a few feet from Blake. He was unmoving, and his head was turned away from the thief.

Blake crept closer to the resting warrior to wake him, but Owen's eyes were already open, his gaze fixed on the standing man. Blake retreated slightly, not wanting to be caught between Owen and the knife-wielder.

The man took a few more steps and it became obvious that he was headed toward Moirin, where she lay alone beyond the circle of bandits. Owen rose silently to his feet, leaving his axe behind, and he stepped to where the man loomed over Moirin's sleeping form.

Blake too stood up, but more slowly. He did not possess Owen's agility, and struggled to be as quiet. He stayed to the side and he could see Owen draw near the man. Both figures were bathed in bright moonlight, and Owen's hair appeared white in the gleam.

The man shifted the knife in his hand, and lowered the weapon to strike.

Owen seized him around the torso, pinning the attacker's arms to his sides and covering his mouth to prevent him from calling out. The man tried to wrench his body away, but Owen overpowered him, pushing him face first to the ground. Owen jammed his knee in the small of the man's back, keeping pressure until finally the attacker relented, going limp against the ground.

Moirin was awake. She did not stand, but surveyed her would-be attacker from where she sat. Blake was struck by how remarkably unfazed she was by this attempt on her life. She pulled a cloak around her shoulders, and crossed her arms. Her dark eyes shone in the moonlight, and Blake drew closer.

He recognized the subdued man as from within the bandit ranks, but did not recall meeting him.

Owen turned to Moirin, seeking instruction. The bandit's mouth was momentarily uncovered and he cried out, waking the other members of his company.

Aeron approached first, her sword drawn.

"What is the meaning of this?" she asked, rubbing her eyes. Her voice was cracked with sleep, but she was clearly alert.

"One of your men tried to kill Moirin," Owen said. He grabbed the aspiring assailant by the back of his shirt, hauling him to his feet. The bandit tried to escape, but Owen pulled him back with a casual severity. "Do you have any idea why he might want one of ours dead?"

Aeron's eyes widened slightly. "This is Seph. He joined our ranks two years ago, after his wife was executed by King Alderic." She gave a half smile. "I was right in my guess that you are fleeing the king, after all."

"Why do you say that?" Blake asked, suddenly nervous. Yet he knew there was no reason for fear; Aeron and her outlaws were as much an enemy of the king as they were.

"Though name Moirin is uncommon, I knew I'd heard it before. But, I didn't make the connection with Seph," Aeron answered.

Moirin was now standing, her cloak still wrapped around her. She studied Seph's face in the bright light of the moon, while Owen held him steady.

"I do not recognize this man, nor does his name sound familiar," she said finally.

"We passed each other in a hallway once," Seph spat. "Though I doubt you would remember me."

"You would kill me over a brushing of shoulders?" Moirin laughed.

"I would kill you for the one you stole from me." Tears filled his eyes, as a violence grew within him. "Before her death, my wife swore her innocence to me."

"Who was your wife?" Moirin asked, a mocking coolness permeating her voice.

"She was a cook at the castle," Aeron addressed Moirin, though her eyes remained locked on the restrained Seph. "She was hanged by the king for poisoning your husband."

"And you would lay the blame on me for your wife's murder of my husband?" Moirin asked, directing an icy stare toward Seph. "It seems I should be the one holding the knife."

"She swore to me that she had nothing to do with it. She was on her way to the gallows when she told me; she had no reason to lie." He glared at Moirin. "Besides, I would have seen her killing any of the king's kin as a victory, and she knew this. She would have been bragging," he retorted, breath seething between his bared teeth. "She told me that the only other person who could have poisoned the food was his wife."

"You have no evidence I have done anything wrong," Moirin responded. "You would take the word of a murderess and a liar. She killed Severin and was justly punished for her sins."

She stepped closer to Seph, as her voice lowered in a teasing tone. "Worst of all, she was a mediocre cook."

Seph lunged at her, exploiting a momentary lapse in his guarding, but was quickly subdued by Owen. On the ground, he hissed up at her a series of curses and condemnations. Moirin looked down at him with an expression far removed from pity.

Aeron looked between Moirin and Seph, the very image of control as she viewed the conflicting parties. She motioned for Owen to stand aside. He nodded, and let go of Seph, who stayed on his back.

"Stand up," Aeron commanded.

Seph looked up at her for a moment, before slowly complying. He dusted the grass and dirt off of his clothes, and stood before her. His chin was raised, and his eyes did not hesitate to meet those of his leader.

Blake was impressed by the transformation that overcame Seph at the word of his commander. He had in a matter of seconds gone from a man seething with rage, to a self-controlled follower hoping only to maintain the respect of his leader.

Aeron looked him over, murmuring as she considered her options. She ran her palm across her chin, clearly unhappy with the choices she had been given.

"I understand you will want us to depart," Moirin spoke up. "We will not stay in the company of our enemies. It is as unsafe for you as for us."

Aeron shook her head, her arms crossed. "Nothing has changed." Her words were chosen with obvious deliberation. "Seph acted against my orders and he will be punished. You saved Ian, and I promised you our protection. We will see you to Rieville but, after that, we'll go our separate ways."

Moirin lowered her head in grudging thanks, while Owen watched Seph warily. Despite Moirin's acceptance of the offered assistance, Owen remained edgy, as though he could leap into action should Seph so much as twitch.

Blake felt lost in the occurrences. From what the cellarman had told him of Moirin's late husband, he understood that Prince Severin was no friend to the king's cause. Prince Severin had hoped to take the kingdom for his own, though this was precluded by the prince's untimely death through poisoning.

Had Prince Severin ascended the throne, Moirin would have become queen of Vesia: the very end she sought. Moirin was above all else pragmatic, and he could not imagine she would assassinate so powerful an ally.

Blake looked at Moirin, but her face was unreadable. Despite the bandit's accusation, Blake was no closer to understanding the truth than he had been the day before.

Aeron confiscated Seph's weapons and ordered him to join the night watch, where he would be guarded by two others. Blake returned to his bedroll, and found himself gradually drawn back into slumber. Despite the apprehension that now pervaded the group, he had no trouble falling asleep.

He could rest easy, because he knew Owen would not sleep at all.

The next morning, they rose early and Ian prepared a modest breakfast. Blake and Owen joined the bandits for the meal, though Moirin did not eat with the rest. Instead, she ate some of the provisions they had brought with them from Fellridge, perhaps not trusting the bandits' loyalty to Aeron's command.

Returning to the well-travelled path, she rode at the front of the company beside Aeron, while Seph rode in the middle of the pack; flanked by his companions, and watched on every side.

Blake resumed his position beside Owen at the back of the party. Neither said a word to the other, as they trod steadily along at the pace set by Aeron. He frequently glanced ahead to Seph and Moirin, and wondered what he would do were Seph to experience another violent outburst. Likely nothing, Blake was very content to leave the fighting to others.

Owen seemed relaxed in the saddle, his slackened body nodding with the movements of the steed beneath him. The wear of sleepless nights was showing, Owen's face appearing more drained of life than usual. Blake was again struck by the difference between the warrior's current, sedated state, and the blindly ruthless bearing that could seize him within a moment of hostility.

"Surely Moirin would have more to gain by Prince Severin's survival. After all, they shared the goal of removing the king from power." Blake broke the silence, looking to Owen for a response.

Owen smiled slightly before responding, his voice low.

"These things are rarely as simple as they seem."

"Her hatred of King Alderic seems simple enough," Blake pressed.

"You think she hates him?" Owen asked quietly. "She may love him, for all I know." He paused, his eyes fixed on the road, before continuing. "You assume that Moirin's desire has always been to merely overthrow Alderic, and return the land to a less war-drunken rule. It was not. In Moirin's eyes, Alderic was once an instrument of attaining power, before he became nothing more than an obstacle to overcome. Still, I could be wrong."

"Are you saying she killed Prince Severin?"

"I am saying that Moirin is forceful, and that if anyone can bring about Alderic's downfall it is her. However, do not be so ready to place your absolute trust in her, or to ascribe more gallant motives to her actions. She is resolute in pursuing her goals, and loyalty is not among her virtues."

Blake was silent again. The truth about Prince Severin's death did not matter. Owen showed no intention of leaving Moirin's side, and Blake owed her the debt of his life and freedom. He did not understand what Owen meant in describing King Alderic and Moirin's relationship so, nor how Moirin could once have planned to use King Alderic as a mean of gaining power, but thinking on it longer would do him no good. They were in search of the liogan weapon, and that was all that mattered.

When they stopped to rest that evening, Blake approached Moirin. She had the map out again, sitting far apart from the others. She muttered quietly to herself, as her fingertips traced a line across the cloth.

"Where are we going?" Blake inquired.

Moirin sighed, her eyes finally leaving the map. "I do not know." She set the cloth on the ground between them, and indicated with her finger the next marking. "It says 'Split Oak', and there is this triangular shape, but there is no mention of a town or person. I find myself doing little else but look at an incomprehensible mark on a useless piece of fabric. Perhaps if I stare long enough, the answer will appear to me, but the hour grows late and I am still as lost as before."

Blake gave himself over to study of the markings. While Moirin had previously been secretive regarding the map, she now seemed receptive toward help. Blake would have liked nothing more than to say that he knew where they should ride, but the symbol beneath the word was as foreign to him as it had been to Moirin.

She pulled out a second map, one of Vesia, which she had acquired in Brecktvin. "There is a large town nearby called Rieville. Aeron has chosen it as the place where we part ways with the bandits. We will be able to restock our provisions, and ask the inhabitants for assistance."

"I would imagine Seph's attempt to take your life last night was unsettling to say the least."

She shrugged nonchalantly. "There things are bound to happen on occasion. If I spent my time worrying about every person who carries a grudge against me, I would be left unable to act."

It was hard for him to imagine so little being made of the attempted killing of a noblewoman.

That night, Seph was again guarded by the two bandits on the night watch. This did little to assuage the tension surrounding his attack, but Blake knew that Owen was in need of sleep. The circles beneath the warrior's eyes were darker than before, and his hands had resumed their fevered trembling.

Blake offered to keep watch over Seph and Moirin, and wake the warrior immediately if there was any threat. He could not tell if Owen actually trusted him, or whether he was simply in no position to refuse, but Owen accepted the offer.

Blake stayed next to the sleeping warrior, leaning against the roots of an ancient tree. He would be able to wake Owen up quickly, should the need arise.

The night was calm, the forest flooded by the light of the nearly full moon, and the pale blue illumination of the trees surrounded Blake. He found himself enjoying the brief moment of tranquility, hidden within the hunt for the weapon.

The last embers of the fire were slowly dying, a deep and vivid red peering out from beneath charred wood. The wind picked up and a haunting whistle filled the air, as the breeze filtered through branches and leaves.

Owen stirred beside him, before becoming still again. He had done this periodically through the night: briefly waking, before falling back to sleep. Blake wondered if Owen ever truly slept.

He leaned back against the trunk of the tree. The roots held him, and he felt at ease. The rest of the night passed without incident, and Blake was soon greeted by the pink rays of dawn's light. He knew that as the sun rose, so would those around him, and he enjoyed the last moments of solitude before the others awoke. He breathed deep the cool, misty air, and felt the dew on the grass beneath his hands. He had not slept during the night, but he was refreshed nonetheless.

Moirin and Owen arose ahead of the bandits, and began quietly making preparations for the journey, while a few feet away, Aeron slumbered soundly. Her mismatched armor lay in a tenuously balanced heap beside her, and her body shifted with each deep breath.

Soon, the bandits woke, and the camp was again filled with the noise of talking, and the smell of food being cooked. Ian was again hard at work, providing for the now eighteen outlaws who clamored for breakfast only minutes after waking. Though they were bandits in the woods, they ate better than most city-dwellers.

Seph requested permission to step away from the others, so as to fulfill his body's basic needs. Aeron allowed him to leave, but ordered one of her bandits to accompany him. She took the obligation of protection seriously enough and would keep Moirin alive, even at the cost of her follower's freedom.

"We will take our leave of them at the next town," Moirin reminded Owen in hushed tones.

Breakfast was finished, and the horses were saddled and ready for leaving. However, Seph and his attendant had yet to return to the site. Aeron glanced around, her annoyance evident. Her armor was on, her hair tucked loosely in the back of her clothing, and she grabbed her weapons. She signaled for one of the bandits to accompany her, as they set out in search of Seph.

Owen was on guard, his eyes scanning the tree line. It seemed his tension was catching, because Blake felt a small rush of anxiety, and he could see Moirin's hand resting on the hilt of her sword.

They waited in silence, until heavy footfall signaled an approach. Aeron broke into the clearing, a man's sagging body slung across her wide shoulders. She carried him with ease, yet the greater burden she bore could be seen within her eyes. She gently laid the body down on the flattened grass.

Blake saw the bloodstain on her shoulder even before he saw the deep cut that traversed the man's throat.

He recognized the body as that of the bandit assigned to accompany Seph. The woman who had followed Aeron into the woods returned empty handed, telling her leader that there was no sign of Seph anywhere.

Aeron cursed.

Blake could see the knife sheath at the dead bandit's hip was empty. Seph must have taken his guard's knife and turned it against him.

"I am sorry," Aeron said mournfully, directing her words to the body lying prone on the grass. "Seph's never been our strongest fighter; he shouldn't have been able to overpower you."

Seph and the bandit had left the campsite nearly an hour before. He could have gone in any direction, and his distraught mentality made it difficult to predict his actions. Still, Aeron dispatched two scouts to go in search of Seph.

Blake looked to Moirin.

"We will proceed to Rieville," Moirin said, "but keep on your guard; Seph may be closer than we think."

The bandits buried the body in a shallow grave in the woods, and returned to the path leading to Rieville.

By afternoon, they reached a small farmhouse a few miles outside Rieville, which the bandits used as a hideout. There, the group divided as Moirin, Blake, and Owen continued toward the town.

Aeron decided she would accompany the trio to the town, as she had business to take care of in Rieville and her supplies needed restocking. She kept her horse by Moirin's, leading the way.

"What are you looking for anyway?" she asked casually.

"I am not sure what you are referring to," Moirin responded, her words clipped and her eyes fixed ahead.

"The map you carry, I've seen you studying it over the past few days," Aeron continued, ignoring Moirin's obvious unwillingness to discuss the topic further. "I would imagine it must be important, if a lady such as yourself is willing to risk her life to find it."

Moirin let out a sharp laugh. "Did you not hear Seph's accusation? I am far from a lady."

Aeron smiled, but seemed puzzled, while Moirin's trivializing tone only deepened Blake's persistent uncertainty. He looked to Owen, but found his companion was returned to the stoicism that kept him mute.

21

Rieville lay before them. It was considerably smaller than the imposing Brecktvin, and its red brick buildings and cobblestone road appeared to be in good condition. Green trees lined the streets, and the inhabitants strolled at a leisurely pace, unencumbered by the frenetic energy of the city.

Once in the town, they parted ways. Owen stayed by Moirin's side, protecting against Seph's possible return. It was unlikely that he would be in Rieville, as Seph had not been in possession of a horse, but it was an outcome Owen was obligated to guard against.

Blake went to the blacksmith, while Aeron went her separate way. The four of them agreed to reconvene at the tavern, where they would spend the night before departing in the morning.

King Alderic had confiscated Blake's tools, leaving the thief feeling oddly vulnerable. He had not been this long without his instruments since the day he had acquired them. He brought the blacksmith his request, outlining in detail each piece he lacked.

Hours later, newly crafted tools in hand, Blake stepped back out into the street. His ears were ringing from the sound of the hammer and anvil. His lungs felt dusty with soot, and the cool breeze was a pleasant change from the stagnant heat of the forge.

The bright blue sky was lit by a shimmering sun, and Blake breathed deep the fresh air. He found he was almost enjoying himself.

Blake was on his way to the tavern when he came across Owen, who was wandering aimlessly through the streets, his seeing eye staring absently through the people who passed him.

It may have been his imagination, but Blake thought for a moment that Owen was almost relieved to see him.

"Where is Moirin?" Blake asked, surprised she was not by Owen's side.

Owen shrugged one shoulder. "She went alone in search of 'Split Oak', insistent that I would only draw attention. She gave me little choice in the matter."

Moirin was doubtless correct; Owen was tall, gaunt, and covered in scars. In a town like Rieville, such things would not go unnoticed. However, Blake knew that Owen was uneasy without Moirin in his sight.

They walked together in the direction of the tavern, Owen's pace becoming more natural as he kept by Blake's side.

"Have you been to Rieville before?" Blake asked.

Owen nodded. "A few times."

This surprised Blake; for all its charms, Rieville did not seem to be a place of much importance.

They passed a collection of people, gathered to watch a juggler, when Owen suddenly pushed forward into the crowd, lightly seizing a hooded figure by the shoulder.

The woman wheeled around to face him. She was shrouded in a thin linen cloak that was the vibrant blue of lapis lazuli. When she saw the face of the man who had accosted her, she removed the hood from her head and smiled.

"Viscountess," he greeted her with a slight bow. Had Blake not known him better, he would say the warrior looked almost pleased. It was the first time since Blake had met him, that Owen appeared remotely lighthearted.

"Owen," she said, returning the gesture in like. A humor undercut her formality. "It has been a long time since I've seen you. To tell the truth, I am surprised to be seeing you at all."

"A long time. You look the same as the day I met you," he responded. "Though, I fear underground imprisonment has not favored my countenance."

She turned to Blake. "And who is your companion?" Her eyes skimmed him from head to toe, and she smiled. Her lip hitched to one side, her unguarded grin charmingly askew.

"This is Blake, he was being held for execution in Alderic's prison." His words returned Blake to the present, and the thief commenced a brief bow as if compelled by the introduction.

"Blake, this is the Viscountess Nahia."

She grasped his hand in greeting. She had bronze skin, and pale eyes that creased at the corners in a confident smile. Her brown hair was lightened by hours spent beneath the sun, and it fell loose about her shoulders.

"What brings you to Rieville?" she asked, looking between Owen and Blake.

Blake automatically opened his mouth to speak, but was silenced by a quick but stern look from Owen.

Nahia's smile was unchanged. "I take it the reason for your journey relates to Alderic." She nodded to herself. "I will ask you nothing more, though I hope I can enjoy your company in town despite our differing allegiances."

"What are you doing in Rieville?" Owen asked. "If I remember correctly, you avoid returning home."

"True enough, I rarely have reason to come home," she responded. "Do you know the Earl of Eskemn? He and his advisor have had a difference of opinions regarding the earl's wife, which ended in the challenge of a duel. In the heat of the moment, neither man truly realized how unwilling either was to risk their lives. They agreed to, instead, have their champions duel to decide the outcome of their dispute."

"And you are the earl's chosen?" Blake asked.

"I am," she responded brightly.

"When is the duel?" Owen asked.

"At sunrise tomorrow. We will meet outside the old town gate."

"We are intending to spend the night in Rieville, perhaps we can accompany you," Owen said.

"I would certainly be glad for it." She smiled, turning her gaze to the thief. "Can I expect your attendance?"

Blake was taken aback by her interest, and did his best to formulate an unruffled response. "It would be my pleasure." He immediately worried that his reply had been overeager.

He glanced down. The hem of her slate grey skirt was tattered, where it rested on her boots. He looked up again, to find her eyes still on him.

He felt his cheeks flush as she watched him, her smile growing. She spoke to Owen, though her gaze remained on Blake, "I have a few matters to attend to in town, perhaps I will see you at the tavern this evening."

"Of course," Owen responded, while Blake nodded wordlessly.

After Nahia's departure, Blake turned to Owen. "Who is she?" He glanced back to ensure they were not overheard.

"Nahia? She is a close friend of Alderic's." Owen shrugged. "She is likely the only friend he has ever had."

"Was it not risky telling her that I was in the prison? She may be inclined to return us to Ashen Castle."

"It is true that we should exercise caution in her presence. However, Nahia rarely intervenes in the affairs of others, save on a whim."

"She hardly seems like a noblewoman of the king's court. After all, she is in the countryside fighting impulsive duels," Blake mused aloud.

Owen chuckled under his breath, the sound surprising Blake. "It is common knowledge that she is the sole heir to a fortune rivaled only by that of the king. Yet you are correct, she has never concerned herself with the politics or behaviors more fitting of a noble." He shrugged. "She lets her wealth sit, unused, while she travels across the kingdom in search of adventure."

"And such a one as she is friends with the king?" Blake asked.

The lightness to her aspect was nothing like the grim, punishing demeanor he had glimpsed in his brief interactions with King Alderic.

"Their friendship is certainly odd. Even his past bloodshed, seen by most as detestable, does not appear to diminish her liking for Alderic."

"And she is a good fencer?" Blake asked, trying to make sense of her willingness to duel.

Owen shook his head. "She is a good fighter, but unsuited to the technical aspect of dueling, as engaged in by the nobility. You see, in a nobleman's duel, they fight only until a drop of blood is drawn. The swordplay is complex, requiring great patience and finesse. Nahia lacks these qualities, more inclined to fight underhanded. Much like yourself, a knife is more her weapon of choice."

"So, why would she be asked to duel on another's behalf?"

"I do not know. Perhaps the Earl of Eskemn wishes to gain favor. However, he should know better than to tangle with Nahia. Where Alderic wrestles with morality, Nahia experiences no such struggle. Though she may not seem it, she is dangerous."

Blake felt Owen's warning was directed more at him than at the absent earl, so he ceased his questioning. They did not speak much to one another as they continued through the street. Once at the tavern, Blake spotted Aeron sitting at the bar, drinking from a tankard of mead. A man in the tavern had recognized her, and was trying to goad her into arm-wrestling. She shook her head adamantly, but he would not leave her alone.

Finally, she stood, the man eagerly following her lead. Blake watched from across the room, as she silently gestured, holding her fists up just beneath her chin. The man took the signal, preparing himself for attack. He took a quick step forward, jabbing with his right fist. Aeron did not attempt to move, letting the blow land on her cheek, shaking it off before driving her fist toward his left eye. Her knuckles connected with the side of his head with a sickening thud, and the man fell to the floor, unconscious. Aeron wiped her knuckles on the side of her shirt, and resumed her place at the bar, stepping over the challenger's recumbent body.

The tavern was filled with the honeyed smell of mead and wine. Spilled drinks had over the years sunk into the unfinished wooden floorboards and the scent rose up, imbuing the air with an amiable, soothing sweetness.

Blake sat beside Aeron on the now vacated stool. The server brought him a tankard of mead, and he thanked her with a polite smile.

"That happens often?" he asked, turning his attention to Aeron.

She shrugged indifferently. "Sometimes. I don't go into town much, and most of the people I meet on the road are being attacked by bandits." She laughed heartily at her own joke. "Even if they recognize me, they aren't looking for a challenge." She looked at Blake, her mind seeming to search for something before she spoke again. "Now, I think Moirin mentioned you were a swindler and street thief."

"That certainly sounds like the description she would give me. I have always loved performing sleight of hand before an audience, but people are too quick to associate these forms of amusing trickery with the ways of liogan. For this reason, I practice my art running rigged games in alleys, scraping together money as it is wagered. It is not as profitable as I would like, so I engage in more traditional methods of thievery as required by an empty pocket."

His mind turned back to Hugh, and he felt the familiar pain growing in his chest. "I didn't often pick pockets, though I trained a pickpocket to work with me. I would distract a crowd with a game, while he lifted their purses."

"Where is he now?" Aeron asked.

"Gone. King Alderic executed him by hanging." Blake paused, tipping the tankard of mead to the side. "In life, he wanted nothing more than to learn the art I so cherished, but I was an unwilling master to his studious pupil. I may not have been the teacher he deserved, but it pains me to know that he spent his final moments in this world thinking I had abandoned him, leaving him upon the mercy of a heartless king."

"And you travel with Moirin to avenge your friend's death." Aeron clapped him on the shoulder with a force that nearly knocked him from the chair, her sense of her own strength doubtless compromised by the alcohol she had already imbibed. "Blake, I wish you luck with whatever you're looking for."

She winked clumsily, hinting at her knowledge of the map. This was somewhat less than secret given her earlier interrogation of Moirin.

Blake drank deeply from the mug before him. In the back of his mind, he wondered where King Alderic was at that moment. Their inability to understand the map may have placed them out of the king's path and temporarily out of harm's way. Though, were this the case, it would be so much the worse for their undertaking.

When Nahia arrived, she and Owen sat down at a table in the corner of the room. The sun was beginning to set, and there was still no sign of Moirin. Blake and Aeron joined the pair at the table.

Nahia smiled at Blake as they approached, her eyebrows raised a little as she took in Aeron's appearance. She stood and shook the other woman's hand.

"You must be Aeron, the bandit queen," she said, a note of admiration in her voice. "I have heard tell of your many adventures."

Aeron sat down. "I can only hope you are not a law keeper, self-appointed or otherwise."

"Nothing could be further from the truth," Nahia said. "Tell me, is it true that you once, single-handedly, fought off a lynching mob of seven men?

I heard that by the time you were through, they had been robbed of their money and weapons, everything but the clothes on their backs."

"That's not entirely true," Aeron said, leaning forward against the table, her eyes crinkling. "I took the clothes as well."

At this they both laughed, and Nahia ordered a round of drinks for the table.

They passed the time in idle chatter, carefully keeping away from the purpose of their journey. While Aeron may not have been acquainted with the exact nature of their errand, she seemed to pick up on their secrecy in the presence of Nahia.

An hour later, Moirin entered the tavern and joined them at the table. Her eyes met Owen's, and she shook her head. Her search for information had been unsuccessful. Her eyes lighted on their new companion, and the muscles of her jaw visibly tightened.

"Moirin," Nahia greeted her plainly. She stood to take the other woman's hand in a brief and polite shake. Blake was struck by the sudden lack of warmth in Nahia's expression. "I see you are doing well."

"You appear to be the same," Moirin responded, her words unnaturally measured. Her eyes turned to Owen and Blake, wordlessly seeking explanation.

"Do not worry," Nahia laughed, inferring the reason for Moirin's glance, "they have told me nothing of your journey, nor would I want to know." She grinned. "Your secrets are safe from Alderic, as they have always been."

"I am sure you can understand my need for discretion in such mixed company," Moirin said, looking pointedly at Nahia.

Nahia kicked back in her chair, and inspected Moirin lazily. While the words had undeniably been chosen to attack her character, Nahia gave no indication that she was injured by the remark. She tilted her chin up, and the smile dropped from her face as she began her response:

"My loyalty to the king is well known, and I do not make any secret of my allegiance." Her eyes narrowed. "Your motivations, too, are clearly understood."

Nahia turned to the others sitting at the table, and her mood lightened. "Still, there is no need for discord this evening. You cannot tell me where you are going, but perhaps you can tell me about your journey from Ashen Castle prison to Rieville."

Blake told her of their time in Brecktvin, though careful to leave out any mention of their own interactions with Geils, while Nahia listened with rapt attention. She propped her chin on her right hand and with her left, she turned her glass of water back and forth in semi-circles on the table; the curved edge traded rhythmically between her index finger and thumb. Her attention to the story did not slip, and the movement of her hand on the glass seemed unconscious.

"To think how many died at Geils' hands," she mused, after he had finished the tale. "Fear of liogans has left a deep mark upon the minds of the people."

"Have you ever seen a liogan?" Blake asked.

Nahia's mouth half opened in surprise, and her glass momentarily stilled on the table. She paused before answering, her fingers gradually resuming their absent-minded task. "I believe so, though it was only once."

While it was not expressly forbidden to discuss liogans, it was understood to be an unmentionable topic amongst company. Blake had ignored this, noting the openness with which Nahia discussed the subject.

"What was it like?" he pressed.

She shrugged. "I am afraid my story verges on the mundane, as I was not witness to a particularly incredible act. A few years ago, I was returning to my estate on foot. It was a new moon, and I could barely see ten feet ahead of me. A man's horse had gone lame on the road. I don't think I would have given him a second thought, were it not for the way he glanced around to ensure he was unobserved. Luckily, in the darkness I evaded his gaze. He knelt by the horse, and it seemed as though the air thinned. There was a flash, like a spark, and the man's very hands were briefly aglow around the horse's foot. When the man rose again, the horse placed its weight back on the injured foot, cured of its lameness. The man resumed his place in the saddle and the two galloped away."

She paused. A faltering smile grew across her lips. "In all my years of exploring the outermost reaches of the kingdom, I have only once glimpsed the liogan ways. My guess is that whatever skill in controlling magic remains will die with the few remaining, hidden practitioners."

"Why does King Alderic not seek to use these liogans? Imagine what the king could accomplish, were his raw power aided by the ancient ways of magic," Blake asked.

Blake was the only one of those seated at the table who knew that a liogan had been used to secure Lord Wesley's fortress. He decided against revealing this information, as it would only remind the others of his earlier fault.

"I think the practitioners today are weakened by their lack of practice and bonding," she responded, leaning forward. "In the past, liogans reinforced each other, strengthened by their comrades and community. They would have learned from and protected one another. Today, any who are not killed in childhood must live in hiding; the magic that was once their strength has become their undoing." She watched Blake's response. "I noted a few eccentricities in your movements reminiscent of the more highly skilled gambling men who roam Conrisia. I would guess you might have a personal stake in the fate of liogans."

"I look to a day when I can perform replicating the appearance of magic for entertainment, without fear of misunderstanding and death," he stated.

"You may have a long wait." She smiled, sympathy in her eyes. "Although, I suspect if your skill of trickery is strong enough, you may find the dangerous connection to be of great advantage."

Blake leaned back in his chair. His eyes stayed locked on hers, and she returned his gaze unflinchingly. He may have missed seeing her uneven smile, but there was something calming about the solemnity with which she regarded him.

Moirin crossed her arms, clearly ill at ease with Nahia's presence. The motion caused the fabric of her shirt to hitch, and the key came loose from the wrapping in her pocket. Within a second of the key falling, Moirin had snatched it back between her fingers, and hidden it safely within the paper wrappings.

Nahia raised her eyebrows, clearly amused by how agitated Moirin was in her presence. A grin grew across her face, as her eyes narrowed with an innocent playfulness.

"What do you have there?" she asked.

Blake could tell she had asked purely to put Moirin further on edge, and could not help but smile at the immediate animosity this provoked in Moirin, who glared at Nahia.

"That is none of your concern."

"You're right." Nahia laced her fingers behind her head and leaned back. "Besides, I doubt it is anything worth my while."

Moirin's lips drew together, not taking the bait. "We have a long day ahead of us. It is best we all get some sleep." Her eyes turned back to Nahia. "You ought to rest; tired eyes make for a slow response during a duel. It would be a shame if any harm befell you."

Nahia laughed loudly, drawing the attention of a few of the tavern's patrons. "I will take that under advisement," she responded, still chuckling.

Moirin did not indulge Nahia's amusement, turning on her heel and proceeding up the stairs, followed by Aeron. Owen too took his leave with a small nod to the viscountess. Blake could tell he did not want Moirin to be too long out of his earshot. He protected her with the single-minded devotion a dog shows a bone.

"Would you show me something?" Nahia asked, once the others were gone. "I have always been fascinated by such subtle talents as pickpocketing."

"Of course. Better yet, why don't I teach you how to implement a few tricks?"

Nahia nodded, her eyes never leaving his face. Blake kept his own downcast, focused on the unsteady movements of his own hands. She propped her chin on the heel of her palm as she watched him, pushing her hair to the side. As Blake demonstrated the diversions beneath her watchful gaze, he found that it was, perhaps, fitting that he turned to discussion of distractions employed by pickpockets and ways to use a mark's sense of control to advantage.

An hour passed this way and, with the others gone, Blake knew it was only right that he too should retire. He set his palms against the table, and rose to stand. He was surprised when he felt Nahia's hand light on his wrist for a moment.

"It was a pleasure to make your acquaintance, Blake," she said.

She looked at him, and he was struck by the earnestness in her eyes. It was only a small shift from the humor of her typical countenance, but he could feel his throat catch at the unexpected change.

He nodded, unsure of how to respond. Climbing the stairs to the second floor, he found himself too nervous to cast a glance back at Nahia, instead intently focusing on each step that lay before him.

22

Alderic led his soldiers through the narrow path leading to the base of the mountain, on the other side of which lay Linwood. The sun was beginning to set, and he kept the horses at a steady pace, hoping to reach the mountain before nightfall.

Callum rode beside him, the chain mail beneath his breastplate jangling lightly with each step his horse took.

Without warning, an unknown man ran out in front of the king's horse, narrowly avoiding being trampled. Alderic pulled back on the reins, while Callum dropped down from the saddle, seizing the intruder by the elbow.

Callum held him there, as the king surveyed the man. The man gave no struggle as he watched the king dismount, though he seemed to be in the grips of agitation.

"My king, I must speak with you," the man cried out, when it seemed he could wait no longer. He wore the traditional garb and headdress of the bandit tribe that Alderic knew roamed those parts of Vesia.

"What is your name?" Alderic asked, admittedly confused by the bandit's presence.

"I am Seph. Only one day ago, I counted myself as one of Aeron's bandits," he responded, breathless. "I come to you bearing news of your brother's wife."

"What is this news?" the king asked.

"Moirin and her two companions have taken shelter with the bandits. Aeron is guarding them against you."

Alderic knew of Aeron. Every so often, he would hear complaints of her criminal activities distressing citizens who had lost precious cargo to the bandits. Still, Aeron's outlaw tribe rarely gave him trouble, and apprehending them had never been a priority for the king.

Alderic gave Callum the signal to release the man. There was little risk, as the former bandit was surrounded on all sides by the king's loyal soldiers.

"Why are you telling me this?" Alderic's eyes narrowed. "Do you hope to gain royal favor?"

He shook his head adamantly. "I seek only revenge. My wife was a cook in your kitchens, loyal to her king until the very moment she was wrongly hanged for the poisoning of your brother." Seph's eyes filled with tears. "I wish only for Moirin to suffer the way my wife did in her final moments."

"What information do you have for me?" Alderic asked, tiring quickly of Seph's overt sentimentality.

"The bandits will rest for the night in a farmhouse a few miles outside of Rieville, it is the only residence beside the road leading to the town's gates. I have no doubt Moirin and her companions will be with them."

"Very well, do you know anything else?" Alderic asked. "Do they have in their possession a key?"

Seph shook his head. "I have told your highness everything I know."

Alderic drew his lips together, and took a few steps before the traitorous bandit. He sighed, before returning his gaze to Seph.

"How long have you been under Aeron's leadership?" Alderic asked.

"Five years."

"Has she protected you and provided for you? Have those among them risked their lives to shield you from harm? Have you done the same for them?"

"I could not have asked for a better leader," he admitted reluctantly.

Alderic drew closer to Seph, looking down coldly on the errant bandit. "Do you know what I will do when I find Aeron and your companions?"

"You will kill them." A hot rage burned in Seph's eyes, and his body shook. "They have harbored a fugitive, and must pay the price."

"Would you ask me to spare any one of your companions?" Alderic spoke quietly.

Seph shook his head in response. "I am content to know that you will mete out justice as is fitting. You are a wise king, and they will pay for their killings and robberies. Besides, I would let one hundred of them die to see

Moirin swinging from the gallows, her body twisted by a cruel wind. That depraved woman is long overdue her punishment."

Hearing these words, the king felt bile rise in his throat. Despite their often-antagonistic relationship, he would not hear her spoken of so.

Alderic turned back, nodding at one of his soldiers, who dismounted, and pulled from her saddlebag a length of rope.

When he comprehended what was about to happen, Seph made to run away. Callum grabbed him, holding him tight as the soldier looped the end of rope around Seph's neck, throwing the other end over a sturdy tree branch, before securing it to the pummel of her saddle.

"If I am as wise a king as you say, would it not be wrong for me to punish so selectively?" Alderic said, as he surveyed the terror-stricken bandit. "I doubt there is a robbery in which you did not partake fully, and I cannot rightly spare you from the fate you would have me dispense to any other of your kind."

"Please," Seph begged through tear-filled eyes, "I have given you everything I can."

Alderic's thin lips twisted into a smile. "Perhaps this experience will bring you closer to your wife. You will join her in the afterlife at least."

Seph sobbed as the rope tightened around his throat. The soldier urged her mount, and the horse walked slowly forward, while Seph was pulled from his feet. He kicked for a while in the air. His hands were not bound, so he tried to pull himself up on the rope, easing the pressure on his neck. Standing in the saddle, the soldier struck the back of his hands with the flat of her sword, causing him to lose his grip and swing uncontrollably.

When Seph's body was finally still, he was taken down from the tree. Alderic gave orders for the body to be brought with them. Two soldiers slung the body over the back of a saddle, tying it down with the same length of rope used in the hanging.

Alderic led the soldiers toward Rieville. While this route would divert them from the swiftest passage to Linwood, it would only delay them by a day. The time could be quickly made up, and Alderic would not risk losing the chance to possess the key. While Alderic had planned to simply take whatever he found in Linwood, the key would enable him to move more quickly toward the liogan weapon.

Callum whistled lightly as the horses jogged forward, by all appearances in good humor. It had taken Alderic years to accustom Owen to killing, and the process had left the previous knight broken in mind and spirit. The king could not take credit for how quickly Callum had acclimated to the blood-soaked profession.

There was something of the cavalier in Callum's aspect, allowing him to kill seemingly without remorse, yet this nonchalant attitude was tempered by a fierce loyalty to the king. And for this reason, Alderic was tolerant of the bearing displayed by his second.

23

B lake woke, his back sore from sleeping on the bed. It seemed his body had grown accustomed to the firmness of the earth beneath him, and the straw-packed mattress offered him little but discomfort.

Within seconds he realized a persistent knocking at the door was the reason for his early awakening. He pulled himself from the bed and opened the door, where Moirin greeted him with the command to meet in the room below.

Owen had slept there, his bed by the window, and was awake when Blake closed the door. After a quick shave and face washing, Blake joined them in the deserted tavern.

The room was dark, as the sun had yet to rise, and the embers from the previous night's fire still burned in the hearth: flickering red the only light in the room. The smell of mead greeted his nostrils, though too early in the day to be an enjoyable scent.

Nahia had forgone renting a room, instead sleeping the night in the corner of the tavern. It seemed a common enough practice, as other patrons were dispersed across the room in states of repose. Nahia was still asleep, her hair falling across her face, and a rapier tucked between the crossed arms on her chest.

Blake approached, and shook her shoulder gently. Reaching out the touch her, he experienced more nervousness than he had felt during the entire journey. When he tapped her shoulder, she started and the sheathed rapier slipped an inch before staying fast in her arms. After travelling with Owen and Moirin, he found it unusual to see someone who could slumber soundly, unguarded.

She stood, and shook the last of the sleep away. Through the haze of awakening, she managed a half-smile at Blake, who found himself inelegantly stepping back to join the others. She took the little water that remained in the glass into her palm and splashed it across her face, wiping it away on her sleeve.

There was something about Nahia's reckless bearing that made Blake uncomfortable, but in a manner not entirely unpleasant.

She glanced out the window. "The sun will rise soon. I had best make my way to the gates." She reached across the bar top, filling her canteen and drinking deep, before leading the group from the tavern.

They reached the stables and loaded the horses' saddles with their belongings, before setting out for the old town gates.

When they reached the gates, Nahia stepped forward, her eyes searching for her opponent. There was a small grass clearing between the trees and the road. Blake assumed this was to be the place of the duel.

The Earl of Eskemn was there to greet her and they exchanged a few quiet words.

The earl was a small, rotund man. His eyes squinted, even in the low light of early daybreak, and he glanced around nervously.

The earl's adversary approached on horseback accompanied by his champion: a tall man, dark haired and barrel chested. The champion dismounted, his feet thudding against the ground as he landed, while the earl's advisor stayed on horseback, regarding the small group with the same anxiety displayed by the earl himself.

Nahia and the earl's champion shook hands. Blake heard the man introduce himself as Frederick, and Nahia offered a small, polite bow as she introduced herself. Though neither Frederick nor Nahia smiled, they showed each other no animosity.

Signaled by a word from the earl, they stepped back, each walking in opposite directions as the spectators moved out of the way. Nahia walked until she reached the tree line, and Frederick until he had reached the dirt road of the city, though only a relatively small space lay between them.

By agreement, the earl called a start to the duel. At his sign, both parties advanced, their weapons drawn. Neither made an immediate movement, instead hanging back and watching their opponent carefully.

Nahia hesitated for only a moment longer, before abruptly discarding any show of reserve and lunging forward. Her weapon flashed as the tip surged toward Frederick's torso. Frederick knocked the weapon from its intended path, returning with his own attack.

Nahia protected herself, diverting the blade, before relaunching an assault.

Frederick slipped by unscathed again.

This failure to strike caused her to pull back a little, resuming her consideration of the man before her. He seemed grateful for the break, mirroring almost exactly her contemplative stance.

Blake understood what Owen had meant about the differences between a nobleman's duel and a fight. The movements were small and controlled. Neither combatant used the shoves, punches, kicks, and grabs that were commonplace in a brawl or street fight. Moreover, he could not help but feel that Nahia was somehow holding back, her struggle with restraint was almost palpable.

They moved forward again. It happened too quickly for Blake to fully follow the movement of the two weapons. All he knew was that Frederick's blade pierced Nahia's sleeve, while hers had brushed his torso, the end catching in the fabric of his shirt.

Blake held his breath in anticipation as he watched both swords withdraw. Frederick and Nahia each took a step backwards, as they brought their blades back to their sides.

Both blade tips were stained with red.

Nahia looked down, and Blake could see a mark grow from a pinpoint to stain the sleeve red with blood. Similarly, Blake could see blood steep into Frederick's shirt, where the fabric rested against his stomach.

Frederick and Nahia exchanged a look, and Nahia shrugged. From this, Blake understood that neither knew who had landed the first hit. He was similarly at a loss.

Blake turned to Owen for clarification, but the warrior only shook his head.

The earl and his advisor spoke in whispers, before they turned to their champions. "It will be decided on the drawing of second blood," the earl proclaimed in a shaking voice, the oddness of the words seemingly not lost on their speaker.

While the announcement was strange to Blake, the champions did not seem surprised by the order. Dutifully, Nahia and Frederick resumed their starting points. The injury Nahia sustained was to her unarmed side, and was unlikely to impact her ability greatly.

Frederick gave no indication that his cut was paining him particularly, and his movements seemed in no way hampered by the superficial injury.

At a word from the earl, they surged forward again. To Blake their movements seemed emboldened by the injuries they had inflicted on the other. There was no wavering as their weapons clashed, and the meeting of steel rang out in the open space.

Nahia was unrelenting, driving Frederick backwards until he tripped on his heel. He fell to the ground, catching himself on the palm of his left hand. Nahia seemed poised to strike, but she drew back. She touched her elbow, and her fingertips came back red with blood.

She held her hand up to signal the end of the duel, and pulled Frederick to his feet. She clasped his forearm in a gesture of good will. Her cheeks were flushed, and wisps of brown hair clung to her forehead with sweat.

Nahia must have noticed Blake staring at her, because she returned his gaze offering a wink that made him turn his face away in a burst of uncharacteristic shyness.

She offered her apologies to the earl, with a slight insincerity. The earl seemed to take the loss in stride, though his disappointment was evident. He shook the hand of his advisor, their dispute settled, though Blake was still unsure of the exact terms the duel had been set upon.

After bidding the earl, Frederick, and the earl's advisor farewell, the three travelers and the bandit queen mounted their horses and set out away from the town. Nahia would journey with them until they reached the road leading to her estate.

24

The bandits knelt on the floor of the farmhouse, while Alderic's soldiers paced behind them, watching for any aggressive movements. Aeron's followers had put up an honorable fight but, evenly matched with the soldiers in number, their lack of battle training meant their swift defeat.

Badly beaten and stripped of their weapons, the bandits looked on the king with almost uniform disdain. Moirin was not among the bandits, nor was there a sign of her loyal companions. The dark confines of the farmhouse had begun to smell of spilled blood, and Alderic was quickly losing patience.

"I see your leader, Aeron, is not among you," the king spoke.

Alderic stood at the center of the room, looking out across the faces that turned impertinently towards him.

"This need not be difficult," he said. "I know that you have been harboring a woman and her two male companions. Any of you who have information on where I can find them, speak now."

The bandits remained silent; they would not trust him so easily.

Alderic sighed. "I have allowed you to maraud unchecked for all these years, and I do not have the time to bring each of you to trial. You can either help me now and receive a pardon for your past sins, or remain against me and perish."

The bandits looked up at him, but not one made any movement, nor opened their mouth to speak. In spite of himself, Alderic was impressed by Aeron's training of her followers.

Alderic grew impatient at their continued defiance. "Speak or die; it is not complicated. If you choose silence, you will see each of your companions killed, powerless to do anything but await your turn."

Alderic would not wait any longer. It would only stand to see how the bandits would conduct themselves in the absence of their leader.

25

Nahia spoke over her shoulder to Owen, as her horse jogged alongside Blake's. Blake could not help but be aware of her presence at his side every second of the journey, so he kept his eyes fixed ahead. Her laugh drew his attention and, though he did not look at her, he could picture her lopsided smile.

When they came to a split in the road, Nahia took her leave. She leaned over in the saddle to wish Moirin luck on her journey and lost her balance slightly, steadying herself against the other woman's shoulder.

Moirin forcefully shook off the contact, and drew her horse out ahead of the others, putting distance between herself and the departing viscountess.

Nahia bid farewell to Owen, Aeron and Blake, before turning her horse toward the narrow, winding road that led to her estate.

Blake could not be sure, the leaves of the trees cast her in moving shadows, but he thought that she looked back at him over her shoulder as she rode away.

He hoped she had.

Moirin was forthcoming in her reluctance to rejoin the bandits, but the only road leading from Rieville passed the farmhouse, so she had no choice but to accept Aeron's company until that point. If Aeron was uncomfortable with Moirin's obvious dislike of the bandits, she gave no indication, instead cheerfully riding beside as they approached the hideout.

They reached the fence encircling the farm. The farmhouse was a tall, wide wooden building set atop a rolling green. They intended to offer their thanks to the bandits and say farewell to Aeron, so Blake and Owen began to dismount.

"Stop," Aeron said. The gravity of her voice sent a chill down Blake's spine, and he immediately complied. "Stay in the saddle, and be ready to leave at any second."

Even Moirin gave no resistance.

"There should be someone at that post," Aeron said under her breath, pointing to the far side of the fence. She dropped down from the horse. "They would not have left without me," she mumbled, breaking into a run toward the gate. She flung open the rickety wooden entry and ran across the grass, barreling into the house.

Blake could not see into the home, but he saw Aeron freeze only a step or two past the doorway. The muscles of her back pulled tense, and her hand clenched the wooden frame. Blake glanced at his companions, and saw that Owen was already hastening to Aeron's side, his axe drawn.

Blake dismounted. He took his sword in unsteady hands, and followed Owen's lead carefully. He could not imagine what would bring Aeron to a dead halt and cause Owen to come to her side, visibly prepared for a fight. Anxiety flooded his stomach, as he pushed the gate open hesitantly with his foot. He winced as the hinges creaked, and he tried to slow the swinging motion of the gate.

He could see Owen had lowered his axe, but Aeron had not moved from her place in the doorway. He walked to where the pair stood motionless, and peered into the room through the space between Aeron's shoulder and Owen's elbow.

What he saw caused his heart to nearly stop. The walls and floors were splattered crimson. The red color overwhelmed Blake's vision, but it was not until this crushing effect had faded to the background that his eyes were finally able to see the destroyed figures scattered across the room. The black fabric of Aeron's followers clothed the annihilated bodies. Aeron had likely lost every one of her bandits to the massacre.

Owen brushed past Aeron's still unmoving frame into the room.

Blake watched him carefully, to see whether Owen would undergo the aggressive transformation that violent imagery had previously ignited.

He did not.

Owen hung his head, and his shoulders sagged, as he walked through the wide room. His boots tracked blood with each step, as he checked the bodies for a sign of life. His search was fruitless, as all were dead.

Blake was better able to see into the room now, and his eyes were drawn to a dark outline against the wall. Owen walked toward it and nudged the very lowest point of the object. This set the form swinging back and forth. In its movement, it passed briefly through a shaft of light coming from the cracked roof. It was another body, and a rope extended from the figure's neck to the rafters.

The body turned, and Blake could just make out the face as belonging to Seph. His mind raced, as he realized that Seph had likely led King Alderic to the hideout, betraying his fellow bandits.

Aeron seemed to have come to this same realization, and her entire body shook with grief. Blake put his arm around her shoulder, though he feared she would push him away. Instead, she leaned against him. Wracked with sorrow, she was overtaken by a tortured weeping.

Blake could feel his knees buckle against her weight, but he would not move. He pulled her closer to him, and her tears wet his shirt.

Blake watched over her bowed head as Owen continued searching the room, though his attention was focused on the outlaw leader broken beside him.

26

A lderic surveyed the empty hall. He thought Nahia might have been home, though it seemed this had been optimistic. Her woman had simply shown him in, and set up lodging for his soldiers in the servants' quarters which lay largely abandoned, as Nahia kept only one individual in her service.

The manor was cold, the stone walls and floor unwarmed by any fire. While tapestries were pinned to the walls, they lent no welcome to the imposing home. In the corners of some, the cloth had deteriorated and begun to slip from the fixture, leaving these hanging precariously over the floor.

The servant treated the king with sincere respect. While others in the countryside were hostile to his rule, Nahia had always ensured that the allegiance of her servants lay with the king.

He was shown to a bedroom, one of the few bearing typical furnishings. Entire rooms of the manor were bare, nothing but stone floors and walls, while others hosted the strange objects Nahia had acquired during her journeys.

Alderic lay on the bed, and the muscles in his back began to gradually relax, the easing met with an uncomfortable ache. The wool blanket beneath crept up to meet him, and he allowed himself to rest. He was within the walls of one loyal to him, and this was so rarely the case.

Their visit to the farmhouse had not been futile. Though there was no sign of the escaped trio, Seph had not misled them. One of the bandits finally confessed their part in protecting the travelers and received the mercy promised by Alderic. His soldiers dealt with the other outlaws before departing, ridding Vesia of a bandit pestilence that had afflicted the people for many years.

He pressed the heels of his hands hard against his eyelids, pushing until he saw a flickering, white light. He was forced to return to the original plan, having gained nothing through the diversion to Rieville. Moirin was still unaccounted for, and the key was missing. He could only hope to reach Linwood before she did, his chances bolstered by the fact that she was unaware of Linwood as the location of 'Split Oak', at least according to Geils' presumption.

Feeling restless, he rose and left the room to wander the manor. The home was strewn with goods and heirlooms, though none appeared cared for or deliberately placed. It was clear Nahia had not inhabited the manor in some time.

He heard the steady hoofbeats of a horse approaching. Sword drawn, he crossed the great hall, and made his way to the entrance. Alderic stood in the doorway, looking down the steps at the approaching rider.

Nahia swung one leg over the back of the saddle and hopped down to dismount. Approaching the king, her boots tripped carelessly over the dusty stone steps. Without speaking a word, she grasped Alderic's arm in a warm greeting.

"I thought you might find your way to Rieville," she said, smiling as she led him back into the house.

"I take it news of my journey has reached you," he spoke steadily, still fatigued by the lack of rest.

"Yes, though I do not know any specifics."

Callum was in the main hall, appearing unsure of his position. While Alderic had told him that they were unlikely to encounter any danger, he still assumed the role of the king's personal bodyguard, hesitant to leave his master's side.

"This is Callum, my knight," Alderic said, introducing him to Nahia. "Though he has only been in my service for a short time, he shows remarkable promise."

Nahia took his hand in a firm shake. "It is a pleasure to meet you, Callum."

Callum watched her warily, though he showed all the respect due to so close a friend of the king. He executed a slight bow, before deferring to Alderic's instruction.

The king excused Callum to wait with the soldiers. He and Nahia walked to the dining room, where her servant brought them black tea.

Nahia poured the two white and blue porcelain cups full of the amber colored liquid, before resuming her seat opposite Alderic.

"What brings you here?" she asked plainly. "You are not accompanied by enough soldiers to be going to war, and I can see clearly that you have brought only your most capable. I assume your mission is one of great importance."

Alderic leaned forward. He kept his voice low, though they were alone in the room. "I found the map."

Nahia's eyes widened as she watched the king. "You found the map," she repeated the words. "And you believe uncovering the liogan weapon is possible? You were the one who told me it was likely the stuff of legends, posing no real threat."

"Given the consequences, I cannot risk the legend being true." He rested his elbows on the table's edge, leaning forward. "Moirin has the key to the next point on the map."

"And you cannot reach the weapon without it."

Alderic nodded. "I can prevent Moirin from reaching the next point, but I will not be able to progress further without it."

"Do any others travel with Moirin?" she asked.

"Owen and a confidence artist named Blake."

"Who is Blake?"

"A swindler and thief, first arrested for trying to kill a nobleman. He has moderate skill, though with an ability to think on his feet that would make him an asset to any such venture. I recruited him to retrieve the map."

"I take it he was successful."

"He managed to steal the map, something the previous thieves all died attempting." Alderic nearly smiled. "He then had the sense to hide a piece of the map to ensure I lived up to my end of the bargain."

"But you did not," she added, an amusement in her voice. "This surprises me. Ordinarily you uphold your word."

"It was unfortunate, but doing so would have presented too great a risk to the venture." Alderic surveyed her, his curiosity building. "You have an odd interest in someone you've never met. Have you come across this man before?"

"I was hoping I could avoid becoming involved." She considered, before relenting with a small sigh. "I saw Moirin and the three accompanying her yesterday afternoon in Rieville." Alderic was about to speak, but she cut him off with a wave of her hand. "I do not know where they are now, so you need not ask."

"Three?"

"Yes, besides Moirin, there were three others. Owen, Blake, and Aeron, the bandit queen."

"Aeron," Alderic said, "she has, for the moment, escaped the death of the others."

Nahia raised her eyebrows at the mention of the bandits' deaths, before continuing. "Moirin seemed unhappy with her presence, though she was not exactly pleased to see me either."

"Is she well?" Alderic asked, in spite of himself.

"I would imagine so. For the first time since her attempt following Severin's death, her dreams of becoming Queen of Vesia are finally within her grasp. She should have been removed from the castle years ago, by one method or another." She watched him. "It is curious; you knew that you could not keep her cloistered forever."

"It is no more curious than a sudden inquiry after a confidence artist who seems to have sprouted a conscience."

"What will you do now?" she asked, abruptly changing the subject.

"I will move forward to Linwood, in search of something known as 'Split Oak'. I may not have the key, but I can stop them from recovering whatever lies there, rendering their key useless."

"Linwood," she said, laughing lightly. "It is strange, this is the second time the small town has been mentioned in recent days."

"What do you mean?"

"I visited with Lord Richard, and he told me of a man who had come to his doorstep. The man was ragged, having travelled without food or rest for nearly a week. He told the baron of a mysterious entity that brought dread and murder to the town, ritualistically killing residents and all who attempt to escape. They call it the Horror of Linwood."

"This news comes from Lord Richard?" Alderic asked. "It is peculiar that I have not once heard tell of such a monster."

"Whatever your objections to Lord Richard, I believe he is telling the truth." She shrugged. "Admittedly, it was ill luck that brought the traveler to the baron's door, as the man's journey did not continue."

"I would imagine," Alderic said, his tone caustic.

"If you still intend to reach Linwood, you will need to go through the valley," Nahia cautioned. "The mountain pass may be faster, but to travel it with so large a group is suicide. The path is narrow, difficult to navigate for even a single rider. The days are windy, and at night it grows so cold that there are tales of travelers freezing to death having stopped to rest for merely a few minutes."

"I doubt those legends relay fact," Alderic responded.

Nahia shrugged. "Whether this is an exaggeration or not, I know of several who never returned from their journey across the mountains."

Alderic nodded. While he was known to be intrepid, he was not one to take lightly words of warning, or to act in imprudence. He trusted Nahia to not lead him astray.

He took a drink from the cup before him. The tea was strong and acidic, its flavor a mixture of the black tea leaves and delicate orange blossom.

27

They spent the rest of the day digging. The rolling green of the farmland had become a makeshift gravesite, the wooden fence now encircling human-sized pits that were to be filled by the bodies of Aeron's bandits.

Blake knew that Moirin was uncomfortable with the delay. She voiced concern that King Alderic could return at any moment to finish the job but, in the end, she relented. Aeron and the bandits had offered them protection, and she could not deny the outlaws a proper burial.

Owen and Aeron carried most of the bodies from the house into the yard, one carrying beneath the arms, while the other held the corpse's feet. Moving the bodies this way allowed them to keep the blood off of their clothes.

The breath left Blake's body as he watched them bring Ian into the field. Blake stepped out of a grave, and pressed the tip of the shovel against his boot. The pressure of the metal against his toes helped keep the tears from his eyes.

Owen and Aeron knelt to lay Ian gently into the ground. His thin body rested awkwardly in the quickly dug grave, his arms and legs askew.

Ian's hands and knees were covered in blood that, given the cut across his throat, could not have been his own. Blake winced as he realized that Ian had not been the first to die. He would have had to watch his bandit family, those who cared for and protected him, be slaughtered by the king's soldiers before finally facing his own death.

Aeron went back inside the farmhouse. She cut Seph down, and carried him outside. He had been hanged, and there was no bleeding to avoid. She held the body across her shoulders, and set him down at the center of the field.

"Do you want Seph buried elsewhere?" Blake asked as he finished shoveling dirt into Ian's freshly-filled grave.

Aeron shook her head, as she looked down at Seph. "All he ever spoke of was revenge for his wife, and I knew he would do anything in her memory." Aeron said these words, as she looked out at the bodies blanketing the yard. "I'm as much to blame for their deaths."

She took the body back into her arms, and set it down in one of the shallow graves they had dug earlier. They would have made the graves deeper, but the sheer number of bodies made this impossible.

Blake pushed dirt over the body, covering Seph as quickly as he could. Though Aeron's sentiment was admirable, Blake did not want to spend another second looking upon the traitor.

After all the bandits had been buried, Blake sat on the fence, hooking his feet against the lower rail. The sun was setting and they would need to either depart soon, or stay the night. As the sky darkened, a true fear began to seize him. It was easy to pretend that he was courageous enough to face the wrath of the king during the daylit hours but, looking out at the field of newly-buried bodies in the dying light, he knew he could not continue.

During his time in Ashen Castle, he had acted out of necessity. He had broken into the earl's fortress in return for his freedom, and his escape from the prison thereafter was an escape from the hangman's noose. In his meeting with Geils, he navigated the situation, all the while knowing he enjoyed the upper hand.

Something about this was markedly different. Had he been in the company of the bandits a day longer, he too would be occupying a shallow grave, or more likely rotting in the musty confines of the farmhouse. There was nothing a group of outlaws, or even Owen, could do to protect him from the sword of the king.

Escape was the only option: escape from seeking the weapon, and escape from the attention of King Alderic. Blake was not unaccustomed to abandoning a venture when it became too difficult or inconvenient. Indeed, simply going missing had become second nature to him, and should not be too difficult to take part in again, especially given the consequences should he fail to leave.

However, he would need to be patient. Knowing the king was likely nearby, he would continue to use Moirin and Owen for cover. Alone, within close proximity of the king, he could place himself in an even more detestable situation.

Blake looked over, and saw Owen shoveling dirt into the final grave. He felt the flush of shame, something he did not encounter often. In deciding to abandon the company he had pledged himself to, he had shown yet again that he would gladly sacrifice his honor to preserve his own life.

Moirin seated herself by the entryway to the house, her eyes scanning the map in the dying rays of the sun. Blake sat beside her. He did not try to help, knowing that he was already of little use.

Aeron approached, and came to the other side of Moirin. "Will you ever tell me the meaning of your map?"

Moirin sighed. Blake could tell the frustration at her inability to find the next point was mounting. Instead of folding the map away, as she had done in the past, she spread it out flat across her knees.

"Do you know of a 'Split Oak?'" she asked, relenting.

Aeron looked over Moirin's shoulder at the map. "I have not heard of any split oak, but I do recognize the symbol there."

Moirin passed her finger over the strange marking beneath the word. "What is it?"

"A water snake with a triangular head." Aeron smiled. "It is the symbol of Linwood, a small town near the base of a mountain."

"How do you know this?" Moirin asked.

"We attacked a party from Linwood once, a government group. They carried papers that had this mark. It is an odd image, and I asked their leader about the marking. He told me that it was the ancient symbol of their town, now out of use." Aeron shrugged. "It's not something I thought I'd ever see again."

Moirin folded the map and looked up at Aeron. "How far away is Linwood?"

"It is not the distance, but the difficulty. Most would tell you that to reach it you should avoid travelling the mountain pass, instead taking the safer valley path. However, with a group like ours and the threat of King

Alderic, I would risk it. Though the mountain is dangerous, we could put a few days between us and the king."

"We?" Moirin repeated, slightly raising an eyebrow.

"The king has taken from me something very precious, and I will join you in your fight," Aeron responded.

Moirin opened her mouth to counter this, but seemed to think better of it and closed it without speaking. Perhaps she decided Aeron would be useful, or perhaps she took pity on the bereaved outlaw. Either way, she eventually nodded her head in assent.

While the rest of his companions drew together in solidarity, Blake began to withdraw. His sense of self-preservation had not failed him yet, and his mind was made up.

Blake did not know where the king was, but it was clear that he and his soldiers were nearby. It would be reckless to leave the others only to face the king alone. Putting a few days between himself and the king, as Aeron's route promised, he would be all the safer when abandoning the others.

Regardless of what else might transpire, when they reached the town of Linwood he would find a way to quietly leave their presence.

The sun had set by the time they saddled the horses, preparing to ride in the direction of Linwood. They had rested well in Rieville, and were as prepared as they could hope to be in facing the mountain route. Blake also suspected that Aeron did not wish to spend the night so near the place where her people had been put to death. Besides, it was unlikely any of them would sleep that night.

Even as he urged his horse to follow the others, the image of Ian's dead body crept to the forefront of his mind.

28

The land outside the manor lay in darkness, and Nahia's servant had lit candles throughout the home. The soldiers were dining in the great hall, and the servant brought an assortment of roasted meats and vegetables to the travel-weary troop. For the first time in days, the soldiers were able to rest.

The sound of their carousing filled the wide chamber, as the smell of food met the air. Alderic sat at the end of the table with Callum at his elbow. The knight cast his eyes about the room. He seemed apprehensive, despite his king's diminished caution.

After eating a brief dinner, Alderic took his leave of the soldiers. He walked through the manor, enjoying the close spirit of the flickering, heavily shadowed halls. The cool stone and relaxed darkness reminded him of Ashen Castle and, for a moment, he longed to return home.

For much of his life, Alderic's wars had kept him away from Conrisia, and far from Ashen Castle. Though many years earlier he had fulfilled his father's dream of controlling the greatest known kingdom, his soul would find no solace in serene stagnation. His sight had turned to finally learning the truth about the liogan weapon's existence, and he approached it with the same ardor he dedicated to conquering.

Perhaps Moirin's leaving would draw him closer to Conrisia, allowing Ashen Castle to again feel like home. Even far away, her presence lay heavy on his mind, her absence not fully relieving him of his enthrallment. When he closed his eyes, he could see her captivating lips, and the cruel eyes that regarded him with such heartfelt disdain.

The flickering light suddenly extinguished, and he felt himself swallowed by the arching walls. The darkness surrounding dragged him through an ever-narrowing course, tearing at his throat and suffocating him with blinding force. In the absence of light, the hold of Moirin's phantom was undeniable.

A cold sweat formed on his brow and his heart thudded in his chest, gradually slowing as he brought himself back under control.

Gathered, he went to the balcony overlooking the lands of the estate. A candle rested on the table beside him, and Nahia entered with two cups of tea.

The tea sent spirals of steam into the cold air. The coolness of the night allowed each star to shine more brightly, while the moon blanketed the terrain in a silvery blue light. The wilderness surrounding the estate was visible in the pale glow, Nahia's land stretching as far as could be seen.

She set the tray down, and took a seat beside him.

"Where are you returning from, that you met with Lord Richard?" Alderic asked, referring to their earlier conversation.

"The east," she responded. "I passed through Elsin, though I did not have the opportunity to visit the aged king. It appears that trials by ordeal are gaining popularity, receiving the support of King Unger himself. I saw a man who was accused of murder have molten lead poured across his bare hands. The blistered, burnt flesh was accepted by as proof of his guilt, and he was put to death. This seems to have become the new rule of the land." She paused. "There is something else you might find of interest."

"What would that be?" Alderic asked. He could not imagine anything in King Unger's land holding his concern.

"It is a legend, one that appears to be growing in power. The people believe that a high ruler will arise from the ranks of their people, leading them to greatness. They will overthrow you and bring together each neighboring kingdom, protecting and uniting them beneath a single banner."

"Everyone has heard of this prophesy," Alderic responded.

Nahia nodded. "But there is something else, something that lays within in the Elsin kingdom. They call it the Rock of Briggid. It is a test: a way the high ruler will reveal themselves to the Elsin people. There is a large boulder, and lodged within this is a solid, steel ring. They say that whoever can pull free the steel ring, will lead the uprising against the Vesian tyrant."

She paused. "While you might not believe in this prophesy, you should know that Unger's people have fixed their faith to this fabled figure, as have many in Vesia."

"Regardless of veracity, I suppose it is interesting," Alderic responded, the reminder of a challenger for his crown only bringing his attention back to his own weariness.

Nahia studied him. "Perhaps you would enjoy the challenge. You are a king for battle and your value is greatest in times of upheaval. Yet, Vesia has not had a real war in some time, and your skill has resulted in a rarely broken peace. You have withdrawn from the battlefield, and now you focus your efforts on finding a liogan weapon, which may or may not even exist."

"What is your point?"

"I am only saying that you must be tempted to let a challenger rise, even to let the liogan weapon be discovered and put to use against you, if only so you can again face a true contest."

Alderic considered whether to tell Nahia of his suspicions regarding the weapon. The limited knowledge he had of Ethin's activities before the man's death raised more questions than answers, however, if existent, the threat was unlike anything he had seen before.

"Perhaps if the weapon were merely an item of warfare, I would see the value in such a challenge. Yet, I believe the nature of the weapon to be something else entirely," he began. "The people did not know Ethin as I did. His disgraceful bearing and hunger for power are, I fear, reflected in the design of this liogan weapon. Should it exist, it could not be an instrument of honorable combat."

"I remember Ethin well; he is hard to forget," Nahia said. She paused. "I suppose it is true; the people may fear the power you hold, and hate you for the countless deaths your kingdom's expansion once brought, but a civil war with Ethin's handiwork could rip the world to shreds."

They conversed until the candle between them burned down to a stub. Nahia fell asleep in the chair, and Alderic retreated indoors. He would not bother to move her, despite the coldness of the night air. However, he did retrieve a woolen blanket from one of the rooms, and laid this over her slumbering form before returning to his own room.

He hoped he could sleep at least a few hours before his party set out again in the morning.

29

The sun had long since set by the time they reached the base of the mountain, a sprawling form that lay solidly between Rieville and Linwood. Blake looked up, and saw the snow-covered peak surrounded by weathered trees. He could only imagine the difficulty the upcoming journey would entail.

Blake wrapped a cloak around himself, and he could see his breath turn to fog in front of his face. His fingers were cold from clutching the reins, and he tucked them, along with the grasped leather straps, beneath his shirt and against the warmth of his stomach.

Moirin led the group, and Owen kept close behind her. Aeron followed Blake and, while she had expressed her desire to fight King Alderic in fiery tones, it seemed the combativeness had momentarily left her body. Rather than compel her horse forward, she allowed herself to be pulled by the meandering steed.

"We should find a place to rest," Moirin said. "It has been a trying day."

The words were infinitely beautiful to Blake's ears as he contemplated laying his head down.

"Thank the gods. I did not know how much longer I could continue," he breathed.

Though they were still near the base of the mountain, already the chill of the wind crept insidiously through his clothing.

Aeron shook her head. "We will only rest during daylit hours. The nights are dangerously cold and we must keep ourselves and our horses moving."

Disappointment flooded Blake as they continued to trudge onward in the darkness, the path beneath them lit only by the moon. Blake was weary and could easily forget that only the night before, he had slept within the warm shelter of the tavern.

The path began to narrow as they journeyed further upwards. The monotony of the climb caused Blake's mind to wander. He thought again of Ian, and wondered whether they should have left him to die at the stake. Perhaps Geils' men would have garroted him before the flames had a chance to consume his flesh; many years ago, this had been a standard practice. Even had Geils not given his victim this courtesy, Ian would have at least been spared seeing the deaths of his comrades before suffering his own brutal demise.

The feeling of his horse briefly losing footing on the loose stones, before haphazardly regaining control, abruptly pulled Blake from his thoughts, forcing him to focus on the path which lay ahead. His responsibility in remaining aware was not only to himself and his companions, but also to the faithful horse who labored so diligently beneath the saddle.

He reached down, and patted the chestnut steed's shoulder in recognition of the silent effort, without which their task would be impossible. The horse gave no response, continuing to plod away tirelessly on the steep and treacherous path.

He turned his head a little to speak to Aeron.

"What is Linwood like?" he asked.

"I have only been there once, some years after we robbed that government group," she began, a sorrow tinged her voice as she referenced her lost followers. "It is a beautiful town, set at the base of the mountain within the forest." She paused. "What is surprising is the dust."

"Dust?" Blake asked.

"All the buildings and roads in Linwood are made from the light-colored rock of the mountain. The rock powder coats the streets, and the town appears as if it's covered in a fine snow."

"And what of the forest?" Blake asked, curious.

"The forest is lush and green, surrounding the mountain. No other towns or cities are near Linwood. It is completely isolated, but I remember it as a thriving town, completely self-sufficient. They hunt in the woods, fish in the lake, and keep farms along the mountain base. Inside their small, quiet town, they have everything they need."

Blake was glad to hear that Linwood prospered, as this would make it easier to slip away from his companions. The king could not be far ahead, nor behind, given the recentness of the bandits' killing, and the mountain path would only buy them a day or two. Blake's fear of sharing the bandits' fate kept him moving forward, committing him to the treacherous climb. He would be patient, and bear the arduous journey a little longer.

30

Alderic had been travelling the valley for three days. The sunlit hours were cold and brought with them a freezing fog that made the path ahead difficult to see. At night, the air constricted the lungs of the soldiers as they tried to sleep. However, the king was glad to have taken this route. Given the chill of the valley, the mountain path must have been life-threatening.

Tensions were running high within the party. The food supply dwindled, and lack of rest weighed heavily on all. The strain reached its pinnacle when, during a mid-day respite from riding, Alderic's longest serving soldier, Bryan, was thrown to the ground before him by the man's enraged fellows.

"He has been caught stealing food. We saw him eating the last of the meat, hiding himself from us," one soldier made the accusation to the king, while the others nodded fervently.

Bryan lay prostrate before Alderic. Through tears he apologized profusely, nearly incoherent in his babbling. He pressed his face against the cold, damp ground, continuing his prayer for mercy.

Alderic stood, and put the toe of his boot beneath the soldier's chin. He tilted the Bryan's face up, so that he reluctantly met the king's critical gaze.

"Is this true?" Alderic asked.

Bryan nodded, before forcing his own face back to the ground. His lips continued their murmured pleas against the dirt.

Alderic sighed. Bryan had been in his company since the day he took control of his father's army, and the soldier had shown him nothing but loyalty over the years. The punishment for this kind of crime against the other soldiers was death, but the king found he was disinclined to simply execute one of his most devoted.

"I will give you one chance to save yourself," Alderic spoke. "If you can fight Callum to his death, I will allow you to resume your position with no further consequence."

Bryan's eyes widened and he began to stammer thanks, but was immediately silenced by a look from the king.

Alderic turned to Callum, surveying the knight who sat atop a large boulder by the side of the path. "Callum, you can freely choose to accept or decline this challenge. However, should you decline, Bryan will be executed and you will no longer be my knight, instead joining the ranks of the soldiers."

Callum grinned widely, hopping down from the boulder. "I accept the challenge."

Alderic knew he might lose the knight, and that this was not an improbable outcome. Experience often won out over youth, and Bryan had been a soldier when Callum was but an infant in his mother's arms. Yet, Alderic was pleased that Callum was willing to risk his life in pursuit of his ambitions.

Callum had been given his title based on potential, rather than skill. While Alderic believed strongly in the young man, he did not want the knight to become too comfortable with the status he had been granted.

This fight would be as much a test of Alderic as of Callum. He would see whether the intermittent training he had given the knight would be sufficient against a seasoned soldier such as Bryan. In spite of himself, he hoped that he would not lose the knight so soon.

The soldiers formed a wide circle, so that neither combatant could retreat from the fight. Both men were stripped to the waist and without weapons or armor, standing at opposite sides of the circle. Alderic handed each a sword and stood, unarmed, between them to ensure neither man struck prematurely.

The king stepped back, giving the signal to begin. He crossed his arms, and came to stand at the edge of the circle.

The combatants began to prowl at the periphery. The wind had picked up, tinging their uncovered skin white. The sword rattled slightly in Callum's hands, due to cold rather than fear.

Callum made the first attack. He lunged forward, the point of his weapon aimed directly at Bryan's heart. His attack was deflected by the soldier, and the knight retreated quickly, out of Bryan's striking range.

Callum held back, as Bryan neared him. The soldier surged forward, and Callum spun out of the way, though not quickly enough. The blade grazed his side, making a shallow laceration at his rib.

The pain seemed to awaken Callum to the fight, and his eager eyes gleamed. When Bryan attacked again, Callum caught the blade between his arm and his side.

Bryan tried to withdraw the weapon, laying cuts into Callum's arm and ribs, but the knight gave no sign that the injuries were felt.

Callum pulled back his own sword, freeing his hands to grab the hilt of Bryan's blade. He tried to wrest the weapon from the soldier, but was unable to do so. With only a foot between them Callum surged forward, headbutting his opponent.

Bryan lost his hold on the blade. The cold had weakened his grip, and the pain of the head strike left him momentarily disoriented.

Callum took advantage of this lapse and, laying the sole of his boot on the soldier's chest, he kicked Bryan away. This left the soldier unarmed and on the ground, while Callum wielded both weapons.

Bryan rose to his knees, and Callum discarded one of the swords. In a single, smooth movement, he swung the held blade, slicing through Bryan's throat. Bryan died quickly and with little suffering: the most Callum could have offered his fellow soldier.

The circle of soldiers broke, and Bryan's body was carried away immediately. The others were unfazed by the death; many made known their satisfaction with this carriage of justice.

Alderic ordered a soldier trained in medicine to treat Callum's wounds. She wiped away blood, and applied a healing salve made of oil and herbs, to the slashed skin. Strips of fabric were wound around the knight's torso, before his shirt was pulled on over the bandages. Callum looked up at Alderic, a proud grin across his face.

Alderic had not been mistaken in recruiting Callum for his right hand.

Despite the large amount of bleeding, the wounds Callum had received in the fight were shallow, and would heal quickly. He would be ready to fight again the next day if needed. Ordinarily, Alderic would not concern himself with the treatment of injuries, but he felt an obligation to Callum.

While Callum did not yet have Owen's talent, his defeat of Bryan showed he was far from unprepared for battle. With time, his skill would reach that of the former knight, and he did not display the mental weakness that had proved ruinous to his predecessor.

By Alderic's calculations, they had two more days of traveling the valley before reaching Linwood. He would keep his troop moving on, even through the night. The movement would keep the cold at bay, and they would be able to rest in the steadily growing warmth of the valley.

The wind picked up, and Alderic could hear the whistling of the gusts against the mountains that towered so high above. He became aware of something cold and hard against his shoulder. He pressed his palm at the spot, and could feel a small object sewn within a fold of the fabric.

Alderic tore the few stitches, hooking his finger on a small metal piece held fast with thread. He pulled it free. In his palm, he held a small, golden key. Attached by a piece of string was a small note which read:

I could hardly let you leave without this.

It was written in messy, nearly illegible, handwriting he would know anywhere as belonging to Nahia.

He rolled the small key between his fingertips, watching the cool sunlight glint on the gold. The mist fogged the shining metal and wet the skin of his hands.

Though he was disconcerted that Nahia had caught him so unawares, he now held the key to whatever lay at 'Split Oak'.

Linwood was only a few more days' journey away, and he had never been more certain of his approaching victory.

31

Over the days they travelled, Blake's mind was dulled by the unrelenting cold, and his senses gradually numbed. The nights were bitter; his eyes stung, and his ears and fingertips had lost all feeling. Like the others, he wrapped both his blanket and bedroll around him, over his cloak. This helped keep the cold away, if only to the extent that he would not die of it.

During the day, Blake could sleep only intermittently. The brightness, unobscured due to the lack of trees higher up on the mountain, kept him awake. Even through closed eyelids, the light of the sun cut through like a knife.

They set a fire, and melted snow for drinking water, but the heat did little to soothe the weary travelers. There was no comfortable place to sleep on the narrow path and they were forced to set their beds on the uneven ground, between a wall of rock and a steep drop. Blake had awoken with fresh aches each time, and wondered how much longer he could carry on.

On the fourth day, they neared the mountain peak. The path had narrowed, such that they could no longer ride the horses. Blake was shivering violently, as were his three companions. His teeth chattered and, with all his will, he could not stop the shaking of his body. His eyes watered, and the tears froze on his cheeks.

It was midday when they came to a halt. They would rest a moment, but they could not sleep; it was far too cold to risk inactivity.

Moirin undid her saddlebag and brought out their remaining rations. Blake could see the inelegance of her hands as she tried to rebuckle the pack. She was clumsy, and her fingertips were swollen from the cold.

Moirin, Blake, and Aeron set upon the food, knowing it was near their last. Owen held back, watching the others.

"You must eat," Moirin said, pushing a piece of dried meat into Owen's hands.

Owen seemed confused by her request, but took the food that was forced upon him. He raised it to his mouth, but the meat slipped through his fingers, falling to the ground. Owen stared at it for a minute, before picking it back up.

Owen did not try to eat again, merely staring at the food in his hand. His skin was turning blue, and it seemed that he could not bend his fingers.

It was then that Blake noticed what was different about Owen.

"He has stopped shivering," Blake said to Moirin.

"We should move," Moirin said, pulling herself to her feet and turning to Owen. "It will do him no good to sit still in the cold."

Owen nodded, and made to follow Moirin's lead. He struggled to stand, but slipped back to the ground. He stumbled to his feet a second time, but fell again. This time, he caught himself on the rocks, opening up a gash in his arm.

Owen's blood was flowing to the ground, as he tried to stand a third time. Blake wanted to rush forward to help him, but the path was far too narrow. Instead, Aeron reached out and held fast to Owen's shoulder, keeping him from attempting to stand again.

Aeron pulled aside Owen's shirt sleeve and pinched his arm, hard.

"This one's little more than skin and bones," she said. "It's no wonder he's given in to the cold. I'm only surprised he's lasted this long."

Blake cautiously made his way along the edge, coming to Owen's side.

"What will happen to him?" Blake asked.

Aeron looked down at Owen, who stared back at her numbly.

"If we do nothing, he's bound to die." She inspected his arm wound. "It's so cold, his blood's already frozen, but I suppose that's one less thing for us to worry about."

"How can we warm him?" Moirin asked, looking on.

"We need to collect everything we have: blankets, jackets, and bedrolls."

Aeron stood to help Moirin find what they had, while Blake watched Owen. If they were going to warm him, Blake knew Owen would start bleeding again. To protect against this, Blake tore a strip from his own shirt and wrapped it tight around the warrior's bloody forearm.

Owen's breathing was shallow, barely there. It was as if the frailty of his body had become all-consuming. His already pale skin had turned white, and hardened to the touch.

Blake knew then that Owen would die on the mountain. It was strange to think that the former knight had braved King Alderic's service, survived the confines of prison, and fought off the forces of Brecktvin, only to die of cold.

Lost in this despairing thought, Blake was caught off-guard when Owen suddenly bolted upright.

Owen began tearing at his own shirt, stripping the clothing from his eerily composed body. His bare chest was exposed to the bitter cold, a wild look in his eye.

Blake scrambled to stand, trying to hold Owen back and reclothe him. Owen pushed him, and Blake fell backwards onto the very edge of the path. He could feel nothing lay under his shoulder, and he tensed, aware of the steep drop beneath him.

Blake reached his hand out, searching for a hold to bring him back to solid ground. His deadened fingers felt blindly for rescue.

Aeron had rushed forward and subdued Owen. She pressed her arm against his neck, forcing him back to the ground.

He struggled against her briefly, before he stopped, exhausted by the attempt.

Blake's fingers found a jutting rock, and he pulled himself back to safety, his heart hammering. He leaned back against the side of the mountain and watched as Aeron and Moirin wrapped Owen's body in every remaining cloth they had. Though this would keep whatever warmth was left in his body, it also served to restrain him, keeping his arms tight against his sides.

Though the path was narrow, Moirin led the smallest of the horses forward. She brought the steed to lay beside Owen, it's heat warming the deathly cold warrior.

They stayed there for some time. Owen's eyes were closed, and Aeron would pinch his skin twice each hour to check his blood flow.

Finally, they could wait no longer. While Owen's heartbeat had grown stronger, and his breathing had become more normal, he was not yet conscious. Moirin and Aeron tied him to the horse's saddle, still tightly wound in cloth, and they resumed their journey, all but Owen on foot.

On that night, they began the descent toward Linwood. Though the night was bitter cold, by morning the air had warmed a little.

Owen had yet to awaken, but Aeron was encouraged by the warm color gradually coming back to his skin.

"Will there be any damage?" Blake asked. "He's been asleep nearly a day."

"His body should recover," Aeron nodded. "He may be in pain for a little while."

"What about his mind?" Blake asked.

"I'm hardly trained in medicine," Aeron laughed. "My guess: there'll be no more damage than there was before."

32

In the final day on the mountain, Owen regained consciousness. He did not leave the saddle, but he began to move. They unbound his limbs and, though his skin was still tinged with signs of death, he seemed nearly returned to himself.

Blake's muscles ached, and he could scarce believe it when he saw the outline of a town at the base of the mountain. He could see farms by the northern perimeter of Linwood, and the beginnings of the large forest surrounding the southern side of the mountain town. It was already evening, but the four were miraculously energized by the end in sight and their pace quickened as they reached Linwood.

The air was cool, but much warmer than the climate of the mountain they had endured. Based on Aeron's description, Blake had expected to see a lively, bustling town, but found instead that Linwood lay deserted. They rode their horses through the streets, which were covered in a fine layer of hoary stone powder, the color of the mountain rock.

Night had fallen, and sounds of the forest surrounded them, though they were distant. The mountain still towered above, but the surrounding trees brought a warmth, an embrace, to the town of Linwood.

The doors of each residence and establishment were shut. The buildings were made from a combination of wood and mountain stone, and the closed doors were painted bright colors, contrasting with the white-grey rock material.

The stillness of the town sent a wave of tension through the four travelers, as they searched for any sign of human life within the walls. The dusky smolder of evening was curtailed by the glowing streetlights on every corner, which sat on posts high above their heads.

"Something's wrong," Aeron muttered. "It was not like this before."

"Is it abandoned?" Blake asked.

Moirin shook her head. "I think not." She pointed above them. "The streetlamps are glowing. Oil must be refilled regularly, and for not one lamp to be without flame indicates that they are well maintained."

They came to a building at the center of the town. It was made of the same dusty stone material as the others, and its door was painted a bright green. The sign above read: 'The Linwood Inn'.

Moirin knocked on the door, and Blake caught a movement at the window of the second floor. The curtain was drawn back briefly, before being pulled closed. After a few moments, they could hear the shuffling of feet behind the door.

"Who are you?" a feminine voice came through the door. "What do you want?"

"We are travelers in search of rooms for the night," Moirin responded. "It is growing dark, and we are in need of rest. May we come in?"

The footsteps retreated, before returning, joined by others. "Where are you coming from?" a second voice inquired.

"From Rieville," Moirin responded: a half-truth.

Blake could catch a few whispered words, as the two behind the door seemed to debate opening it. "But there are four of them," was responded to with: "We know nothing about them," before the two descended into indistinct murmuring.

Finally, they were gratified by the sound of a deadbolt coming undone, and the green door swung open. A man and woman stood behind the door, and ushered the travelers inside with panicked motions of their hands. With everyone inside, the couple resecured the bolt and the woman stood with her back leaning against the door, as if this were the only way to ensure it was fully closed.

The man began, "I am Nathan, and this is my wife, Hasna."

"We thank you for your hospitality. I do not know how we would have fared in a ghost town," Moirin said, managing to sound distantly polite.

"I see you are all in a sorry state," Hasna said, looking the travelers over, her eyes lingering on Owen's bloodied forearm.

"What happened to Linwood?" Aeron asked. "The town seems deserted."

The man and woman exchanged a weighty look, before Nathan responded, "the town is far from deserted, but our people are afraid to leave their homes or open their doors as nightfall nears." He kicked at the dusty floorboards. "Not that it does much good."

"We all go out to the lake once a day, in the morning..." Hasna began, but trailed off before finishing her sentence.

"What happens in the morning?" Blake asked.

"You may curse the luck which brought you to Linwood," she responded, setting her jaw.

Blake could tell the woman was serious in her concern and, even through his fatigue, he felt fear rise within his breast.

"What keeps your people in their homes?" he pressed.

"This monster," Hasna began quietly, as though afraid of being overheard, "The Horror of Linwood—"

"They should not trouble themselves with this now, they should rest," Nathan said, his own tiredness showing.

Hasna turned to him. "Why wait? They were damned by their mere entry to this town. You know as well as I do that no traveler has yet escaped the clutches of the beast."

"What is the Horror of Linwood?" Aeron asked, her words cutting through the mounting argument.

Hasna cast her husband a final annoyed glance, before turning back to Aeron.

"Every morning, we go to the lake in the woods. We fear this being, this monster. It writes on the walls, calling itself the Beast of Erkynon: child of the death goddess and a mortal man." She took a deep breath before continuing, "one of our people is taken in the night, and the next morning we find them in the lake, their body covered in cuts and markings."

"I someone abducted every night?" Blake asked.

"No, and it's been over a week since the last body. With each victimless passing day, our fear grows. This is why we do not go out after evening, and why no travelers pass through the town." She paused. "At least...they don't get very far."

"Why do the people not leave?" Moirin asked.

"Because it is impossible to travel beyond the woods or mountain base before night falls. A few have tried, and each time we found them the next morning." She did not need to say more for Blake to grasp her meaning.

"If that is all, then we should rest," Moirin stated, seemingly unintrigued by the Horror of Linwood. "We have travelled far, and must take advantage of this shelter." She nodded to Nathan and Hasna. "I appreciate the warning, and assure you that we will be vigilant."

Without another word on the subject, the innkeepers led them up the stairs to a series of empty rooms. Moirin gave the pair a handful of coins in payment.

Whether it was true or not, it was clear that the innkeepers were genuine in their fear of the Horror of Linwood. Aeron and Blake exchanged a brief, confused glance before parting in the hallway. Blake did not know what to make of this supposed monster, only that it had struck angst within the people of Linwood: the deserted streets were proof enough of this.

Each went into a room, except for Owen. Taking bedclothes from one of the chambers, he made a small sleeping place for himself in the hallway, so as to better guard against trespassers.

Blake entered the room. It was a small space, with painted white walls and dark wood trim. The sun had set outside and Nathan provided him with a candle, which he placed on a table by the bed.

It was strange being alone. This was the first time, since they had left Rieville, that Blake had been away from his travelling companions. He closed the door and looked at each of the room's four corners. Despite whatever manner of monster the innkeepers claimed lay waiting in the darkness, he felt more protected than he had in days.

The walls were thin, and he could hear Aeron pacing in the room next to him. She had not slept but a little since they discovered the dead bandits. He said a silent prayer to Sylas, the god of wanderers, that she might find rest that night.

Blake dropped onto the bed, going over in his mind the plan for escape. He had seen briefly a layout of the town from the mountain, and had seen Moirin's map of the area. There was a castle to the south-west of Linwood, the nearest sign of others, and it was to here that Blake would travel. Still laying on his back, he rummaged absently through the belongings he had set on the floor by the bed. He was taking only a few items and some money, not wanting to weigh himself down.

He would leave early in the morning, after taking full advantage of the roof over his head. It would be days before he reached the south-western castle, and he could not pass up a few hours in a warm bed for the sake of expediency.

Footsteps approached rapidly in the hallway, before Blake's door was thrown open forcefully, the wood slamming against the wall. Blake started, as he watched Moirin barrel into the room, lines of anger etched across her face.

"Where is it?" she asked.

"Where is what?" Blake responded, thoroughly bewildered.

She held aloft the brown paper packaging. "The key. It's gone."

"And you think I took it?" Blake forced himself to remain calm.

"Owen would not take the key, and Aeron's hands are so large and clumsy that I would have caught her the moment she tried to steal anything. You, street thief, are the only one who could have lifted the key from me undetected."

Perhaps it was a remaining effect of the freezing mountain air, or perhaps the lack of sleep had taken a greater toll on Blake's mind than anticipated. Either way, it took him a moment to put together what must have happened regarding the key.

The last time he had seen the key was in Rieville, shortly before offering Nahia some instruction in pickpocketing. While it might clear his name, he would not give Moirin this information, as it would only serve to underline his own idiocy.

"Have you nothing to say for yourself? Perhaps it would be better had I left you in the king's prison," Moirin spat.

Blake stood up from the edge of the bed, discarding any pretense of composure. "Do you think for a moment that I would be so foolish as to steal the key and then remain in your company, riding by your side?" he shouted back. "I think these things through and apparently, of the people in this room, I am alone in that."

Moirin pushed him, and he fell back onto the bed. "Yet it is gone," she responded.

The noise had drawn both Aeron and Owen to the door. Blake made to stand again, but he saw Owen's fingers tighten on the axe handle and remained seated, taking a deep breath before continuing in a lowered voice.

"I did not steal your key. Besides, what use would I have for it? I could continue the search without the map, and pursued by both you and the Blackdog King, but that hardly seems a prudent path." He held his hand out. "Give me the packaging."

Moirin handed it to him, doing nothing to disguise her distrust of the thief.

Blake took the candle into his hands, inspecting the worn packaging in the low, flickering light. "It is possible that I can work with this. The key has rested in this paper for years, and its outline is clearly imprinted." He sighed as he felt the strains of commitment wrench him further. "It will likely fail, but I do remember the approximate size of the key. I will redraw this and tomorrow bring the sketch to the blacksmith, so he can create a copy based on these specifications."

Moirin opened her mouth to speak, but Blake cut her off. "The key will, by nature, be difficult to replicate. If we had the lock I would be able to make adjustments to the copy and there would be a better chance of it working."

Moirin looked down at Blake. Her chest rose and fell, and she looked as though she might speak. Instead, she nodded curtly at Blake and left the room, followed by Owen.

Aeron stayed for a moment in the doorway. The light showed the contour of the weariness beneath her eyes, and the care that marked her brow.

Blake offered a perfunctory smile, as Aeron closed the door to his room. He flopped back on the bed, and stared up at the ceiling, the crumpled paper resting against his chest. His plans would be put on hold for one more day. Not because he was reluctant to leave, but because he refused to give Moirin the satisfaction of his untimely betrayal.

He set his elbows on the window frame and looked out into the night. The sun had long since set, and the light of the moon and lamps was cast against the dusted roads, making the town of Linwood glow silver.

He caught a movement in the street. A man left one door, which was closed quickly behind him. He sprinted through the road, white dust flying at his heels. He reached a second home and pounded frantically on the door. Words were exchanged, and the door was opened and quickly shut behind him. Blake could practically hear the sound of the bolt.

Blake climbed into the bed and was soon asleep. He slept soundly through the night, awaking early to trace the shape of the key from the paper. When he was done, he tucked both his tracing and the neatly folded wrapping into his pocket.

He met the others downstairs in a small dining room. It was obvious the innkeepers had not housed guests in some time. They tripped over each other as they rushed to bring breakfast foods to the table.

"Despite the monster, Linwood's offerings are not blighted," Hasna said as she set a loaf of bread on the table. "Our soil is rich, and our animals graze freely on lush, green grass. I doubt even the markets of Conrisia could feed you better."

Blake was inclined to agree. The foods they brought were nothing less than a feast. He consumed the bread, slathered with salted butter, and eggs fried on an iron griddle. He sank his teeth hungrily into fresh beef, grateful to find tender, succulent meat rather than the desiccated, heavily salted fare to which he had grown accustomed.

Best of all, the innkeepers brought to the table a pot of dark, hot coffee. Tea may have been the customary drink in Conrisia and many of the surrounding cities, but coffee was common in the Isle of Ang, and was the treat Blake had been raised to enjoy. He stirred in two spoonfuls of sugar, and a healthy dose of fresh milk. It was almost absurdly sweet, but it was the way he liked it.

Taking the first sip, he was flooded by the overwhelming sweetness and the bitter, roasted taste of the coffee. He drank deep from the cup, and all his senses felt more awakened, as the mild, lightheaded sensation took hold of him. He remembered the sights of his early years. He could see vividly in his mind's eye the fishermen returning with their catch, and drinking strong coffee as they looked out at the water, satisfied with their day's work.

He sat back in his chair, his haggard body feeling warmed and nourished by the drink, which comforted him in a way nothing else had since the day of his capture.

When they were finished eating, Blake noticed the innkeepers exchange a brief and sorrowful look. Remembering Hasna's comment from the night before, Blake stood up from the table.

"Are the townspeople going to the lake?" he asked.

The man nodded wordlessly, his wife taking his hand in her own. "They will be heading there now."

"I would like to go with them," Blake said, his curiosity about the state of the town and Horror nagging him beyond his ability to withstand it.

He looked to the table, where his companions sat. "As would we," Moirin added, speaking for the others. She rose, setting her napkin down on the tabletop. "Thank you both for this breakfast. We have not eaten this well in a long time," she said to the innkeepers.

They walked with the innkeepers down the street, where many townsfolk were converging on the small road. Few people spoke, the procession holding a mournful atmosphere.

As they passed through the street, people filtered out of their homes, joining the movement toward the lake. In the doorways sat the older children, who appeared to be caring for the younger. The children watched as the adults walked past the businesses and houses. Some watched in silence, others cried, but all seemed to grasp the gravity of the custom.

The walls were scrawled with writing. Already, a few of the townsfolk who stayed behind were busy scrubbing the words away. As they passed, Blake could read what little remained legible.

I am the child of Erkynon.

Blake remained silent as they continued the journey to the lake. He felt his anticipation growing as he walked with the others. He knew of Erkynon, as well as any in Vesia did, though he knew only little of her Beast. He remembered some stories that the demigod would raise the dead, but he could recall little else besides.

The crowd surrounded the lake, and it felt as though they were collectively holding their breaths. The lake was vast, and Blake could not see the other side well from where he stood. After a time, a shout was heard, and a word was passed through the crowd until it reached the place where the small band of travelers waited.

Aeron shifted to the side, while Owen looked across the lake. He was no longer bleeding, though the blood-soaked fabric was still tight around his forearm.

The innkeepers bowed their heads with the others of Linwood, and Blake looked to Hasna for clarification.

"There is no body this morning," she said, her tone a mixture of regret and relief. "We will wait for the next day."

It was a strange way the people of Linwood had adopted. It was as though they feared delaying the inevitable more than they feared the deaths of their own. The crowd dispersed, making their way back to the town in a less orderly fashion than they had employed in their trip to the lake.

When they returned to the town, parents pulled their children into their arms, and men and women returned to work.

Blake was given directions to the blacksmith, while Moirin and Owen went in search of information on 'Split Oak' and Aeron set out to find the nearest tavern.

Blake watched Aeron leave, troubled by the sorrow that accompanied her. He would be gone by the next morning, and knew he should not worry himself with the others' affairs. Still, he found himself following her, compelled by an indistinct force.

"Why don't you accompany me to the blacksmith?" he asked, touching the crook of her arm.

Aeron shook her head. "I'd prefer to be alone right now with a strong ale."

Blake was tempted to let her go, but instead he pulled on her arm, bringing the woman to a halt. "I may need protection in my errand. I am, after all, reluctant to become the next victim of this self-proclaimed demigod."

Aeron looked at Blake critically, before relenting. "Once the key is made, I'll continue my journey to the tavern."

Blake responded, "I swear, I will ask nothing more of you."

They made their way to the blacksmith who, Blake was relieved to see, was stoking a fire for the day ahead.

Having braved the bitter cold of the mountains, and the subtle coolness of Linwood, the dry heat of the blacksmith's forge came as a welcome relief to Blake. As soon as he crossed the threshold, it was as though he were drawn into a fiery embrace that warmed every inch.

Blake explained the task to him, and showed him the figure he had drawn that morning. He felt foolish holding out his simple outline, all the while understanding the difficulty of the thing he asked.

The blacksmith nodded, unperturbed by the strangeness of the request. He was a young man with blond hair tied into a thin, tight braid. The lightness of his hair was smudged with dark streaks from the soot, and so early in the day his cheek already bore a swipe of black ash, showing where he had absentmindedly brushed his hand against his face.

Blake waited with his back to the wall, while he and Aeron watched the blacksmith work. Even the bandit queen seemed to forget her sorrows, becoming entranced by the process unfolding before them.

The blacksmith found a strip of metal previously set aside, and hammered it down to approximately the thickness Blake had specified. From that point, he used a series of instruments to match the shape Blake had drawn on the piece of paper.

Blake watched this development closely. He had deliberately made the outline slightly wider than what he believed to be the specifications of the key. While he would eventually need the copy to be the correct thinness, he would be better able to make adjustments if the metal could be filed down when he had the lock in front of him.

In the midst of these thoughts he remembered that by the next morning he would be far from Moirin and the others, unable to fit the key to the lock. He felt the flush of shame creep over him, but there was nothing to be done. He had decided long before that cowardice would triumph over his better nature, and knew that this would leave Moirin's charge unfulfilled. It was a price he would gladly pay for his life.

He compensated the blacksmith for the work and took the fresh key into his hand, the metal still warm from manipulation. Stepping outside, he felt his lungs pull in clean air, met by the coolness of the outdoors.

He turned his attention to Aeron. She still had a distant look on her face, no longer able to forget her pain in the practiced movement of the blacksmith.

They went to the tavern, and sat on the ground by the side of the street. Aeron drank from a tankard of ale, while Blake enjoyed another cup of cloyingly sweet coffee. The piping hot liquid warmed his hands as he held the white clay cup between his bare palms.

The tavern had been empty, Aeron and Blake the only patrons within sight. The streets were similarly deserted. Though daylight was still upon them, the people of Linwood wasted no time out of doors, as though afraid night would come but a minute early. Those passing through passed quickly, before secreting themselves away. The two travelers sat by the light dusty street, looking out at a row of colorfully painted doors.

"What are you thinking about?" Blake asked Aeron, breaking the silence that had stretched between them since their departure from the blacksmith.

Aeron kept her eyes fixed on the street. "I feel I failed them. It's my fault they were in the farmhouse, having just given shelter to an enemy of the Blackdog King."

Blake said nothing, knowing his words would do little good.

"They were lucky their deaths were by the king's soldiers," Aeron continued. "Had they been caught by vigilantes, their deaths would have been by torture or public spectacle." She let out a bitter laugh. "I should thank King Alderic."

Blake put his hand over her shoulder, resting his coffee cup against the side of his knee. "They know you could not have served them more loyally, nor worked harder to ensure their welfare. You took us in out of obligation, and there is no reason for you to feel shame. You acted with the honor and integrity of any great leader."

He was accustomed to speaking in such a way that ran contrary to his own actions, but never before had it cut so near to his life's blood. His own cowardice sprang to mind and he could no longer meet her eyes, so he kept his face downcast as he left his hand where it lay.

"I am glad you're here," Aeron said, relenting a little. "Even with your refined ways, you're different than Moirin or Owen. You remind me a little of the ones I lost." She looked at him with a smile. "But don't let it get to your head."

In spite of himself, Blake laughed. He kicked a small stone into the road with the toe of his shoe. It hopped a few times against the cobblestones before coming to rest. Given the desertion of the streets, the stone lay undisturbed.

He felt the weight of Aeron's head against his shoulder, but nothing could compare to the burden he felt in his chest. This pain served only to steel him further against the sentimentality that would stay his actions. No sense of loyalty or honor could sway him from his chosen path.

He swirled the coffee in his cup, watching the liquid brush rhythmically against the sides.

He hoped he was doing the right thing, though he knew it to be something else entirely.

They returned to the inn as night was just beginning to fall. It was easy to see that they were the last people in the streets as the sky turned to a brilliant shade of red, fading gradually into black. By the time darkness came, they were ensconced in the safety of the white-grey rock walled lodgings.

Alone in his room, Blake pulled the pack onto the bed, emptying it over the blanket. He would only take with him what he needed, and he sorted the items by order of necessity. He had a small amount of money, a cloak and blanket, as well as the weapons Moirin had given him outside the castle walls on the night they escaped from the king's prison. He repacked only these items, the bag's weight now halved.

He set the pack in the corner of the room, where it would be out of the way should he receive an unexpected visit from one of his companions. The smell of food drifted up the stairs, and Blake could feel himself beginning to salivate. After the sumptuous breakfast, his imagination filled with the vast possibilities dinner at the inn presented.

He joined the others downstairs. The dining room was empty apart from them, and they sat around the same table as directed by the innkeeper. A fire burned in the hearth, warming the room, and lighting the walls with a soothing glow.

In the light of the fire, Blake could see Aeron's eyes staring back from the circles that marked her unrest. When Blake looked at her, she shot a bright smile his way, though there was something empty in its nature. She was the one he felt the most guilt abandoning. The smile dropped slightly from her face and she returned to her absent study of the table, digging her thumbnail into the crease of the wood.

Moirin stared into the distance, the flames making her dark eyes appear black. It was obvious her mind was still on the map; Blake doubted there was a time when the mysterious document strayed far from her thoughts. A frown was across her lips, and a small crease formed at her brow.

Blake sat down in the chair opposite Moirin's, and he slid the replica key across the table. "It will need to be filed down once we have the lock, but it should be around the right thickness." He shrugged, not wishing to make much of his skill. "Working the key from this point will be simple, and there is even a slight chance that the key will work in the lock in its present state."

Moirin picked up the key, and looked it over.

"I am sorry for my accusation last night," she said, barely concealing the struggle through which the words found life.

"I understand."

"I did not believe you to be trustworthy, yet you continue to show yourself to be surprisingly invaluable to this effort," she said. "I hope you can forgive my mistake."

Blake nodded, though he silently begged her to quit her praise.

He turned his attention to Owen who sat beside her, reserved as usual. He was surprised to find his stare was met with one in like. Owen's eyes searched his face, avidly looking for something Blake could not distinguish.

Blake wondered if Owen could sense his intention to leave, or whether he was simply prone to study of his companions. Either way, Blake grew uncomfortable having his gaze returned, so he let his eyes wander the room, eventually drawn in the direction of the kitchen by the clanging pots and pans.

The door opened and both innkeepers came through, bearing food haphazardly on a wide wooden tray. Nathan set a hot bowl of soup before each guest, and a fresh loaf of bread at the center of the table. Hasna brought them salted butter, water, and ale.

"Is there anything more we can offer you?" Nathan asked.

"This is in excess of anything we could have expected," Moirin responded.

"In truth, it has been many months since we had any guests," Hasna said. "We are pleased to practice our hospitality."

The sadness in the woman's voice reminded Blake of the town's struggle with the monster somewhere outside the inn's door. The couple returned to the kitchen, leaving their guests alone with the warmth of the food and fire to draw their minds from the troubles which lay ahead.

The soup nourished both the bodies and the travel-weary wills of the group: potatoes, carrots, broad beans, and barley stewed in a hearty tomato broth. The bread was heavily crusted, and when Aeron tore it in half at the center, it released a puff of steam and the rich, yeasted smell of fresh baking.

Blake heaped butter onto a handful of bread, and dipped the piece into the broth, soaking it through and melting the butter to a shimmering puddle. When he bit into it, the bread was tender, releasing the savory warmth of the soup and the salty fat of the butter in a single, delicious mouthful.

As Blake split a boiled carrot piece in half with his spoon, he wondered if he was making a mistake by leaving. As the hour of his departure neared, it was difficult to avoid a sense of regret. Here, in the warmth of the fire, filling his stomach with cooked vegetables, he had regained his sense of safety. He thought for a moment of going upstairs, and unpacking his bag; his companions would be none the wiser.

However, his mind was again besieged by images of the slain bandits. It was altogether too easy for to picture himself among the dead and, for this reason, he knew he must depart. No thrill of adventure nor sense of indebtedness could justify sharing their fate.

After dinner, they sat by the fire a while. Owen began lightly humming a song to himself, and Blake found he recognized the old tune. It was a country song of harvest, strange to hear from one such as Owen. Blake remembered how Moirin had described Owen before his service to Alderic: the young man filled with joy, and wondered if he was glimpsing this underlying nature.

As Owen continued humming, Blake joined in, quietly singing the words:

"Leaves of red and golden wheat Dance in the breeze, mark harvest's feast Bring bread and ale into the field So we can share the ample yield

Kind farmer sing and children play Make bright your eyes this autumn day"

Owen looked up at Blake, his lips almost smiling. The hint of humor appeared almost tragic on as mangled a face as his.

"I am surprised a Conrisian knows this song," Blake said.

"I am from elsewhere in Vesia," Owen reminded the thief, tilting his head slightly to the side. "Though I have not been home since," he added.

Blake wanted to ask more about Owen's life before King Alderic, but hesitated to pry too deeply. He would be gone soon, and it would do him little good to know such things.

Aeron spun a triangular piece of wood back and forth across the hearth, paying little attention to the exchange between Owen and Blake. The piece was charred from its brief time in the fire, and left her fingertips smudged with the ashes. He could tell her mind was occupied by her executed comrades, and he wondered what she would do if she ever came across the Blackdog King and his soldiers.

The hour grew late and Blake excused himself from their company. He paused at the bottom of the stairs and cast a final glance upon the gathering, knowing it was likely the last time he would see any of them again.

Back in his room, Blake moved quickly, he wanted to put as much distance as he could between himself and the others before sunrise. While King Alderic should not arrive for at least one more day, he did not want to be found sharing Moirin's company were the king's soldiers to arrive in Linwood any earlier. Without further hesitation, he wrapped himself in the cloak and threw the pack on his shoulders.

He did not fear the Horror of Linwood. While he did not doubt the sincerity of the townsfolk's fears, he would not allow this to inhibit his actions. Though he had faith in the gods, in all his travels through the cities of Vesia, he had not once seen signs of a demigod. Even the single liogan he had come across was less than impressive in his show of skill.

He would not be able to go out through the hallway, because Owen had set his post there. Besides, the front door was heavily secured by the innkeepers, and he would not be able to barricade it behind him. Despite the spinelessness of this act, he would not willingly put their lives in danger.

He opened the window slowly, wincing at the scrape of the wood in its frame. He was on the second story, and the fall would only be around ten feet. With no fear of injury, he concerned himself with the sound he might create upon hitting the ground.

In the room, the windowsill was at the height of his sternum. He set his palms on the edge, and jumped slightly to bring himself onto the wooden ledge. He straddled the sill, one leg in the room and one leg out.

Looking down, it seemed he was higher up than ten feet. He slipped the pack off, and hooked it over the toe of his boot. He brought his other leg outside, and turned to face the inside of the room. He lowered himself out the window, so he was holding on by his fingertips. He dropped the pack to the ground, relieved to find that it made only a slight thud.

He looked down to ensure he would not land on the bag, before letting go. He fell to the side, rolling from his right ankle to his shoulder. He stayed still a moment on the ground to ensure he had not drawn attention to himself. The streets were empty, and he had no reason to fear discovery.

Standing, he brushed his clothes off, and pulled the pack back onto his shoulders. Blake looked back up at the window. Even should he change his mind, he doubted anyone would open their doors this late, and the window sill was far out of his reach.

The night was cool and still in the embrace of the valley, a pleasant change from the harsh conditions they had withstood on the mountain. His bones ached at the memory, and he shook the chill that had spread over him.

The streets were silent, as each man, woman and child had tucked themselves behind bolted doors. The street lamps continued to burn, though Blake found himself resenting the glow they cast, as it only increased the likelihood of his discovery.

He began his walk to the stable where the horses were kept, referring to his mental mapping of the town. All the streets looked the same in the darkness, as the different colored doors were difficult to distinguish in the lamplight.

The streets abandoned, the stars shone all the brighter. It had been many years since Blake had taken the time to look up at the night sky in earnest. He took a moment to do so then, remembering how fragile life could be: a cruel reminder that, had the timing been different, he would be dead twice by King Alderic's hand.

Blake cast a final glance at the vast expanse of the sky, before returning his attention to the empty street. Walking along the road, he was suddenly aware of the sound of footsteps behind him. He prayed he was merely hearing the echo of his own steps resounding through the dark street. Still, he reached for his dagger, preparing himself for a fight.

The footsteps quickened, falling out of pace with his own, as they grew closer.

His heart thudded frantically in his chest, and he readied himself to confront his follower. Before he could turn, he felt a sharp pain radiate from a single point at the back of his head. He had been knocked senseless before, and the thought that he must have been struck crossed his mind as his vision faded to a familiar oblivion.

33

Alderic reached the town of Linwood in the early hours of morning, his tired soldiers fortified by the knowledge that soon they would rest indoors. They masked their weariness well, keeping their backs straight and their eyes diligently focused on the road ahead.

The only one seemingly unaffected by the long journey and lack of sleep was Callum. He kept doggedly by the king's side, his eyes flitting to Alderic every few minutes in hypervigilance. Instead of being exhausted by the hardships, he displayed more vigor than ever. Yet, Alderic was sure the knight's caution concerning his king would fade as he became more battle-tried.

They rode into town, and saw the streets deserted. It was early yet, and light was only just beginning to sweep across the land. Painted doors lined the streets with color, and the horses' hooves clapped against the dusty cobblestones, sharp in the still morning

They continued through the empty roads, and Alderic could see that the windows of the bottom floors in each house were boarded up. He remembered Nahia's tale of the Horror of Linwood, and wondered how much truth this fantastical tale held. He would not waste time waiting to be greeted, and immediately sent one of his soldiers to climb the bell tower.

She rang the bell; the tolling echoed through the streets, and Alderic brought his soldiers to a halt. He dismounted and handed his reins to Callum.

Doors began to open, and Alderic could see faces look out timidly through windows and doorframes at the Blackdog banner borne by the soldiers, before the townsfolk filtered into the streets. They saw the Alderic's ring, and the bronze sword by his side: the signs of his kingship. After only a moment's hesitation, they crowded to stand before him in a sea of ragged clothes and exultant faces.

They pressed their hands to him, touching his clothing and his hair. Some wept, and their mumbled entreaties fell over each other, dissolving into an indecipherable murmur.

Alderic was unsure of how to react to this greeting. At first, his fingers sought the hilt of his sword. Their closeness set him on edge and instinct urged him to protect himself; usually Vesians greeted him with fear or hatred. However, it was clear that the people of Linwood intended him no harm. Their words were either praise of his kingship, or pleas for help.

One man fell to the ground before the king, and soon the others followed. Alderic stood before the prostrate villagers, their clothing covered in the rock dust of the streets, trying to make out the nature of their appeal to him.

Unwilling to lose another minute unnecessarily, he took an old man by the shoulder and pulled him to his feet.

"Tell me why your streets were deserted when we arrived, and why your people were cowering in their homes," Alderic said, letting go of the man. He wished to hear Linwood's account of this Horror.

The man kept his eyes downcast. "We are terrorized by a beast that takes our people in the night. We can only thank the gods that your highness has come."

"What happens to them?" Alderic asked.

"In the morning, we find them in the lake, dead." Tears rose to the man's eyes. "Everyone here has lost someone they love to this monster."

Those same words were often applied to his own reign, and struck deep within Alderic. He looked out at the gathering crowd. Faces were upturned towards him, their eyes desperately searching for the promise symbolized by their king.

Alderic was well aware of the legendary status his exploits had reached. In the eyes of the people, he was omnipotent. In hours of need his villainous nature was transformed to a means of salvation. No one was stronger than he and if he could not defeat the monster, they were truly without hope.

"Very well," Alderic responded with a sigh. He would not leave Linwood in a state of distress while it lay beneath his protection. Besides, it had been too long since he had faced such a distinctive adversary.

"When did this begin?"

The old man answered. "Nearly one year ago. Since then we have lost twenty-five of our people. They are found covered in cuts and markings floating in the lake."

"The markings, do they mean anything to you?"

"There have been messages," a woman said from the back of the crowd, diverting from his question. "It writes on the walls at night, calling itself the true child of Erkynon."

At the mention of the Beast of Erkynon, Alderic felt his heartbeat suddenly quicken.

Only weeks before, his hands had touched the well-worn pages of the book, his eyes dwelling upon the symbols and illustrations, the carefully written words of the tale.

Alderic lived in hope that the Beast of Erkynon would be revealed, that the legend of Death Sin would prove true. Alderic had always kept his faith in the gods, yet he feared that this single legend would not match the expectations he had built upon since childhood.

He took a deep breath, unwilling to believe too quickly in Death Sin's existence in Linwood.

"It is an old story," the old woman explained. "The goddess of death, Erkynon, fell in love with a mortal man and birthed a child. It is a demigod who wanders our world, while within it lies the power to bring the dead to life. One who cannot be killed, yet bleeds when cut."

"I am well-aware of the legend surrounding the Beast of Erkynon," Alderic said. The corners of his mouth twitched downward. "It is an intriguing tale, but it is difficult to believe any human could think themselves to be Death Sin."

The old woman lowered her voice. "Truthfully, your highness, there are many among us who believe it too."

"I will rid you of this monster, though I was brought to Linwood by other matters. I am searching for a group of travelers, two women and two men. If they arrived in town, it would have been in the past few days. If anyone has any information, speak now."

A man came forward, clutching a cap in his hands. His knuckles turned white as they pulled against the fabric. "My wife and I own an inn." His voice trembled as he spoke. "Last night, two men and two women spent the night in our establishment."

"Describe them." Alderic responded.

"Well, one woman was older, very large and strong, puts a true fear in you just looking on her. I was half-afraid for my chairs." He laughed uncomfortably, "The other was rather small. She had brown skin, and dark eyes, with long hair she kept in a braid tied with string. Not very pretty, but I suppose that is not for me to say."

The innkeeper rattled on with his descriptions, Alderic becoming increasingly annoyed with the man's disorganized speech.

"Of the men, one was tall and pale, with very long, light hair. He had a cut on his face, going right across a dead eye. Real wiry, but somehow looked close to death's doorstep. The other was smaller with brown hair. Seemed quiet. Nothing notable about him, I'm afraid. Although, I suppose it I were pressed, I would say—"

Alderic interrupted him, not wasting a second more on the man's nervous ramblings. "Where are they?"

"When we saw your highness through the window, we went to rouse them. You can imagine our surprise when we found they were gone. They had paid for the night anyhow, so we didn't think too much on their leaving," he responded.

The innkeeper offered to lead them to his establishment. Alderic gave the signal for his soldiers to stay, while a tilt of his head prompted Callum to accompany him to the inn.

They searched the rooms, but the travelers had left nothing of significance behind, much as Alderic had expected. The innkeepers apologized profusely for not having stopped them, but Alderic stepped into the street, refusing to indulge them.

He turned to Callum, who leaned in the doorway.

"Find them."

Callum nodded, obvious excitement building within him at the chance to test his mettle. He took his leave of the king, and Alderic watched from the doorway as Callum deployed soldiers in search of the outlaws. A few were held back, sent instead to gather information from the people of Linwood regarding the 'Split Oak'.

If the outlaws were to be found in Linwood, the novice knight would find them.

Alderic did not believe that Moirin would be imprudent enough to stay in Linwood, had they already located 'Split Oak' and retrieved whatever lay there. Regardless, he held the golden key. This would cripple their efforts, assuring him enough time to focus on ending the supposed demigod that terrorized the town of the mountain.

Alone, he made his way to the lake. The dirt path turned to grass, and he tied his horse's reins to a nearby tree branch. Proceeding on foot, he enjoyed the soft give of the ground beneath his well-worn, black boots.

The water was surrounded by a dense circle of trees, hidden far from the view of the town. He reached a point where all he could see was the arching green of the trees surrounding him, and the blue sky reflected on the lake's surface.

The smell of water and decaying leaves filled his senses, and he breathed deep the brisk smell of the forest, his weary chest welcoming the restorative air. He walked the long perimeter of the lake, hoping for some sign of a frequently trod path into the woods; some indication of where the monster's hideout lay. He found none.

The king sat by the side of the lake. Sunlight glimmered on the water, and a warmth filled the unmoved air. He pulled the boot from his right foot, followed by that of the left. He then undid the buckle of his belt, and drew it away from his waist. The secured weapons were carried along, as he set the leather boots and belt on the ground beside him. Alderic stripped off his remaining clothing, laying them by his weapons on the shore. Naked, he stepped into the water.

The lake rose to meet him. He walked until his feet could no longer reach the rich mire below. He dipped his head beneath the surface, and swam to the center of the lake. The cold of the clear essence soothed his muscles, sore from the weeks on horseback. The lake embraced his chaste body with its tranquil waters.

He stayed there for some time, enjoying the play of the water on his pale skin. From the center of the lake, he looked out into the forest surrounding him. He had nearly forgotten his reason for coming there, when his attention was drawn to a flickering light deep within the woods. He narrowed his eyes, identifying the light of a fire shining out from between the trees.

He swam to the far bank of the lake, that closest to the source of the light, and came to stand on the shore. His black, wet hair clung to his shoulders and back, and his bare feet were coated with mud. He walked into the woods, twigs and stones digging into the soles of his feet with each step.

He continued in the direction of the light he had seen, though he had yet to see it again. He walked until, finally, he was gratified by the sight of a small home, surrounded on all sides by dense, rising trees. Alderic could see again the light of a fire through an open window.

He retreated back through the woods until he reached the lake, marking the place with a white stone. He would confront whatever lay within the woods alone, but to do so unarmed would be reckless.

Given the width of the lake, it would be quicker to swim back across. He stepped to the water's edge, diving below the surface where the lake was still shallow. The mud and water-grass skimmed his bare chest, as his body arced back toward the surface.

He swam to the opposite side, where he clothed and armed himself. His body still wet, his shirt dampened and adhered to him, as he fastened the belt around his middle. The bronze of his sword was cold, and he ran his finger unthinkingly along the gouge at the hilt.

Soaked strands of jet black hair fell into his face, clinging to his skin, and he brushed them away impatiently, as he walked along the lake's edge to the place by the woods he had marked with a white stone.

The sword tapped at his knee, as he travelled through the wood. He made slightly more noise, as the sticks cracked beneath his boots. This forced him to move more slowly, careful to conceal his presence.

He could see the clearing, and the small home within. He stood still at the edge, as he watched a figure emerge from the house. The figure, whom he was able to identify as a man, carried a small blade. He set the blade in a tree stump by the side of the house.

The king could see the man more clearly. There was nothing about him that suggested a demigod or liogan, but he knew it was impossible to tell by sight alone. Alderic stayed hidden, reluctant to engage too hastily with the Horror of Linwood.

34

Blake had woken briefly, and felt the sharp pain of a shoulder digging into his stomach as he was jogged with each step the person carrying him took. A burlap bag was tied around his head, and his nostrils filled with the dusty smell of jute. His hands and feet were roughly bound, and the rope dug into his flesh. He tried to struggle, and he felt a hard object strike him twice in the head, before he succumbed to unconsciousness again.

The second time he awoke, he was first aware of the searing pain that filled his skull. His hands were bound, this time behind his back. The bag was still over his head, but he could tell it was not well secured at the neck. He lowered his forehead toward the ground, and caught the edge of the bag between his knees. Raising his head, he was able to slip the jute sack. He blinked as his eyes adjusted to the new surroundings.

He was in a small room, the walls made of a rough, rotting wood. There was no furniture in the room, save for a single, lopsided chair. Sunlight filtered in through a window secured with iron bars, and the streams of light were blurred by rising layers of dust in the air.

The door to the room was slightly ajar. Blake crawled on his knees, ignoring the throbbing behind his eyes, and turned his head sideways to look through the doorway. He was off balance, given the hands tied behind his back, and steadied himself with his shoulder against the wooden frame.

He could see a man sitting on the floor in front of a roaring fire. His head was half-shaven, the hair crudely cut from his scalp, and he was dressed in rags covered in black stains. Tears spilled across his cheeks, causing a mixture of dirt and soot to become wet and run in lines down his face.

Blake could hear a quick, repetitive speech coming from beneath the man's breath. It had the intensity of a curse, and the devotion of a prayer. Blake pulled back silently, afraid to disturb his captor.

In the corner, as far as he could get from the door, Blake began a sightless examination of the ropes that bound him. While Blake had never much enjoyed the escape arts, he was not entirely untrained. When he was bound, he had been unconscious and had lost the advantage of controlling the application of the knots.

Nevertheless, his fingers strained to touch the ropes and, from the feel of his bindings, he was able to quickly identify the point of attack. He wedged a jutting knot beneath the toe of his boot and pulled his wrists back, all the while trying to separate a part of the rope with his index finger. He pulled harder, relieved when he felt it loosening. He shifted his wrists, trying to gain a more advantageous position, and offered a silent entreaty to the gods, as he felt the knot beginning to give.

As if sensing his prisoner's progress, the captor entered the room, his long hair on the side of his head falling forward to cover one eye. Blake hid the loosened knot between his wrists, turning them against each other to increase the tension of the rope. The man approached, and tugged at the ropes on his wrists and ankles. Satisfied they were tight enough, he backed away.

"Why have you brought me here?" Blake asked. He spoke in as quiet and unthreatening a tone as he could manage, afraid of angering the man. He was simply relieved that his loosening of the knot had gone unnoticed.

His captor turned away wordlessly. Blake watched, helpless, as the man left the room. He did not have time to return to his escape, before the man came back, carrying with him a large knife, and small bowl filled with black ink.

The knife was silver, and bore strange symbols along the blade. Blake did not recognize any of these markings, but they filled him with a sudden sense of dread, as if all the warmth had left his body, and his heartbeat faltered within his chest.

The man pulled Blake roughly to his knees and tilted his face up. He pushed against Blake's chest, until his captive was backed up against the wall, forced to kneel straight by the boards pressed against his back. The half-shaven man dipped his fingers into the ink, and began to draw intricate symbols on the left side of Blake's face and neck.

Blake's heart was pounding and he held his breath, too afraid to make any motion. He could feel the wet pigment drying on his skin, and his thoughts turned to the companions he had left behind in the interest of self-preservation. He was struck by the irony of the situation, and wished with all his heart that he had not left their company. If there was a lesson to be learned, it was truly too late.

The man set down the pot. Blake tried to sink back to his heels, but was prevented by the wall behind him. The man grabbed him by the shirt and pulled him back up, steadying him forcefully against the boards.

Keeping his hands on the fabric, the man tore the shirt down the middle. He picked up the ink pot, and resumed his illustration on the left side of Blake's chest.

Looking down, Blake could distinguish the symbols written across his skin. While he had not seen the victims found in the lake, he remembered what the innkeeper had told him of their year long struggle against the beast, and of the markings the bodies bore.

"Erkynon," Blake whispered.

The man stared at Blake. "Mother," he responded under his breath. The word came, husky, from the back of his throat, as if pulled from his lips involuntarily.

His worst fears confirmed, Blake felt his entire body go numb. It was as if the will to fight or escape had left him in one breath. He felt himself under renewed scrutiny from his captor.

"Why are you doing this?" Blake asked, as the Horror of Linwood looked over the markings he had already made.

There was no response.

Perhaps a direct approach was not what was called for.

"Perhaps there is a way I can better serve you. A child of a god, you should not concern yourself with so lowly a one as me," he said, regretting the tremor in his voice.

The Horror of Linwood took up the knife, and set the blade against Blake's lips. The man shook his head wordlessly, undeniably urging his prisoner to silence.

Blake nodded his submission, and the blade was withdrawn. The man took up the ink pot, and continued his painting of the torso. The ink was cold against Blake's flushed skin. The man took the silver blade, and made an incision from Blake's ribs to his navel. Blake winced as he felt the skin slit. Red blood blended with black ink, as it flowed into the lines drawn on by the captor's fingers.

The Horror of Linwood took some of Blake's blood into the ink bowl, and turned his attention back to Blake's face. He took the blood and ink, and began to illustrate his victim's left temple with the mixture.

Blake shivered, his shirt hanging in tatters off of his shoulders. He worked at the knots with his fingertips, but the attempt was slow to progress, as he was barely able to move without attracting the eye of the menace.

The dusty air clung to the inside of his throat, and he wanted nothing more than to expel it in a single, great cough. He was forced to stifle this urge, as he could only imagine the consequence that would follow, should he inadvertently harm the drawing of the symbols.

Blake could not be sure, but he thought he heard the sound of a creaking floor board in the other room. From his glance out the window, he had concluded that they were far removed from the civilization of Linwood, and he had trouble imagining anyone well-intentioned would make their way to this home.

His captor had detected the sound, and he abruptly stopped drawing. The man looked into Blake's eyes, and Blake responded with a look of confusion. The Horror of Linwood held a crooked finger to his lips in warning.

He took the wide, ritual knife in his hands, holding it tight and concealing it against his side. He rose slowly from where he had crouched in front of Blake, and walked to the door. He rolled his feet, from heel to toe, as he walked, making no sound.

Blake watched him peer cautiously through the door, and waited only a moment before resuming his attempt to loosen the knots. The man's back was to him, and he stood at the opposite end of the small room, giving Blake some comfort in knowing he would see his captor approach him before the man would notice the slackened bindings.

With a final glance back at Blake, the man stole into the other room, closing the door behind him.

35

Alderic had approached the house after he saw the inhabitant retrieve the silver blade from the tree stump. He stepped through the stone circle outside the house door, and past the threshold. He found the room empty, though a fire still burned in the hearth. The wood that made up the house had fallen into disrepair; ceiling planks were split down the middle, ready to fall, and older beams looked as though they might crumble at the lightest touch. It was impressive that the house was still standing.

He heard a movement behind him, and turned. A figure came through the doorway, not stopping when he saw the king, and Alderic drew his sword as he stood face to face with the stranger.

The man before him was a terrible sight to behold. His bones stuck out at the elbows and shoulders, visible through ink-stained and ragged clothing. His head was half shaven, with the exposed side covered in bizarre cuts and blisters, while on the other side the tangled hair fell past his shoulder. His brow was contorted in agony, and his face stained with grime and fresh tears.

Alderic was most struck by the hollow of the man's cheek bones, set beneath dark pits in which bloodshot eyes lay. The eyes stared up at him, as the man's back hunched over. His movements were feral and he looked up at the king, as though preparing to strike.

"Are you the one who leaves the bodies in the lake? He who calls himself the Beast of Erkynon?" Alderic asked.

His baritone was measured and calm, easily conveying his authority over this vagabond who, despite his life removed from society, was nonetheless one of the king's subjects.

The man looked defiantly at Alderic, his small, emaciated body not tempering the intensity with which he watched the king.

"Do you know who I am?" Alderic asked, his tired tone nonetheless dominating. He would not tolerate defiance from his subjects.

The man's eyes travelled to Alderic's ring, which bore the blackdog's visage. He hesitated, before nodding back. His hands found each other, and twisted back and forth in a wringing motion, all while his eyes remained locked on the face of his king. The fingers of his right hand were blackened with ink, which smudged across his skin as his hands knotted together, the joints becoming visibly distorted.

"I cannot allow you to continue needlessly killing my people," Alderic was strangely sorry to be speaking the words, but he knew it could not be otherwise.

The man's glare flickered and faded above his cavernous cheeks, and he nodded in subservience. In that moment, it was as if his very soul cracked in half; overwhelmed by the ruler who stood before him. His eyes left the king's face, as he fell to his knees before Alderic's boots, hitting the floor with a snapping sound.

"Forgive me, forgive me, forgive me," the man whispered through tears, his voice pleading to the floor boards. "My king, my god. To live is anguish. Please do not leave me to suffer."

The man's hair on the unshaven half of his head fell forward. His shoulders heaved with sobbing, before suddenly becoming very still. His breath came steady, and he lay his hands by his sides, palms facing upwards toward the king.

Alderic stepped down on the man's hair, pinning his forehead to the floor. Sighing, he unsheathed his sword. He paused only a moment, looking down with pity on the wretched beast who was prostrate before him.

Alderic swung the blade down, quickly severing head from shoulders. The man's body slumped back, while the head rolled in a semi-circle, leaving an arc of blood on the floor, still anchored by the hair trapped beneath Alderic's boot.

A sound came from behind the door through which the man had entered. Stepping over the still body, Alderic pushed the door open, but found the room empty. Loose rope bindings lay scattered on the floor, and splashes of fresh blood and wet ink stained the ground.

Whomever the man held hostage had clearly freed themselves, breaking through the window to the outside. They left behind a trail of blood, which led across the windowsill and onto the grass below.

Alderic had no interest in pursuing the vagabond's captive, and returned to the room where the body remained. He lay the body on a small cot in the corner of the room, setting the severed head beside the shoulders. He covered the corpse with a tattered blanket, and offered a small prayer to the death goddess herself.

The dead man was not the legendary demigod. Were he truly the Beast of Erkynon, Alderic's blade would have shattered against the skin, rather than easily slicing through the gaunt neck. The Beast of Erkynon would bleed when cut, but a killing strike would destroy the weapon while preserving the Beast.

A great king attempting to behead Death Sin was a risk. According to the legend, it could awaken a terrible power within the demigod. Alderic had felt no such threat; instinctively, he had known that this pitiful soul was not the child of Erkynon.

The king could not help but feel disappointment. Despite himself, he had hoped the legend was true. He had indulged the fantasy that such a beast could roam the earth, carrying great pain though invulnerable to death.

Alderic exited the small house through the front door. He made his way back to the lake, and from there to Linwood. He knew the people would be looking for proof that the beast had been slain, but Alderic had never in his life taken a trophy. He found the practice tasteless, and would not stoop to such foul depths for the sake of Linwood.

36

B lake sprinted through the woods. He could feel the blood dripping from his stomach, and ink was swept into his eye as he sweated. Still, he could not slow his pace. He only prayed he would not arrive too late.

He had been trying desperately to undo the knots, when he heard his captor exchanging words with someone. Pressed by an overwhelming curiosity, he had dragged his bound and bleeding body to the partially open door. Again, he braced his shoulder against the doorframe, so he could glimpse into the other room.

He could see his captor's back, and perceived the frenetic energy that caused his hands to wring. However, Blake was more interested in the dark, looming figure who had intruded upon this forest hideaway.

It was the Blackdog King.

The familiar alarm had filled him as he beheld the king. But, he was more surprised to find this fear was mixed with an odd sense of relief. King Alderic's presence built horror within Blake, from even before the moment they met, impressing upon the thief the totality of his power.

Yet, if anyone could be trusted to annihilate the threat, it was King Alderic.

That his life had lain in the king's hands was paradoxical in a way that, by that point, seemed almost mundane. Though, Blake could still appreciate the peculiarity of this turn of events.

To use the king's presence to his advantage, Blake had needed to work quickly with the ropes, and be free and away from the house by the time the king was through with this supposed Beast of Erkynon. Otherwise, he would only trade one menace for another.

After a moment's struggle, he had freed himself from the wrist bindings. The ropes at his ankles were more challenging. His nails had been shredded by the removal of the tight cord at his wrists, so he had used the combination of his fingers and teeth to remove the ankle bindings.

Once he had freed himself, he still faced the challenge of the barred window. Luckily, the wood around the bars was near rotted. Blake had stood on a chair, and given the iron a swift kick. The bars fell out of the window frame, onto the grass outside. He knew the sound would not go undetected so, pushing the chair away, he had leapt through.

Upon hearing footsteps approach, he had hidden himself by the corner of the house, out of sight of the window. It was only after he had heard the footsteps retreat, that he began his dash into the woods.

Linwood finally within view, Blake realized how little thought he had given to a plan during his frenzied sprint away from the king. His only objective was to find his companions, and ensure that they were not harmed by King Alderic's soldiers.

King Alderic was clever enough to know that they had made it to Linwood, Blake was sure of it. He could only hope that Moirin would have taken them into the safety of the mountains.

Blake waited at the outskirts of the town, hoping that something would occur to him. The front of his shirt was torn, and he was still covered in blood and ink. As many of the markings were on his face and neck, he knew there was no way for him to remain inconspicuous.

Blake may not have known where Moirin was headed, but he knew the direction in which she would not journey. Staying to the outskirts of Linwood, he kept his face downturned and wrapped the ripped shirt across his still bleeding stomach, tucking the end into his belt. It would at least hide some of the markings.

He kept near the cover of the brush, passing several of King Alderic's soldiers who rode by on horseback, unheeding of the disheveled man who hunched and limped along the edge of the road.

He continued walking, and for some time did not come across any more of the king's soldiers. Though relieved, he worried that he was only drawing farther away from Moirin and the others.

As he staggered along the path, his attention was drawn to the clash of weapons nearby. He quickened his pace as he searched for the source of the noise. He could not be sure, but there was a depth to the ringing of steel he could have sworn belonged to an axe.

At the side of the road, Blake came upon Owen fighting with an armed man. Aeron and Moirin were nowhere in sight, nor was this opponent attended by any of the king's soldiers.

This man was dressed unusually. Unlike the soldiers, he wore chain mail across his torso, a visible breastplate, and brown leather gauntlets protecting his wrists and forearms. His head was covered by a dark metal helmet, and he swung his sword in a wildly aggressive manner.

Blake kept to the side, out of the way of surging weapons. His pack, knife and sword had been taken from him during his kidnapping and without these, he was afraid to involve himself in any fighting. Though, it was not only a lack of weapons that caused his reluctance to engage in combat.

The armored man launched a new series of forceful attacks, each skillfully deflected by Owen. Despite the failure of any of these strikes to produce a hit, the armored warrior seemed undeterred. In fact, it seemed that with each attack his determination grew ever stronger.

Seeing an opening, Owen used the blunt of the axe to knock the man to the ground. Blake could see the familiarly unsettling insanity shining from the light-haired warrior's eyes, and he knew that the man in armor would be dispatched within seconds.

The helmeted man scrambled backwards, his sword fallen from his hand. He clambered back until his shoulder ran up against a large boulder, and he could go no further. He raised the gauntlet of his right arm to try to block his execution. The chain mail rose with the motion of his arm, uncovering his stomach.

Blake caught sight of the shirt beneath: a canary yellow fabric. He had only seen that vivid a fabric once in his life. The ground spun, and he was half-convinced his eyes deceived him. Still, the color was unmistakable.

"Stop!" Blake shouted. He feared that Owen, in his present state, would be unheeding of the word.

Owen looked in the direction of the cry, his eyes landing hazily on Blake. Though his head was turned, he continued the downward motion of the axe.

He could not be controlled in combat, and the descent of his weapon said as much.

However, the minor distraction allowed the helmeted man to roll out of harm's way. The mail covering his shoulder snagged between the axe and the boulder, but he pulled against it, breaking the fine metal links and freeing himself. He grabbed his sword from the ground and stumbled to his feet.

As the man tried to make his escape, Owen chased after him. He raised his axe as he neared his prey, preparing to strike again.

Blake ran, placing himself between Owen and the armored man. His heart thudded in his ears, and his nostrils filled with the scent of his own blood, trickling as it did down his stomach. He knew he could not count on Owen to spare him, but he stood firm.

Owen raised his axe in threat, and Blake closed his eyes. He had seen the sheer aggression in Owen, and was sure that the warrior would strike him dead at any moment. He counted in his head, and when he reached ten he reopened his eyes.

Owen looked back at him, his face returned to removed sedation.

Owen's opponent had fled, leaving the two of them alone in the empty street, facing each other. Blake was uncomfortable beneath Owen's blank gaze, and shifted his feet slightly against the dirt of the road to mask this disquiet.

"Why did you stop me?" Owen asked. His words might have been taken as accusatory, but he spoke with a faded resignation.

"The shirt he wore," Blake said, fully aware of how ridiculous his reasoning would sound, "it belonged to Hugh, the man who was brought with me to Alderic's prison."

"The man who was executed?" Owen asked.

"At least that is what I was told. I know it might not be him, but there was something in what little I could see of his face that was familiar. You must understand, if there is even a chance it is him, I could not let him die a second time by my own failing," he said.

Owen said nothing in response, but nodded his head, his eye turned away from Blake. He wiped the blade of his axe in the grass, and put it over his shoulder. He began to walk, and Blake followed him.

Blake went over in his mind every small detail of the masked warrior. He tried to summon a single piece of evidence that the man was indeed Hugh. With each attempt at recollection, the vision he held in his mind became increasingly distorted.

Despite this, he was near certain of the man's identity.

"Perhaps that is your friend," Owen said after silence had hung between them for a few minutes. "If it is, he has suffered a fate far worse than death: he has become the king's new knight, my cursed replacement. More terrible than a death of the body, being Alderic's knight means a tribulation of the soul."

Blake said nothing, his thoughts returning to what little he knew of Owen's time serving King Alderic, and the acts he had been forced to commit on the king's behalf. He had trouble imagining Hugh willingly partaking in such carnage. Yet, if he was still by King Alderic's side, he must have known about the bandit massacre. Blake wondered whether Hugh had participated in the slaughter.

"Moirin found 'Split Oak', but it was too late," Owen spoke, his voice cutting through Blake's musings. "There was a place at the root where a hole had been dug. Only moments before the fight, I overheard two soldiers speaking about a box that had been recovered."

"And he has the key," Blake sighed.

"Since it is no longer in Moirin's possession, we can only assume it to be so," Owen responded. For the first time, he looked over Blake, stating matter-of-factly: "You are covered in black markings, and your stomach is cut."

"Is it?" Blake smiled, happy to jest a little. "It has been a strange morning. I was kidnapped by a man who thought himself the son of the death goddess. Certain that I would end my journey face down in the lake, I was rescued by none other than the Blackdog King himself."

"When you were missing this morning, we were told by the innkeepers that you were likely taken by the monster that terrorized the town," Owen said, seemingly ignoring the reference to King Alderic. "Though I did not share my suspicion with the others, I thought you left of your own accord."

"Was there reason for such a conclusion?"

"There was no indication that anyone forced their way into the room, and the scrape of your boot on the wall made me think you had climbed from the window yourself."

"Yet, you did not tell the others of my cowardice," Blake responded with a mix of suspicion and relief.

"It did not matter either way, I don't want them to think poorly of you. This is the task we have chosen, and you were thrown into it by circumstance. I could not blame you for rethinking your position." He looked at Blake as they walked along the road. "Does your presence here mean you have chosen to continue the journey?"

"In so far as we can make it." Blake laughed.

They carefully avoided King Alderic's soldiers and kept a steady pace, not wishing to draw unwanted attention. Blake found his thoughts returning to Hugh.

"Why would King Alderic make Hugh his knight? It is true that he was the son of a farmer; he was used to labor and physically strong. However, from what I remember, Hugh had no discernable skill in a fight."

"Nor did I, though likely even less than your friend," Owen responded. "Alderic does not choose his knight based on prowess in battle. He saw a quality in me that he could exploit, something he could use to turn me into the killing instrument he wished to command. I am sure he must have noticed something in your friend that he could similarly utilize."

Though Blake did not say it aloud, he was well aware of the trait of Hugh's that could be easily exploited. Hugh's loyalty was intense, doubtless more so in the hands of the king. Blake shuddered to think to what use this ardor could be put, were it shaped by the hand of a powerful master.

"From a pickpocket to a knight," Blake reflected. "If it is true, this is certainly a fantastical turn of events for Hugh."

Owen stopped and put his hand on Blake's chest, bringing him to a halt in the middle of the road. "You must understand that I cannot allow the king's knight to live. If our paths cross again, I will kill him."

"He is not a bad man, but he is inexplicably driven to do the will of whomever he follows," Blake responded. "I have lied to him, taken his loyalty for granted, and left him for dead. I cannot do so again."

"So long as you understand I will do what I have to."

Blake nodded in response, though knowing he had little choice in the matter. They continued their journey, and came to a neglected crossroads where Moirin and Aeron waited.

Aeron's eyes widened when she spotted Blake, clearly relieved. "What happened to you?" she asked, laughing while she clapped his unmarred shoulder. "You're near covered in ink."

Blake explained the story behind his kidnapping by the Horror of Linwood, and inadvertent rescue by the king. In this retelling, he chose to leave his act of abandonment from the narrative.

As he spoke, they journeyed along the forest's edge, and Blake gradually realized that they were not leaving the perimeter of Linwood.

"Why are we not putting distance between ourselves and King Alderic?" he asked.

"The only chance we have of finding the next point is by following Alderic. I am sure the information is contained in the box, and without it we are lost," Moirin responded.

"There is another option," Blake said.

"Which is?"

"Assuming he has it, King Alderic may not have tried the key yet. If I can gain access to the box, we could both learn the next location and simultaneously prevent him from doing so."

Moirin sighed. "It is not a bad idea, and no more foolhardy than attempting to track and circumvent the king."

Blake was nervous, hoping he was not putting himself in over his head in a desperate attempt to undo the wrong he had committed against them. He knew his key copy would doubtless need work before it could open the lock, and that this would be impossible without the box.

"The king will be guarding it closely," she said.

"First, we will need to find where he is staying," Owen interjected. "Moirin, there is one weakness of the king you can easily exploit."

Moirin looked at Owen pointedly, though the meaning of the glance was lost on Blake. Moirin jutted out her jaw in annoyance. "Perhaps."

They reentered the town walls, careful to keep hidden. Blake kept the hood of his cloak over his face, to obscure the markings. Moirin led them to an area of Linwood, far from the center, where King Alderic's soldiers were not yet present.

They reached a well and Blake pulled off his torn shirt, wetting it. He scrubbed the ink from his face, before cleaning the black markings and drying blood from his chest and stomach.

Looking at his reflection in the water, he noticed a black sign on his left temple that would not wash away. He could not see it clearly in the rippling surface, yet a distinct image surged to the forefront of his mind: a symbol made up of overlapping curved and straight lines, wrenched together in a grotesque arrangement.

At the sight, his breath grew cold, and he felt the press of his life's blood become momentarily faint.

He wet the shirt and tried again to remove it, but he found the mark held fast. He could not give it much thought, as there were more pressing matters to attend to, but he felt a chill run down his spine as he touched the place with his fingertip.

He bought a new shirt from a merchant, and could only hope the shallow cut on his stomach would not reopen and mar the fabric. Once he had collected himself, he joined the others as they worked out the finer details of procuring the box.

It took them little time to find that King Alderic had appropriated the inn for his temporary headquarters. Soldiers lined the walk outside, and the smell of mead and cooking food filled the streets. Getting inside the inn would not be too difficult, but the pervading presence of the military left little room for error.

There were ten rooms on the second floor, and Blake doubted the king would keep the box in any room but his own. Looking up, he was rewarded by the sight of the king, in a room at the western corner.

After night had fallen, Blake and Aeron stole to the side of the inn. There were soldiers in the street, but at the moment there were none on the west side of the building. Blake came to stand beneath the window, with his back to the wall, while Aeron stood beside him. He kept his eyes on bell tower, where Owen and Moirin waited.

A tiny light flared beneath the bell: this was their signal that King Alderic had left the room. Aeron laced her fingers together, and Blake placed one boot in her grip. She lifted him up, and he felt as though he would topple over, and scrambled to grab hold of the windowsill with his fingertips while his feet felt blindly for her shoulders. When he found his footing, he experienced a short moment of equilibrium before Aeron pushed against his feet, propelling him over the ledge.

He pulled himself into the room, the windowsill digging into his side. He landed with an unceremonious thud on the floor, and gasped as sudden pain reminded him of the cut across his stomach. He looked around to ensure he was alone and, finding the room empty, he pulled himself to his feet. While the bedroom was unattended, it would likely not stay that way for long.

With a sense of urgency, Blake began his search of the room. He had no idea what the box looked like, and he gripped the key copy tight in his hand. He scanned the room, looking for any clue as to the object's whereabouts. The mere act of standing in the king's chambers caused him repulsion, and his fear mounted with each second the box was not within his hands.

He hunted fruitlessly for a few minutes, before catching sight of a tightly wrapped bundle in the corner. It lay beneath a saddlebag, and he removed it delicately from its place of hiding, careful to not let the covering items make a sound as he replaced them on the floor.

He sat at the edge of the bed, and unwrapped the cloth gingerly. A brass box fell into his lap, and he turned it over in his hands. It had a small lock at the front, and he carefully placed the key into it. The metal of the blacksmith-made key snagged against the beautifully crafted golden lock.

He shifted the key, and tried to turn it, praying that this replication would defy the odds.

Unsurprisingly, the lock would not budge. Stealing the box would alert the king to their continued close proximity, but it seemed he had little choice. Putting too much pressure on the lock could trigger a failsafe that would damage whatever lay within, and he could not risk this possibility.

He was preparing to leave through the window, when he heard the handle of the door turn. He looked to the bell tower but saw no sign. He sought their attention with a brief wave of his arm before instinctively diving behind the opening door. His hiding place would last as long as the door stayed open, and he could only hope that Moirin and Owen were aware of his predicament.

The wood of the open door pressed nearly to his face, and he knew his presence would be revealed all too soon.

A heavy tread indicated King Alderic's entrance. Blake could not help but notice that, for the second time that day, he was observing the king while concealed behind a door. Though, this time, the king's presence brought neither reprieve nor salvation.

As soon as King Alderic closed the door, they would lose possession of the box and the soldiers would be sent out to hunt down Blake's companions. Blake would doubtless be executed promptly, and his rescue from the Horror of Linwood would be for nothing.

He began to prepare himself for death's embrace, when a shouting erupted downstairs. Blake heard the king's weight shift against the floorboards, and the sound of his bronze sword being drawn from its sheath.

37

Alderic heard the shouts coming from the bottom of the stairs and he reentered the hallway, his sword gripped loosely in his hands. He was confident his soldiers could handle any threat they encountered, but he remained ever prepared to fight. The sound of footsteps came up the stairs and two of his soldiers approached, a third individual held tight between them.

Alderic re-sheathed his sword. The figure was hooded, but he knew there was a reason the soldiers had brought the intruder directly to his door. The creeping sense of unease that threatened to swallow him left no doubt as to the person who stood before him.

"Moirin," he spoke the name like a curse.

Alderic took the cloak's hood and pulled it back, his fingertips skimming Moirin's hair, and revealed her cold, upturned face. Her eyes glinted back at him, nearly smiling despite the dispassionate twist of her mouth. She said nothing, and did not waver in her steady gaze.

He nodded to the soldiers and they let her go, taking their leave in turn. Alderic stepped to the side, allowing her entry to his room. She stepped past him in the narrow doorway, her shoulder brushing against him as she passed. The cloak dragged on the ground behind her, and she pulled the fabric up slightly to keep it from catching on the coarse floorboards.

At the brief physical contact, he could feel the dead thudding of his heart in his ears. He took a deep, shuddering breath to keep himself in control.

"I'm surprised to see you here," he said. "You did not put up much of a fight, practically handing yourself over to me."

He began to circle her, taking in every aspect of her appearance. His body slinked, predatory with each step, carefully considering the adversary who stood before him. Her demeanor bothered him, far too casual for the circumstances.

"Perhaps I have grown to miss you," she responded, her tone offhanded.

Alderic let out a bitter laugh, stopping only inches in front of her. "This I doubt very much. Tell me why you are here."

"Could you ask me to leave?" she asked.

With that, she closed the short distance between them. She lay the flat of her hand on his chest, and with the other she stroked the dark hair away from his face. Her fingertips brushed his cheek, carrying the errant strand behind his ear. She brought her hand to rest just above his collarbone.

Alderic's heart raced, and his mind reeled. Her light touch sent a tremor through his entire body, and his left hand clutched futilely at the air to hide his state.

Despite his disquiet, the king knew he could not allow this hostile act to go unanswered. He reached his right hand out, and grasped Moirin by the throat. His fingertips sank into the soft flesh, and he could feel blood pulsing within his hold.

A sudden horror filled him, and his vision was clouded by the pressure bursting within his brain.

"I should have thrown you into servitude the second my brother was in the ground," he whispered roughly into her ear.

"If you did, it would only be so I could serve you myself," she responded, her voice strained by his grasp.

Alderic's breath came in ragged torrents. His skin crawled where he touched her, but he was having trouble letting go. His repulsion was not assuaged by passion, and a sickening feeling crept through his right hand, and drowned his entire body in weakness. At any moment, he felt as though his senses might drift into a void from which they would never return. His sight would turn to darkness, and he would be gone.

Overwhelmed, Alderic stepped back and released Moirin's neck from his grasp. His grip would leave a bruise, and he found himself glad to have made a mark that she could not hide behind treasonous eyes.

Moirin rubbed the red that deepened around her throat as she looked back at him.

"Run!" Moirin said.

The door slammed closed, and Alderic saw Blake burst forth from the shadow. The thief clutched the brass box in his hand, and he sprinted across the room.

Moirin slipped through the window and Blake flung the box down to her, making to follow her lead. As he clambered for the opening, King Alderic seized him around the waist, and slammed him down onto the hard floor.

Blake felt the air leave his lungs abruptly, and the metallic taste of blood filled his mouth. The back of his head had hit corner of the wall, and a pressure burst forth between his eyes. His vision swam, as he struggled to regain his breath.

King Alderic's back was turned to him, as his sight was directed out of the window and into the street, watching Moirin's retreating figure.

Blake pushed himself slowly to his feet, hoping to take advantage of the king's momentary inattention. His movement was noticed immediately, and King Alderic's head whipped back in the direction of the thief.

The king's eyes blazed dark and his nostrils flared, as he looked down at Blake. The criminal was of little use to him one way or the other, and they both knew it. King Alderic grabbed the front of Blake's shirt, and pressed his knuckles into the thief's stomach. The knife slash from that morning reopened, and blood seeped into the newly purchased shirt.

Blake tried to fight back. He felt lightheaded, as King Alderic's knuckles ground into his lacerated skin, and he saw the knife drawn from King Alderic's belt. He flinched at the bright flash of steel, and his mind raced as he struggled to find a way out. He could not overpower the much larger and stronger man, nor could he free himself and flee. His only recourse was underhanded combat.

He pulled away from the struggle, and reached upwards. He slid his fingers through the raven locks of the king's hair, and used the hair he grasped to pull the king's face down to meet his. He pressed his teeth against the corner of Alderic's mouth.

Blake bit down, and could taste the Blackdog King's blood rise in his mouth.

The move was unexpected, and Alderic's hold slackened for a moment. A restriction rose in Alderic's breast as he felt pain radiate from where the thief's teeth cut into his skin. Yet it was not this ache that halted his heart and stayed his hand.

He could feel Blake's warmth against him. The thief's saliva blended with his blood, and Alderic could feel Blake's breath hot against his cheek. He wanted to act, to finish this fight, but their mere closeness immobilized him.

The knife he held dropping to the floor. Alderic heard the clatter of the blade, but it seemed somehow distant. Numbness spread through his body, inundating his muscles with the same incapacity.

Blake drew back quickly. He could see King Alderic's eyes still widened in surprise, and a flush was creeping across the pallid face. He had little time to escape, so he freed himself of the weakened king and ran toward the window.

Blake had one leg over the sill, when King Alderic regained himself enough to retaliate, picking his knife up from the floor. He grabbed Blake by the wrist, and tried to drag him back into the room.

Blake was determined to flee and threw himself out of the window, still suspended by the held wrist. His shoulder was wrenched as his weight strained against the king's grasp, so he grabbed the windowsill with the other hand as he tried to work his wrist free.

The king's heart was pounding, and his legs felt as though they might give out at any moment. Thinking through the haze, he decided to let go. He took his knife and impaled the flesh between Blake's thumb and index finger. The blade sank through to the hilt of the knife, pinioning the thief's hand to the windowsill. He let go of the wrist and stepped away wordlessly, watching to see what Blake would do. The thief would choose to either cripple his hand, or suffer the wrath of the king.

Blake felt the knife enter his hand, and the pain blazed white hot through his vision. He considered holding on, but knew only a second more, and the king could decide to pull him back in. Closing his eyes, he let go of the window, and fell down to the street. He could feel the blade tear through the soft skin, cutting through muscle.

Pain surged through his legs, as he struck earth. He pulled himself to his feet, bracing his bloodied hand against the ground, and ran toward the bell tower. Blood streamed down his forearm, staining the road with splatters of red. He could feel the agony in every inch of his body and he ran, half-blinded by pain, through Linwood.

Alderic watched Blake race through the street, until he could see the figure of the thief no more. He wiped his mouth with the back of his hand, effectively removing any trace of the criminal. He turned to the empty room and leaned against the wall, allowing his head to drop back. He rubbed his closed eyelids with the heels of his palms.

He had allowed himself to be distracted and incapacitated twice by this anxiety. He cursed himself, vowing to never let such vulnerability cripple him again. Still, he had made similar oaths in the past.

In a moment of clarity, he remembered something he had noticed upon seeing Blake. It was a small symbol, borne on the thief's left temple. He could not recall the exact image, but he knew he had seen the marking somewhere before. Though his memory was unclear, Alderic had the distinct sense that it was of great significance.

Alderic went into the hall, and assembled the soldiers. He deployed a few to search for Moirin, Owen, and Blake. He knew he would not find the next location without the box. Even should the soldiers fail, he had faith that their paths would cross again soon, even as they neared the eastern edges of Vesia.

Moirin had rejoined the others in an alley behind the bell tower, and they were ready with horses when Blake arrived. He grasped the pummel of the saddle with his uninjured hand, and pulled himself onto the horse's back. He landed awkwardly, and straightened himself using his elbow.

"How did you get there so quickly?" he asked Moirin.

"It was obvious that you would not have enough time to leave with the box, but I didn't want you distracted by this inevitability," she answered, as she turned her horse toward the abandoned road. "As soon as you were through the window, I went into the street and waited for a signal from Owen."

Under the cover of darkness, they rode out of Linwood. From a distance, they could hear the rousing of the soldiers. King Alderic must have ordered their pursuit.

Blake looked down at his hand. By some miracle, he could still move his thumb and fingers. Relief filled him at the realization of his luck; his livelihood could have been lost to him forever had his hand been irreparably damaged. He wrapped it loosely in the front of his shirt, and kept himself in the saddle, though still slightly off balance.

The moon was rising, and the pale light illuminated the road before them. As they departed Linwood, they exchanged the silvery dust of the streets, for the soft darkness of the surrounding forest.

"I know of a place where we will be safe from the king, and can work to open the box without interruption. Larian Castle is not far from here," Moirin said as they continued into the night. "The baron is sympathetic to our cause, and can protect us for a short while."

38

They travelled three days before laying eyes on Larian Castle, tucked in a vale and surrounded by lush greenery, the air pleasantly warm. Behind the castle rose a dark, jagged mountain, and it appeared the edifice was carved directly into the rock side. It was this same castle that Blake had first seen on the geographical map, and to which he had originally intended to flee.

In the three days, they had seen no sign of King Alderic or his soldiers, and even Blake had begun to rest easy in the assumption that they had escaped his searching.

"I have not been here in many years, as Alderic kept me cloistered in Ashen Castle following Severin's death," Moirin said as they rode toward the towering castle. "I look forward to again seeing the baron and baroness. They are formidable allies, with enough wealth to provide opposition to the king's rule."

A brief, stony ascent brought them to the twisted metal gates that barred their entry. Moirin spoke to the porter, and a message was relayed inside.

They waited, Blake's horse shifting nervously beneath him. The warm air was filled with a mist that lay like a blanket in the valley, sparkling in the light of the afternoon.

The gate opened, and they were ushered inside by guards. The men did not lower their weapons, as they surrounded the four travelers. They held long spears and kept their distance. The sharp blades hovered only inches away from the newcomers.

A figure appeared on the steps to the castle, signaling the guards to lower their weapons.

The threat dissipated, Moirin dismounted first and walked up the steps. Blake watched, as she and the man spoke in undertones, before she motioned for the others to join her.

Blake cautiously looked over the armed guards, before stepping down clumsily from the saddle, his hand throbbing as the cut began bleeding anew. The horse's reins were taken from him by an attendant, and he met Moirin with the others on the steps.

"Silvius has passed away. His son, Lord Richard, is now baron, and has agreed to speak with us," she said quietly, as they were led into the castle. "I have never met him before, but if he is anything like his father, he will gladly give us shelter from Alderic."

"Lord Richard," Blake mused. "It is strange for a baron to use his first name so. Is it a show of humility?"

"Perhaps," Moirin answered, after considering this for a moment. "However, I suspect through linking his first name with the title, even the most causal of addresses bears signs of his status."

They were led to the great hall. Tapestries covered polished stone walls, and the afternoon sun streamed through stained glass windows. Blake was struck by the difference between this well-groomed castle, and the near dilapidated state of the king's own home. While King Alderic's drenched walls crumbled from years of neglect, here not a stone was out of place.

They were led further through the hall, to where the baron stood, and they were brought out before him. Each showed him the deference he expected, apart from Aeron who watched him with her arms crossed.

Blake kicked her lightly in the side of her leg, and she took her cue. She bowed her head like the others, and hunched her back, better masking her intimidating figure.

Satisfied, the baron approached. The man appeared to be near his fifth decade, with deep creases showing at the corners of his eyes. His brown hair was brushed back, and his skin was clean shaven, but for a groomed moustache. Most striking were his high and sharp cheekbones, which drew attention to the shining blackness of his eyes.

He smiled as he walked out to greet them better, a row of straight, white teeth showing. His face fell seamlessly into the pleasant folds that extended from his eyes to his cheeks, putting each of his visitors at ease.

"I hear you seek shelter in my home." He nodded, as if to himself. "I would be glad to have guests of your esteem."

"We thank you for your immense generosity, My Lord," Moirin said, bowing her head.

Blake noticed how at ease Moirin was in Larian Castle. Surrounded by the trappings of nobility, he saw no trace of the discomfort she had shown in the company of Aeron's bandits.

Lord Richard laughed, speaking to Moirin. "Think nothing of it. My father thought very highly of you, and I would do his memory a disservice should I turn you away."

"I am sorry to hear of your father's passing," Moirin said. "He was a great man."

"My mother is gone as well. Both were killed by the king for their attempts at rebellion," Lord Richard said, pacing solemnly before them. "He sent an assassin to ruthlessly take their lives in the night. I only pray they did not suffer much in their final moments."

"It is a tragic thing," Moirin responded. "I too have lost family to the king. My husband, Severin, was killed by Alderic."

"I have heard rumors that the king murdered his own brother," Lord Richard said, looking at Moirin. "It seems we are bound by a common enemy."

He offered her a small, sad nod. "I'm sure you are all weary from your travels. Servants will show you to your rooms, and it is my hope that you will join me for dinner this evening."

"We would, of course, be honored," Moirin responded.

"I can assure you, the honor is all mine. I do not often entertain visitors from Conrisia, my castle being situated near the outskirts of the Vesian kingdom. If there is anything you require, ask and it shall be granted."

He gave a small signal with his left hand, and they were led away by servants.

Blake marveled at the wide expanse of the halls they were led down, well-lit and fastidiously adorned to give the castle a lavish texture. Finally, they were brought to an unused wing, where they were each shown into separate chambers.

Alone in his room, Blake found a wash bowl and soap had been set in the corner of his room. He stuck his hand in the basin, and found the water to be piping hot. He knew his body was sorely in need of cleaning, but he began by washing his injured hand. He scrubbed at the open tear, and the water turned from pink to red. He winced as each motion brought greater pain, but he carried on. He had seen others suffer from infection in the streets, and knew too well the risks of an unclean wound.

Perhaps the servants had seen the sorry state in which he entered the castle, because a change of clothing and fresh bandages had been laid out on the bed. He stripped off his clothes, and ran a hand across his grimy face. He cleaned himself as best he could using the reddened water, scrubbing again the cut on his stomach, careful to keep the water from dripping onto the floor.

Satisfied he had done all he could, he bandaged the injured hand and made his way to the bed. There, he passed a large mirror set against the wall. The polished surface was speckled with grey tarnish, and he looked carefully at his reflection.

Much had changed since the days, only weeks before, when he and Hugh ran games in back alleys, lifted purses from travelers, and tested the locks of poorly guarded homes. His stomach bore the shallow wound inflicted by the Horror of Linwood, and the strange ink marking on his temple had yet to wash off. Meanwhile, a bruised lip and cut hand were proof of his latest meeting with King Alderic.

In under one month, his face had grown careworn and his body battered. It was the cleanest his skin had been since they began their journey and he struggled to recognize the man in the mirror.

He wondered if Hugh would.

He had not thought much on his old partner since their brief meeting during the fight with Owen. The new knight had given no sign of recognition when Blake saved him from Owen's axe. Then again, the masked helmet made discerning the knight's expression challenging. Despite this, there was something about his bearing that made Blake sure of his identity.

Blake sat down on the bed. Not only had he been told that Hugh died, but he had believed it wholeheartedly. He had felt Hugh's absence from the living world. His mind turned back to Owen's words, his proclamation that a life as King Alderic's disciple was a fate worse than death. Blake could not accept this.

The sun was setting, and the light filtered through stained glass, casting the walls in a colorful, fractured glow.

He pulled the white, folded shirt on over his head. Already, a small stain was growing at the sleeve, where blood seeped through the bandage, but Blake could not worry about that. He pulled on the rest of the clothing, and lay back on the bed. His eyes closed, and felt himself drift into sleep. The walls of Larian Castle could hold off King Alderic for a little while, and Blake would make the most of this sense of safety, transient as it was.

His dream began as an indiscernible swirl of images, each blending into the next forming a shifting abyss. Hands reached forth from the void, gripping him and threatening to drag him through the chasm. His very soul was seized, and he struggled desperately against the threat of death.

There was a darkness, a subtle violence to the visions that left his brow drenched with sweat, his heart thudding numbly in his ears.

He awoke with a start. The sun had set, and the room was lit only by a single flame. He could feel something dripping across his cheek, beneath his eye. His reached a trembling hand to touch his temple. The fingertips were wet, and he pulled the candle from the bedside table toward him.

In the low, flickering light, he could see his fingers stained black. The substance was the color of ink and sticky as blood. He stood, carrying the candle to the mirror, and examined himself in the faint light. He could see the dark liquid streaming from the symbol at his temple.

He touched it again, surprised to feel no pain. He knelt by the basin, dampening the cloth in the then cold water. He wiped the substance away from his temple, until only the cryptic mark remained. He felt panic rise as he looked again at his reflection, the haunting shadow on his face the only proof that so strange an event had even taken place.

There was a knock at the door, and he took a final look in the mirror, before answering. Blake spilled out inelegantly into the hallway, where his companions greeted him.

"We have been called to dinner," Moirin said, looking composed as ever.

Blake nodded. He did not wish to mention the extraordinary incident, still unsure of what it meant. Instead, he silently followed their lead toward the great hall of Larian Castle.

He could see Owen's arm bore a new bandage, though the wound had ceased bleeding the day before. Each of his companions had been given a change of clothing as well. The clean and pressed apparel helped mask their fatigued bodies and tattered nerves.

As Blake walked, he straightened his clothing and ran a hand through his hair. He was damp with sweat and water, and sure that in his current state he was less than presentable. He could hear Aeron laugh to herself as she watched him fuss over his appearance.

"Are you afraid the baron will see a hair out of place?" she asked, still chuckling.

Blake rolled his eyes.

The dining hall blazed in the warm light of torches, and a wide table stretched nearly the length of the room. Already, the servants were laying an assortment of foods across the long boards, before scurrying back to the kitchen only to return seconds later, their arms laden with fresh dishes.

They were shown to the table by servants. Aeron and Owen stayed beside Blake, while Moirin took a seat opposite. Soon Lord Richard joined them, followed into the hall by his bodyguards. He was dressed in a white shirt, black trousers, and a scarlet jacket. He sat down beside Moirin.

"I hope your quarters are satisfactory," Lord Richard said.

"Exemplary, thank you," Moirin responded.

A man with short, grey hair came to sit at Lord Richard's other side. He too looked at Moirin as he seated himself, and she smiled at him.

"Ajed, it has been too long," she spoke, addressing the newcomer.

Ajed nodded curtly. "Indeed, it has."

It seemed to Blake that Moirin expected him to say more, but Ajed immediately turned to the food before him. Moirin appeared bemused by this coldness, and was left to converse with Lord Richard.

Blake filled his plate. He had not seen such a bounty of food in his life. He felt as though he could not eat quickly enough, barely stopping to wonder if he was making a spectacle of himself. Looking around, he was relieved to see Aeron had applied herself to the food with a similar enthusiasm, though Owen ate at a more measured pace, picking guardedly through the fare.

Lord Richard surveyed the group with curiosity. He steepled his fingers, resting his index fingers against his bottom lip, barely touching his teeth. His eyes were sharp, as he turned his attention to Blake.

"And where do you come from?" he asked.

Blake swallowed his mouthful of food too quickly, and coughed before answering, "the Isle of Ang."

"Moirin tells me you were a thief and swindler, condemned to the gallows," Lord Richard informed him, something distinctly grasping in his gaze.

Blake could feel himself stiffen slightly. "She is not incorrect, though the charge was attempted murder of a nobleman," he answered. Blake carefully enunciated each word, Larian Castle conjuring his finest dialect.

"Do you have ambition beyond existing as a street thief? Your presence in this illustrious company would indicate such."

Blake paused. Often, he expressed his aspirations only to regret it almost immediately. However, he remembered Nahia's response, and there was an authenticity to Lord Richard's regard that caused the words to spill from his mouth.

"I can perform illusions." He hastened to clarify, "I have no liogan skill, but through trickery I can make the appearance of enchantment."

"Solving a problem through mundane means, though made to appear as if by magic. It is certainly a dangerous ambition." Lord Richard smiled against his fingers, his eyes crinkling pleasantly. "You will have to perform for me during your stay. I am always looking for a new form of amusement, and I must admit you intrigue me."

Blake felt relief well up in his chest. "I would like nothing more. It is not often I am able to perform for a knowing audience." Even as he spoke, he searched his mind for an illusion impressive enough to satisfy Lord Richard's curiosity.

Lord Richard looked at Blake a moment longer, before turning his attention to Aeron. Blake did not know why, but he sensed a shift in the baron's otherwise pleasant demeanor.

"And this is the bandit queen, Aeron," Lord Richard said.

Aeron nodded in response.

Lord Richard looked her up and down, tilting his head slightly as he took in her appearance. "You are everything the stories make you out to be." A hardness glinted in his eyes. "Because you accompany Moirin, your life is safe within these walls, but do not think I have forgotten the riches your bandits have stolen from me in past years."

"We have robbed so many, that you'll have to remind me," she answered, casually defiant. "It must not have been a particularly large cache, given my forgetfulness."

Lord Richard's eyes narrowed as his lips tightened into a slight, teasing smile. "And where are your bandits now?" he asked slowly, though it was clear he knew the answer.

Aeron made to stand, but Blake put his hand on her elbow, silently urging her to stay seated. They were surrounded by Lord Richard's servants and bodyguards, and provoking animosity would likely not bode well for them.

Lord Richard did not wait for a response from the bandit queen, before facing Owen. "Of course, this man needs no introduction. Broken by the king, though many believe you will outlive the man himself." The smirk was back on Lord Richard's face. "You seem different than when I last saw you, fighting by King Alderic's side to crush an uprising on my land. You had both eyes, if I recall." He laughed. "The king truly left you a wasted fragment of the warrior you once were."

Owen remained silent. He did not appear to be intimidated by the harsh words of the baron, simply uninterested in forming a rejoinder. He continued with his meal, barely looking up when addressed.

Blake observed Owen's reticence, and felt himself losing his own appetite. Something made him gradually uneasy about Lord Richard, and their stay in the castle. Yet, he was sure they must be safer under the baron's protection than outside the walls, where they would be exposed on all sides to the searching of King Alderic's soldiers.

Blake could sense a disquiet growing, even within Moirin. She looked at Ajed a few times, appearing disheartened when she found he ignored her completely, keeping his eyes downcast. She seemed desperate, and even looked to Blake a few times, as if seeking some elusive reassurance.

When the dinner was finished, they excused themselves to their rooms. The baron wished them a restful night, and took his own leave. They kept close together as they proceeded through the dimly lit hallways, this time unaccompanied by servants.

They entered their wing of the castle, starting when Ajed stepped across their path. He grasped Moirin by the forearm, and drew her to his side.

"You should not be here," he whispered, an urgency in his voice.

Moirin pulled her arm back. "What do you mean?"

"Lord Richard may have the title now, but he is nothing like his father. If you stay, you and your companions will suffer."

"Yet, you remain faithfully in his employ," she countered.

"I have a duty towards the people, and am honor bound by the memory of Silvius." Ajed bowed his head. "There is something you should know about Lord Richard, perhaps only a suspicion, but it will make you understand why you must leave."

He whispered into Moirin's ear, his words inaudible to the others.

Moirin nodded as she listened, sorrow crossing her face. "If it is true, it is a matter of great shame," she said once Ajed had finished speaking.

Blake glanced at Aeron and Owen, noting that they seemed as confused as he was.

Ajed's voice shook with age and sorrow. "Stay the night." He looked across the tired faces. "But leave in secret at daybreak, before Lord Richard awakens."

With this advice, Ajed swept past them, walking quickly down the hall. Moirin made to halt him, but seemed to think better of it. She took a candle from the hallway, and led them mutely to her room, locking the door once they were all inside.

She sat down on the edge of the bed, still not speaking. She ran her fingers through her hair, touching the top of her braid. Owen sat down in an armchair, and Blake seated himself on the floor with his back against the wall.

Aeron remained standing, looking down at Moirin. Her arms were crossed, clearly unsettled by the baron's hostility toward her.

"Silvius was a great leader, a kind and hospitable nobleman. Given my years in the forced seclusion of Ashen Castle, I led us here with the belief that he lived, and that we would benefit from his protection. I have known Ajed many years, he is not one to spread falsehoods. If he says we should rid ourselves of Lord Richard's company, I trust him absolutely."

She looked around at her companions, and found no disagreement.

"In the meantime, we should rest ourselves and try again to open this," she produced the brass box from her bundled belongings. "The key is still stuck in the lock," she said, and turned to Blake. "Is this something you can handle?"

"I can try," he responded.

Blake retrieved the tools from his boot, relieved they had not been taken during his abduction in Linwood. The mere thought of the Horror of Linwood brought back the memory of his earlier dream and the black blood that had flowed from his temple. He shook off the chill that spread through his body, focusing instead on arranging his instruments.

"I had the blacksmith put together a facsimile of my equipment, though they are of a much poorer make than those I lost to King Alderic." He laid the tools out across the bed. "I am afraid to tamper with the lock, as what we have seen of the Ethin's work leaves me with the impression that he would put safeguards in place at every turn. If I do anything wrong, it could destroy whatever lies inside. Nevertheless, we should be safe if the key will turn."

He took into his hands a small metal file. His right hand still injured, his grip was loose and painful. He removed the key from the lock, and began to file away any pieces that stuck out improperly from the body. After each adjustment, he tried the key in the lock again.

It still would not budge.

Owen and Aeron returned to their rooms. Neither had been sleeping of late, so they were advised by Moirin to take full advantage of their comfortable quarters. This left Moirin and Blake alone with the box.

"I once saw a similar container, a small box with a twisting top that released acid if it was opened improperly. The contents were completely engulfed." Blake spoke, mostly to himself.

"Do you need help?" Moirin asked absently, looking out the window across the night covered valley.

"No," Blake answered, his pride a little wounded by the question.

He continued filing, the pain in his hand increasing with each movement.

"Why did you tell Lord Richard that King Alderic killed Prince Severin?" he asked suddenly.

Moirin turned back to the room, her eyebrows raised. "You know why."

"To gain his trust," Blake responded as he continued working with the key.

"Yet, this is not why you asked. You wish to know if I killed my husband, as Seph and others have asserted."

"Did you?"

Blake was surprised to find himself speaking so bluntly with Moirin. Even at his most confident, he found her undeniably intimidating. Had the pain in his hand not been so distracting, he would never have spoken to her in such a way.

Moirin sat down on the bed, resting against the headboard. She crossed her arms and looked at Blake. The thief kept his eyes downcast, preoccupied with his work.

"If I told you that Severin died by my hand, would you abandon us in a foolish attempt to distance yourself from the Prince of Vesia's murderer?"

Blake shook his head, "I was just curious. It seems that he was no supporter of King Alderic's rule, so I have trouble understanding why you would kill a potential ally."

Moirin sighed. "Perhaps someday you will understand. Things are never as simple as they appear, and circumstance calls for a hard heart and a strong hand. It is not unlike when you left your friend to die so you could save yourself the noose. These tasks are not pleasant, but they must be done."

She paused, before continuing, her words more carefully chosen than before.

"Yet, what you say is true: Severin was always a threat to Alderic. He alone could have dismantled the kingdom from within, but Severin was a dangerous man. He lacked Alderic's discipline, and would have endangered all of Vesia were he made king."

"Why was he so dangerous?" Blake asked.

"Severin was a man of strange and dark impulses. He and Alderic shared strengths, both of body and intellect, to the extent that the only person capable of controlling Severin was Alderic. However, the love Alderic bore his brother made him either unwilling or unable to assert authority over him. This leniency on the part of Alderic was what made Severin's mere existence so menacing."

"Yet many Vesians believe King Alderic killed Prince Severin."

Moirin shrugged. "The people hold beliefs about the king, and it is true that some will do anything, no matter how wicked, to gain power."

Blake wondered whether it was of herself she spoke.

"Severin was a strikingly attractive man," she said, half musing to herself. "In my entire life, I have never met another who neared his beauty. The people often describe him as having been divinely handsome, though even this could not do his appearance justice."

Blake tried the lock again, and this time he felt the pieces give beneath his fingers. He raised the lid cautiously, while Moirin watched opposite. He almost regretted opening the box so soon, as he knew it would bring an end to this unguarded, honest conversation.

He could feel a contraption shift on the other side of the lock. He brushed it lightly with his thumb, and felt something sharp push back. He had successfully opened the box without the safeguard deploying and, rather than tamper with the precautionary measure, he pulled what lay inside free and handed it to Moirin.

He closed the box again and set it on the table a few feet away. He believed it to be secure, but he would not risk a misjudgment.

What had lain inside was a small metal plate, made of what appeared to be a gold alloy. It reflected the light of the candle, as Moirin stooped to examine it. The surface was covered with labyrinthine markings. It showed a pathway leading through the seeming maze, and there was a name written at the bottom.

Rowena

Moirin placed it beside the map, running her finger over the writing on the plate. "I now know the place, but there is a problem: this path through the labyrinth seems to extend from nowhere," she said, frowning. "Yet, at the end of it should lay the liogan weapon."

39

There was no sign of Moirin or her companions. Since the death of Silvius Larian, Moirin had no allies within the easternmost parts of Vesia, and Alderic knew she could not turn to the late baron's son, Richard, for assistance.

After all, to accept Lord Richard's protection from the king would be to exchange the danger of lying beside a lion for that of placing one's head in its open mouth.

The nearest place where she might find refuge was Elsin, ruled by King Unger, and it was to this kingdom that Alderic led his soldiers. As it was with each of the lands bordering Vesia, the nature of the relationship between the two rulers was dictated by Alderic, who only allowed Unger to keep his crown for as long as it suited the Vesian's interests.

Yet, it was from Elsin that talk of an uprising spread. In this kingdom lay the Rock of Briggid, of which Nahia had spoken: the challenge that would identify the Vesian king's destroyer.

He led his soldiers up to the gate of Unger's castle, where they were immediately received by the porter. Alderic knew that none in Elsin would deny him. His soldiers were seen to, and led by servants to sleeping quarters, while the horses were brought to the stables.

Callum stayed by Alderic's side, as they entered the throne room. The castle was adorned in ancient embellishments, and the throne was surrounded by ornamentation that greatly exaggerated the power of its occupant.

Servants stood in each corner of the room, watching the young Vesian king and his knight with hesitation. They seemed unsure of how to attend to this visiting ruler, and instead held back to await instruction.

Callum stared at the servants. While Alderic was at ease assuming authority within this foreign castle, the knight seemed tentative in these unknown surroundings. He kept his hand on the hilt of his sword, and kept glancing toward the door.

"Compose yourself," Alderic muttered to the knight. "Stay on your guard, but do not allow the Elsin to think you agitated."

Though it was the middle of the night, Unger had been roused from sleep, and summoned to his own throne room to personally welcome the Vesian king.

He was wearing a long black shawl covering his night attire. Servants appeared to have rushed in making their king presentable, as his clothing was in disarray and the crown seemed as though it were lain carelessly on his head. Unger's people were more concerned with not keeping Alderic waiting than with properly attending their own king.

Unger was in the midst of his eighth decade, and the years had been truly unkind. His back had warped, and he had taken to walking with a cane. His hair was greyed, and his face had descended into deep, twisted wrinkles, each conveying the torment in which they were produced.

"I thank you for your hospitality, even at so late an hour," Alderic spoke politely as he took in the haggard appearance of the aged king.

Unger bowed his head to Alderic. With the movement the crown nearly slipped from his brow, but was steadied by the servant at his left. He was helped into the throne, his discomfort at being awoken so late evident, and he handed the cane to his servant who set it to the side.

Alderic watched the troubled movements, a slight crease forming at his brow. "May I ask of the reason for your affliction?"

While he had not seen Unger in years, the aged king had not seemed so stricken with ailments at their last meeting.

Unger laughed, a shallow wheezing coming between chuckles. "You, ruthless child, are the reason for our afflictions." His tone grew more serious. "Every king and queen fears the day you come to their kingdom and claim it for your own. We fear we are no different."

Alderic was one of the few royals who referred to himself simply. He was reminded of the royal pretension which caused Unger to use 'we,' and sighed inwardly.

"I have no desire for Elsin at present. Tonight, I ask only for your shelter and cooperation."

"Granted, of course," the Elsin king spoke, watching, through narrowed eyes, the young Vesian who stood before him. "Our kingdom is at your disposal. But, you already knew that."

Unger steadied himself in the throne, as he looked down on Alderic. "We can offer you more than simply shelter. There are many lovely women and men of the Elsin court who find you pleasing to the eye. Should you want a companion for the night, it can be easily arranged."

Unger paused and smiled with knowing. "Though, we have heard tell that such affection would leave you paralyzed with fear. Of course, we never believed these rumors, so unbecoming for such a strapping young conqueror."

Unger laughed lightly, before descending into a fit of coughing. Alderic tensed at the mention of such weakness, but decided to disregard Unger's words. While the Elsin king was insolent, Alderic would not waste time on such base affronts.

"There is one more thing I must inquire of," Alderic continued.

"You may ask us anything," King Unger responded, a bitterness pervading his words. The uttered phrase could have been an offered kindness but, from Unger's lips, they were nothing but a regrettable truth.

"My late brother's wife, Moirin, do you remember her?"

"We have a vague recollection." Unger nodded, appearing wearied by the late hour.

"She is no longer at the castle, and I wish to have her returned to me. Has she passed through your kingdom?"

"She has not. A lady of such closeness to your highness would be remembered, and we would have been told of her presence."

Alderic drew his lips together and surveyed Unger, who sat stooped, barely able to support his own insubstantial bodyweight. He stepped closer to Unger, watching as the other king reflexively edged backwards.

"Should you hear anything of her whereabouts, I am to be informed immediately," Alderic spoke, a quiet aggression to his tone.

"Of course, we will do everything in our power to return Moirin to your highness," he said with a pained smile. "We have heard of her...*importance* to you."

Alderic nodded, recognizing the forced gesture while ignoring the taunts Unger sprinkled liberally into his speech.

"I thank you for your cooperation, and wish you peaceful rest," he said, all the while knowing Unger would not sleep another second that night.

Alderic turned on his heel, after offering the traditional half-bow, and left Unger seated on the throne. His cloak swept across the floor, while Callum followed close behind.

"Keep your eyes open," Alderic muttered to his knight. "There is something changed in Unger beyond his physical infirmity."

An eager smile appeared on the Callum's face. "Yes, my king."

40

Moirin and Blake had fallen asleep in her room, Moirin across the bed and Blake propped up against the headboard, when they were woken by Owen and Aeron. Moirin slipped the gold plate and map into the pocket of her skirt, and Blake put the box into one of the packs, thinking it might become useful later.

Aeron and Owen had already saddled the horses, and prepared everything for their departure. The sun had not yet risen, and the vast valley surrounding them still lay in darkness. All but a few servants were still sleeping, and they were careful to avoid those awake as they made their way to the gate.

The early morning air was cool, and Blake looked out at the remnants of night covering the valley. He would sorely miss the feel of a soft bed and the warmth of the hearth, but he trusted Moirin's decision to leave. With the aid of the metal plate, she knew their destination, though the location of the labyrinth remained a mystery.

The travelers stepped thorough the stone arch overhanging the gate, leaving behind them the comforts of Larian Castle. Blake's breath caught, as spear-wielding guards suddenly rushed forward from behind the portal. They surrounded the small band, their weapons held out, and forced the horses to huddle together, nearly knocking the riders from their backs.

Lord Richard stepped from the shadows at the top of the stairs, coming to stand in the castle doorway. Even in the dark, a wide smile could be seen stretching across his face.

"I cannot imagine you would so impolite as to leave without properly thanking me for last night's hospitality. Allow me to rectify your misstep."

Lord Richard signaled to a guard, and pointed a thin, delicate finger at Moirin.

The guard put down his spear, and stepped through the line, the circle yielding to let him pass. He seized Moirin by the elbow, and pulled her roughly from the saddle.

Owen sprang down from the back of his horse, grabbed the guard, and pried him off of Moirin, throwing him to the ground. He held out his axe, warning the others against approaching. His bright hair shone out in the low light, and his eyes held that same intensity that kept any attacker from approaching.

Aeron seized Blake's reins, pulling his horse outside of the circle of guards. She forcibly pushed him to the outskirts, positioning herself between the thief and the points of the guards' spears.

Guards crowded forward and Aeron was unable to reach her sword to arm herself, however, she made do with the tools available to her. One guard attacked her with a spear and she wrested it from his hands, sticking him in the throat with his own blade.

Blake tried to move forward to aid the bandit queen, but she only tightened her hold on his reins, keeping him out of harm's way. There was nothing for Blake to do but watch as Aeron kept the guards from nearing him.

The spear-wielding men were hesitant to attack, and Lord Richard seemed to realize he could not compel the guards onward. They kept their line, trepidation written across their faces. Lord Richard looked directly at Blake as he gave a second signal, directed toward the sky.

Blake watched, from horseback, as two archers appeared in the turrets. They directed their arrows inwards, toward the courtyard, and drew their bows taut. Blake called out to Aeron, as he could see Owen was already aware of the additional offensive.

At the prospect of becoming riddled with arrows, before being sliced to pieces by the spears, the travelers had little choice but capitulate to Lord Richard. They were disarmed by the guards, and led back into the castle.

Blake looked back into the courtyard, mournfully surveying the mere paces they would have needed to ride in order to secure their freedom. Those paces could just as well be miles for all the good it did them.

Back in the great hall, they were made to sit on the bench. Guards stayed at each corner of the room, watching their prisoners for any sign of resistance.

Lord Richard entered the room, followed dutifully by Ajed. Ajed looked at Moirin, sorrow and reproach in his eyes, as he kept to Lord Richard's back.

Lord Richard smirked, looking at each in turn. "I suppose my anticipation of your early exit was unexpected." He shook his head, as he paced the stretch before them. "But, I cannot allow you to leave. I have far greater plans for you here."

Lord Richard called forward a scrawny young woman. He handed her a piece of paper. "You are to relay this message to King Unger of Elsin, and no others." He placed his hand on her shoulder, and stooped slightly so his eyes were level with hers. "Be sure you do not fail me in this," he whispered, though loud enough that Blake could hear the words.

The messenger nodded, her jaw clenching nervously as she stepped away. She placed the paper in a satchel, and departed the room.

Lord Richard faced Moirin. "I think the Elsin will be very interested in acquiring you. It is said that you occupy a privileged place in King Alderic's esteem, and it is time to see whether these whisperings hold any truth."

He sat down in a chair before them, placing his chin in his palm. His eyes were mockingly earnest, and he wetted his lips before continuing.

"I mean you no harm, Moirin, as you are no good to me dead. However, King Alderic must pay for his crimes against my people. My father and mother raised two rebellions, and both lost their lives for these fruitless efforts. King Unger shares my feelings toward King Alderic, and he will doubtless pay well to have you in Elsin."

Moirin smirked back, unwilling to yield for even a moment. "You claim you avenge your parents' deaths, yet the whisperings you trust so implicitly have also told of your exhuming of the late baron and baroness." A look of disquiet appeared on Lord Richard's face, and she continued. "From what I hear, their bodies were moved from your family's gravesite to unmarked paupers' graves in town on the very same day you took the title that once belonged to your father. These rumors tell more, besides."

"What more do they tell?" Lord Richard asked, looking distinctly nervous.

Moirin smiled, tilting her face to the side. "They say that no assassin of the king took your parents' lives, rather their killer was someone closer."

Lord Richard's face blanched, and his lips drew into a tight line. "You would accuse me of so heinous a misdeed?"

"I would," Moirin responded, her gaze never wavering from Lord Richard's face.

Lord Richard frowned for a moment, before his mouth twitched upward at the corners, breaking out into a bright, carefree smile.

"So it may be," he said with a grin, "Yet it hardly matters. I want King Alderic dead, and selling you to the Elsin serves this ambition."

Blake glanced uneasily between Moirin and Lord Richard. It occurred to him that both had committed cold-blooded murder, and willingly allowed the king to shoulder the blame for their sins. He was unsure what to make of this, but he found himself fascinated by the depraved smile that distorted the baron's face as his transgressions were unmasked.

"Why would you turn to Unger?" Moirin questioned. "Though you feign devotion, it is obvious you do not share your parents' noble cause, nor the Elsin's justified hatred of the Vesian king. You must be after something more, something nefarious, and therefore turning to Unger is a mistake. Alderic is in possession of far greater wealth and power, and would be better able to give you whatever it is you crave."

"The Blackdog King is not known to appease his enemies," Lord Richard responded, "and he has made his distaste for me known in our previous crossing of paths; I am the last person he would seek to placate. Besides, what I seek lies beyond that which can be purchased."

When it was clear no response from Moirin was forthcoming, Lord Richard stood up, and walked in front of the bench. He looked at each of his prisoners closely.

"Moirin holds the key to dealing with the Elsin; I will not harm her for now. As for the rest of you, I have no such obligation to keep you alive." A lascivious smile lit upon his wrenched lips. "It will likely take a few days to receive word from Unger regarding the sale. In the meantime, I imagine I can find all kinds of ways to entertain myself."

The four were led from the great hall by guards, and pushed into Moirin's room. Blake heard the door lock behind them. The beauty of the early morning sun through the colorful panes played again on his vision but, in the light of day, he could see that the windows were iron-barred behind the intricate stained glass.

Owen stayed by the door, listening to the movements of the guards at their post, while Moirin sat at the edge of the bed. Her face was drawn, and she toyed absently with the sleeve of her dress. Her eyes stared at the floor, and Blake could see she was trying to think of some way to escape the hold of Larian Castle.

Blake sat down beside Aeron on the floor. Her hand was stained with the guard's drying blood, and he tried to smudge it away with his thumb.

"Why did you defend me?" he asked quietly.

"Would you rather I had left you to the guards?" she asked, laughing.

"Why?" he asked again.

Aeron's face grew more serious, her eyes thoughtful as she considered the question. "I am so used to protecting others, and I suppose you remind me of them."

"The bandits?"

She nodded. "You have that same way. Protecting you must be second nature on my part."

"Thank you," Blake said.

She said softly, "it seems that a swindler could get us far from here, safe from Lord Richard."

The words were spoken in encouragement, but Blake felt them as a millstone around his neck. He nodded, and allowed himself to rest a moment longer.

41

Hours passed before Blake heard a sound in the hallway. The door clicked open and Lord Richard entered, accompanied by three guards. Blake could see more armed men lining the hallway outside. Lord Richard was clothed in the same scarlet jacket he had worn the previous day, a white shirt that lay open at his neck, and black trousers tucked neatly into shined boots.

He grinned as he entered, deep laugh lines appearing at the corners of his eyes. If Blake did not know better, he would say there was a pleasantness about Lord Richard's face. Similarly, there was an easy manner about his speech, a sweet murmur to his words that could lull even the wariest of opponents into submission.

"This is the last time you will enjoy such luxury in your accommodations. I hope you have made the most of it," Lord Richard said, looking across the faces of his prisoners.

Owen had stepped away from the door when the men entered, every muscle in his body tense as his eyes followed even the subtlest movements of the guards.

Lord Richard stood before Owen, who seemed as though he were ready to strike. The baron came closer, his face only inches away from that of the warrior.

"Owen," Lord Richard spoke, his voice low and firm. "We have met before. I know you, and you will obey me." He placed his hand against Owen's jaw, shoving the former knight until he was backed up against the wall. Lord Richard's next words came in a fleeting murmur. "Your mind and your companions will tell you to resist, but it is of no use. I am your master, and you shall submit entirely to my will. I will accept nothing less than absolute surrender."

Lord Richard brought his lips to within inches of Owen's left ear. The baron whispered, his words inaudible to the others, his fingertips turning white as he pressed them forcefully against Owen's face.

Blake watched as a change came over Owen. The former knight seemed to be intently listening to the words whispered rapidly to him, his eyes widening ever so slightly.

"You are mine to control," the baron said, a gentle lilt to his voice.

Blake remembered what Moirin had said about Owen's need for a leader. She had told him that Owen would gladly place himself back in King Alderic's service, if it meant submission to a strong hand. Blake wondered if what he saw before him was a reflection of the warrior's requirement for a master.

Lord Richard turned his attention from Owen, a final push against the jaw in his hand knocking the warrior's head hard against the wall. Before even pausing to appraise Owen's reaction, Lord Richard's eyes keenly scanned the room.

The only one who had not stood when he entered the room was Moirin. She crossed her arms, and looked up at Lord Richard, her eyes cold. She made no move to stand, wordlessly trying to provoke Lord Richard to action.

This minor act of hostility seemed to amuse, rather than perturb, their captor. He walked leisurely to her, and tilted her head to the side so he could better examine the bruising King Alderic had left on her neck. Letting go of her chin, his thumb absently skimmed the fabric at her collarbone as he looked down at her with a show of pity.

"I only have you for a few more days, and I am sure I can offer you better than you will receive as Unger's purchase." He hooked his pale, delicate hands beneath her shoulders, and pulled her to stand. "You would not be so rude as to refuse my hospitality." He slipped his arm around her waist, clasping her roughly against his side, and pinning her elbows against her own ribs.

The lines of guards peeled from the walls to follow, as Lord Richard, dragging Moirin along, led the small procession through the castle and back to the great hall. They were seated on a bench, facing the center of the room.

Aeron struggled against the guards, but stopped when blades were drawn. Blake was surprised to see that Owen was entirely accepting of his captivity. He seemed to have grown meek in the brief custody of Lord Richard, obeying the commands without resistance or objection. Lord Richard had asserted his authority over the warrior, and the will to oppose seemed to have fled Owen's body.

Blake, himself, was forced to be compliant. He lacked Aeron's strength, Owen's battle skill, and Moirin's power. Submission to the more formidable opponent was a practice he had adopted many years before, as he found it indispensable to his own survival.

Lord Richard pushed Moirin to sit. She struggled against him, until he drew a knife and held it to her throat. The silver blade glinted, and Blake's eye was drawn to the intricate sapphire studding at the handle. Despite the circumstances, he could not help but admire the impressive craftsmanship of the weapon.

"I would rather sell you to the Elsin, but I will not hesitate to cut your throat," Lord Richard murmured to Moirin.

He removed the knife once he was sure he would receive no further resistance from Moirin.

"I have, for your delight, a rather novel diversion." Lord Richard announced turning back to the room.

A servant entered, carrying a large object bundled in black silk cloth, and tied with a red lace ribbon. She bowed before Lord Richard, presenting him with the parcel.

Lord Richard accepted it, a slick smile rising to defile his lips. He silently dismissed the woman, before turning back to his benched captives.

"I was given this device by a friend." He unwrapped it slowly. "It is so simple yet, if the tales are true, it is something to be admired."

He drew from the black silk an object made of untanned leather. It appeared to be a boot, though only loosely arranged, and he held it out so each of his captives could see.

Lord Richard summoned a servant, who carried a basin filled with water. The servant set the basin on a table, and Lord Richard submerged the leather design into the liquid. He spread his thin fingers out, and pressed it beneath the surface, ensuring every inch was wetted.

Leaving the leather to soak, he dried his hands on a cloth and stoked a fire in the hearth. The flames quickly overtook the thick logs of wood stacked within, and Lord Richard used a poker to bring the flames to a head.

The fire blazing, he turned his attention back to the four captives sat on the bench, his eyes on Owen. "I think our warrior here would make a fine candidate upon whom to test this device." He moved closer, articulating each word with a motion of his hands. "You see, the leather will soften in the water, fitting nicely on your leg. I will hold your leg over the warmth of the fire, and it will tighten." He drew his hands into opposed fists. "It will tighten until the bones in your ankle and foot are pushed and pulled from each other, rupturing the threads that hold the bones in place." He looked at the leather softening in the basin. "I believe everything is ready, so if you don't mind," he said, indicating for Owen to stand.

Blake watched Owen carefully. The half-blind warrior stood, submitting his person entirely to the will of the unstable Lord Richard. It was as if Owen was drawn by some otherworldly force, powerless to resist the destruction of his own body by the hand of the lunatic baron.

Blake could not stand by and watch. Without thinking, he stood, stopping Owen in his tracks, and approached Lord Richard.

"Test it on me."

Lord Richard was unmoved, his dark eyes narrowing.

"Your willingness is strange enough to rouse suspicion. I would rather test it on this legendary warrior, who appears to me as little more than an obedient pup."

"What satisfaction would that give you?" The words were falling from Blake's lips faster than his mind could work. All he knew was that he must convince Lord Richard to choose him; he had to shield Owen from the baron's depravity. "Indeed, he is a warrior. You need only look upon his face to see the evidence of his past wounds. Yet he is willing to risk the loss of his foot.

"Do you think he will scream? Do you think he will cry out for mercy?" Blake pressed on. "Do you truly believe a single tear will fall from his sightless eye? No, he will give you nothing."

"You make as if you are with me," Lord Richard mused. "Yet, what cause have I to trust you?"

"It is my own self-interest you can trust," Blake responded, seizing on a truth known to both himself and the baron. "If you are left unsatisfied by the test of this boot, you will need to find new ways to keep yourself entertained. I would rather you test your device on me, and spare all of us further misery."

Whether Blake's words of entreaty affected Lord Richard, he could not say. However, Lord Richard looked upon Owen again. The warrior had a look of detachment from the happenings around him, and Lord Richard's eyes crinkled at the corners in a growing smile.

"I want you to ask me again," he said, his eyes wandering lazily over Blake.

"What?" Blake was confused by the strangeness of the request.

"Ask again."

"Try it on me."

"No." Lord Richard circled around Blake. "Ask again."

"Please, spare Owen and use me."

"Still, no." Lord Richard's pacing continued "Ask again."

"I beg of you," Blake pleaded. "Use me."

"Closer, but my answer remains no. Ask again." Lord Richard grinned. "I knew there was a reason you were different, and I am glad to see I was not mistaken."

Blake's mind reeled as he tried to fathom what it was the baron was after. He could tell Lord Richard was enjoying the exchange immensely, but with each time he asked, he found his own resolve waning.

Unable to come up with another idea, Blake dropped to his knees, his hands on the cold stone ground. He bowed his head, assuming the demeanor of a beggar in the presence of royalty. "Please, do not do this to Owen."

Lord Richard reached down and took the hair at the back of Blake's head between his fingers. He pulled back hard, forcing the thief's eyes to meet his own.

"Ask again," he murmured.

"Please." Blake could manage no more than the single word.

Lord Richard's eyes narrowed slightly as he looked down, his fingers still pulling Blake's hair. He sighed, and half-nodded.

"Very well," the baron said, releasing Blake from his grasp. "I would not waste my own time on this twice when there are other diversions I could pursue." Lord Richard sighed. "If you so desire, you may be the first."

Blake stood, and two servants seized him by the arms, ensuring he would not struggle. Blake had no intention of fighting back. He would not stand a chance against Lord Richard without assistance, and Owen's seeming severance from reality made the warrior useless to his companions.

Blake was brought to the edge of the small, wooden table. Lord Richard forced Blake onto his back, where he was tied to the table by the two servants. The baron yanked the travel-worn boot from Blake's foot, and pulled the fabric of his trousers over the knee, exposing the bare skin of Blake's calf.

Once Blake was securely restrained, Lord Richard removed his red jacket, and rolled up his shirtsleeves to the elbow. He pulled the device from the water and shook the excess liquid into the fire, where the drops hissed and steamed, as he came near to Blake. He sat down on a stool, and took Blake's ankle into his hand.

Blake felt the device wrap around his foot and calf. The wet leather clung to his skin in a repulsive manner. It was cold and covered in a fine slick that coated his leg. He could feel his heart beat faster as the soaked device cooled his blood.

When everything was in place, Lord Richard bound the leather tight with thick cords. Already, Blake could feel the circulation to his foot lessening, and he became acutely aware of the throbbing veins struggling against the sudden constriction.

Lord Richard set the thief's foot down and, from the corner of his eye, Blake could see Lord Richard rake fire onto the stone outside the hearth. Blake's heart was pounding, and he felt suddenly light-headed. Silently, he cursed himself for taking Owen's place in the boot.

Blake looked at his companions. Owen's good eye stared back at him, almost as blank as it's damaged twin. His face was unchanged by the scene of despair before him. In that moment, Blake understood why he could not let Owen be tortured by Lord Richard. Owen was helpless beneath the baron's influence and Blake felt obligated to protect him, just as Owen would shield him, were he more able.

Moirin sat on the bench beside Owen. As she watched Blake, she appeared distressed by the scene before her. Yet, there was something calculating about her regard of him, as though her mind was not fully on the torture that would soon be inflicted by Lord Richard.

Aeron was physically restrained by three guards. He was sure she could shake them off if needed, but there would be nothing she could do, and nowhere they could go. One guard had placed the point of his sword against her shoulder, and it drew blood as she resisted, the red liquid streaking her clothing.

Blake nodded slightly to her, hoping she would stay in place. He hated to think that he would cause her harm. He did not know if she understood the signal, but she ceased fighting the men who restrained her.

Lord Richard had come to stand behind the table to which Blake was bound. The baron seized the edge and dragged him toward the hearth, the table scraping against the stone floor.

Lord Richard held Blake's tightly bound leg with iron tongs over the fire, fastening it to a metal rail, so the restrained thief could not pull back.

The heat from the fire was low, and it was some time before Blake felt the warmth of the flame creep through the thick rawhide. At first, it was nearly comforting; he no longer felt the sickly cold and damp against his skin. It was replaced by a gentle heat that seemed to soothe his constricted limb.

This moment of calm lasted only a moment, before Blake could feel an uncomfortable tightness growing around his leg. The bindings were already taut, but a new pressure was rising. The heat caused the leather to contract around his leg and foot, squeezing his muscles, and slightly pushing the bones of his foot and ankle against one another.

His calf was also wrapped in the leather and, while there were no joints to contort, his muscles were squeezed tight, and it felt as though his foot would be suffocated. The constriction increased, and Blake realized he was holding his breath. He let the air out, shaking, from his lungs. He gasped as the leather tightened further. In his mind's eye, he could see the bones of his foot pressed together, grinding at the joints. He knew it was likely too soon for this to occur, but the pain was excruciating and Lord Richard's description of what would happen to him played through his mind.

He could hear the sound of screaming and profanities, and he realized they were coming from his own lips. He looked to Lord Richard, who was watching him curiously, his fingers steepled against his chin.

Blake dropped his head back to the table, staring up at the ceiling. He lifted and dropped his head again and again, each time increasing the force with which he struck the table. He tried to separate his mind from the sheer agony that radiated from below his knee, rippling through his entire body. A sharp ache welled between his eyes, and his sight flickered to darkness.

Through this insentience, Blake was granted reprieve from the baron's amusements, though it was not to last.

When he awakened, he was unbound, lying on the table. The boot was being cut from his leg by Lord Richard, while Aeron looked on with concern. The leather of the boot was dried, and Blake could only assume the baron had removed the apparatus because it could shrink no further.

Lord Richard's hands were now on his bare leg. Blake was vaguely aware of the fingers pressing into his flesh, but it was as though he allowed himself to feel nothing. He kept his sight averted, afraid to see what had become of his brutalized limb.

"Not exactly what I had hoped for." The disappointment was clear in Lord Richard's voice, as he allowed Blake's leg to drop against that of the table.

Unsteady, his bare foot numb against the floor, Blake was supported by the shoulder of a servant. He followed Lord Richard as the baron beckoned Aeron, Moirin and Owen to come with him, their obedience assured by the armed guards in their wake. Lord Richard led them to a small room on the second floor of the castle.

The servant deposited Blake onto the stone floor, where the thief stretched the leg out in front of his body, still reluctant to examine the damage done. Another servant set Blake's boot beside him.

Lord Richard looked down at the half-conscious Blake. "I had a thought. You say you are skilled in performing feats of illusion, and I have something of a challenge for you. Tomorrow morning, Owen will use his axe to remove Aeron's head. See if you can reattach it and bring her back to life." He paused, briefly drawing his lower lip into his mouth. "If you can, I will offer you my sincerest congratulations, and you will have spared the life of your companion. After all, I would not execute her for a second time. If you cannot revive her, then justice will have been served, and Aeron will have paid the debt she owes for past crimes." He laughed, as he perceived the distress on his captives' faces. "Either way, I am sure to be entertained."

He crouched down on the floor before Blake. He reached out a pale, graceful hand, and brushed Blake's sweat soaked hair from his brow. He cradled the thief's cheek in his palm for a moment, his eyes contemplative as his gaze remained fixed on Blake.

"Perhaps you now curse your bravery and wish you had let your friend bear the punishment." Each word was tenderly formed between his lips, the kindness in his manner at odds with the cruelty of his desires. "I am sure it is difficult to prepare so remarkable a feat as the one I suggest while your mind recovers." Lord Richard edged closer so his lips were inches from Blake's ear. "They did not try to rescue you from your anguish. It will be interesting to see if you repay that benevolence in like."

Blake pulled back from Lord Richard's hand abruptly, his head knocking against the wall behind him. A splitting pain shot through his head. He could not remember much from earlier, but he wondered if he had indeed been successful in rendering himself unconscious.

Lord Richard rose to his feet, and surveyed the others. "You will be woken tomorrow at sunrise, and the execution will go ahead. It is up to you whether the bandit queen survives," he said, looking again at Blake.

"I hope you enjoy your new room," he said. "Think of it as a harbinger, rasping its desperate tale of what is to come."

These words spoken, he exited the room. Behind him, a servant closed and secured the door. The lock fell into place, and light filtered through the fortified windows, landing on the dusty surfaces and odd contraptions which filled the space.

Blake was unsure of what Lord Richard had meant in referencing the room as a harbinger. However, as he looked around for the first time, the baron's intentions became disturbingly clear.

A large metal casket lay in the center of the room. Moirin swung open the lid, revealing an interior lined with thick spikes. She ran her fingers along the points, pulling her hand back as one drew blood. Hers was not the only blood in the casket, and Blake could see dried pools of the rust colored substance at the base of each spike. Blake could see where one would be impaled on all sides by the sealing of the coffin.

Moirin swung the lid closed with a clang, causing Blake to flinch.

Chains hung high on the walls, dried blood and scratch marks indicating their previous occupants. Aeron picked up thumbscrews from a table, and spun them between her index fingers, as she surveyed the room. She passed Owen, who stood watch by the door. He had not spoken a word, nor did he seem to shield against Lord Richard's men anymore.

Aeron joined Blake on the ground, and pulled his bare foot into her lap. She inspected the flesh closely, offering him a small smile.

"You are lucky. Though I am sure it is painful, nothing's broken."

Blake gathered the courage to look at the tormented leg. Bruises had already begun to form, painting the skin with vivid purples and blues. It appeared not as his limb, but as a piece of a dead thing. He moved his toes in succession, and Aeron clasped her hands warmly around his foot.

"See how it feels tomorrow, but it'll probably be more painful than it is today." She smiled. "Still, you'll heal."

Blake dropped his head again against the wall behind him. The sharp pain behind his eyes returned, and his entire body seemed filled with weariness. Yet, he knew he could not rest. He looked to Aeron, who said the words on both of their minds.

"Tomorrow, my life's in your hands and I'm not sure there's a trick to get out of this." She looked at him intently. "If I can't be saved, I blame only myself. I always knew it would end like this." She smiled. "Well, not exactly like this."

Blake could not find words to respond. Instead he turned his attention to the wall. His mind struggled to formulate a plan, or even a comprehensible thought, but he found himself lacking. It was as though every voice in his head had been cut away, leaving him in an eerie silence.

42

Alderic studied a map of the area surrounding Linwood. He was still sure that Elsin was the nearest settlement to Linwood that Moirin could possibly consider safe. Yet she was not there, nor was there any sign she had passed that way.

A knock came on the door, and Alderic gave permission for entry. Callum walked into the room, his eyes wide and a slight flush to his cheeks, as though he had run there.

"I was walking through the castle, when I happened to overhear a conversation in which I have no doubt you will be interested," he spoke. "A woman was speaking to King Unger. She said she is a messenger from Larian Castle, and that her master has taken possession of Moirin and three other outlaws. A Vesian baron named Lord Richard wishes to sell Moirin to King Unger."

Lord Richard's actions did not surprise Alderic, the baron was far from idealistic and would do whatever he considered necessary to ensure he was protected from Alderic, free to pursue his questionable exploits. It was left only to be seen how Unger would handle the information.

Alderic placed his hand on Callum's shoulder in wordless thanks and strode from the room, the knight following. The Vesian king walked quickly, but he masked anything in his manner that would suggest knowledge of the message.

They found Unger on his throne, speaking quietly to a small assembly. When those in attendance saw Alderic enter, they retreated to the corners of the room, leaving the path between their aged king and the young conqueror clear.

"I am leaving soon in search of Moirin. I have taken advantage of your immense hospitality for long enough," Alderic said smoothly. "My soldiers and I will depart at sundown."

Unger nodded with forced gravitas. "We are glad to have had the opportunity to show you the kindness Elsin has to offer, and welcome your return at any time." He struggled to stand, the cane slipping twice from his trembling hand. "We wish you luck in your search for your late brother's wife."

Alderic felt his artificial smile tighten, and his eyes narrowed as he watched two servants step forward to assist Unger. He sensed Callum shift by his side, and saw the knight's hand reach for a weapon. With a small shake of his head, Alderic stilled the hand, and the knight stood at ease beside the Vesian king.

Unger came to meet Alderic in the center of the room, his cane bearing half his weight as he hobbled forward. His lips twitched, and he could barely conceal his happiness to see the invading king depart his castle and land.

Alderic clasped Unger's arm briefly in thanks, before removing the cane from the feeble king's hand. Unger's expression grew confused as his body wavered, his withered legs trembling and looking to fall. Alderic reached out, grasping the elderly king by the elbow. He steadied him for a moment, before lowering him to the floor at an excruciatingly slow pace.

Unger's eyes grew wide, as his body angled to the floor. He was helpless to stop the sinking motion the Vesian inflicted on him. His cheeks drew red points of humiliation as his defenselessness was displayed to a room of his most trusted friends and advisors.

A servant moved forward to intervene on Unger's behalf, but Callum half-unsheathed his sword in warning. The servant bowed her head, murmuring an apology as she retreated from before the knight.

Alderic stood, looking down on the elderly king. His large frame loomed ominously over Unger.

"You are still king because, until now, it has been convenient that you remain thus," he hissed to the fallen Elsin. "My sword has been well-bathed in the blood of kings, and I will not hesitate to add your soul to those in the underworld by my hand."

"We do not understand your sudden animosity towards us," Unger stammered, still feigning ignorance.

"The next time you receive secretive word from a messenger, be more careful that you are not overheard. It was foolish to attempt hiding this from me."

"You would take some vagabond's word over ours?" Unger's eyes were wide.

"It was my knight who reported this to me, and I would take his word against that of one thousand of your men," Alderic responded. "Your attempts to resist my authority are pathetic. You are king in name only, and any power you have exists solely at my discretion."

"You think our people would be so quick to submit to you?" Unger said, a sneer growing on his face, despite his absurd position on the ground. "You know nothing of our people. In the city center stands proof that our wills shall not bow to the tyranny of the Blackdog King."

Though Alderic was well aware of the moniker given to him by the people, until that moment, no one had ever used it in his presence.

"You doubtless refer to the Rock of Briggid, the symbol predicting my inevitable downfall," Alderic said. "I am surprised to find the Elsin king himself allows the fate of his people to rest upon mere myth."

Unger's eyes widened, as if taken aback by the Vesian's knowledge of the rock, before descending into uncontrolled laughter. "It does not matter what you know," he wheezed.

"Of which rock does he speak?" Callum asked, ignoring the hysterics of the Elsin king.

"The Rock of Briggid is just an old tale," one of Unger's advisors responded, stepping forward. "It's a local legend, nothing of enough importance to concern your highness."

"Speak," Callum said.

"There is a loop of steel formed within a large boulder," the advisor continued, clearly ill at ease speaking to the knight. "The story says that whoever can pull free the steel ring, will overthrow the tyrant king, and bring peace to the world." He winced as he spoke the word tyrant, looking sheepishly at Alderic.

Unger spoke up, his eyes fixed unwaveringly on Alderic. "The ring shall be pulled free by one made an orphan, if not by your hand than by your will." He laughed again. "Vesian, your days are numbered."

"Enough! You will lead me to this rock," Alderic said, seizing the advisor. "The Elsin place all their hope in these tales. You wait for a savior, rather than strengthening your land. It is time these fantasies are put to an end." He turned to Callum. "Bring King Unger with you."

Callum pulled the lame king to his feet. Unger tried to resist, but the knight easily overpowered the frail man.

The crown fell from Unger's head, striking the stone floor with a resounding clang. A servant rushed forward to pick it up.

"Leave it there," Callum said, staying the servant.

The knight secured the aged king, dragging him along in Alderic's wake, while the crown lay untouched upon the floor of the Elsin court.

Unger was tied to the saddle, his horse led along by Callum's, as they followed Alderic and the advisor to the city square. They attracted a trail of the Elsin people as they made their journey and by the time they reached the square, a large crowd had formed.

The skies had darkened, and frigid rain was pouring down. This did not deter the Elsin people, who allowed their clothing to soak through as they kept their eyes on Alderic. Even through the downpour, the young king could see the pain and fear on their faces as they watched him approach the fabled rock.

"You see how they gather?" Unger said, blinking through the rain. "They will not stand for your tyranny. We draw power from the Rock of Briggid, a power that you, with all the strength of the Vesian army, shall never grasp."

"Still your tongue," Alderic commanded, turning to Unger. "Soon enough, you shall see that I need no army to cripple the spirit of Elsin."

Unger spat to his left, and Callum pulled abruptly on the reins, causing the Elsin king to lurch forward in the saddle.

Within moments, Alderic would be standing before with the sacred boulder that prophesized his demise by the hand of an Elsin. However, he felt no apprehension as they drew near; he was merely wearied as he took in the terrified appearances of those who crowded to glimpse him through the deluge.

The trembling advisor brought Alderic to the place, before hastily retreating. Alderic now stood before the boulder, the distant gathering encircling him. His soaked hair clung to his face, and he pushed the wet strands from his eyes.

Half of the steel ring stuck out from the rock, the other half seemingly poured into the crevice, where it had hardened. He ran his thumb over the curve of the metal looping. The cold ring was slick with water and worn by the elements, its arcing turn smooth to the touch.

He could feel the loathing directed at him, as he caressed their symbol of freedom. The object upon which the Elsin people had rested all their hopes, their dreams of a kingdom free from the threat of Vesia. Even through the heavy rain, he could hear murmured prayers and oaths as the metal lay beneath his hand.

He stepped away from the rock and returned to his horse, retrieving a hammer from beneath a strap of the saddle. Coming back to stand before the rock, he gave the hoop one more glance, before bringing the head of the hammer down to strike the protruding ring squarely at the top.

Hammer met steel with a clash. The sound ripped through the heavy rain like a peal of thunder, and the ring sparked bright as it was driven down into the boulder.

Alderic could feel the force of the blow tear through his arms as he pulled back. His ears rang with the resonance of the assault, and his fingers ached as they tightened around the handle.

He held the hammer aloft, prepared to strike again, but saw that this was unnecessary. The force of his swing had cracked the stone in half, the two pieces rolling slightly away from one another. The steel was exposed, but still lay firmly within the rock.

Alderic kicked against the hoop, forcing it from the halved boulder. He reached down, and retrieved the liberated steel ring. He held it high above his head so that all those gathered could see. His eyes locked with Unger's, the latter looking on, helpless to halt the dismantling of the Elsin prophesy.

Alderic dropped the ring to the ground, crushing it into the mud with the heel of his boot. The bright steel disappeared, engulfed in grime, and Alderic watched as the crowd gradually dispersed. Their fallen faces faded away as they departed into the downpour.

Unger slumped in the saddle, his royal garments plastered to his body by the freezing rain, emphasizing the frailty of his frame. His horse was pulled forward by Callum, as they made the journey back to the castle. Unger gave no more resistance, allowing himself to be led in silence, his tears blending with the rainfall.

When they returned to the castle, they stopped in the courtyard. Unger's advisors had disappeared, leaving the Elsin king alone with Alderic and Callum.

Alderic was the first to dismount. He left the reins of his horse with Callum, as he circled to where Unger sat, untied but still in the saddle. He took the feeble king from horseback into his arms.

Alderic carried him through the halls. King Unger weighed little more than a small child, his thin skin covering trembling bones. It was as if all the vulnerability of the Elsin land was reflected in the frail body of their king.

In a way, Alderic pitied the decrepit king, and regretted taking such action against the spirit of the Elsin. King Unger had protected his land with fierce devotion, showing nothing but love for his people. He was simply no match for the power of Vesia; he was no match for King Alderic.

The Vesian deposited Unger on the throne. Alderic stepped back and cast a critical eye over the sopping wet, skeletal king.

"I trust I can leave you here for now," Alderic said. "Five of my soldiers will stay behind in Elsin to ensure nothing untoward occurs in my absence."

"What will you do with us?" Unger asked through a dry cough. "Will we lose our kingdom?"

Alderic shook his head. "You will continue to be king for now, but you are to do as I say. I will not tolerate any talk of an uprising, and demand a vow of absolute allegiance."

"You have it," Unger said sullenly.

"My soldiers will ensure that, this time, you are kept to your word," Alderic responded.

"We thank you for your generosity," Unger said, pausing as if considering his next words carefully. "You have shown us leniency, so I shall offer you a warning. We are a land filled with those orphaned through your past wars. For your own sake, you should not rest easy having merely destroyed the Rock of Briggid."

Alderic turned on his heel, leaving King Unger without his cane, stranded on his throne in the empty room. The ailing king called out to the conqueror, but his pleas landed on deaf ears.

Alderic returned to his room, and changed into fresh attire. He had just begun another examination of the map, when Callum knocked on the door.

"Assign five of the soldiers to stay behind," Alderic ordered. "They are to keep King Unger under constant observation, ensuring he makes no decisions that go against Vesia."

"I understand. When do we depart?"

"Immediately. We do not know how long the outlaws will remain in Lord Richard's custody. He is a contemptable and unpredictable man, controlled only by his own degenerate impulses."

Callum departed to fulfill Alderic's command, leaving the king to look over the papers. There was only one mark remaining on Ethin's map, a single unvisited point. On the parchment, it appeared to be the three markings indicating a spring, but without the final piece, the spring could be anywhere.

The advantage of Lord Richard's capture of Moirin and her companions was the delay of their search. For, so long as they were detained in Larian Castle, whatever lay within the brass box would remain stationary.

It was still raining when the sun began to set. The conditions were far from ideal, but Alderic refused to delay their travel to Larian Castle. The horses were saddled, and his soldiers were assembled, save for the five left behind.

Alderic looked over the soldiers who were to accompany him, taking note of those Callum had selected to stay behind. The king was pleased to see that Callum had chosen well, and that those who remained in Elsin were both highly capable of the task ahead of them and dispensable to the king's immediate journey. With no delays, they would reach Lord Richard's castle by morning.

43

At midnight, the door of the torture room opened slowly. None of the occupants had been sleeping, each far too apprehensive for rest. Blake tensed, lifting his head painfully to view the newcomer. Ajed stepped into the room, closing the door behind him.

Ajed stood before Moirin, who sat atop the closed casket. "I am glad to see you have all made it through thus far." He turned his attention to Blake, his brow furrowed. "I am truly sorry for the damage inflicted on your leg."

Blake waved away the concern, though even the nonchalant gesture caused him to ache. "Nothing appears out of place."

Ajed nodded, before turning back to Moirin. He frowned as he looked on the prisoners with pity.

"There is no aid I can offer you." He sighed, the weight on his heart apparent. "Lord Richard has many faithful to him; he has even begun to turn the guards and servants against me. The exits are always under watch and, even now, I am guarded by one of Lord Richard's men who waits for me outside this room. I have risked much coming here, and live each day on time borrowed against whatever usefulness I still hold for the baron."

He looked back to Blake. "I ask, though I believe already knowing the answer, whether there is anything you can do to fulfill Lord Richard's challenge, and spare the life of your companion."

Blake was silent for a moment before answering. He wanted desperately to make it so, but he could see no way around Aeron's death.

"Every part of the execution is controlled by Lord Richard: the blade, the place, and even Owen," he said, casting a reproachful glance toward the humbled warrior. "Without control over even one of these components, I cannot see a way out."

Moirin stepped down from the casket, extending her hand to Ajed.

"I thank you for your loyalty to the memory of Silvius. He was a noble man, and you have done him great justice."

Ajed's eyes filled with tears at the mention of his deceased master, and he nodded to Moirin in thanks before departing; there was nothing more he could offer the captives.

The next morning, a sharp knock came at the door. Blake could not remember the moment he had fallen asleep. He had been so sure the night before that no rest would come, yet he was startled awake by the sudden noise. Looking around he could see Aeron had also just awoken, though Moirin and Owen had the composed weariness of remaining awake the entire night.

Though he had hoped a plan would come to him in the night, no such miracle had occurred. He thought only of holding off the execution for a moment more, praying that the stolen moments would yield to him some scheme by which Aeron might be spared.

Blake sprang up, wincing as pain tore through his brutalized leg. He grabbed an object from the table, shoved it in his pocket, and stepped past his companions, meeting the guard at the door.

"May I speak to Lord Richard privately?" he asked.

"No, it is time," the guard responded forcefully.

"Please, I promise you he will want to speak with me," Blake urged. "He will be angry with you if I am denied this."

The guard looked him over. Finally, he nodded silently.

Blake winced as he forced his boot on over his abused leg, and followed the guard from the room. The door was locked behind them, and Blake could see Aeron's troubled face through the small, barred opening.

The guard led him through the hall, pain filling every step Blake took. They reached a closed door, and the guard knocked twice, before gaining admission.

The chamber they entered was lavishly decorated with patterned rugs, and crimson curtains framed stained-glass windows. Lord Richard lounged in an armchair looking vaguely amused to see Blake standing so inelegantly in the entrance.

"You may wait outside," Lord Richard said to the guard, his eyes never leaving Blake.

Lord Richard indicated for Blake to sit opposite, only a foot away. The baron watched as Blake limped to the chair, the corners of his lips pulling into a smile as he beheld the lasting effects of his leather contraption.

"What brings you here?" he asked. "I will not allow your friend a stay of execution, if that is what you are seeking."

"It would make no difference," Blake responded. "You know as well as I do that the challenge you present is impossible to fulfill."

Lord Richard leaned back. "Indeed, though I am surprised to find you accept defeat so readily. Why are you here?"

Blake pulled from his pocket the device he had brought from the torture room. Looking on it for the first time, he saw it was made of two metal bars, set parallel by two long screws. On one of the bars lay sliding metal pieces, long and narrow.

"I would like to know what this is," Blake said, passing the contraption to Lord Richard.

The baron laughed as he received the instrument, turning it over in his hands. "You do not expect me to believe that such curiosity is genuine."

"No, but you'll tell me anyway." Blake knew he was being over-confident, but he had nothing to lose. Besides, there was something about Lord Richard, an aspect that made Blake sure the baron would indulge him.

Lord Richard cocked his head to the side, and looked inquisitively on Blake.

"Why should I do such a thing?"

"You would know that better than I," Blake responded.

Lord Richard smiled. "You aren't wrong." He clasped the device, warming the metal in his palm. "I find you interesting, more so than the others. They are battle-tried, wearied by their struggles and broken by the search for power. You are different, though if you spend much longer in their company you may find yourself similarly tried."

"It is far better than following your path, which leads only to depravity and despair," Blake responded.

He looked on Lord Richard, a question needling the back of his mind.

"Have you ever had a wife or husband? Taken a lover?" Blake asked. "Do you care for anything beyond these amusements?"

Lord Richard grinned, leaning forward. "It seems I understand you far better than you understand me." He pressed his fingertips to his chin, considering as he spoke. "These contraptions provide me with more pleasure and entertainment than a man or woman ever could. I have no interest in human flesh, beyond how much pain it can withstand. Anything else is mundane."

At this Lord Richard laughed, running his delicate fingers across his face. He rolled his crisp, white shirtsleeves to the elbow, and took the device back into his hands.

"You wish to know what this is?" His eyes were hard despite his still grinning mouth. "It is an early design of my own. Not very successful, so I suppose I keep it for sentimental reasons. It was meant to cause pain with no lasting damage by driving these loose pieces between the bones of the hand, compressing the soft tissues. I was overzealous in my first uses of it, and broke bones of the few unlucky."

He smiled, as if lost in a memory. "I remember a man named Thomas. I broke both his thumbs using this device. After the bars were removed, I'm sure one trained in medicine could have set the bones. Instead, I cut them off completely.

"I left him alone to recover and the next morning, I found he had amputated all the fingers on his own left hand, before cutting off the hand completely. He had tied a belt around his arm, to stay the blood, and he had thrown the severed pieces to the far side of the room, as though he wanted nothing to do with them."

"Did he survive?" Blake asked in spite of himself.

Lord Richard nodded. "He did. Given your running about with the nobility, you may have even crossed paths."

"I think I would remember a thumbless Thomas."

The baron chuckled. "Indeed."

Lord Richard's attention was brought back to the device. "While clumsy, and undoubtedly flawed, I feel there is a certain beauty, a simplicity to the design. It has been years since I held it in my hands."

Blake's teeth were set on edge by the tenderness with which Lord Richard discussed his invention, but he felt unable to look away.

"Shall we have a demonstration of its use now?"

Blake shook his head. "My hands have suffered enough damage."

"I did not mean on you," Lord Richard answered quietly.

There was a small table beside them, and Lord Richard pulled it into the space between. He propped the instrument on the table surface, righting it when it fell to the side.

"Poor craftsmanship," Lord Richard said with an almost indulgent tone.

He set his hand between the bars, putting the metal pieces, long side down, against the back of his hand. He tightened the screws until the pieces were set very lightly against the flesh between his finger bones.

He looked up at Blake.

"Now, you are to turn the screws. Be sure to keep the bars level, otherwise it will not work."

Lord Richard's expression was earnest, but untroubled. There was no doubt in Blake's mind that Lord Richard truly intended for him to enact this punishment.

Blake was surprised to find himself hesitating. After the pain he had endured at the baron's hands, he should rightfully be seeking reparations, but his fingers shook slightly as he reached forward and touched the rusted screws.

"Do not be afraid. Tighten them," Lord Richard insisted, seeing Blake's tentativeness.

Blake's eyes met Lord Richards for a moment, a jolt of anticipation coursing through him before he began a half-turn of one screw. He could not work them both at the same time, given the state of his right hand, so he alternated between the turnpieces.

The bars were coming closer together, and Blake could see the metal pressing into the pale, delicate skin. Lord Richard's bones were steadily becoming more visible, as the flesh was crushed. He looked again at Lord Richard's face, and could see the signs of pain appear; the baron's usually grinning mouth was drawn into a thin line.

Blake tightened the screws further. He could have ceased, but he realized that he wanted to cause Lord Richard agony. Blake had not yet been stopped, and he would close the bars until the metal pieces pierced the flesh, pinning the baron's hand to the dreaded contraption.

The skin was taut, and Blake could see Lord Richard's breath becoming ragged. A swell of warmth filled his chest, as he continued the cursed work.

Finally, the baron placed his hand on Blake's, stilling the tightening of the screws.

"Enough," Lord Richard said quietly.

Blake pulled back, looking again at Lord Richard. The other man's face was paler than before, and a slight sweat was forming at his temples. Lord Richard took the device into his lap, gently unscrewing the bars until he could pull his hand free.

He set the instrument down on the table between them, and turned his hand back and forth. Already, deep marks were forming in a band across the back of his hand. He looked at Blake, a smile again lighting on his lips.

He stood, and Blake did the same. Lord Richard took Blake's chin in his affected hand and pressed his lips to the thief's brow.

Lord Richard's mouth was cold against Blake's skin, and Blake flinched as he felt the baron's sweat slick on his forehead.

"We are more alike than you think. Should anything happen to you, I would be truly sorry," he said softly.

Without another word, Lord Richard opened the door and summoned the guard to bring Blake and the others to the grand hall. Blake had stalled the execution for as long as he could.

As he was led back toward the torture room, Blake reflected on their predicament. While he may not be able to manipulate the execution itself, there remained options. He knew he would need to make use of whatever else was available to him.

Rejoining his companions on the path to the great hall, Blake kept tight to Aeron's side. He whispered in her ear, his words inaudible to the guards who followed them.

"I cannot bring you back, but there is someone who can prevent the execution from taking place. Someone who could in an instant end the lives of all Lord Richard's bodyguards and servants before killing the baron himself."

"If you mean Owen, it is unlikely he will turn against his new master," she muttered back.

"I will admit, it is a poor prospect. Yet, I believe that once the axe is in his hands, I can help him along the way," Blake said, praying he was not giving her false hope. Though, he could not help but feel that it was better for her to face death with the belief that she might be saved, than in a state of complete despair.

The bright light of morning illuminated the hall, and Blake could immediately see the changes Lord Richard had made during the night. In the center of the room stood a hinged wooden contraption, which had a space for the neck and wrists to be held fast, much resembling a pillory.

As soon as Aeron saw the restraints she tried to bolt, but was set upon immediately by the guards who followed them. Her arms and legs were held tight, as she was forced toward the center of the room. Her neck was set into the large opening, and her wrists placed in the two dips inches away from her face. The hinge was closed and no matter how much she struggled, she could not break free from the contraption.

Lord Richard sat the remaining three captives on the bench, opposite the restrained bandit queen. He paced in front of them, glancing back and forth between Aeron and the others. His lips parting to reveal white teeth in a lustful smile that set his captives on edge.

"Before we begin, there is one more matter to attend to," Lord Richard said.

Two guards dragged the casket into the room, and Blake shuddered as he remembered the impressive iron thorns that lay within. Blake wondered which of them was ill-fated enough to be thus condemned.

Lord Richard looked at each of his captives in turn, before bringing his gaze to the corner of the room, where his late father's faithful advisor stood.

"Ajed," Lord Richard began, as his guards seized the startled man, "did you think your midnight visits to the prisoners would be overlooked? Do you think yourself so indispensable to the running of my affairs that I would not punish such blatant disobedience? You are a traitor, and this should have been done long ago."

"Lord Richard," Moirin said, standing.

One of Lord Richard's bodyguards forced her back into her seat and stayed beside her, sword drawn, to ensure there would be no further attempt at intercession.

Lord Richard looked briefly at Moirin, before turning back to the trembling Ajed.

"My lord," Ajed stammered, "I, only—"

"Silence," Lord Richard commanded with a wave of his hand, "I have heard enough of your words to last me twelve lifetimes."

The baron crossed the room, throwing open the lid to the casket, revealing the blood-rusted spikes within. Two guard pulled the struggling man forward, forcing him to recline across the lower row of barbs.

Ajed's chest heaved as tears rolled down his face. It seemed he had not yet been pierced by the sharp points he lay across.

"Please my lord, for the sake of your father, do not do this," he pleaded.

Lord Richard laughed. "There are no words that would better secure your fate."

With this, Lord Richard pulled down the lid of the casket. Blake could hear the spearing of flesh, as cries of agony rose, distorted by the layers of metal.

Lord Richard set his shoulder against the foot of the casket, pushing it across the floor. The iron grated against stone as it was shoved forward. Blood streamed from the box, streaking the floor crimson, and twice the baron's boots slipped in the growing pool. Lord Richard pushed the casket into the roaring hearth, where flames lapped the metal sides.

Aeron could not see the fire, due to her restraints, but she closed her eyes. She allowed her neck to rest against the hinged board, no longer trying to glimpse the scene of destruction.

Though he was seated, Blake felt distinctly unsteady. He looked to Owen and Moirin, both of whom stared, motionless, at the casket. He wanted to shout for help, to stop the burning of Ajed. In that moment, he realized the true extent of their helplessness.

Blood hissed and Ajed's cries increased in fervor, before ceasing completely with a rattling groan. The smell of burning flesh and hair rose from the hearth, filling the air of the great hall. Lord Richard gazed contentedly upon the fire-consumed casket before turning back to those assembled.

Lord Richard glanced at Blake from across the room, their eyes briefly locking.

"There are far worse ways to die," he said gently.

Blake believed him.

"We are moments away from justice for my people, and a great test of skill." Lord Richard's fingertips stroked his forearm absently as he spoke. "Reanimation of the dead, especially reattachment of a severed head is a feat that even most powerful liogan would likely struggle to perform." The baron turned to Blake, an aberrant shine in his eye. "Remember that I will enjoy nothing more than to continue the work I began on you last night."

Blake looked to Moirin, but found her eyes were still fixed on the flame-engulfed casket. He tried to shake the sense of incapacity Ajed's death had inspired, as he set his mind on his burgeoning plan. As unlikely as success was, he could see no other way.

He swallowed, his throat sticking, rose shakily to his feet, and came to stand beside Aeron. He could not see her eyes, as they were obscured by the long, dirty mess of hair that fell across her face and onto the floor, but he placed his hand on her shoulder in reassurance.

Lord Richard brought Owen to stand beside Aeron, pressing the warrior's own axe into his hands.

Owen stood, dumbly, before Blake. He held the axe, but made no move. He appeared to be waiting for instruction from Lord Richard before he dared so much as adjust the grip of the weapon in his hands.

Blake noted the docility in his demeanor; Owen found it a relief to turn himself over, body and soul, to a strong commander, to no longer have to decide for himself. Blake remembered Lord Richard whispering, and a shudder ran down his spine.

The half-blind warrior raised the axe over Aeron's head. He would wait for Lord Richard to give the final order for the beheading.

Aeron's eyes were closed as she waited for the inevitable axe-fall, while Moirin and Blake looked on in horror. It seemed that their fearful anticipation gave Lord Richard pleasure, as he visibly reveled in the delay.

Blake knew the word would come soon enough, and that he had no time to lose. The axe was in Owen's hands, and this alone was half of his plan. His only hope was to turn Owen on Lord Richard by creating a violent act, igniting the animalistic urge that could consume the warrior's meekness.

"Bring down the axe," Lord Richard said.

The very second that Lord Richard ordered the beheading, Blake kicked Owen square in the back. He put as much force as he possessed into the action. His body ached, as he rested all his weight on the injured foot, and he could feel Owen's lightness as he shoved him forward. The blow sent the former knight hurtling into the baron.

No change came over Owen. He did not stop the fall, but the axe head fell flat between his chest and that of Lord Richard, causing both men to fall to the ground. The warrior righted himself immediately, and stood beside the capsized baron, looking blankly at Blake.

To Blake's dismay, Owen was Lord Richard's to command. The thief panicked as he realized he was only seconds away from tasting the edge of Owen's axe: Lord Richard only need give the order. His attempt to use Owen's trauma to his advantage was the height of foolishness, and Blake realized that it would likely cost him his life.

Blake was distracted from this morbid thought by a commotion near the castle entrance. He could hear clashing weapons and shouting followed by sudden silence, broken only by the approaching tread of boots.

He looked at Lord Richard, but the baron merely shrugged in response.

King Alderic swept through the door, his knight at his heels. Eight soldiers had followed him into the castle, while the others remained outside to secure the remainder of Lord Richard's guards.

Lord Richard was still sitting on the floor, where he had been thrown during the altercation between Blake and Owen, his head resting against the bench. His hair was tousled, and a small trickle of blood ran down his forehead. His smile was wide as he watched Alderic subdue his bodyguards, and he let out a jovial laugh as he sat up against the leg of the bench.

Two soldiers released Aeron from her restraints, and tried to place her in shackles of their own. She threw the two soldiers to the ground, but was overwhelmed when the weight of three of their peers came down upon her.

Moirin too was captured by the soldiers, though she did not attempt to fight back.

Blake did his best to keep out of the soldiers' reach. The king's knight broke through the ranks, and headed straight for him. His breath caught, as he looked upon the face of his old partner, though he had little time to react, as Hugh was advancing on him rapidly.

Blake scrambled across the tabletop, but Hugh caught him by the heel. Blake kicked back, landing a few blows on Hugh's torso. He was surprised to see that his strikes did little to slow the knight.

Hugh grabbed Blake's injured leg. Blake collapsed in agony as Hugh's grasp tightened around the devastated muscle. Suffering rolled through his entire body, as every nerve was set afire by the knight's wrenching of the damaged flesh. Hugh was then able to take him by the shoulders, and haul him to his feet.

Owen, however, remained untouched. The axe was gripped loosely in his hands, though he gave the impression that he would make short work of any attacker with the courage to approach. It appeared King Alderic's presence had brought forth the fight that Blake's kick had failed to.

One soldier advanced, his steel sword drawn. He lunged, and was struck down instantly by Owen's axe.

The fierce nature of the warrior did not deter King Alderic, who motioned for his soldiers to stand down. He took his own bronze blade in his hand, and drew near his former knight. When he came within striking range, Owen swung the axe out.

The blade missed King Alderic by inches, snagging instead the edge of his cloak. The Blackdog King smiled at the near contact and with one hand he undid the clasp at his throat, letting the cloak fall to the ground.

Owen stepped back, blindly climbing to stand on the bench. The axe rested in the space between the two men, while the king's brazen blade held back, as if stalking its prey.

Lord Richard still sat on the floor with his back against the bench where Owen stood. King Alderic paced only a foot away from the seated baron, while the warrior's axe was poised dangerously close to Lord Richard's head. Despite the apparent risk, the baron seemed unfazed by his surroundings, and made no attempt to remove himself from harm's way. He smiled as he took in the scene unfolding around him, more amused than afraid.

Blake caught a glint in Owen's eye. It was something separate from the drive that engulfed him during the fight. There was a reflective aspect to this flash, and Blake realized why both men took their time approaching. There was an intimacy to their knowledge of each other's movements. King Alderic had instructed Owen in the art of fighting, and Owen had been King Alderic's dutiful apprentice. Both were doubtless among the most skilled warriors in the world, but they were nearly ineffectual in each other's presence. In order for one to gain the upper hand, they would need to act unpredictably.

It was King Alderic who seized the opportunity. He slammed his boot against the center of the bench, causing the wood to break in half.

Owen leapt out of the way, but King Alderic was ready for him. Surging forward, he seized Owen's axe, and pulled it roughly. Owen was thrown off balance, and King Alderic dragged him to the ground. He pushed his heel against the warrior's neck, until the fallen man stopped struggling.

Blake saw the defiance leave Owen's body, witnessing the depletion with a sense of sorrow. Still, though their only hope died with Owen's heart, he knew it was for the best that Owen ceased before any real harm came to him.

Hugh was holding Blake's upper arm tight, his fingers leaving marks on Blake's skin. Blake jerked away reflexively, and Hugh pulled him closer.

"Hugh, why are you doing this?" Blake asked, pleading.

"My name is Callum," he responded coldly. "Hugh died the moment he was left on the mercy of the hangman."

Blake looked into the knight's face, searching for some spark of familiarity. He sought the loyalty Hugh had shown over the time of their partnership, but he found it had been replaced by a fanaticism for the Vesian king. Blake would receive no pity.

King Alderic pulled Owen to his feet, and a soldier drew out shackles, proceeding to bind Owen's hands. When the half-blind warrior was safely secured, King Alderic passed the task of Owen's guarding to a soldier. King Alderic himself placed the restraints on Moirin's wrists, while Aeron and Blake were similarly bound.

The king passed a hand into the pocket of Moirin's skirt, retrieving the small metal plate. Moirin's jaw clenched as King Alderic looked down at the golden disk that had once lain carefully hidden in Linwood. Any chance they had of diverting him with the empty brass box was gone.

Through all their tribulations, they had managed to survive. Against the odds, they had found the final piece to understanding the map, and it now lay in the King Alderic's hands.

44

The king stowed the piece, and offered an appreciative nod to his four captives. He looked again at the dismantled restraints in the center of the room, and the blood that streaked across the floor leading to an iron casket in the fire, from which emanated the scent of burning human flesh.

He turned back to the room, his eyes lighting on the baron. Lord Richard was still on the floor, askew beside the broken bench. His hair was disheveled, and his clothing in a state of disarray. From the ground, he watched as the king approached him; he made no attempt to stand or retreat.

Alderic seized the front of Lord Richard's white linen shirt, and hauled him to his feet. The king pushed him against the table, thrusting his palm against the baron's chest.

Lord Richard fell back against the surface, his eyes still crinkled pleasantly in a grin as he looked up at Alderic. A slight laugh escaped his lips, as he stared down his king.

"Lord Richard," the king growled, "Your depravity is evidenced by a single glance." His tone lowered as he inched toward the baron. "I have warned you before that your degenerate pastimes will not be tolerated in my kingdom."

"Calm yourself, Blackdog King," Lord Richard responded, his voice jovial. "Your precious Moirin is unharmed, I saw to it myself. As for the others, they are a thief, a bandit, and a traitor, respectively. You can hardly fault me for amusing myself with these villains."

"And who lays in the fire?" he asked.

"Do not concern yourself with him; he was no friend to your highness. Justice has been meted out. It is no different than those rulings given by the vigilantes of Vesia who thrive in the absence of true order."

Lord Richard's betrayal of the previous baron's cause had gained him adversaries. In truth, despite their mutual hatred of each other, Alderic and Lord Richard shared many common enemies.

"This cannot go on," Alderic responded, undeterred.

"What are you going to do?" Lord Richard asked.

Alderic unsheathed his sword, and lay the point of the blade against Lord Richard's neck. The bronze point sat against skin, as the king weighed his options. He had no desire to kill Lord Richard, but it seemed his warnings had been ignored by the baron, and he could not tolerate such obvious disregard of his authority within Vesia.

Lord Richard appeared to sense the king's hesitancy to kill him, and he let out a laugh. His flesh jogged against the sword, and a droplet of blood appeared on his throat.

Seeing the blood, the king withdrew the weapon and set it back in the sheath. He had never encountered difficulty disciplining the nobles of his land, but Lord Richard could not be threatened because he did not care about consequences. While the king was reluctant to admit it, he was at a loss handling the wayward baron.

Lord Richard lay back, his fingers reaching the small laceration at his neck. His fingertips dipped into the growing crimson pool, and he drew the bloodied digits down his neck and across his chest. The red lines disappeared into the open folds of his shirt, and he looked down in admiration at his own blood-painted skin.

Alderic watched the display, aware that a failure to deal with Lord Richard adequately would undermine his authority. He drew back his fist before connecting it solidly with the side of the baron's head, the sound of the strike echoing through the hall.

Lord Richard fell back against the table, unconscious. His head rolled to the side, and his hand fell away from the blood on his chest, peaceful as he lay across the wide boards. The lines of his face relaxed, and he appeared almost handsome in the ease of his stupor.

Alderic turned to the guards. "He has some kind of torture room, does he not?"

The guards were silent, but a voice sounded behind him. "He does."

It was Blake who had spoken. Alderic offered the thief a half-nod, before turning back to the unconscious deviant.

Alderic called forth three of his soldiers. "Find the room, and bind the baron there. You are to stay behind in Larian Castle to ensure he is not freed by his servants or bodyguards." He turned to Lord Richard's servants. "Clean this room, and bury whoever is within the fire."

He led his soldiers and the four captives from the great hall, casting a final glance across the blood streaked floor, scorched iron casket, and dismantled pillory.

A cart sat in the center of the courtyard, hitched to two horses. The prisoners were, one by one, led into the small wagon, and their hand shackles fastened to metal hoops protruding from the sideboards.

He would not dispense with the captives. There was nowhere nearby for them to be imprisoned, and he could not afford to send away any more soldiers. Besides, Moirin and her companions have proved useful in the past, so they would be kept chained to the wagon, carried along to the final point.

Alderic led the party from Larian Castle, guided by the information gleaned from the metal plate. His journey's end was finally in sight.

45

The rain had stopped, but the sky was still overcast. Lightening flashed in the distance, crawling in streaks across the clouded atmosphere before dissolving away. The horses' hooves splattered mud with every step, and the wood of the cart was slick with damp.

Blake pulled surreptitiously against his bindings, but found they held fast. He glanced at Moirin, whose eyes scanned the surroundings absently. It seemed she had embraced their failure with resignation, recognizing the futility of trying to escape the hold of the cart.

"Where are we headed?" he asked her quietly.

"The village of Rowena, though it hardly matters now. Even if we could free ourselves, King Alderic has all the pieces required to find the liogan weapon," Moirin responded.

The thief turned silently back to the road ahead.

Earlier that morning, Blake had forced his damaged foot into his boot. Since it seemed that he would not be required to walk in the near future, he brought his foot up to meet his hands, and grasped the leather at the side of the boot to pull the shoe off of his leg. It stuck, and he put the toe of his other boot against the heel, pressing it to the side of the cart as he dragged the article from his leg.

The skin felt hot, and he pressed the side of his bare foot against the bottom of the cart. The cold damp soothed his tortured appendage, and he took a deep breath as the cool spread through his veins. He moved his toes a little, grateful to be free of the confining boot.

Aeron was bound near the back of the cart, and she was roughly jostled with each stone and dip that the wheels encountered. While Blake resented their capture by the king, he knew that without the ruler's intervention

Aeron would be laying in pieces on the floor of Lord Richard's hall, though she would be lucky if that was all. Having met the baron, he doubted the man's depraved amusements would have ended upon her death.

Owen's head was bowed, his long hair falling across the shackles at his wrists. His shoulders were crumpled beneath the weight of his failings, and his eyes did not venture to meet those of his companions.

Blake wished he could offer the broken warrior some comfort, let him know that he was not to blame for their capture. In spite of himself, Blake was angry at Owen for failing to slay either Lord Richard or King Alderic. He was also embarrassed by his own miscalculation regarding Owen's mental state, an error which had left Lord Richard alive and well.

King Alderic sent Callum to the back of the company, to better keep an eye on the prisoners. The knight brought his horse around and followed the cart closely, keeping a watch over the individuals bound therein.

Blake welcomed his old partner's presence. He now had an outlet for the unjustified sense of betrayal he felt towards Owen.

"What's wrong, Blake?" Callum spoke between upwardly curving lips. "Can you not find a clever way out of this? Perhaps if you leave the others to die, you can save your own neck."

The barbed words achieved their purpose, and Blake felt their cut as surely as he would the blade of a knife. The eyes of the once presumed dead man looked back at him with a grin. Rage filled Blake; he could feel the tension behind his skull, straining to take control.

Blake was surprised when Owen's knee pressed against his shin. The pressure applied to the damaged tissue sent pain hurtling through his body, clearing his mind of emotion. He cursed beneath his breath as the ragged nerves surged, but was grateful for the moment of clarity which the ache brought him.

He nodded to Owen in thanks, but his fellow prisoner only looked away.

Blake looked to Callum. "Saving you was impossible. Anyone else would have done the same," he protested.

"I would not have left you there," Callum said quietly, and Blake knew it to be true.

Callum was loyal to a fault. The knight would have died trying to pry the bars away with his bare hands, sooner than leave a friend to die.

"It seems my betrayal has suited you well," Blake said, ignoring the familiar guilt, "as you've so readily assumed the office of king's dog."

"Better the king's dog than a thief's lackey," Callum responded coldly. "Blake, you are so often sentenced to death that it seems the gods themselves seek your execution."

Blake glared back as Callum looked down with a slight smirk.

"What are you doing back here? Don't the Blackdog King's boots need shining," Aeron interjected, her eyes firmly fixed on Callum. Even bound to the cart, the bandit queen seemed determined to protect Blake.

Callum looked on the prisoners a moment more, before turning back to the road. He stayed beside the cart, but his focus was on King Alderic.

Blake slept as they were carried along in a direction only the king and Moirin understood. It was dark when he woke, and his neck was tender from resting at an angle. In the light of the moon he could see Owen's staring, vacant eye.

Callum still rode behind them, his horse's steps paced and even in the pale glow. It was only because Blake had known him for so long, that he could perceive how tired the knight truly was. Watching the king's captives from the saddle, Callum was vigilant. He held upright and stiff-necked, but there was something in the hang of his shoulders that betrayed a bone-weariness even a zealot's enthusiasm could not mask.

Blake's mind returned to an earlier time. Hugh had been in his company for only a month, when they were nearly caught stealing a pure silver weathervane from a duke. Instead of running away, they had hidden themselves on the flat rooftop, lying on their stomachs until nightfall. They successfully made away with the silver but for the next week, Hugh did not sleep even a moment. Blake tried to convince him they were far from danger, but Hugh had become extreme in his vigilance. In time, this guardedness faded a little, but Blake would always remember the fatigued alertness that had so strangely come over his partner.

Blake craned his neck over the edge of the cart. He could see the cloaked king tirelessly leading the pack of soldiers through the darkened road.

Inside of the cart, he was not the only one with sight fixed on the king. Moirin watched King Alderic through half-lidded eyes. Her head dipped with each jolt of the cart, and even chained to a small wagon she maintained an elegance that Blake found inexplicably chilling.

The liogan weapon she had risked her life to find would soon be within the Blackdog King's grasp, yet she seemed to take the loss in stride. She had claimed that this weapon was the only thing that could challenge King Alderic's rule, and Blake wondered what was to blame for their failing. Had they been a mere day ahead of the king, perhaps the weapon would be in Moirin's possession.

He tried to imagine Vesia divided by war between Moirin and King Alderic, but all he could picture was the destruction they would leave in their wake. He could practically smell the burning homes, and taste the blood in the air.

As morning broke, they passed shepherds gently guiding flocks in their shared direction. Even in the early hours of day, the sun beat down on the earth, and Blake could feel his shirt soaking through with sweat. His lungs were filled with the dust kicked up by the horses. The feel of the thick air was suffocating, and he pulled ineffectively against the chains.

As if crossing an invisible border, the dry dirt of the landscape dwindled, replaced with lush verdure. The branches of trees hung low, laden with green leaves and ripe fruit. The dirt beneath the horses' hooves grew softer, the dust replaced by fragrant soil and fresh mud.

Blake could see shepherds drawing water for their flocks at the base of a fall, which sprang from the side of the mountain. Water poured down over dark rocks, and the spray sent a light mist through the air that lit in colors as it passed beneath the sun's rays. Dashing over water-worn stone, it came to pool at the base in a blue swell that reflected immaculately the clear sky above.

The cart had come to a halt near the waterfall, and King Alderic dismissed his men to find food and drink. Callum clearly wished to stay behind and keep watch over the prisoners, but the king insisted the knight accompany the soldiers to find sustenance.

King Alderic would watch the prisoners himself.

Small homes, made of wood and tented canvas, comprised a nearby village. Blake guessed that these were the homes of the shepherds. From far away, he could see the people greet the soldiers, the exchange seeming amiable enough.

Blake looked over the edge of the cart. In a tree, a blackbird seemed to watch him as it bobbed its head. The bird began to sing and the sound uplifted him, despite his circumstances.

Alderic knelt at the edge of the spring. The clear water rippled under his fingertips. He cupped his hands together beneath the surface, and brought the water to his face. He watched as the dirt from the day's travel was carried from his skin. Similarly, he cleaned his arms, before bowing to drink from the fountain. His throat was dry, and the water soothed his need.

The king retrieved a leather flask from a supply-laden horse and filled it at the spring. He brought it to the cart, holding it out to Moirin in a gesture of benevolence. He knew she would be tempted to reject the offering, but he also knew his captives would soon be overcome by thirst.

She hesitated for a moment before taking the flask from his hand. Her unwillingness to accept any kindness from the king was evident, but her thirst left her unable to refuse the offer. She drank, before handing the flask to Blake, who sat across from her. In time, the flask had been taken from by each prisoner, and Alderic left it in the bottom of the cart, within their reach.

His eyes rested on Moirin, and he felt the familiar uncertainty. His desire was tempered by terror of his own reaction, and any fondness he might feel for her was mingled with an acute sense of loss. She stood as testament to the demise of his only brother, of Severin, and with every glance the hurt began anew.

In spite of himself, Alderic sought Moirin's gaze, and was disappointed to find that she kept her face turned resolutely away from him, her eyes downcast. Alderic's throat felt suddenly dry again, as his sight traced the gently curving line of her neck, lazily trailing the copper skin, until he could take the image no more.

He turned his attention instead to Blake's hand, which rested on the edge of the cart. Alderic noted that the knife wound he had inflicted was beginning to heal; it no longer bled, though the hand bore significant bruising and a slash severing the flesh between the thumb and index finger.

The bare foot of the thief rested awkwardly on its side, propped against the opposite thigh. A web of overlaid bruises dappled the skin purple, black and yellow. The bones seemed in place and intact, as there were no unusual protrusions, but the damage done was readily apparent.

Alderic did not know the cause of the injury but, given Lord Richard's debauched indulgences, he was able to guess the nature of the incident. Though previously the king had not hesitated in ordering the thief's death, he felt sorry to have in some way caused the man to endure such bodily perversion at the hands of the baron.

Blake saw the king staring, and self-consciously tucked the bare foot under his other knee, wincing as the abused flesh was squeezed between his leg and the bottom of the cart. His ankle was exposed, and he knew he could not hide the degradation of the torments suffered within Larian Castle.

Alderic's eye was drawn to the mark on Blake's temple. He had noticed the strange symbol in Linwood, but since then had not thought much on it. He stepped closer and took Blake's chin in his hand, so he could better see the mark. Blake tried to resist, but Alderic forcefully turned the thief's face to the side.

Alderic surveyed the oddly curving lines, and was struck by a sense of recognition. Understanding filled him, and he let drop the thief's chin. He knew the symbol but it seemed strangely out of place, so far from the confines of dusty pages.

It was one of the marks of the death goddess, Erkynon, illustrated in the book he had so often read. Alderic was surprised he had not known it immediately in Linwood. Yet, he was sure the mark was not meant for living flesh. This was the symbol painted in ink and blood on the skin of a human sacrifice, one who would be made to serve the death goddess in the afterlife.

Regardless of what life he led, what good or bad he accomplished in the living world, upon his death, Blake would be of Erkynon. He would be forced do the grave bidding of the underworld for an eternity, with no hope of salvation.

The king pitied the thief. No matter what misdeeds Blake had performed, the countless trivial crimes he had committed in the past, Alderic knew he could not deserve such inhuman punishment.

Alderic stared at Blake, wondering if the thief knew anything of his condemnation: that the judgement rightly belonging to his soul had been stolen from him.

Blake looked back, nothing in his eyes showing knowledge of his heinous fate.

Owen's axe lay strapped to the king's saddle, and Alderic could see his former knight's eyes instinctively seeking out the weapon. He could not bear to look upon the shattered warrior, and instead turned his attention to the only prisoner unknown to him, assuming her to be Aeron, the bandit queen. He noted her unwavering, defiant stare and, in time, he returned her gaze. His black eyes looked idly through hers.

Callum returned early and pulled the king aside.

"There is a woman in the village whom you should meet," he said. "She has a story that may be of interest to you."

Alderic instructed the knight to keep close watch over the prisoners. The king armed himself lightly for entry to the village of Rowena, taking only his sword and a single knife, before making his departure.

Callum sat down on the ground, leaning his back against the trunk of the blackbird's tree. He left the chain mail on, though he was already sweating through the bright yellow shirt beneath. The dust had turned thick with perspiration on his forehead, and he wiped it away with the back of his hand.

Blake wished he could have saved Hugh's soul from the corrupting clutches of the king. Yet, within the shielded eyes he could see burning the same unbridled enthusiasm that had so often irked him. Hugh had found a place for his loyalty, his zealot's fervor. As the king's knight, Callum fulfilled every desire Hugh's simple life as a thief's apprentice had left unmet.

"Are you finally satisfied?"

Callum was silent for a moment, seeming disquieted by the prisoner's candor. Blake found himself praying that the other man would leave the question unanswered, as he already knew Hugh's response. However, Blake knew he never had such luck.

Callum looked up at him, squinting against the sun's rays filtering through the canopy of leaves. A smile grew on his face, as his eyes met Blake's.

"Yes."

Blake was then sure that Callum would as soon die in King Alderic's service as he would take a breath of air.

"Do you remember this?" Blake said. A small, thick leaf had fallen from the tree into the cart. Blake held it in his hand, closed his fingers over the leaf, and showed it to have disappeared upon reopening his hand.

Callum picked up a similar leaf from the ground and copied Blake's motion. His practiced movements were adequate to trick the untrained eye, if a little clumsier than Blake's.

"I wish I were better trained," Callum said, his tone accusatory.

Callum took out his sword and balanced it on his knee. Blake could see a stain of blood near the hilt, and he thought back on the dead bandits.

"Still," Callum began, a slight smile growing on his face, "it has worked out for the best, would you not agree?"

The warm breeze swept through Callum's hair, as he kept a steady eye on his former partner. Blake turned away, his back now facing Callum to the extent his shackles would allow. The gentle wind cooled him, bringing his body relief where his heart would find none. His eyes turned to the prisoner beside him, and he remembered Owen's meeting of Callum in Linwood; Blake should have let the warrior's axe swing put an end to the devoted knight.

46

Alderic followed Callum's directions until he came to the outside of a small dwelling. He ducked his head beneath the overhanging canvas, and saw an old woman sitting in the center of the room, tending absently to the hearth. The sunlight came through the canvas in a muted, golden glow.

"I am King Alderic. I was told you have information of interest to me."

"I know who you are," she responded, without once looking up from her work, "and I know why you are here; you want to know about my granddaughter."

"Your granddaughter?"

"I told that young man who was here earlier. I hoped he might help me find Alyssan." She finally turned to face Alderic. "After all, if the king and his soldiers can't locate one poor villager there's not much hope for his rule."

Alderic was mildly amused by the old woman's directness.

"Why would I be interested in finding your granddaughter?"

She laughed. "I do not know in the slightest. I told the story to your man, and he thought you might want to speak with me personally." She leaned back. "Imagine, the king taking interest in my only granddaughter."

"Tell me what you told the knight," the king responded.

"Alyssan likes to wander, ignoring her responsibilities here. She should be married by now, if you ask me, but never mind that. Alyssan was travelling the hills and, one night, she came home, saying she had found something. The next day, under the first rays of the sun, she took five others with her, and they all went to the small mountain above the spring." She paused, drawing in a deep breath before continuing. "They never returned. I have waited for them there every evening, but they never returned."

"What do you think happened to them?"

"People have stories," she scoffed. "Say they abandoned Rowena in search of better fortunes."

"You do not believe this?" Alderic inquired.

"No, Alyssan wouldn't have left me here without so much as a word: something happened to them."

Alderic thought on this. It was strange that six villagers could disappear completely in the hills, but he did not see how it related to Ethin's map.

The small mountain from which the spring stemmed was too inexact a location to feature on the map. Alderic already had suspicions about the starting place of the labyrinthine markings, though they had yet to be substantiated.

"Tell me about the spring," he said, abruptly changing the subject. Alyssan's disappearance may have been uninteresting to him, but he would take advantage of the old woman's knowledge.

"There is little to tell. It provides water for our people and flocks."

"Does nothing lay within?" Alderic pressed.

The old woman thought on this a moment, before responding. "There's a place in the spring, beneath the mountain, filled entirely with water. All our people know not to venture beneath the rock, lest they become trapped and drowned."

Alderic nodded. He could feel his heartbeat quicken as he thought on her words. He had the confirmation he needed.

"Thank you for your time," Alderic said, leaving the home.

"Please find her," the old woman called out after him.

As he returned to the spring, Alderic took out the metal plate. The bright gold surface shone, reflecting light into his eyes, and he tilted the plate to better examine the engravings. He could see the village name of Rowena, which had brought him to this spring, and a series of path markings that seemed to originate from nowhere. In that moment, he understood their starting place to be hidden inside the mountain, accessible through the water of the spring.

The soldiers had set up a camp outside the canvas village and the prisoner cart was brought to the new site. Blake watched the green of the spring gradually fade from view, as they were dragged from the spot by the steady step of the laboring horse.

The midday sun shone down, and Callum approached the cart with provisions tucked in his arms. He begrudgingly passed food to each of the king's prisoners, along with a fresh flask of spring water.

Blake watched the other man closely and, when Callum finally reached him, he shot forward and grabbed the knight, pulling him toward him.

Callum fell against Blake and struggled to right himself, cursing the sudden strength of the bound thief.

"Release us," Blake begged, first grasping Callum's shoulder with his shackled hands, before finding a better hold by his side. "King Alderic will kill us as soon as he knows we are of no use." Blake's eyes filled with tears as he sought some spark of kinship within Callum. "You must protect us."

Callum pulled back. "I owe you no protection," he responded. "However, our previous association means I know you better than most." He grabbed Blake's wrists, exposing the dagger the thief had lifted from the knight's side. "You forget, I am well aware of the deception you so eagerly employ."

Callum pushed Blake back, the thief's shoulders colliding with the side of the cart. Callum slammed the handle of the dagger against Blake's bare foot, causing the thief to cry out. Blake rubbed the foot as he watched Callum leave them, an air of triumph encompassing the knight.

"I am sorry he noticed the dagger," Moirin said. "Though, bound to the cart and surrounded on all sides by soldiers, I am not sure so small a weapon would have aided an escape."

"Perhaps not, but, during his fight with Owen in Linwood, a few links of his mail shirt were broken." Blake opened his hand to reveal three curved slivers of metal. "Callum fell too easily for such misdirection, though I suppose this only shows my failing as a mentor. I can use these to open the locks on our shackles, though it will not solve the problem of the soldiers."

King Alderic was making preparations to take his leave from the camp. From the corner of his eye, Blake could see Moirin watching the scene unfold.

"If we are to move, we must do so quickly," she whispered, her sight not leaving the far away king. "Alderic will depart alone to seek the weapon." She looked at Blake. "You should be the one to pursue him."

Blake's breath caught in his throat; he could not imagine why he would be chosen for so crucial a role.

"Why me?" he said.

"You're from the Isle of Ang, right?" she responded. "You're likely the only one of us who can follow where he leads."

He did not understand, but from Moirin's expression he knew disagreement was not an option. Despite their previous differences, he trusted her judgment, and knew she had not chosen him on a whim.

Blake nodded. "Very well, but I do not see how I can slip away unnoticed."

"We'll distract the soldiers," Aeron said.

"Focus first on freeing yourself," Moirin said to Blake.

Blake twisted the metal pieces together, bending the amalgam into the approximate shape of a pick. Looking at the lock, he could see he was lucky, in that only one part would be needed. The small, knotted piece was painful against his fingertips and the thin metal offered no hold, so he wrapped the fabric of his shirt around the end to provide something to grasp.

Finally, he felt the lock give, and he silently removed his shackles. He huddled beside Owen, to conceal the movement of his hands, as he worked to free the warrior. Owen's lock proved more difficult than his own, but, eventually, he felt the restraints come free. They each stayed in their same corners, so as not to draw the attention of the soldiers.

Blake had just removed Aeron's shackles, when he saw that King Alderic was leaving the site. Blake motioned to Moirin, who remained bound to the cart.

"There is no time to free me. Aeron and Owen, you are to cause a distraction that will occupy every soldier, while Blake makes his escape." She sighed. "You cannot begin the distraction right away. We must wait until Alderic has traveled far enough that he will not be drawn back to fight."

She looked in King Alderic's direction before turning to Blake. "He is headed back to the spring, so do not concern yourself with the exact path he travels. If you run, you will make it." She grasped his forearm briefly. "You must find the liogan weapon."

Blake nodded and pulled his boot back on with some difficulty, while they waited for King Alderic to adequately distance himself from the site.

After a few minutes had passed, Moirin nodded, and Aeron sprang from the cart. The bandit queen struck down a soldier, who had not yet drawn his weapon. She took his sword, and freed Owen's axe from the king's saddle.

Aeron threw the axe to the cart, where the head lodged in the side.

Owen picked up the axe, but made no move. Moirin had to practically kick Owen from the cart, but once he saw Aeron attacked on all sides, he joined the fray, sending many of the soldiers running for cover.

Blake saw his opportunity, and dove into the brush. The branches scraped him, but he was safely out of the brawling soldiers' sight. He sprinted through the woods, until he could no longer hear the sound of swords and fists clashing.

He kept running, his foot throbbing with each fumbling step, until he could see the spring. As Moirin had predicted, King Alderic was only just approaching the water's edge. There was a palpable change in the air as he neared the green of the spring, and Blake found a place to hide himself.

The king removed his belt, containing a sword, knife, and two water flasks, and slung the looped leather strap over one shoulder and across his chest. He wound a length of extremely thin black rope around his arm, fastening it with a simple knot.

King Alderic waded into the water and swam until he reached the sheer rock face that towered over the shimmering pool. There, he dipped beneath the surface and out of Blake's view.

47

Alderic swam as quickly as he could, acutely aware of the stone above him. He knew that he had passed the turning point; even if he were to try to return to the safety of the spring, his lungs would not carry him there. He had no choice but to press on, though he would not have wished it any other way.

Just as the last of the air left his lungs, he could feel himself rising involuntarily to the surface. His head left the water, and he was able to breathe freely in the cold damp of the mountain cave. The astringent, mineral smell of the hollow met his nostrils, and he inhaled deeply as he tried to supply his body with much needed air.

He was surrounded by darkness, the lack of light preventing so much as a flicker or shadow from guiding his way. He dashed his palm against the surface of the water, and listened as the ripples extended outward. The water stretched on all sides, and he continued to swim in the opposite direction of the spring.

After a short while, his blindly searching hands came to a rock ledge. He moved sideways against the stone perimeter, feeling for a handhold. His fingers numbed against the slick surface until, finally, he found edging within reach. He secured his hands over the ledge, and pulled himself from the water.

His clothes were soaked through and he pushed clinging hair away from his face, though in the absolute blackness of the surroundings it did little to aid his sight. He felt for the flasks on his belt, and took the lighter of the two into one hand. He removed the watertight cap, and shook the contents into his lap.

He removed his shirt, and wrapped it around the knife blade. He opened a small container which had fallen from the flask, and put a few drops of Fisherman's Ruin onto the fabric. Though the fluid was outlawed in most of his kingdom, he had found no substitute that neared the sheer volatility of Fisherman's Ruin.

He took a piece of flint and a small coin made of steel, and struck them together repeatedly. He produced a spark which flashed as it ignited the fuel on the shirt. He knew the wetness of the fabric would regulate the burn, giving him at least three hours of the flame.

As the shirt fabric flared, he could see he was inside an arching cavern within the mountain. A glance at the metal plate indicated a passage only a few feet away. He replaced the fire-starting items in the flask and pulled himself to his feet.

Holding the makeshift torch, he could feel the metal heating up, but the bone knife handle made the warmth bearable. The flickering light cast shadows across the hollow, and he progressed slowly through the labyrinth of stone channels that riddled the mountain, guided only by the reflecting metal plate.

48

Blake waited a few minutes before following Alderic into the spring. He was careful to find the exact place where the king had submerged himself, though Blake was hesitant to go beneath the water. Raised on a peninsula off the mainland, he had grown up by the sea. He was a passable swimmer, though he had never reached the skill of most on the Isle of Ang.

Still, he realized, this was the reason Moirin chose him. Few in Conrisia would ever venture into water; the rough tides dashing against the cliffs made the activity nearly unviable. Though he was a better swimmer than most in Vesia, he doubted his own ability to follow where the king led.

His thoughts turned to those he had left behind, his companions who at that very moment were risking their lives to buy him this opportunity. He said a small prayer to the divine wanderer, Sylas, and took a deep breath, before plunging beneath the surface.

The temperature of the water decreased as he swam farther from the sunlit pool, and deeper into the rock-encased space. He felt the last of the air leave his body, and reached his hand up. He felt nothing but solid stone above him. He kicked his feet out, propelling his body forward, his fingers skimming the rock ceiling.

He could feel a pressure building behind his eyes and his lungs struggled against his will. He closed his eyelids tight, hoping the strain would distract him from his body's raging, unmet need to breathe.

He remained fully clothed, and he knew this was slowing him down. He had unthinkingly followed the king's lead in this, and severely regretted his decision. The water pulled him back, and the neck of his shirt dragged against his throat.

Just as he was losing hope, his fingers slipped from the rock edge, his hand finding cold air in its stead. He pushed himself up, gasping when his face reached the surface. He tread water for nearly a minute, as his breath came back, quick and shallow. His head reeled and he felt sick, his heart hammering out of his control.

When he had collected himself, he realized he was in complete darkness. He swam until he found a ledge and, with much struggling, he pulled himself out of the black depths of the water.

Without light, he would not be able to navigate the space within the mountain, let alone find the place where he had entered. Without light, he would be trapped in the cavern.

He felt for the ground, and crawled on hands and knees across the slippery, wet rock surrounding the obsidian pool. From the corner of his eye, a flicker of light caught his attention. He thought it might have been an illusion but, after staring into the darkness for some time, he caught a second glimpse. There was no mistaking it: the light of a flame was reflecting off the arcing stone.

Cautiously, he felt his way to the side of the water nearest the light. As he drew closer, the light became clearer. While he could not see it's source, he could just make out the ground beneath him. Seizing his courage, he stood up and began his journey through the passageway from which the light came.

Blake could only assume the flame was borne by King Alderic, and he knew that if he was close enough to see the light's reflection, King Alderic would be able to hear any misstep Blake might make. So, while he could not see well, he fastidiously avoided the loose stones scattered on the path before him.

He rounded the corner joining two passages, and was met with the direct light of the flame. His heart pounding, he ducked back behind the crook of the passage. He had seen King Alderic's back, and Blake uttered a silent prayer that King Alderic had not noticed his presence.

He waited, holding his breath, until he could hear the king's footsteps carrying him away from where Blake stood. He let out the ragged breath, and waited patiently before continuing.

He followed King Alderic through a stream, which had flooded one of the passageways. The surface only came to Blake's waist, but he chose to swim in the shallow depths, so as to avoid the noise that came with wading through the black water.

As he moved, it occurred to him that he had not yet considered what he would do if he found the liogan weapon. King Alderic had the torch and the plate, leaving Blake travelling blind to the path. Blake could not, by any easily conceivable means, reach the cache first.

Blake could not fight King Alderic for possession of the weapon, because that was a fight he would be bound to lose. This left him with only one applicable skill: he would find some means to steal it.

He slowly pulled his body from the water, aware of the faint dripping sound that came from his soaked clothing, and looked around for any sign of the king. The torch was far away now, the light only faintly visible. He hoped he would be able to catch up discreetly.

As he left the water, he felt a hand grasp his neck and drag him roughly to his feet. A blow landed on his stomach, and he was dropped, doubled over, onto the hard ground. King Alderic grasped his hair, and turned Blake's head to face him.

"Did you truly believe you could escape my observation?" he asked, his fingernails digging into the thief's scalp. Blake pulled back, and King Alderic let go. He hauled Blake to his feet, and pushed him ahead on the path. "As you made it this far, you might as well see how close you came to finding the map's end."

Alderic shoved the small of Blake's back, driving the limping thief forward through the passages, until they reached the place where the torch had been left burning. The flame had yet to dim, and Alderic knew it would last at least until he reached the weapon's resting place.

Alderic had been aware of another presence in the mountain since the thief had emerged from the spring, though he did not know it was Blake who followed him until their near collision. He could have killed Blake, but decided against it. He was undeniably impressed by the tenacity and courage of the thief, and this was enough for the king to allow him to see the journey through.

He also felt sorry for Blake, as he thought again on the endless damnation the thief would face in the afterlife. Blake's fate was sealed by the symbol on his temple, and Alderic found himself reluctant to perform the execution that would condemn the thief's soul to eternal service of Erkynon.

As they moved through the flickering passages, the ill-fated swindler broke the silence that had stretched between them.

"There is one question that has needled my mind since laying eyes on your knight, Callum," Blake said, testing his luck against the king.

Alderic pushed Blake forward by the shoulder. "What would that be?"

"I was told that Hugh was dead, that he had been hanged only shortly after my departure for the fortress," Blake said. "Why was this misinformation relayed? Everything I have seen indicates that you would not torture someone if you had nothing to gain by it. I was condemned to the gallows; what use was served by my belief that Hugh had died?"

Blake could hear only silence as they walked along, before the king finally responded.

"That was upon Callum's request: he asked that news of his death be spread." King Alderic paused. "He wanted no part of his past life. He would not respond to Hugh, so I granted him the new name of Callum."

"He would destroy his very identity because of me," Blake mused.

"He would extinguish himself, so great was your betrayal in his eyes. Ordinarily, I must accustom a new knight to act as I direct, at times without remorse. There was no need for me to prepare Callum so; your apathetic exploitation, followed by apparent betrayal, left him vulnerable to such command. Your considerable self-regard shaped him into a worthy knight."

Blake's mouth became dry, as regret filled him. It was too late for such sentiments, as he would doubtless be killed by the king in mere moments, but he offered a silent entreaty to the gods that Callum would forgive his past failings.

They spoke no more and the king navigated the passageways silently. The marked chamber in the mountain was only a few feet away, and Alderic could sense a stifling decay in the air as they drew near.

A small aperture in the cave wall, near to the ground, stood as the entryway to the chamber. Finding a stone jutting from the wall, Alderic unraveled the rope from his arm, securing it to the protrusion.

Alderic had Blake go through first. He could not risk the other man trapping him in the chamber by cutting the rope, which tensed as it bore the thief. Blake disappeared from his view, and Alderic could hear a thud as the thief reached the floor of the cavern.

Alderic followed, the rope straining to support his weight. The cord did not extend all the way to the ground and Alderic let go. When he reached the bottom, and shone the light of the torch, he found a twelve-foot drop from the end of the rope.

He noticed the scent that filled the closed space. It was the type of rot he encountered all too often and, as he looked through the room, his eyes fell on several corpses. Each was in a state of forced repose by the far side of the chamber.

He saw the thief had immediately moved to the center of the room, where the piled goods lay. Blake was sorting through objects quickly, a desperation to his movements. Alderic approached, and Blake reluctantly stepped away from the treasure.

Hidden in Blake's hand was a small, metal object: an item of much importance to the Blackdog King should the words of the dead cellarman be believed. He tucked it in his pocket.

Alderic kicked through the piled goods. He recognized most of the collected objects as valuables stolen from Ashen Castle, but there was nothing he was unfamiliar with, nor anything signifying a greater purpose.

Alderic moved to stand beside the corpses and stared down at the bodies. The old woman of Rowena mentioned that her granddaughter had entered the spring with five other villagers, yet there were only four bodies in the chamber.

The stagnant cave had preserved the bodies relatively well. Though the air smelled of decay, the skin had not sagged, and they looked as though they could have simply been asleep.

Blake came to the king's side. "Their fingertips have turned," he mentioned.

Alderic brought the torchlight closer, though he did not touch the bodies. He could see the skin at the fingertips had darkened considerably, their tint a deep, unnatural blue. This was something he could not account for, even given his many years of contact with the dead.

"There were six," the king answered. "Two who entered the cave are missing."

Blake turned his eyes to the small aperture where they had made their entrance. Twenty-five feet above, it seemed hopelessly far away.

"Perhaps the missing two never entered this chamber."

King Alderic shook his head. "Each of the four bodies has been propped against the cave wall. I doubt they died in identical positions. Someone was here when they died, and moved them out of respect." He looked to the entrance.

"Then how did they depart?" Blake asked. "I don't see how they could have reached the break so high above."

"The old woman in the village said they were travelling in the hills when they disappeared. There must be another way out, a way that leads through the mountain." King Alderic responded, casting light around the room. "Though, I suppose finding an escape is your specialty." The words were spoken with a distracted bitterness. "We should leave, there is no sense wasting a moment more in this tomb."

"What of the liogan weapon?" Blake asked. "Will you leave here without it?"

"The weapon is not here. Either one of the two villagers has taken it, or it was never here to begin with." King Alderic sighed, and ran a hand through his hair. "Ethin was a vile man and a poor leader; it would not surprise me if his final act in this world amounted to nothing more than deception."

"Still, you followed the map here," Blake pressed. He knew that he ought to embrace the king's willingness to leave the mountain, his task unaccomplished. However, there was something about King Alderic's demeanor that troubled him. Despite himself, he was curious as to why the king was so cautiously accepting of defeat.

"So I did." King Alderic looked away, continuing his search for the escape found by the missing two. "Yet, I suppose I was also in search of something long since gone." The king's thumb absently touched the gouge mark in the hilt of his sword.

A crease formed across King Alderic's pale brow, and Blake could see the furrow beneath the flickering, warm glow of the torch. Blake felt an odd sickness grow within him, as the king's vigor, and warmongering spirit, was replaced for that instant by a careworn despondency. He felt himself pitying the forceful ruler. Blake looked again at the king's mauled hilt, and found that the small, metal object he had tucked into his pocket weighed against his very soul.

49

A slight whistling noise caught Blake's ear. It was faint, but the sound was distinct from the silence of the cavern. He could not locate the source, as the feeble noise was distorted by the chamber, so he began to move through the room, hoping that the sound would grow stronger as he neared its origin. He stepped past priceless heirlooms and the corpses of the villagers, until he finally noticed a delicate increase in the volume of the wavering whistling.

He reached the wall and King Alderic approached, bringing with him the light. Blake could make out an outlet low in the stone, roughly broken through. He knelt by the aperture, and could hear the whistling coming from the portal.

The break in the wall was small but, given the size of the four dead they had found, it was not unreasonable to assume that the missing two could have made their way through so narrow a space.

"I think I can hear wind," Blake said.

King Alderic nodded. "You may go first."

Blake crept through and felt the light scrape of the stone as he only just managed to pass. He could scarcely believe that he was abandoning more treasure than he had seen in his lifetime. However, in that moment, his concern lay more with the king. He steadied himself outside the aperture, and watched for the flickering torchlight.

King Alderic was forced to break away more stone before attempting to cross to the other side. He was released into the crudely constructed passage, similar to those that had led them to the treasure chamber.

"The metal plate shows that the mountain is filled with blind halls and chambers disconnected from the destined path. It seems that, by luck, the villager had stumbled upon one of these detached tracks leading from the mountain side," King Alderic said.

Blake stepped forward, the ground unstable beneath his boots. King Alderic was behind him and the light was poorly cast, leaving the thief to make his way in near darkness.

His ankle wrenched to the side as he stepped on something soft. The pain caused him to lose his footing and he fell, his elbow connecting solidly with the very thing that had caused him to trip. He scrambled away in a panic, as Alderic shone the light of the torch.

It was a human, a man who lay face down on the ground. Alderic grasped the shoulder, and turned him over. Blake backed away as far as he could, loose stones digging into his palms, until he met the wall.

Shaken by the king, the man's eyelids flew open. The light of the blazing knife torch illuminated the supine figure. He made to scream in terror, but no sound came out. It was clear that he was too startled to speak. King Alderic picked him up, and threw him over his shoulder.

Even with the weight of the body on his shoulder, the king held his hand out to Blake, and helped him to his feet.

"Thanks," Blake said begrudgingly. He was caught off guard by the unexpected kindness from the Blackdog King.

King Alderic nodded curtly at Blake, and the two continued their journey from the chamber.

King Alderic held the torch with one hand, and steadied the man across his shoulder with the other. Unlike the passages they had travelled before, the ground was dry, and the air grew warmer and fresher the further they progressed.

After nearly an hour of travel, which he sensed was uphill given the ache in his shins, Blake saw a cool light filtering through a crack in the stone of the mountain's side. A steep climb led the way to this gap in the rock. The whistling sound was piercing, gusts of wind battering the side of the mountain.

The king began his ascent toward the light. His boots slipped on the rocks, bearing his weight and that of the barely-conscious body across his shoulder. He anchored his elbow on the edge, momentarily blocking any light from entering the cave, as he stole from the confines of the mountain.

Once King Alderic was no longer within the cavern, Blake began the stony climb and after a few slips he reached the top. He held onto the side of the rock, but found himself unable to pull through. The muscles of his arms strained, as they tried to haul his dangling body at so odd an angle. He briefly caught King Alderic's eye as he struggled, kicking against the stones under him, and feeling them tumble away beneath his feet.

Suddenly, he felt a powerful grip tighten around his wrists, and he was propelled upwards, past the stone, and onto the green grass of the mountainside. King Alderic set him down, and Blake dusted himself off, his shoulders aching from the force with which the king had dragged him through.

Blake looked up at King Alderic. He had been given no reason to suspect the king would spare him, let alone aid his escape from the mountain. Yet, there he was, freed from the constricting underground course.

King Alderic turned his attention to the man they had brought from the caves who was now sitting up and staring ahead, though he moved restlessly at every sound made by Blake or King Alderic.

Alderic crouched before the man, and passed his hand before the other's face.

"You cannot see anything, can you?" Alderic asked.

After a momentary pause, the villager shook his head, tears springing to his useless eyes.

"What is your name?"

"Francis," he responded, his dry voice cracking.

Alderic removed the heavier of the flasks from his belt.

"This is water," he said, pressing the flask into his hands. "Drink, then tell us what happened in the treasure chamber."

Blake sat down on the grass beside King Alderic, watching Francis carefully. He was surprised by King Alderic's courtesy in dealing with the blinded villager, but he supposed the king was seeking information only feigned benevolence would bring.

"Alyssan, one of the women in the village, told us she had found a way into the mountain. She had brought a lamp into a secret hall beneath the hills, and told us there was something we should see." A sad smile appeared on his face. "She had marked the place where she had entered, and we left the village at daybreak. There were six of us who went into the mountain.

"She showed us these passageways she had been through before, and she led us to this room with all kinds of treasure."

"What happened to the others?" Blake asked. King Alderic looked over at the thief, his eyes neutral.

"There was something in the room, amongst the treasures. Caris found it. It was a small silver vial, so small that it fit in the palm of her hand. I think the metal was pure, it made a beautiful ringing sound when she tapped it with a chalice. Caris pried open the lid." Francis' voice broke, and he buried his face in his hands. He began to sob, his entire body shaking with the effort.

"What happened when Caris opened the silver vial?" Blake asked gently, sensing that the king was growing impatient.

Francis shook his head vehemently. "I don't know what happened. The others tried to take it from her, but she would not let go." He drew in a shaky breath. "There was this sound. It was like the pop of wet firewood as it enters a blaze. This terrible noise escaping their mouths. The second it happened, they were dead. It was as if their souls simply fled their bodies."

"But you survived," Alderic interrupted.

"Caris and I survived. I was standing right beside the others, but for some reason I was spared. I couldn't bear to see my friends scattered around the room, so we brought them to sit against the wall. We planned to come back for them, to bring their bodies from the mountain. Caris was distraught by what she'd done.

"We began to leave the way we'd entered, but Caris went back to the chamber and retrieved the silver vial. I asked her why she would take that cursed thing, but she said she might need it. I didn't question her, and began to lead the way out. I felt a blow at the back of my head." He touched the place, wincing at the pain. "I think she must have hit me with something. When I woke up, I began to crawl away from the chamber. I had a canteen filled with water, though eventually it ran out. In the darkness of the mountain, I didn't realize I lost my sight."

Alderic left the villager with the flask, and walked to the edge of the mountain, casting his gaze into the expanse of valley below. A few feet away, the Fisherman's Ruin consumed the last of the torch.

Blake brought himself to the king's side, wincing as weight shifted onto his injured foot.

"Ethin told the truth yet," King Alderic muttered, half to himself.

"Whatever lies within that vial, is it really so powerful?" Blake looked at the king questioningly. "It only killed four, and that would seem to have been an accident."

"Whatever occurred in the mountain is not a display of the liogan weapon's full power," he responded. "The weapon was undirected, and the villager who found it has not yet learned its use. The weapon appears to defend itself and its master against any threat, however small. When the villagers tried to take the silver vial from Caris, it struck out blindly in protection."

King Alderic sighed, brushing the windswept hair from his eyes. "The real power of the weapon will be far greater."

"You would truly do away with, rather than utilize, such an obvious advantage?" Blake asked, unconvinced.

"It will bring nothing but destruction. I would eliminate this liogan weapon both to continue my rule, and to protect those within Vesia, even from themselves."

From the stories Blake had been told about King Alderic, he could not believe this to be true. Even as a child, he had imagined the young king to be a cruel barbarian, killing any and all who stood in his way. He had been so sure that the king lacked even the most basic humanity. It was difficult to reconcile this godlike icon of power with the sorrowful man who stood beside him.

"Yet, Ethin is regarded as a savior of those who would be free of your rule. It seems unlikely that he would create a weapon of savagery, when that is the very trait others despise in you." Blake did not know where he found the courage to speak to the king with such aggressive candor, but he braced himself for the repercussions.

Surprisingly, the king appeared merely tired by the questioning. "There are many things about Ethin that the people do not understand. It is true that my father taught me to be ruthless in the face of adversity; I learned from him the art of warfare, and to gain power primarily through military action. I may be savage, as you say, but I derive no enjoyment from needless bloodshed.

"Ethin had other ideas. He tried to establish himself as a leader, but he lacked the ability command. Frustrated, he claimed to have developed a new method of warfare: a departure from the battlefield. He said he could cause even the most powerful kingdom to crumble from within.

"I know nothing of the liogan weapon's effects, beyond the fact that it is clearly capable of protecting itself. Yet, I knew Ethin," he said, pausing. "Nothing good could come from one so corrupted by the thirst for power. He would sell his soul for the taste of blood, yet this desire to kill was surpassed only by his own cowardice. You can imagine how ill-suited to power such a one would be."

Blake thought on this. He did not want to believe that the familiar image of Ethin conjured by the folktales of Vesia was so divorced from the man himself. Yet, there was something in King Alderic's demeanor that left little doubt of his honesty.

"The Vesian army is unrivaled," Blake said. "How could anyone believe that your rule would be threatened by so small a weapon?"

"Knowing so little of the weapon's effects, I cannot predict the outcome. It is possible that I would be victorious, likely even. However, Vesia will suffer for it. I cannot shield every territory from a weapon I do not yet understand," Alderic admitted with regret. "My father taught me that there is honor to be found on the battlefield. This is a belief that Ethin did not share, and I will not allow such underhanded means to destroy the kingdom I have bled to build."

Alderic looked Blake over. "You may think me cruel, as countless other do, and it is true that I have committed pitiless acts. However, you must understand that there is no measure I would not take to ensure the prosperity of my kingdom."

Blake was surprised to hear King Alderic speak so forthrightly, when the ruler had previously shown him nothing but disdain. He reached into his pocket, his fingers lighting upon the cold metal piece that lay within. Yet, Blake found himself hesitating to act, as he understood the significance it held for his ruler.

Taking a deep breath, Blake grasped King Alderic's hand in his, and quickly pressed the small object into his palm. He released the king, and let his own hands fall awkwardly to his sides.

Alderic gazed down and turned the item over in his hand. It was the piece gauged many years ago from his father's sword, a small bronze round bearing the insignia of his family: a blackdog with glowing, ruby eyes.

Blake watched him with curiosity, understanding in part the importance so small an object held for the Vesian king. Blake found his mind returning to his own family whom he had not seen in many years. He could only assume that they still lived on the Isle of Ang, basking in sunlight and the brisk breeze of the sea, all the while blissfully unaware of the peril in which their land could soon find itself. Casting aside his preconceptions about the nature of the king, Blake knew what he must do to protect them.

"I know you have no reason to trust me, and you yourself have deceived me in the past," Blake began, the words hurried. He saw the king turn to him, breaking from the hold of the blackdog. "However, if it is truly your intention to shield Vesia from this liogan weapon, I give you my word that I will aid you in any way I can." Blake bowed his head. "You are my king, and I swear on my honor that I will follow you as a faithful subject."

Alderic looked down at Blake, unsure of whether to accept this offer of loyalty. His eyes moved to fix on those of the brazen blackdog he held in his palm. Not since his childhood had he seen the ruby eyes shine back at him. They were just as piercing as he remembered them, and his fingers folded protectively over the bronze piece.

There was no reason to believe that Blake would keep his pledge of loyalty. The thief had shown himself more than capable of deception when it suited him, and had risked his life on multiple occasions in his opposition of the king.

Blake lacked the cleverness that Alderic had seen in thieves and confidence men in the past, including many of those who died in the trial of escaping the prison. Despite this lesser talent, Blake had shown himself to possess a scrappy resolve that had kept him alive and thriving.

"You may be saying this to save your own neck," Alderic said, "and as you say, there is no reason for me to trust you."

"Owen told me you have an eye for character, and that you can shape the man to fit the role," Blake responded, raising his chin in challenge. "Perhaps he was mistaken."

Alderic paused, his eyes again lighting on those of the blackdog.

"Very well," Alderic answered with a sigh, though knowing that in Blake's eyes he was yielding. "I suppose a man like you could be useful in procuring the silver vial, though know that at the first sign of treachery, I will not hesitate to separate your head from your neck."

"I am aware of how you reward betrayal," Blake responded, his mind returning to Owen.

Alderic glanced back at Francis. "We will deliver him back to Rowena and join my soldiers. Caris could not have travelled far, as she is likely tired, hungry and on foot."

Blake pulled Francis to his feet, and they began the journey down the treacherous mountainside, Blake limping along as King Alderic led the way.

Blake did not know whether he had done right in pledging his devotion. He watched King Alderic descend the mountain, the setting sun making the steep, stony path exceedingly dangerous. Yet, he observed a solemnity in the king's bearing that quieted his fears. The thief had secured himself to the ruler of his land in protection of its people. For the time being, that was enough.

Epilogue

1

Alderic entered the blacksmith's workshop and was met by the heat of the blazing furnace. He took his brazen sword from the sheath, handing both the weapon and the gauged piece to the blacksmith. He watched as the metal was heated, reshaped, and the insignia set in place.

Days had passed since his visit to the treasure chamber, and in that time, there had been no sign of Caris or the silver vial. His soldiers thoroughly searched the land surrounding the mountain, but they had recovered nothing yet. Without resolution, Alderic was left with no choice but assume that the weapon might fall into the hands of his enemies.

He looked upon the newly whole bronze sword, and saw the ruby eyes staring back from the shadowy face.

He would protect Vesia with every drop of blood, with every breath of life. Whatever chaos the liogan weapon threatened, he was ready.

2

Blake was consumed by the despairing depths of a nightmare. The darkness clung to him, and he could feel wet ink streaming from the symbol at his temple. His entire body ached, yet he was without hope of reprieve. He fell to his knees, feeling the ground beneath him give, pulling him further down.

The night wound around him like tendrils, trying to drag him beneath the earth itself, and he could do nothing to break its suffocating hold.

A light cut though the shadows and a woman approached. A sheer, grey cloak was draped around her bare shoulders, and the diadem at her brow glinted like ice. She was infinitely beautiful, and Blake could feel the tears upon his cheeks as he took in her sight.

The woman stood before him, taking his face in her hands. In that moment, the suffering left him and it was as though his body was bathed in pure light.

"I am Erkynon," she said, her voice gentle. "I pity you, Blake, for you know so little of the fate awaiting you in the underworld."

Blake could hear her words, but he only wished for her to touch him again, to draw away his misery.

"I can help you," she said.

"How?" Blake asked, his voice trembling.

Erkynon stroked the intricate symbol on his temple, and the ink ceased its drenching of his skin.

"Never before has this symbol been placed on one whose heart still beats, and I was unsure of what it would do. This mark has bound you to me, allowing me to speak to you. Though you walk amongst the living, your soul belongs to me. You are torn between this world and the next, a true inhabitant of neither."

She touched his temple again. "This symbol will be your damnation or your salvation."

"Tell me what I must do, so that I may live," Blake begged.

"You have heard of my child," she began. "You must find it and bring it into its birthright. Once it has used its gift, I shall release you."

She looked down upon him, condolence in her eyes. "Take care you are not killed. If you die before awakening the Beast to its power, you will be condemned, enslaved to the underworld."

She stooped and placed a kiss upon Blake's brow. The place where her lips met his forehead was cold, as if caressed by frost.

Blake awoke with a start. His clothing was drenched with sweat, his hair matted against his forehead. For days, he had been troubled by these dreams: pressing visions that wracked his soul. He had been waking up more exhausted than he had felt upon falling asleep.

His mind swam, and he pressed his hands against his closed eyes. He might not be able to make sense of the change that had come over him, but of one thing he was certain:

The Beast of Erkynon roamed the earth, and Blake knew where it could be found.

THE END

Don't miss out!

Visit the website below and you can sign up to receive emails whenever Livia E. De Souza publishes a new book. There's no charge and no obligation.

https://books2read.com/r/B-A-YBXFB-DJZDD

BOOKS 2 READ

Connecting independent readers to independent writers.

Also by Livia E. De Souza

The Blackdog King
The Blackdog King

Standalone
The Sons of Saints

Watch for more at https://www.liviaedesouza.com/.

About the Author

Livia E. De Souza lives in Connecticut, where she writes speculative fiction. Read more at https://www.liviaedesouza.com/.